12/29/93   12/13/93 6 T
11/99   ME
01/08 JBD

Family Values

A NOVEL

Lawrence David

SIMON & SCHUSTER

New York London Toronto Sydney Tokyo Singapore

SIMON & SCHUSTER
SIMON & SCHUSTER BUILDING
ROCKEFELLER CENTER
1230 AVENUE OF THE AMERICAS
NEW YORK, NEW YORK 10020

DESIGNED BY KAROLINA HARRIS
MANUFACTURED IN THE UNITED STATES OF AMERICA

1 3 5 7 9 10 8 6 4 2

LIBRARY OF CONGRESS CATALOGING IN PUBLICATION DATA

DAVID, LAWRENCE
FAMILY VALUES: A NOVEL / LAWRENCE DAVID.
P. CM.
I. TITLE.
PS3554.A9166F36 1993
813'.54—dc20 92-37166
CIP
ISBN: 0-671-73215-3

FOR BARRY AND ELIZABETH DAVID

In growing up together, families are apt to lose a certain mutual regulation as a group. As a consequence each family member has somehow lost the self-control appropriate to his age and status in the family. Instead of controlling himself and of serving the mutual regulation of the group, each member has searched for and found substitute controls, areas of autonomy which exclude the others.

—ERIK H. ERIKSON
Childhood and Society

1 9 7 0

T H I S is to be the Wallace family's last shopping venture into the Wayland town center. In eight days they move to a larger house in Concord, two towns, thirty miles away. Sandy Wallace is surrounded by her five children. The only member of her family not here is Dean, her husband.

"There's going to be so many of you in the car there'll be no room for the groceries," Sandy jokes and she pulls out of the driveway, onto the narrow road that winds through a forest of pine trees. The kids are quiet with the excited anticipation of this weekly grocery shopping, each gets a frozen dinner of his choosing and a package of candy. They rush about the aisles playing hide-and-seek while Sandy fills the cart with food.

Kyle, Sandy's oldest at eleven years, switches on the car radio. She reaches over and switches it off. "No, Kyle, not while I'm driving, it's too distracting."

She drives past the Goldblatts' house. Wendy waves and Sandy honks the horn in response. Kyle switches on the radio again. Loud music pounds out of the speaker.

Sandy reaches over and switches it off for the second time.

"If you can blow the horn, why can't I play the radio?" he asks.

"I was blowing the horn to say hello to Mrs. Goldblatt," she explains.

"You could've waved," he says.

She adjusts the rear-view mirror. "I suppose I could have, but I didn't. Now let's not make an issue out of it."

"Maybe I want to make an issue out of it," Kyle argues.

"Yeah," Tom agrees.

"What's an issue?" Hal asks.

Sandy drives. She drives a VW bus, sky blue with a white vinyl interior, mud stains from the kids' shoes all over the backs of the seats.

The kids are eager to move, each looking forward to having a bedroom of his very own, not having to share. In Wayland, it's been two boys to each room, bunk-bedded, Tom bunking over Blane, and Hal, in the room that was once Kyle's alone, bunking over his eldest brother. Tina, the baby and only girl, sleeps in the small spare room.

Sandy, too, looks forward to the move, both a symbolic and literal shift from a middle-class life to a more upper-middle- or possibly lower-upper-class life. However, the Concord house is larger. Sandy realizes the housework will most surely be doubled.

"If they don't want us to play it, why do they put it there?" Kyle asks.

"Put what where?" Sandy asks, knowing full well he means the radio.

"The radio. Why can't we have it on?" Kyle asks again.

"Put it on—put it on!" Tom breaks in. "I bet Tina wants it on. Don't you want it on, Tina?"

"I'm putting it on," Kyle says defiantly.

"Fine, I'm taking you all home and we won't go shopping at all. How's that for a fun after-school treat?" Sandy says and they all moan loudly.

"Just because you're the one who drives, we have to do what you want," Kyle sulks.

"That's right," she responds.

Everyone else remains quiet, fearing she really will take them back home, to be deprived of this weekly shopping ritual.

Sandy doesn't know what she's going to fix for Dean and

herself. Her big decision for the day: Meal Planning. Sandy's everyday obligation to prepare a balanced meal from the four basic food groups. In Sandy's mind she pictures a large, blank menu-planner, teasing her, pressing her for information regarding the night's entrée. Maybe fish, Sandy thinks as she drives. A salad, then fish. She doesn't know; maybe breaded fish and stringbeans, maybe carrots . . . crescent rolls . . . dinner would be easier if she only had to make one meal for all of them, but the kids won't eat what Sandy and Dean eat, and Dean doesn't have the patience for them after work anyway, would "haul off and crack their heads" if they argued or were too noisy. Besides, Dean and Sandy's dinner together gives Sandy a nice break from the kids as well.

"Tom's making faces at me, Mom," Hal chirps.

"Stop it, Tom," Sandy says.

"I wasn't doing anything," Tom answers.

"Were too," Hal says.

"Well, stop it anyway," Sandy says firmly.

"You're such a liar, Hal. Such a baby," Tom says.

"I'm not a baby," Hal retorts. "Tina is."

"You are too a baby," Tom repeats.

"Will you both be quiet?" Sandy says.

"He did it," Hal says.

"You're both going to sit in the car if you don't keep quiet starting now," Sandy declares.

"Leave me in the car with him and he'll be dead," Tom threatens.

"No, you'll be dead," Hal says to Tom.

"Enough," Sandy says and she drives through the town center, past the Town Hall, the library covered with ivy, the high school, then the elementary school the kids currently attend.

Considering the boys' age differences, it shouldn't be Hal and Tom fighting. Tom's eight years old and Hal's four, whereas Blane and Tom are only one year apart. Tom was born only thirteen months after Sandy had Blane. She had always expected them to be the rivals, but they're not. Blane's nine, Sandy's second child. She finds it easier to remember the kids by their birth order than by anything else. Dean and Sandy are always introducing them as "Kyle our number one son, Blane our number two son, Tom our number three son, Hal our number four son and Tina, our princess."

When the boys ask Sandy what they were like as babies, it gets confusing—when who learned to walk, when who spoke at so many months—Sandy never recorded the dates, cannot recall milestones but only general behaviors: Kyle always slept through the night with no problems. Blane was a bed wetter until six and a thumb sucker until eight. Tom was a crier, all night, all day for his first two years, constantly in need of being held. Hal loved to climb out of his crib while they slept and explore the dark rooms alone. And Tina, still a baby now, just a few months over one year, is the only girl, there's no mixing her up with the boys.

Tina sits in the car seat next to Blane, in the "back-back," the row of seats behind the back seat of the van. Blane hasn't said a word so far this drive.

"How's Tina back there, Blane?" Sandy asks.

"She's fine," Tom says.

"I asked Blane," Sandy says.

"She's all right," Blane replies. "Where will we shop in the new town?"

Sandy glances in the rear-view mirror, catching Blane's puzzled expression. "In a supermarket like always, why?"

"Do you know which one?" Blane asks.

"A supermarket, dummy," Tom answers.

"Will they have Quisp?" Blane asks.

"Yes," Sandy replies. "They'll have Quisp."

Blane nods his head solemnly. "Good."

"At preschool today, Heidi swallowed a bottle cap," Hal says.

"She did not," Tom argues.

"Swallowed a bottle cap, uh-huh," Hal says.

They drive by the post office. Sandy reminds herself to stop by later in the week, give the postman the family's forwarding address.

"What's going to happen to her, Mom?" Hal asks.

"What? To who?" Sandy asks back.

"Heidi," Hal says. "Weren't you listening?"

Sandy takes a breath. "Oh, I'm sure she'll be fine. Just don't go swallowing any bottle caps."

"Okay. I won't," Hal says.

"You're making it up anyway," Tom says. "That didn't happen."

"Did so."

"Then what did it look like?"

Hal puffs out his cheeks, eyes wide, gasping. Kyle turns around from the front seat to get a good look. Blane watches. The older brothers laugh.

Hal smiles. "That is what she looked like."

"Looks more like Nana Lilly when she was almost dead before," Tom comments.

Sandy stares ahead at the road, concentrating on her driving.

"That is how Nana Lilly looked," Tom continues. "Her face went all crazy and then she fell down in the living room." He leans over the front seat by Sandy's face. "Remember, Mom?"

"Yes, I remember, now sit back please. I can't drive with you leaning over me."

"But Nana Lilly didn't swallow a bottle cap," Kyle says critically. "It's hardly the same thing."

"It looked the same," Tom defends, then, "Mom, promise you won't let her do that again if she decides to move in with us, okay?"

Sandy pulls the VW into the supermarket parking lot, searching for a space. Sandy had hoped to have a guest bedroom in the new house, a room for visitors, but after her mother's last heart attack, Sandy and Dean decided they'd try to convince Lilly to move in with the family. Sandy doesn't want her mother to end up in a nursing home; actually thinks it might be nice having her mother around, acting as their live-in baby-sitter; giving Lilly the family to interact with instead of sitting alone in her apartment all day.

"Why do you always park so far away?" Kyle asks.

"There are no other spaces, honey," Sandy says. "What else can I do?"

"I see one closer," he says.

"Well, I don't," Sandy says and she pulls into a space before Kyle can point another out to her. The fact is that Sandy is a bad parker, refuses to park next to other cars for fear she'll hit them. She just eases the car into an empty parking space and hopes others won't pull up too close beside her while they're shopping, making her departure all that more difficult, possibly nerve-wracking.

The kids unbuckle their seat belts, clicks heard all around. Blane unstraps Tina from the car seat and Sandy reaches into her pocketbook for her list and it's not there. She realizes she's forgotten it, has left it pinned to the refrigerator door. She'll just have to shop by memory.

"Okay. Everybody choose."

Sandy stands and watches as the kids assault the frozen food aisle. Foggy cold doors swing open, their little hands grabbing at frozen food entrées and side dishes. Tina sits in the seat of the shopping cart, clutching a bag of potato chips with both hands, banging it against the cart's steel grille side, crushing all the chips. Sandy will have one of the boys exchange it for a fresh bag before they reach the checkout counter.

The boys toss their meals into the basket. Kyle wants the turkey and gravy, Blane the spaghetti and meatballs, Hal the chicken, and Tom tosses a Hungry Man Dinner into the cart and Sandy reaches for it. "Come on, Tom, you won't eat all of this."

"I will too," he protests.

Sandy holds up the box, pointing out its contents. "You're going to eat the peas and carrots and the mashed potatoes?" she asks skeptically.

"Yeah, why not?" Tom says.

"If he gets a big dinner, I get one too." Kyle heads for the freezer again.

"No one's getting a big dinner," Sandy says and Kyle stops, staring back at her. She shakes the box at Tom. Frost is forming on the cardboard around her fingers. "If you won't eat this stuff when I cook it for you at home, why should I believe you'll eat it now, young man?"

"Maybe you cook it bad," Tom says.

Sandy gives Tom a look and walks to the freezer door, pulling it wide. "Now pick out something else," she tells him.

He sticks his chin up at her. "I want that one. I'll eat it all. Just buy it for me, Mom," he pleads.

And the other kids stand staring at her, wondering if she'll give in to him, and Tom rushes at his mother, yanking his frozen dinner selection from her hand and backing away, staring her in the eyes, matching her cold look.

"Fine," Sandy says. "You put it back yourself."

"I will not," he says.

"Just do it," Kyle says.

Blane wanders off looking toward the candy selection. Tina kicks her legs out at the food piled high in the cart. Hal watches Tom and Tom stands holding the box. Sandy stands holding the freezer door open and she reaches out toward Tom for the dinner. "Come on—"

Tom clutches the dinner to his chest like a shield, unwavering.

Sandy releases the door and it swings shut. Other shoppers pass by as she approaches her son, reaching out to him.

Tom backs off. "Get away from me. Get away," he says.

Sandy reaches her hand out to him. "Now you put that back and let's get going. Everyone's waiting. I have milk and ice cream in the cart that I have to get home." She moves toward him as he rushes around her to the checkout counter. Sandy lurches after Tom, grabbing his arm, yanking him back to her. The box drops to the floor and she grabs it.

"There," Sandy says in triumph. "Now pick out something else."

"Ouch, you hurt me. You pulled my arm out," Tom says. He's cradling his arm like a wounded animal.

"She did not," Hal states.

Sandy turns away and looks for the freezer where the Hungry Man Dinner belongs. She opens the door and places it back in, leaving the door ajar so that Tom may select another entrée. "Come on, Tom, you know there are plenty of others you like just as much. I'm sorry if I hurt you, now pick out a dinner so we can go home."

Tom stares at her, slowly walking toward the display. He says nothing, defeated, or maybe Sandy really has hurt him, and a wave of guilt hits Sandy as he takes the door from her, holding it open himself. He points up to the top shelf for the chopped sirloin dinner.

"Get me that one," he says softly, his eyes glassy, and Sandy looks down at him and realizes that she *has* hurt him, that she's handled this completely wrong, and she reaches up to the shelf for the dinner Tom's selected and thinks that maybe she should let him have the big dinner, why did she make it into such a big problem? What harm is there in letting him have it? And Sandy pauses for a moment, trying to decide what to do—what is her best, next, most appropriate move—when all of a sudden Tom smiles. His eyes go wide and he grabs the door, slamming it on Sandy's wrist, throwing all his weight against it, trapping her hand in the freezer, her watch cutting into her skin.

"Godamnit, Tom!"

And she pushes at him, trying to shove him away from the door, but a pain is growing in her wrist, surging through her arm, and she stands there in shock as Tom looks up at her, grinning like a monster. Sandy looks at her wrist caught in the door, bent awkwardly and twisted against the cold glass, her palm flattened against the window. Kyle and Hal rush at Tom, grabbing him and Tom shoves them back, running off across the market down the bread aisle.

The pressure on Sandy's wrist is released and she withdraws her hand from the freezer, trying to move her wrist but she cannot and a man in a white smock comes over, "Are you all right, madam? Are you all right?" and other mothers and other children gaze at Sandy, wire carts pushed up, circling around Sandy as tears stream down her face and Tina cries, Sandy hears Tina crying somewhere far away, distant, and her wrist is swelling and Sandy holds it in her good hand, trying to move it but she cannot, she cannot move it and all her children stare, all except for Tom, who has run off on his own down the bread aisle, and a woman reaches toward Sandy's face, dabbing a tissue at Sandy's nose and eyes, tears running out of her eyes and frozen dinners thawing in the cart.

■

"Everything will go smoothly if we can all just cooperate and do as we are told," Dean says to his children, but they pay him no mind. He stands on the front yard of what was once his home, but has now been sold to a younger couple, a couple with only two children much like Sandy and Dean were when they first moved to Wayland eight years ago.

Moving men in gray sweats lift sofas, tables, lamps and rolled Oriental carpets from the house, loading the furniture into bright orange vans. Sandy, still inside packing the kitchen, tries to decide which foods to take and what to leave behind. Obviously they'll have to eat out tonight.

Tom, Hal and Kyle rush across the front lawn, weaving between the legs of the moving men, ducking behind boxes piled high in the driveway. Dean thinks that maybe he should send the kids inside to run about; now that the fragile items are packed and the house is empty, the kids would probably be better off in there, less chance of them hurting themselves or being an encumbrance to the movers, causing one of the men to stumble, making the whole move go awry.

As it now stands, a glitch in the planned smooth move has already occurred: Blane's teacher, Mrs. Freeman, failed to forward Blane's school files to Concord. Blane waits after school in his empty classroom while Mrs. Freeman prepares the final records for transfer. Sandy gave Mrs. Freeman the directions to the house in Concord. Blane's teacher will be dropping him off there later this afternoon.

Standing on the lawn, the movers, his children, his belongings swirling around him in a chaotic rush, Dean almost feels as if he's the man come out of nowhere; life with his parents being nothing more than a vague memory. Phil Wallace died when Dean was fifteen, never living long enough to see his son graduate high school, Boston University or Cornell Business School. Dean was raised in a two-bedroom, four-room, one-story house and here Dean now stands moving into a new home of three stories and sixteen rooms. As he said to Sandy upon finalizing the purchase of the new home, "I'm thirty years younger than my father was when he died and I have a house over three hundred percent larger. All accomplished completely on my own with no help from my family."

"I'm sure your family would have helped you if they had been around," Sandy replied, not sure what kind of response her husband was fishing for.

"But they didn't. They died and I did it all on my own for us. Now that's something a man can be proud of. Are you proud of me?"

Phil and Lynda Wallace hadn't anticipated having any children, but then, at the age of forty-five, Lynda became pregnant. Phil was fifty when Dean was born. Fifteen years later he died of a heart attack while at the printing plant where he worked as the bookkeeper. Lynda Wallace died six years later, leaving Dean alone, a senior in college. He married Sandy the following year, in 1954.

Nothing but Phil Wallace's old .22 caliber rifle has made its way from Phil and Lynda Wallace's home in Somerville to Dean's homes in Newton, Wayland or now on to Concord. No antique clocks, worn blankets, silver candlesticks or needlepoint cushions, only a dirty rifle Dean keeps as proof of his father's existence. The rest of his parents' belongings: their brass bedframe, the manual lawn mower, his mother's sewing machine and the house itself were all sold, Dean using the money to pay funeral expenses, outstanding debts and college tuition payments.

Hal crashes into Dean's leg, clamping his small arms around his father's calf, "We're moving! We're moving!"

Dean smiles, placing a hand on Hal's shoulder, steadying his son. "That's right, now don't get in the way." Hal releases Dean's leg and rushes off. Dean glances from the empty house to the lawn littered with cardboard boxes, mattresses, the dishwasher, end tables. He wishes he was in his office. He hates taking a day off from work.

Blane waits in the empty classroom after school. Mrs. Freeman's driving to her home to pick up Blane's final year-end report card so he can be transferred.

Blane hates the house his family is moving into. Dean and Sandy love the new house, as do the other kids. They like its big reproduction Colonial look: pale blue-gray with black shutters, white trim, a large porch off the back, a small wing for Dean's den at one side. A carved-wood burst of white sun rays frames the top border of the bold red front door, welcoming visitors to the Wallaces' new home. Blane finds the house creepy, large and sprawling with many rooms and long hallways.

Mrs. Freeman is having her first baby. Blane's family has too many kids, so now they're moving to a new house where they'll all fit and have their own rooms. Blane's been sharing a room with Tom. Tom steals money from Blane's mechanical elephant bank but Dean and Sandy never believe Blane when he tells on his brother.

Blane sits at his homeroom desk. All the other kids are out, so the school's empty. Blane lifts the lid of the desk and looks in. It's empty, he's packed his notebooks in one of his mother's shopping bags from the market. The books are by the door so he can leave the second Mrs. Freeman's back.

Blane gets out of his seat and sits at Gregory Till's desk. He opens the lid. Greg's desk is filled with junk. Blane might break something he hates him so much. Greg comes over to Blane's house to be his friend and he ends up playing with Tom. "You only like to read and watch TV," Greg said. "Tom likes to have fun and play."

Sandy has made attempts at getting Blane to play with them but Blane refuses, wants his friends to himself, doesn't like sharing with his brother. Greg and Tom play Smash-Up Derby outside on the driveway while Blane stays in the bedroom, reading his books about Snoopy, Charlie Brown, Linus and Lucy.

Blane starts poking through Greg's desk. Wacky pack stickers taped all over the inside of the lid. Crust toothpaste and Bone Ami and Vomit and Spic and Spit. Blane reaches under Greg's notebook and finds a squirt gun, a red one with water already in it. Blane gets up and takes it over to the sink, unstops the plug at the back, shaking the water out. Blane then goes over to the door and puts it in his paper bag. Greg can't tell on him because he isn't supposed to have it in school anyway.

Blane gets an idea and looks over the classroom, then walks to the front of the room to Pamela Tubb's desk, deciding to steal all the squirt guns from all the desks, not only Greg Till's— Tom's friend's squirt gun—but all of his classmates'.

He has twenty-five minutes: Mrs. Freeman will be back at four and it's only three-thirty-five now. So Blane checks out every desk, looking under notebooks, workbooks, in pencil cases for those tiny squirt guns you win at the carnivals in town. Blane lifts the bottom of his shirt away from himself, holding it out like a basket, carrying all the guns in it, and he checks the last desk. It contains no gun and the clock reads four. Blane's got nine squirt guns, plus Greg's makes ten. They're all different colors, some broken, some leaking drops out on his shirt, but Blane takes them anyway, shaking the water out in the sink, then putting them in his bag by the door. He hurries back to his seat.

Blane's brothers and sister are moving to the new house with his parents and then he's going there with Mrs. Freeman. "It's only two towns away," Sandy reassured him when Blane spoke to her over the phone in the school's main office. "The car ride won't be long."

A couple of weeks ago Dean and Sandy took the kids over to the new house for the first time, giving the boys a tour of the upstairs, pointing out their assigned rooms. There was the master bedroom at the top of the stairs, Tina's room beside that, Kyle's across from hers, then Tom's, Hal's, the guest room (or Lilly's room if Sandy could convince her mother to move in with the family), and finally, at the far end of the hall, was Blane's room, facing north, toward the back of the house. The windows, shaded by large pine trees, let out onto the roof of the porch one floor below.

Dean and Sandy say they like all the kids the same, but Blane has his doubts. He asked his mother if she likes all food the same, TV shows or clothes the same, and she said, "No."

"Then how can you like us all the same?"

"It's different."

"Do you like all your friends the same?"

"No, not all of them."

"Then how can you like all of us the same?"

"You're my children. I love all of you equally. Differently, but equally."

"Then how do you love me differently?"

"I love you because you're Blane."

And Blane doesn't understand what that means.

Blane has ten squirt guns in his bag. He has ten squirt guns and wonders if any of them are dripping water out, messing up his stories and pictures. He wonders if squirt guns were real guns and if the water was real bullets if kids would really shoot each other when they were playing. Blane wonders if you gave a kid a real gun and told him it was a squirt gun and then when the kid fired it and killed someone if the kid would be a real murderer.

And then this thought crosses Blane's mind: What if someone tells on me? All the kids get together, figure it out and they tell? What happens next? Can they get him or does it not count since he moved and he's not at this school anymore?

Blane looks over at his paper bag. A dark wet streak grows

down one side all the way to the bottom corner. Blane stands, hurrying to the bag, dumping the guns out across the floor. They clatter everywhere and Blane grabs at them, picking them up. He has to put them back quickly before Mrs. Freeman finds him and can tell his parents what he's done, the crime he's committed, but Blane can't remember which guns go in which desks or which desks he took them from and Blane drops all the guns in the first desk he sees. He places all the guns in Pamela Tubb's desk.

Blane sits back at his seat. Mrs. Freeman's not back in the class yet and it's four-thirty. Blane wonders if maybe Mrs. Freeman's having her baby and has forgotten all about him, leaving him stranded, never to catch up with his family at the new house.

"Blane?"

Blane looks around. Mrs. Freeman stands in her long coat, holding Blane's report file. Blane places his hands on the desk, looking back at her. "Uh, hello, Mrs. Freeman."

"What did you do all this time?" She smiles at him.

"I don't know," Blane says. "Nothing."

She walks up to him and puts a hand on his shoulder. She's wearing an orange-and-green-checked maternity dress. She touches Blane's hair.

Blane looks up at her. "I don't want to move. I hate the house I'm going to. I do. It makes me sick."

Mrs. Freeman leans over and pulls Blane's head to her stomach. She kisses his forehead. "You'll be fine, don't worry." Blane feels the baby kick from inside her and he pulls away, frightened, looking up at Mrs. Freeman for some reaction but she's still pretty and smiling and Blane wonders if his mother ever looked so pretty when she was having a baby, when she was having him, but he can't remember, has no way of knowing.

Mrs. Freeman puts her hand on Blane's head. "It's time to go, fellow, let's get your things." And Blane gets out from behind his desk and takes his jacket off the peg by the door, putting it on.

Mrs. Freeman comes over. "Your mother tells me you're going

to have your own special room in the new house. Can you tell me about it?" Mrs. Freeman turns off the lights. Blane picks up the bag with his notebooks, wondering what Pamela Tubb will do with all the guns in her desk. Will she be afraid or fearless for having so many guns?

Mrs. Freeman takes Blane's hand, leading him out of the dark classroom, into the empty hall.

"Aren't you going to tell me about your new room?" she asks.

1 9 7 1

" I F Mom and Dad were smart enough to have stopped after me then there'd be enough money so I could have a sundae and large fries and onion rings instead of just a small fries and only a cone."

Kyle, Blane and Tom sit in one of the beige vinyl booths in the Friendly coffee shop, and Kyle, having made his remark and detailed his feelings concerning his desire for a large fries, side of onion rings and sundae, resumes scanning the menu for other options.

Blane and Tom glare at their older brother, who sits facing them. Their mother gave Kyle the money, one ten-dollar bill, so each is dependent upon their older brother to divide it up fairly.

"We each get three dollars to spend and then we have to give the rest of all of it for a tip," Blane calculates and informs his brothers.

"But what if I don't spend all of my money," Tom asks. "What if I only want to spend one dollar? Then I get to keep two dollars for me."

"No way because then I get to decide because Mom gave me the money to take care of."

"Let me see the money then," Tom demands.

"I'm holding it," Kyle asserts.

"Let me have mine. I want to pay for myself."

The waitress stands by the booth in a gray dress with puffy

sleeves and a ruffled white apron around her waist. "Are we ready to order?"

Each brother orders and the waitress departs, leaving Blane calculating how much each brother has left to spend on dessert. "Because you both ordered large drinks and large fries now you can only order a small dish or cone."

"You're not having any of my fries," Kyle counters.

"Or mine," Tom joins.

Sandy deposited her three eldest children at the local Friendly coffee shop while taking Hal and Tina across the parking lot to the professional building to see their pediatrician for tetanus shots. Handing Kyle the ten-dollar bill, "You can each have a sandwich and a soda and something for dessert. You can meet us at Dr. Severt's office in forty-five minutes or so at around four-fifty-five to five o'clock."

The waitress brings the colas—two large, one small—distributing straws to each of the brothers. "And anyway," Blane says, clutching his wrapped straw in one hand while his brothers crumple the wrappers and deposit them in the glass ashtray, "Mom and Dad didn't stop after you because you obviously weren't what they wanted so they had to have more kids to get what they wanted."

"Yeah," Tom agrees. "You sucked so they wanted to try to get better kids."

"They must not have liked you," Kyle says to Blane, "and you either," he says to Tom, "because they had more kids after both of you too, so if I wasn't what they wanted neither were either of you."

"Mom always tells us she loves us all the same." Blane selects the dessert menu from the stand clipped to the side of the booth. "She said she loves us all the same but different."

"You think she'd really tell you if she didn't want you?" Kyle asks incredulously.

Blane says nothing, admitting defeat, deciding over the choice of sundae toppings: butterscotch, strawberry, marshmallow, chocolate sauce, pineapple and hot fudge.

"But if they didn't want us," Tom says, "why wouldn't they just get rid of us at the adoption place where we bring Christmas gifts at Christmas?" Ever since Tom was displaced as the youngest, most spoiled son by Hal four years ago, and then Tina arriving three years later, Tom has noticed a significant decrease in the number of gifts received. No more plastic handcuffs or battery-operated green-and-red-lit yo-yos upon his asking. On weeknights, his father brings home special gifts for Hal and Tina but Kyle, Tom and Blane are forgotten. And unlike Kyle, who had the benefit of their parents' undivided attention for two years, Blane not only never had his parents to himself, but he was displaced as the youngest after only one year with the birth of Tom.

"If anyone wasn't wanted it was you," Kyle tells Blane. "You're the one they had a kid the soonest after."

"They waited four years after me," Tom says with a note of triumph in his voice.

"Two after me," Kyle says, "and three after Hal."

Blane ponders the point. The waitress appears with their meals. Two cheeseburgers with two orders of large fries for Kyle and Tom. One regular burger with small fries for Blane. "At least I have money left for a sundae," he declares.

1 9 7 2

L I L L Y can't make the bed and Sandy should know this. Sandy should have known and done it for her. Lilly thinks that just because she made Sandy make their bed when she was a child, now Sandy has her mother making the bed in Sandy's house, handing Lilly a pile of clean sheets folded neatly. "Here, Mother, will these do?" They were standing in Lilly's room, facing each other across the bare mattress on Lilly's new bed, Sandy's old guest bed.

"Oh, of course they will," Lilly accepted graciously. "Sheets are sheets are sheets."

"Do you need any help? I could get one of the boys to help you out," Sandy offered.

"Sandy, I don't think making a bed will put me out too much. Now you go take care of my grandchildren," Lilly instructed her daughter.

"Just asking, Mother," Sandy replied.

And her daughter was just asking, as if Sandy couldn't have known that she should do it for her mother. Dean came by her apartment with a small van and loaded Lilly's entire life up into that dirty truck. Now it all sits in the damp basement of this house.

"It's not a basement, it's a playroom," Sandy told Lilly, as if that made it any better. "It's carpeted and you know that. Everything will keep fine," she explained.

"And the kids will poke through my things. Toying with all my things," Lilly replied. "Putting my things in their playroom and they'll play with my antiques as if they were toys." Sandy, rolling her eyes at Lilly, had the nerve to say, "It's just junk, Mother. Just broken relics from every home you've lived in through your life." And that was that and Lilly sent her daughter off to discipline her children. Sandy didn't even have the courtesy to insist that she make the bed for her own mother. The homes Lilly has lived in during her life. The apartment on Commonwealth Avenue where she grew up with her parents and her brother, Schroeder. The apartment in the North End where she lived with Hugh for the three years they were married, and finally Schroeder's apartment in Brookline where she moved with Sandy after leaving Hugh. The very same year Lilly took a job as a bank teller, a job she held for thirty years.

Lilly's been collecting things from all her homes, old oil lamps, woven rugs, painted furniture, embroidered tablecloths. But Sandy doesn't want these things:

"Oil lamps are dangerous," Sandy says.

"The rugs are frayed."

"The furniture has rotted."

"The tablecloths have yellowed."

Lilly never let Sandy talk or visit with her father once they moved to Schroeder's. Hugh would pound on the wood door to the apartment with both fists, shaking the walls, rattling the photos of Lilly's family on the table by the door, and Sandy and Schroeder and Lilly would stare at the door, saying nothing to each other as Hugh screamed louder, demanding to see his daughter, calling attention to the apartment, letting the neighbors know that Lilly was a woman who had left her husband, that she was a "divorcee" in the days when no decent woman got divorced, back in 1938. And Hugh would keep hollering and pounding on the door, sometimes cracking bits of paint off the door's white frame and Lilly would take Sandy by her small hand, leading her into their bedroom closet, telling Sandy that her father would kidnap her and never give him back. "Listen to him pounding on that door," Lilly would say. "He wants to kill us. Your father's a killer—that's why we had to leave him—he's a maniac." Lilly would reduce Sandy to tears, Sandy begging her mother to protect her from him as Lilly sat Sandy down in the corner of the closet and shut the door, protecting the child from Hugh's hysterics. Then Schroeder and Lilly would sit silently on the sofa in the living room, waiting out Hugh's fit until they could hear his screams become sobs as he began crying and pleading with Lilly to let him see his daughter. After Hugh had cried himself out, Lilly and Schroeder would hear his shoes shuffle away from the door, down the stairs and out into the street as he made his shameful retreat back across town to his lonely North End apartment. Later, when Sandy was older, she'd ask Lilly why she left him and Lilly told her daughter it was because Hugh used to beat Lilly but that Sandy was too young to remember it. That was the truth about Hugh as far as Sandy and Schroeder were concerned. The truth to Lilly was that she divorced Hugh because Hugh wanted to touch her and make love to her and it made Lilly sick. The touch of Hugh's hands made Lilly nauseated, to be touched in those places, his hands were so big and hairy.

Dean and Sandy let Lilly bring a few of her own things up to the new room. Lilly selected the white velvet chair that belonged to her mother and the vanity table and footstool that she's used since she was nineteen years old, probably the only things that will remain nice once the kids get their hands on her antiques in the basement.

This is a big house though, plenty of rooms for everyone and certainly the largest place Lilly's ever lived.

Lilly sits on the edge of the unmade bed. The bottom sheet is half on, half off. Two diagonal corners in place. The other two waiting to be stretched taut. Lilly can't take care of herself anymore and Lilly knows that Sandy likes that; likes to remind Lilly that she can't survive without her daughter by her side. Sandy phoned Lilly last week, for the past couple of years Sandy had been trying to convince Lilly how helpless she'd become.

"Mother, you can't even do your own shopping. You can't lift the bundles," Sandy said.

"That is simply not true," Lilly insisted.

"You've said so yourself several times," Sandy said.

"I just can't carry the heavy bundles. I can manage the light ones though," Lilly said calmly.

"So what are you going to live on? Paper towels and toilet tissue?" Sandy snapped back. And Sandy had made her point known and Lilly, finally, after years of arguing, willingly consented to being moved to Concord, instead of protesting and being forced, possibly into an old age home. But then again, Lilly could only agree. She no longer worked and Dean was paying her monthly rent, and since her Social Security check was barely enough to cover utility and food expenses, if Sandy and Dean decided it best for Lilly to move in with the family, refusal was hardly an option.

"Good, I'd hate to think you'd have another heart attack alone there in that apartment," Sandy added. "It could be days before anyone found you. Think about what happened with Dean's mother."

A few years back, Lilly was fortunate enough to have had a heart attack while visiting her daughter. Dean was away on business and at ten o'clock at night Lilly collapsed on the living room floor, facedown. Sandy had to call an ambulance and a sitter so she could go to the hospital with her. Kyle, Blane, Tom and Hal sat perched on the stairway, watching as Lilly was loaded onto a stretcher, wheeled through the hallway and out the front door. During the ride to the hospital, Sandy held her mother's hand and cried how much she loved her, begging Lilly not to die and Lilly didn't. Lilly lived. Lilly's living, and now she'd like to take a nap in her new bed once it's made.

Lilly lifts one of the sheet's corners, pulling at the elastic with her fingers, and she looks down at the pattern. Yellow daffodils with orange shoots leaping from their petals. Sheets that match the daffodil wallpaper covering all four walls of the room. Lilly stretches the elastic toward the corner and a pain grips her fingers. She lurches forward. The sheet snaps back to the center of the bed, flowers sprouting from all over the sheet, a pretty pattern. Lilly sits on the edge of the mattress, rubbing her hands, soothing the pain. She notices Blane run into his room.

"Blane," she calls after him.

He reappears in the doorway of his room. Their rooms face each other, both at the far end of the house.

"Yeah?" he asks.

"Where do you think that should go?" Lilly asks, gesturing over to the white velvet chair.

"I thought we were supposed to put your stuff in the playroom?" he asks.

"Did you know that's over eighty years old?" Lilly tells him. "It was your great-grandmother's favorite chair."

"I didn't know her, did I?" Blane sits beside Lilly on the bed.

"Oh, no." Lilly shakes her head. "She passed away long before you were born. She was crossing the road one day. You know, the cobblestone streets at Haymarket? And a horse and buggy came around a corner and . . . " Lilly stops, staring at the wall.

"She was run over by horses?" Blane asks, his interest piqued.

Lilly nods. "That's right." She pats Blane's head, then smiles. "That was long before there were cars. Now where do you think it would look best?" She directs Blane's attention back to the chair in question.

He looks at it blankly. "I don't know."

"Do you think it would look nice by the window? Or would it be better at the foot of the bed by the nightstand?"

"I don't know." Blane stands, pulling his striped alligator shirt down, hands shoved deep into the pockets of his jeans. "You can sit in it anywhere."

"Well, you must have an opinion. Think about it. Use that smart bean of yours," Lilly tells him.

Blane walks past his grandmother and looks at the chair. "It looks fine where it is, I guess," he says.

"Then what do you think about these sheets? I think they're pretty," Lilly says. She points to one of the flowers, "They're daffy dills. Daffy dills," she repeats and she smiles at him. Blane looks at the sheets tangled over the bed. "Do you want me to help you make it?"

"You don't know how, do you?" Lilly asks.

"I do my own."

"That's certainly good of you, saving your mother the trouble."

"It's on the chore chart. I have to do it to get my allowance each week," Blane explains.

"Oh, I see," Lilly responds, wondering if her daughter makes her own bed or assigns that off to one of the children as well. She looks from the bed up to Blane. "But you don't mind making my bed too? Do you have schoolwork you have to get to?"

"No."

"That would be nice then," Lilly tells him with a smile. "I enjoy your company. It was so lonesome living alone. I hope you grow up and marry a nice girl and have a nice family so you never have to be alone. You don't know how nice it is to be close to you kids, watching you grow." And Lilly stands, getting off the bed while Blane reaches out, taking the sheet and so easily stretching the elastic around the corner of the mattress with his nimble fingers.

"You're such a good boy," Lilly says, sitting in the white velvet chair, putting her feet up on the little hassock, "always have been, never a nuisance when I used to have you over for sleep-over visits. Now when we visit, you won't have to come into Brookline—I'll be right across the hall." Lilly laughs, remembering when she was younger, still working. On weekends, when there were only Kyle, Blane and Tom, Sandy and Dean would drop each one of the boys off separately for a "one-weekend-a-month-visit-with-Nana." The grandson would stay over from Friday night through mid-Sunday morning when Dean would pick the child up, to be returned to the suburbs.

The boys would sleep in Schroeder's old room, giving Lilly the temporary security of knowing she was not living entirely

alone. "Nice to have a man around the house again," she'd say
to each of the boys, kissing them on their cheeks as they stood
upon arrival in the apartment's doorway.

Kyle enjoyed visiting Lilly for the weekends, enjoyed walking
along Commonwealth Avenue, sundaes at Baileys Famous Ice
Cream Parlour and touring the old Grannery graveyard, viewing
the tombstones of famous Boston politicians as well as Mother
Goose. Tom preferred taking the trolley cars to walking. He
enjoyed watching the Red Sox play at Fenway Park. Lilly would
purchase two grandstand tickets, insisting upon sitting by the
exit ramp, always wanting to be prepared in case of emergency
and a speedy exit became necessary. Once Tom and Lilly had
located their seats and the game had begun, Tom took a ticket
stub from his grandmother and ran off on his own, hoping to
catch a foul ball. Lilly sat watching along with the loud crowd,
cracking shelled peanuts, waiting out the nine innings until Tom
reappeared to be taken out for hotdogs after the game. Blane
kept to the apartment for his entire weekend in Brookline, eating
in rather than being taken out to coffee shops or delis, watching
TV rather than going to a movie show. Lilly would leave him
locked in the apartment while she walked down to the market
to pick up the ingredients for the cookies to be baked while
watching the lineup of Saturday night shows: *Jackie Gleason, My
Three Sons, Hogan's Heroes* and *Petticoat Junction*. Lilly would
sit on the couch, Blane's head resting in her lap, and she'd stroke
his hair as the donkey-shaped sugar cookies sat on the cooling
rack, waiting to be eaten.

Blane carefully smooths his hands across the bottom sheet,
eliminating any wrinkles, then spreading the yellow blanket
across it. Within a few minutes Lilly will be able to take a nap
and get a good rest. And when she wakes, it will be dinnertime;
Sandy will have it ready for her and the kids. Sandy's making
Lilly her favorite meal tonight, pot roast and potatoes, softening
the blow of taking away Lilly's final illusion of independence:
having her own place to call home. Lilly no longer simply relies
on her son-in-law to pay the rent on the apartment in her name,

but Dean now owns the roof over her head, the floor under her feet, and the pot roast and potatoes Lilly will be so gratefully enjoying this evening.

Blane folds the blanket and sheet under the mattress, carefully, neatly tucking the corners. Lilly stands and walks up behind him, kissing the back of his head. "I'm glad I'm here with you."

■

Sandy and Dean Wallace had only intended upon having two children, one boy and one girl, but after giving birth to Kyle and then Blane, still wanting the elusive girl baby, Sandy became pregnant again. Nine months later Tom was born.

Having thus spent over half of the last four years of her life pregnant, giving birth to three boys all within three years of one another, Sandy said no more and Dean, wanting a girl but not yet financially able to support three—let alone four—children, agreed.

Four years and two promotions later, Hal was born.

Sandy and Dean couldn't believe that out of four pregnancies not one girl arrived. Sandy felt that they'd been cheated, that they were being punished by fate. Dean, in order to prove his wife wrong and demonstrate that they could control their family destiny, told Sandy he wanted to have one more child with her and he was sure this baby would be a girl.

So Dean, upon receiving the promotion to executive vice president of his division, celebrated by impregnating his wife. Nine months later, Tina was born.

■

Hal's seven party friends encircle him on the family room's carpet as Hal unwraps the first of his birthday gifts. Tina sits by Hal's side watching with envy as her older brother unwraps the presents, somewhat comforted by Hal's decision to make her the recipient of all the unwrapped packages' bows and ribbons. Hal hands his sister a green bow that she immediately plants in the center of her pink-and-white-flowered jersey. "Look, Mom, Look! Green!"

"That's right, that's green," Sandy replies from her seat on the couch and Tina smiles.

Hal lifts the unwrapped present high over his head. "Mr. Potato Head!"

Lilly, sitting at Sandy's side, claps her hands for the present. Sandy tells Hal to say thank you. Tina's eyes are fixated on the red bow decorating a round box. Hal lifts the present before him, tearing at its locomotive-patterned paper.

Kyle sits at the kitchen table, feebly entertaining his junior high math homework while alternately taking bites from a piece of birthday cake and watching his brother's sixth birthday party. Sandy arranged to have both Blane and Tom sent off to friends directly after school so she could run the party without any major interruptions but she asked Kyle to come home immediately after school so as to help out with the party games.

"Why can't you have Nana Lilly do it? I have homework," Kyle moaned over breakfast this morning.

Sandy simultaneously closed both Tom's and Blane's lunchboxes. "Because Nana Lilly cannot keep up with eight wild five-year-olds playing Duck, Duck, Goose, Hot Potato, and Pin the Tail on the Donkey."

"Why can't Dad do it? Blane and Tom get to go to friends, why can't I?"

"Because you're older. That's how older children act—they help out their younger brothers. Now quit complaining."

The cake, decorated with smeary icing pictures of Winnie-the-Pooh, Piglet and Eeyore, sits half eaten at the kitchen table's center. Dirtied Winnie-the-Pooh paper plates, cups and matching napkins lay scattered across the paper Winnie-the-Pooh tablecloth along with the two abandoned party hats worn earlier by Sandy and Kyle. More clapping and Kyle looks over to see his grandmother, cone hat perched atop her wavy gray hair, applauding the Play-Doh factory Hal has unwrapped.

"I once had one of those," Kyle calls and Sandy shoots him a look—*Don't you spoil this for your brother*—then tells Hal to thank the gift-giver but Hal has heard his brother's remark and he turns his head.

"But mine's newer and better," he shouts and he turns back to his guests.

The fourth Play-Doh factory Kyle has seen given at a Wallace family birthday party and, no doubt, in a year or two or three he will be witness to his sister receiving the same. First there was his own Play-Doh factory, then came Blane's, then Tom's, and now Hal's, and Kyle sits through all of their parties quiet and helpful like older brothers do, trying to remember a day when he wasn't an older brother.

A Wallace family once existed composed solely of his mother, his father and his self, existed for two years and one month, but the only memory Kyle has of this family is faint, dreamlike, and Kyle isn't sure if this memory is indeed a memory or if he's imagined the incident.

Kyle sits at a tall brown wood table and the table is a small circle. He sits in a tall sunny yellow wood chair, the chair's sunny yellow squared arms meeting the edge of the circular brown table. At one side—his left—is his father. At his right sits his mother and they make a triangle of three faces. His mother and father are smiling and eating spaghetti with meatballs and he tries to curl the spaghetti around his fork but he cannot, the spaghetti won't stay and keeps slipping through the prongs of the fork and Kyle keeps trying and trying, watching as his parents eat and twirl their spaghetti so easily, listening to their chatter, trying to be a good boy and not interrupt like he's always been told by his mother and father and so he twirls and twirls his fork to no avail when finally his mother catches his gaze, turns to him and takes his hand gently in her own, positioning the fork in the middle of the white plastic plate where they twirl it together. The pasta magically catches within the prongs of the fork, and when his mother releases his hand Kyle lifts the full fork from his plate to his mouth, both his mother and father applauding.

Lilly applauds Hal's fourth gift: a stuffed Fred Flintstone doll. Hal shakes it in the air. "Yabba-dabba-doo!" And then all the kids are yelling, "Yabba-dabba-doo!" except for Tina, who retreats to her mother, scared. Sandy stands, shushing the children, asking Hal to move on to the next gift.

A word problem concerning a bucket of nuts half full, a bucket of bolts two-thirds full, and an eight-by-ten board confronts Kyle but his mind is focused on a day when he was no longer an only son but was one of two sons, an older brother. An eight-month-pregnant Sandy and a one-year-old Blane napped side by side in the master bedroom while Kyle was supposedly napping in his own room, but Kyle, not interested in napping, ventured downstairs for a snack. Finding a large box of cereal, Kyle placed the thin cardboard box on the stove, switching the burner dial up high as he had often seen his mother do. Within seconds the box was growing a flame up its side. Kyle, panicking, knocked the box off the stove with a spatula, then watched as the fire burned over one side of the box, then put itself out. Kyle kicked at the box with his foot, then flipped it over with the spatula, examining its burned side. The picture of the bowl of cereal and pitcher of milk was burned away, leaving only a plate of toast and glass of orange juice. Sandy walked into the kitchen carrying Blane in her arms, taking in the scene: the burned box on the floor, Kyle standing above it with the spatula, a pale blue fire glowing under the front right burner of the stove. Sandy switched off the burner dial and turned on Kyle. "Is this how you're going to act just because you have a brother? What would have happened if the house began burning and I came down to see what was going on? What if Blane was resting upstairs and the fire got to me or him or you before any firemen came? You and I can run out of the house because we can walk but what about Blane? You're not the only one around here anymore. I have to watch out for Blane now and pretty soon there'll be another baby around. You have to be able to watch out for yourself more. You're old enough to do that. I know you are. You could have killed us, do you know that?" Kyle was sobbing, staring up at his mother's swollen belly, and Sandy knelt to him, comforting her son, hugging him toward her with one arm as her other held Blane. Kyle pressed his head up against his brother's body, crying at Blane's back, looking over his brother's shoulder to see his mother's face and see his mother's lips form the words "It's okay, honey. I love you. It's all right now." Several years later—Kyle is seven, Blane is five, Tom is four and a newborn Hal is due back from the hospital in one more day—Kyle informed his brothers that since he was the first son, he was the best son. "I'm the first! I'm the first! I'm the first!" he chanted, whereupon Dean, hearing this and witnessing Blane's and Tom's distress, said, "First isn't any better than second, third or fourth. It doesn't prove to me that you're any better or smarter or nicer than anyone else in this family. First only means that you're older and should know better than to tease your younger brothers."

"Kyle, can you bring in the Hot Potato, please." Sandy gathers torn wrapping paper in her hands, crushing it between her fingers, forming a large, colorful ball.

Kyle slams his textbook shut, picking up the red, potato-shaped plastic toy off the kitchen counter, staring at its white-painted eyes and smiling mouth. He flips the potato over in one palm and turns its dial several times.

The potato instantly begins shaking in his hand, humming, quivering and jittering, and Kyle walks to the family room, handing the Hot Potato to his mother.

"Thank you," Sandy says, giving the dial an additional three twists, and she passes it off to one of Hal's friends. "Pass it around quick. If it stops and buzzes on you, you're out for the next round."

Kyle resumes his seat at the kitchen table, reopening the textbook, relocating today's assigned word problems.

■

Tom notices a piece of egg on the corner of his father's mouth.

"Dad, you have a piece of egg splat on your mouth," Tom tells him.

Dean looks at Tom and smiles. "It's supposed to be there. I'm saving it for later."

Dean and Sandy laugh; she wipes it away with a napkin, then kisses his cheek, soothingly.

Dean looks at the family gathered around the kitchen table, breakfast dishes cleared to the side counter, and he rubs his hands together. "So what did you get me?"

"Dean," Sandy says.

"Maybe we didn't get you anything," Kyle says and Dean laughs.

"Then maybe I'll just have to trade you all in for a better family."

"Yeah, I doubt it," Kyle says.

"You have a wonderful father," Lilly tells Kyle. "Don't tease with him."

"Yeah, don't tease me, Kyle," Dean says and he sticks his tongue out, then looks over at Lilly. "Thank you for sticking up for me."

"Well we did get you a few things," Sandy says slyly and she lifts a big Filene's bag up on the kitchen table. "Tah-Dah. Okay, you kids, run up and get your gifts for Dad."

"Tina, you go get ours," Lilly says.

Kyle, Tina, Blane, Hal and Tom all run out of the kitchen up the shag-red stairs and into their rooms to get their gifts. Kyle, Tina, Blane and Hal are all laughing and Tom runs in his room and shuts the door.

They all went to the mall yesterday morning while Dean fixed the lawn mower. Tom didn't pick his baseball off the lawn and Dean ran over it by accident, bending the blade on the mower, having a fit at Tom.

Sandy drove them to the mall and they all walked around to pick out their gifts, except for Lilly and Tina, who went together, and Blane, who took Hal along.

"We'll meet in front of the Paperback Booksmith in one hour," Sandy said.

An hour later they met back there, all holding bags with stuff for Father's Day except for Tom, who was holding a bag with a box of a model race car. The way Tom justifies it, his father has his own money to buy whatever he wants for himself. Tom also knows that his father thinks Tom's stupid because he doesn't bring home papers to pin on the kitchen bulletin board like Kyle and Blane; those red smiling faces on the tops of their papers grinning at Tom every time he goes to the refrigerator for something to eat or drink. And Tom doesn't do chores like Kyle and Blane, who are always washing the cars or sweeping pine needles off the driveway, making Dean happy. Even Hal sits by Dean's side, watching his father fix broken tiles in the bathroom or clearing weeds from cracks in the front walkway.

Dean smiles anxiously at Sandy and Lilly, waiting for the kids to reappear so he can receive the gifts, hoping he can open them with a gleam in his eyes, showing the family how much he appreciates and loves them. During this silence, Lilly chews on a slice of cold bacon, the only sound in the room. Dean wonders whether the family buys him gifts because they love him because he is their father, or if they buy him gifts because he is their father and today is Father's Day. He takes a sip from his coffee mug. Sandy and Lilly say nothing, sitting. Lilly's chewing has stopped, her hands are folded in the lap of her robe, Sandy's gently hold the edges of the large shopping bag perched on the table, obscuring her face.

Dean speaks. "Do you think maybe we could go to a movie tonight? A new thriller opened up I heard was pretty good."

Sandy jerks her head from behind the shopping bag. "We have the Wooleys' anniversary party tonight, remember? I bought them that vase at the Pottery Shed yesterday."

"That's right," Dean says. "Maybe we can see the movie next weekend."

"Sure," Sandy replies.

"You have a party to go to tonight?" Lilly asks.

Sandy rolls her eyes. "I told you about this weeks ago, Mother, why? Is there a problem?"

Lilly shakes her head. "I was just hoping that the whole family could all go out for Chinese tonight. I was in the mood for chicken chow mein."

"Maybe later in the week," Sandy says, trying to sound kind through anger.

Lilly pushes her chair back from the table, standing. "Guess that means I'll be baby-sitting the kids again." Lilly shrugs, taking a glass from the cabinet by the refrigerator, pouring herself some pineapple juice.

Sandy and Dean exchange a look, then Sandy raises her eyebrows to Lilly. "Did you have something else you were planning on doing so that you couldn't baby-sit?"

Blane, Kyle, Tina and Hal run into the kitchen, giving Lilly no chance to respond; she just takes a sip of the pineapple juice and returns to the table.

Tom gets up from the bed, shoving his hands under his shirt, holding them out like he's hiding a gift or something under it, letting the family think that he has a gift so when he doesn't his father will be disappointed. He walks down the stairs and the family is sitting around laughing, holding their bags from the mall.

Sandy hands Dean a big white box with an orange bow tied around it.

"This is from all of us," she says.

Dean opens the card, reading it. He nods and puts it down. "Very nice," he says. He lifts the box and shakes it by his ear.

"Dean, just open it," Sandy says. "You'll break it."

Dean unties the bow and drapes it around his neck. "How do I look?"

"Don't be dumb, Dad," Kyle says.

"It's my Daddy's Day and I can be dumb if I want to," Dean answers and he opens the box. "Oh, I've been wanting one of these." He lifts out a carved wood deer. "It's a deer." He holds it up and looks at it. "Very nice," he says sincerely. "Very nice. Thank you, everyone," and he leans over and gives Sandy a kiss.

"Me—me!" Tina cries and Tina and Lilly hand Dean his gift. It's not wrapped and he just pulls it out of the bag: a yellow mug, "Dad" scrawled across the side in Tina's messy handwriting.

"I did myself," Tina says.

"I can see. It's beautiful." Dean leans over and kisses Tina.

"Thanks, Lilly. Thank you, little princess." Dean leans over and kisses Tina again.

"Well, who's next?" Sandy asks and Kyle shoves his gift at his father. It's a tie. Dean makes a big deal over it, holding the tie up to his T-shirt, asking if it looks good. Hal hands Dean a statue that states "To the best Dad in the World."

Blane gives Dean two books—one suspense novel and one book on jogging. Dean scans the back covers. "I'll let you read these when I'm through," he says to Blane.

They're finished and the family turns to Tom, and Sandy says, "Tom, don't you want to give Dad the gift you bought him?"

Tom stares back at her. "I gave him the deer with you."

Sandy smiles. "Of course you did. We all gave Dad that deer."

Dean nods at Tom and smiles. "Thank you, Tom, I really like it very much." He looks around the table. "Thank you all for the lovely gifts." He stands, Sandy stands, and all the kids get up and leave the room. Lilly finishes off her glass of juice as Dean and Sandy place the gifts back in the Filene's bag.

Sandy holds up the mug, examining Tina's writing. She looks over at her mother. "This is a very nice gift," Sandy says, and she means it. "Don't you think so, Dean?"

"I think it's great." He takes it from Sandy, walking to the sink and rinsing it out. "I could use it right now for another cup of coffee."

"I'm glad you like it," Lilly says flatly. "We almost got you a hummingbird feeder, but Tina really wanted to go with the mug thing." Lilly stares out the window, looking off into the woods.

Dean and Sandy look at her. "I do like the mug, Lilly, I think it's great," Dean says.

Lilly sighs loudly.

"What is it, Mother?" Sandy asks, again trying hard not to sound too irritated.

A moment of silence, another sigh from Lilly, then, "I was looking forward to chicken chow mein tonight, that's all."

"Mother, I told you about this party weeks ago."

"Well," Dean says, leaning on the kitchen counter, "we really don't have to go to the party. We could just drop off the gift on the way out to dinner. We're really not that close with the Wooleys anyway. And, after all, it is Father's Day."

"Dean," Sandy breaks in. "I would like to go to this party. I've been planning on it."

Lilly tosses up her hands, turning her back on Sandy. "If this is your way of taking things out on me for divorcing your father—fine, Sandy, go right ahead, but I won't play along." Lilly walks into the family room, heading straight for the television.

Sandy follows. "What?"

Lilly switches the channel selector, searching for a program. "You've always had trouble dealing with Father's Day and if this is your way of getting back at me, fine, go ahead, but don't take it out on Dean and the kids is all I'm asking." Lilly selects a Sunday morning local panel show and firmly plants herself on the couch, intent upon watching the program.

Sandy stares at her mother, speechless. Dean watches from the kitchen, unsure of whether to get involved with this or not. Lilly slumps on the couch, shoving her hands into the pockets of her robe. Sandy hovers above her, glaring.

"I'm sorry I'm such an imposition in your lives," Lilly begins, shaking her head, "but after all, I can't drive and unless someone takes me out I have nothing to do but roam the house day in and day out and it was your idea for me to move in with you. I am thankful, but if I did live in Brookline I could at least order in, but they don't have that in the suburbs."

Sandy looks away from Lilly, toward the television where the mayor of Boston talks on about fiscal issues.

Dean can't bear the silence or Lilly's long lament and he takes a sip of coffee from his new mug and says, "We really don't have to go to that party, you know, Sandy, you know that."

Sandy looks to Dean, then to Lilly, then Dean again. "Do you want to go to the movie? Fine. You go to the movie. I'll take Mother out for chicken chow mein." Sandy walks from the room, past Dean in the kitchen, upstairs. Dean can hear the door slam to the master bedroom.

"What movie were you thinking about seeing?" Lilly asks from her seat on the couch.

Tom reaches under his bed and pulls out the model. The box is opened. He's already put a few of the pieces together. Tom sits on the floor and begins assembling the motor, epoxying the carburetor to the fan belt. The engine is the hard part because there are so many tiny pieces and the glue oozes all over, making them gross. Tom thinks that maybe he'll give this to his father when it's done. Maybe he'll finish it today, give it to him later, and just tell his father that he was just waiting for it to dry.

There's a knock at Tom's door.

"Come in."

It's Kyle. He stands in the door staring down at Tom on the floor. Tom looks up at him. "What do you want?"

"You're an asshole," Kyle says.

"Get out," Tom says, putting down the car.

"Didn't get Dad anything. What an asshole."

"I got him this model," Tom says.

"Then why didn't you give it to him?"

"It's not done yet," Tom explains.

"You bought it for yourself," Kyle says.

"Did not, asshole," Tom says.

"Loser," Kyle says. "Loser."

Tom stands. "Get out of here."

"He's going to hate you forever now. Not buying him anything on Father's Day means you think he's a bad father and he'll hate you forever," Kyle hisses.

"Get out of here!" Tom screams and he throws the cover of the model box at Kyle and it hits him on the shoulder. Kyle laughs. "Yeah, you really hurt me," and he turns, "you can't do anything right, you loser," and Kyle steps out and shuts the door.

Tom turns and looks down at the model and he picks up his foot, stomping it down on the car body, crushing the green frame under his sneaker. He lifts his foot off the car and it's all bent and broken and now he can't even give the model to his father or fix it for himself: It's ruined.

Tom walks out of his room, downstairs and into the kitchen. Dean sits at the kitchen table, holding the deer up close to his face, inspecting its details. He looks up at Tom. "This is very nice. Did you help Mom pick it out?"

Tom takes his windbreaker off a hook in the hallway. "I'm going over to a friend's house," he says. "Okay?"

Dean looks at Tom and smiles, nodding. Tom looks back at his father, then at the deer. Dean looks back down at the deer, then back over at Tom and he stops smiling.

"Tom," Dean calls, but Tom turns, pushing open the screen door and walking out of the house, leaving Dean alone to look at the deer the whole family gave him.

1 9 7 3

T H E door to the master bedroom is closed. Sandy crouches on the bed, legs folded beneath her, sitting on her heels as she reads the *Family Circle* magazine delivered in the mail earlier that day. A stack of magazines sits on the bed's headboard: *Good Housekeeping, Better Homes and Gardens, McCall's, Woman's Day, Life, Reader's Digest.* Sandy doesn't have time for books, always picking up a novel, halfway through a chapter only to be interrupted by the kids. Sandy's settled into browsing these magazines overflowing with glossy-faced smiling women in clean antiseptic kitchens and bathrooms, never a crying child in sight.

Sandy reads over a recipe for "Tangy Tangerine Chicken Salad," wondering what kind of a woman would take all that time to bake, skin and dice the chicken, wash and cut the vegetables, then whip up fresh salad dressing. All that bother for a chicken salad sandwich. And none of the Wallaces even like chicken salad. It would all go to waste if Sandy didn't eat it herself.

Sandy turns the page and is faced with an article concerning "Swing Set Safety Tips: How to Teach Your Child to Play Properly Out-of-Doors." Sandy's kids are out-of-doors now, out-of-doors playing at the neighbors, pretending they're in a parade: the neighborhood children lining up their bicycles, pedaling around the block, screaming and ringing handlebar bells. Tina's napping after running around the house all morning. Lilly naps after a morning of watching game shows. A cool breeze blows through the open windows giving Sandy a chill, goose bumps. Her nipples harden and Sandy can feel them press against the cotton of her blouse. She isn't wearing a brassiere, never does when she plans on staying indoors all day, and she reaches up to the neck of the shirt, slowly unbuttoning it down to mid-chest. She reaches in, touching a breast, feeling it grow firm as she turns the pages of the magazine with her other hand. Sandy reads that playground accidents account for four-point-five percent of all childhood fatalities. She closes the magazine and places it on the headboard with the others. She lies back on the bed, unbuttoning her shirt to the navel, drawing it out from the skirt, letting it fall open across the bed, her chest bare.

"Free love" does not exist in Sandy's life. She's read articles in *Life* about people living in communes, sharing everything: homes, money, clothes, children, spouses. Sandy watches these people on news programs: mothers not much younger than herself running half naked through parks cradling newborns in their arms. Is that "free love"? Sandy isn't sure what "free love" is. Is it sex without marriage? Sex without love? Sex without children? Sex for the sake of having sex?

Sandy's blouse is lying crumpled on the carpet with her skirt. Her panties hang halfway down one thigh, leaving the other leg free. *The Joy of Sex* lies open at her side. When Sandy had first heard of the book she had thought it was supposed to be a joke, had thought the title was supposed to be ironic. Not until she finally stood in the bookstore and glanced at its pages did she realize otherwise.

Sandy stares at the drawings of this passionate couple. She attempts to mimic the ways the man touches the woman and the ways the woman touches herself. Sandy studies the picture, then positions her body similarly. Sandy had bought the book secretly two months ago, hoping to surprise Dean with it, hoping it would add something to their usual once-a-week Saturday morning bout of sex: Dean rolling on top of Sandy, doing her, then slipping on his bathrobe and heading downstairs to eat donuts and watch cartoons with the kids. Sandy had hoped that if the book couldn't teach Dean how to give her an orgasm, at least she'd be able to learn how to give herself one, but Sandy's ready to call it quits. She keeps the book hidden in an old hatbox on the top shelf, in the back of her walk-in closet. She could never bring herself to actually show it to Dean, to tell him that she'd bought this book that depicts graphic portraits of a man and a woman doing "it" freely, uninhibited. Sandy had tried to think of ways of broaching the subject: Would it be more or less threatening if she did so while they were in bed? And what would she say after she'd shown him the book and seen the shocked, disgusted expression on his face? All Sandy could come up with was, "It's on most of the bestseller lists; I thought it must be worth reading." So Sandy keeps the book to herself, hidden in the hatbox, only to be read on those rare occasions when she has a moment to herself.

Sandy studies the picture of the close-up of the woman's vagina, a close-up sketch detailing its parts. Text runs along the opposite page, giving an elaborate description of the woman's genitalia, its most sensitive areas for stimulation.

Sandy looks down at herself, then up at the room, catching herself in the mirror on the opposite wall, seeing herself clearly for the first time in a while: this mother of five in her mid-thirties secretly fondling her vagina at four-forty on a sunny Wednesday afternoon, her hands down between her legs while most mothers stand in kitchens baking homemade brownies for their children.

Sandy closes the book and slowly, shamefully, takes her hands from between her legs, sliding off the bed. She turns away from the mirror, gathering her skirt and blouse in her arms, heading into the bathroom to dress.

•

"I want to go too!"

"Why can't I go?"

"Why can't we go, Mom?"

Sandy stands at the kitchen counter, her back to Tina and Hal as she transfers her wallet, lipstick and compact from her everyday handbag into the clutch purse she's chosen to match her outfit this evening. Hal and Tina tug at Sandy's knee-length navy blue wool coat, Hal at its back seam, Tina at its hem. Sandy snaps the clutch shut, clasping it to her side under an arm. "Mother, can't you help me here?"

"I can't chase after them, you know that," Lilly answers from her seat on the family room sofa, and Sandy turns, brushing Tina and Hal away from her sides.

"Why can't we go?" Hal implores. "We'll be good. Don't be so mean."

The car horn honks from the driveway, pressing on Sandy. "Your father and the boys are waiting. We've been over this. It will end too late for you to come. No one your age will be there. Now please let me go."

"I want to go too!" Tina wails.

"Mother! Can't you help me here!" Sandy asks again, breaking free from her two youngest, heading down the hall toward the side door.

Hal and Tina follow on Sandy's heels. "We can go too! It's not too late!"

"I can go! I can go!"

"Let us go! It's not fair!"

"Mommy! Mommy!"

The car horn sounds again and Sandy shuts out Tina's and Hal's cries, opening the door—*'You're a sucky Mom! I hate you!'*—then stepping out and slamming it in their faces.

Tina and Hal run around to the family room window, gazing out as their father pulls the car from the driveway into the street.

The car's headlights shine bright on the dark street as it glides along the road, around a bend and out of sight.

"It's not fair," Hal says, turning to his grandmother. "We're not too little."

Lilly, also left uninvited to a family friend's party commemorating the 198th anniversary of the battle of Lexington and Concord, agrees with her grandson. "No, you're right. It isn't fair. Even though the invitation said the whole family's invited, your mother says that we weren't."

"That's not fair!" Tina echoes her brother.

Lilly scans the evening's TV listing. "Life isn't fair," she instructs her grandchildren. "Most often it truly isn't." She rises from the sofa, placing the *TV Guide* on its seat. She walks into the kitchen. "Now what should I make you two changelings for supper?"

Tina and Hal follow. "What's a change-link?" Hal asks.

Lilly opens a cabinet by the stove. She had asked Sandy to hire a sitter weeks ago when the invitation arrived and she spotted it lying on the counter by the bread box, had asked to be included in on this outing, but her daughter replied that Hal and Tina were too young to go and thus required a sitter.

"You can use that girl Lucy."

"Lucy's away on vacation with her family and you know how difficult it's going to be finding someone for this evening. Everyone's going out."

"I'm sure we all could go to the party," Lilly suggested. "I could watch after them there. That's a solution that would please everyone."

"You wouldn't know anyone at the party anyway so what difference would it make? Within half an hour all three of you would be at me to drive you home."

"The too young and too old get ignored in this household, is that it? I bet even if Hal and Tina didn't need baby-sitting, I doubt you'd let me go."

"But they do, so you're not going and there's no sense arguing this, got it?"

Lilly stares at the assortment of boxes facing her. "How would you like macaroni and cheese," she asks.

"Yes!" Hal and Tina reply in chorus.

Lilly takes the blue box in hand. "And then after we can bake extra-extra-sugary sugar cookies, how about that?"

"Hooray!" Hal shouts.

"Hooray!" Tina shouts.

"Hooray!" Lilly joins in.

"I'm having the window on the way back so don't forget that," Blane reminds his brothers. Kyle and Tom flank him on either side of the back seat as Dean drives and Sandy stares out the passenger side window.

"If other kids aren't wearing ties when we get there, I'm taking mine off," Tom warns.

"You'll leave it on," Dean reprimands. "If you take it off you'll only lose it."

"Good. Then I won't have to wear it again."

"We could just as easily have left you all at home too," Sandy tells her children. "Can't we all just enjoy this evening out together?"

"I'd rather be at home," Blane whines. "None of my friends will be there. Miller won't be there. Alec and Brad won't."

"You have other friends besides Miller, Alec and Brad," Sandy says. "Stop moaning."

"He does not." Tom laughs. "It's only him and Miller and Brad and Alec who eat at lunch together. Never anybody else."

"They're better than the friends you have."

"What's wrong with my friends? My friends are cool."

"They're the stupidest kids in school."

"At least they're not wimps."

"Can you shut them up already?" Kyle pleads to his mother and father.

"Your lunch table's always in trouble for food fights," Blane adds.

"Not always."

"Almost always."

"Is this true?" Sandy asks.

"I'm not staying with them at the party," Kyle says.

"You will if I ask you," Dean replies. "Now we're here and I hope you've got all your bickering done with so we can all have a good time."

"How much past our bedtime is it?" Hal asks his grandmother. The television is tuned in to *Love, American Style*. Lilly sits on the lounge chair while Hal struggles to keep awake on the couch. Tina sleeps at his side, her head resting on the sofa's arm. Lilly reads the *TV Guide*, searching for entertainment alternatives. "I thought you might like staying up late with me."

Having been allowed to defy their mother's wishes and eaten a lot of sweets as well as staying up hours past their assigned bedtimes, Hal and Tina's anger over not being taken to the evening's celebration has dissipated. Come tomorrow each can brag about what they got away with in their mother's absence and prove they rule their own lives and are not held captive to their mother's demands.

Hal yawns into the air. "Is it twelve o'clock yet?"

"It's a little after ten. Don't you want to be up when your mother gets home? Show her you're a big boy?"

"I'm tired."

Lilly glances over at Hal and Tina. Both wear their everyday clothes, neither dressed for bed. Tina remains asleep and Hal's eyes are half shut. Lilly told them they could remain up until the rest of the family returned, demonstrating to her daughter that she can be as unreliable a baby-sitter as any stranger Sandy might hire. "Would you like another cookie?" Lilly asks.

Hal pushes himself off the couch. "I'm gonna go to bed." He grabs Tina's arm, giving it a yank. "Come on, go to sleep in bed."

Tina raises her head, wiping hair back from her face with an open hand. "Mommy home yet?"

"We're going up to bed. Come on." Hal takes Tina's hand and she stands, leaning on her older brother, who slides an arm around her waist.

Lilly watches them walk toward the family room door, her plan to antagonize her daughter ruined. "Hal? Before you go up can you change the channel to number seven, please?"

Hal releases Tina and she totters on, plodding through the kitchen and upstairs. Hal rotates the television's dial until the seven is illuminated with the glowing orange indicator light. "Good night," he says. Hal yawns, turning, leaving the room.

"Good night," Lilly replies. "Make sure Tina's tucked in okay."

No reply and Lilly stares at the television: *The CBS Friday Night Movie*. Lilly realizes she told Hal the wrong channel number. She had wanted twelve, not seven.

On seven, a woman screams in a bedroom as gunshots are being fired through an open window and Lilly has no idea what is going on but is too tired to bother getting up, crossing the room to change the channel to twelve.

"What? I'm under house arrest, is that it? I can't go out without my daughter's approval?" Lilly sat in this very room four hours earlier as Sandy told her mother the phone number where the family would be was written on the pad by the phone.

Channel seven, channel seven, channel seven the glowing orange number reads and if only the strength of her body matched that of her anger she could rise to switch the dial to the channel she wants but it does not, her strength fails her, and Lilly remains in the chair as three men wearing black ski masks burst into the woman's bedroom, one of the men hitting her over the head with a lamp.

■

Their stiff starched white shirts and pressed pants shed, their high-necked silky blouses and straight, below-the-knee skirts removed, Dean has a hard time immediately recognizing his colleagues at CODAT's eighth annual Northeastern Division company picnic, first annual since Dean became division president.

Dean Wallace, at the age of forty, is the youngest divisional president and corporate board member of CODAT, an international data processing company. Dean presides over the Northeastern Division, which may not be CODAT's greatest division in terms of square mile footage, but financially it has been the most lucrative, yielding the highest overall percentage of the company's net profits; a fact for which Dean receives considerable accolades during each of the bimonthly lunches he attends down at corporate headquarters in Richmond.

Dean, only recently having made it to the top, has not yet grown accustomed to his new role as boss, a role that keeps him from having any peers within his own Boston office and puts him in a position of surveying the company on the grander scale of national and international business. "I grew up in a family where nothing was expected of me," he told Sandy the evening after receiving the promotion. "My father died and my mother expected nothing of me, was just happy having me around with no ambitions for me whatsoever and yet here I am. And look at you, coming from your background with your mother and father. Twenty years later, here we are with our own family and own great home, at the top of the world."

Sandy spooned a portion of peas onto Dean's plate alongside the London broil and baked potato. "You've worked hard to do well. It's taken a lot of effort."

Dean leaned over, kissing his wife's cheek, taking her hand still gripping the serving spoon in his own. "You're a great wife and mother. You've made us a great home and I love you."

Dean stands on the edge of the beach at the state park. CODAT employees and their families swim, eat barbecued chicken, play volleyball and run in sack races. Dean watches Kyle, Blane and Tom splash one another in knee-deep water. Hal plays by Dean's feet, digging a hole. Tina, sick at home with an early summer cold, is cared for by Sandy. Lilly refused to come on the picnic outing, claiming "the toilets there are bound to be unhygienic and teeming with diseases."

Dean sits in the aluminum frame beach chair, looking over

Hal's handiwork. "You going to dig all the way to China? Pick yourself up some egg rolls?"

Hal builds a wall of dirt up around the mouth of the hole. "I'm making an experiment."

Dean leans forward, elbows on knees, watching Kyle hold Tom's head underwater, then Tom spring up and shove Kyle under. "What kind of experiment?" he asks.

"Very dangerous," Hal answers gravely and he embeds a small rock in the bottom of the hole.

"Well, be careful then," Dean replies.

Hal, having unpacked the straw beach bag, is surrounded by the colorful plastic toys his father and mother have bought for their children. Red plastic pails, navy blue shovels, sand sifters, geometric molds to create sand castles, plastic boats, an inflatable donut decorated with pictures of starfish and sea horses.

More toys than any child would dare ask for is what Hal has before him, Dean notes, and his eyes scan the blankets of his fellow employees, searching for their children, counting the number of their beach toys.

Dean Wallace grew up in a home without toys. Phil and Lynda Wallace, too old to have a child they found themselves having, raised Dean to act like an adult at an early age and take on the responsibilities of the Wallace home's upkeep. Dean remembers standing, crying in front of a toy store window, pointing to the mechanical dog in the shop window, his father dragging his son away, furious. "You want us to treat you like an adult, then act like one."

Dean regards Hal's toys. More toys than any child dare ask for and more toys than any other CODAT employee's child owns and Dean is at once proud and angry with himself for giving his children so much, all that he never had. Dean eyes Hal's toys, watching his son play in the sand, and he has the sudden urge to take up a pail and shovel and play alongside his son, creating a fantasy world of explorers digging a hole to China. Dean slides off the beach chair, sitting on the old worn blanket that once served as Sandy and Dean's first double-bed blanket.

He picks up a shovel. "I'm going to build a sand castle too," he tells Hal.

"I'm not building a sand castle. I'm making a experiment," Hal sternly corrects his father. "A experiment to explode big rocks all into little bits."

Dean peers into the hole, at the pile of rocks Hal has accumulated for his experiment. Dean picks a small stone from the beach, adding it to his son's pile.

"No," Hal exclaims and he takes the rock out, tossing it down in the sand.

"Can't I play with you?" Dean asks.

"I'm not playing," Hal says angrily. "I'm doing science."

"Can't I join in?"

Hal looks to his father, annoyed by these countless interruptions. "This is mine," and he returns his concentration to the hole.

"So be it," Dean replies with a smile.

The group of fifteen parents watch their children scamper through the woods in search of the treasure that they will then turn in for a first-, second- or third-place prize. The kids, ages eleven through fifteen, search around tree trunks and under bushes for the plastic bags of coins that designate them winners.

Kyle races out from among the pines, waving a bag of shiny quarters. "Hey, what do I win?" He carries the bag over to Marjorie Roache, the organizer of the treasure hunt and director of Human Resources at CODAT.

She takes the bag, examining its contents. "Dean, looks like your son's taken first prize." Kyle beams and the other parents applaud politely.

Dean smiles. "You put money in there, no wonder he found it so quick," and Dean's fellow employees laugh. Marjorie awards Kyle first prize, an inflatable boat for two, complete with a set of oars.

Perry Holtzman's girl, age eleven, runs from the woods screaming excitedly. She is followed only seconds later by Blane, who carries the third of the three sandwich bags. Marjorie hustles the other twenty children from the woods and awards third prize to Perry Holtzman's daughter, an oversized inflatable beach ball, and second prize to Blane, a large raft with a matching inflatable pillow. More applause for the three victors and Dean hears someone say, "Sure looks like your kids cleaned up on the prizes," and Dean looks to see who has made the remark, angry and embarrassed, but sees it was one of the park employees, not one of his own.

"This'll be great down the Cape this summer. We could use it right in front of the house," Kyle says, fastening his seat belt.

"I could use my raft too," Blane says.

"Can I ride it also?" Tom asks. "We can share. They're big enough for two."

"And me," Hal says.

"You better ask before you use it though," Kyle cautions from the front seat. "And you better be careful with it."

"I promise I will," Tom says. "Thanks."

And Dean's sons have reached an agreement over sharing the prizes won but Dean cannot help but be upset with his kids for taking home both first and second prizes. And although he knows he should be proud of them for winning, he says, "You know, it would have been nice for you kids to let others have a chance to win too." He pulls the dark blue Cadillac through the gate entrance to the state park, onto the road. "There were other kids and families that might have liked to have a prize."

"We found them," Blane defends. "Why shouldn't we win?"

And Blane is right but he's wrong and Dean explains further, "You kids have a lot of nice beach rafts and toys, more than you know what to do with. You could have given your prizes to the kids that don't."

"But we didn't even know what the prizes were till after," Blane argues.

"It's more complicated than that," Dean asserts, speeding the car to make it through a yellow light.

"We found them first," Kyle states. "Why did you let us play if we shouldn't try to win?"

Dean keeps his eyes fixed on the road. "Well, not everyone's daddy makes as much as I do. You're very lucky I make as much as I do and can afford to give you nice toys and things."

"Does that mean we have to let other people win just because you can buy us stuff?" Kyle waits for an answer, pissed—he *won* this prize and he *likes* this prize and his father's not going to ruin it for him.

"No, that's not what it means."

"What does it mean then," Kyle demands.

"Just remember that not everyone has as much as you do. Not everyone's as fortunate."

"Don't blame me," Tom says. "I didn't win."

"I didn't win," Hal adds, proudly. "I lost, so I'm good."

Dean flips down the visor, shielding his eyes from the glare. He was attempting to teach his kids a lesson in morals but is no longer sure what his point was, if there ever was one. He drives his children home, altogether confused over how he feels over what they've won, what he's always given them, and what they have naturally come to expect from life. A birthright to be handed everything, for life to come easily, free of worry, free of struggle, free of the anxiety of ever having to make ends meet by doing without the small luxuries of dining out, color television and leather sneakers. "Sometimes I think maybe I spoil you kids a bit too much," Dean says to his carload of boys. "I think you're all a bit spoiled and I'm not sure you appreciate all you have and how hard I've worked to give it to you. Maybe you're all just a bit too spoiled." Dean pulls the car onto a side street, avoiding the heavy weekend traffic on the main roads, his head cleared of his earlier bothersome thoughts. Kyle, Blane, Tom and Hal stare out their car windows, wondering what they've done wrong to deserve such scorn.

■

Philynda, a beagle of four months, scampers across the front lawn, barking at the eight pairs of legs rushing at, then away from her. The kids laugh, glad to finally have a pet the entire family can play with and touch, not a pet to be kept in a cage and just looked at.

In the past there had been individual pets. Pets given as gifts at birthdays or holidays. There were Kyle's gerbils that escaped from their cage, never to be found. Then came Blane's two guinea pigs, Pickles and Tuna, given to him as a birthday gift upon turning eight. Early one morning, Blane found Pickles dead in the cage, rolled over onto her side with Tuna eating out the dead guinea pig's stomach. Blane cried for hours, sitting on the floor by the wire cage, Dean and Sandy trying to comfort him, but sickened themselves by the sight. Sandy took Blane away to the kitchen, forcing him to eat breakfast while Dean buried Pickles out back, then returned Tuna to the pet shop. Tom kept fish. A large aquarium filled with a variety of tropical species: angels, stripers, catfish, goldfish. He spent his entire allowance on the aquarium, purchasing multicolored pebbles to layer along the bottom of the tank, small plants and brush for the fish to swim between, a plastic deep-sea diver with a gold helmet that stood in the tank, blowing air bubbles to the surface. After several weeks, Tom grew tired of the aquarium, its constant need for cleaning, the demand to change the water frequently, and he decided to do away with it all. One afternoon, after school, Tom simply scooped all the fish out of the tank with a small green net, catching them in mid-motion, and he took them into the bathroom, locked the door and dropped them into the toilet bowl. Tom stood above the basin, watching as the fish swam about in a flurry, adjusting to their new surroundings, when he quickly closed the lid and flushed. Like magic, a moment later he opened the lid and the fish were gone. He sold most of the aquarium equipment to a friend at a cheap price.

Sandy and Dean had toyed with the idea of obtaining a new pet for the family, but having experienced less than successful results in the past, they were wary of how to proceed. They finally decided upon a dog—a dog for the whole family to enjoy, not just for one of the kids to call his or her own, but a pet for the whole family; a pet to give the kids a sense of responsibility about caring for something; a pet to keep Lilly company when no one else is around; a pet that will grow as the kids grow, maturing as the family matures.

"Philynda," after Dean's father, Phil, and his mother, Lynda. The only way Dean had of making his parents seem alive to the kids: giving the family dog his parents' names, hoping his children will come to love the pet and through transference the grandparents they never knew. Sandy wasn't concerned with this; actually understood Dean's need to somehow keep an attachment to his parents, if not out of love, then out of guilt for having dismissed them from his life so easily; Dean's parents being no more a burden to him than a family pet, whereas Sandy's parents were forever a burden on her back.

Lilly wasn't offended when Dean announced the dog's name to the family earlier that evening. It gave her an additional opportunity to speak ill of her ex-husband, the children's other grandfather. "The only thing Hugh deserves to have named after him is the mess coming out of that dog's rear."

The sky is dark, lamplight illuminating the front lawn, beaming down at odd angles. Tina charges at Philynda, falling to her knees before reaching the dog. Tom runs over to the beagle, scooping her up in his arms as the dog wriggles to get free.

"Hey, put her down," Kyle calls.

Sandy looks on. Dean interrupts the play. "Tom, that's not how you treat a dog. Let her run on the ground."

Tom gently lowers Philynda to the grass and the dog gives a large bark, wagging her tail happily and running in circles as the family watches, delighted.

"You'll have to be careful about the dog's teeth around Tina and Hal," Lilly warns her daughter. "She looks like a biter."

Sandy walks away from her, sitting on the front steps by Blane. "Aren't you going to play with Philynda?" she asks.

"I'll pat her later when she's inside," he answers easily.

Sandy nods.

Dean, Kyle, Tom, Hal and Tina run after Philynda, following her off the lawn and into the woods where they all stand about in a circle, watching the beagle squat and pee in the brush.

1 9 7 4

T H E Y ' R E gone, off to school, the boys to public schools all over town depending upon their ages and Tina's car-pooled out to preschool. Philynda's out running with the other dogs in the neighborhood, tearing into people's trash. Sandy picks up the morning's dishes from the counter, placing them in the dishwasher, lining up the plates and saucers, all with pretty, leaflike edging. Breakfast is staggered, everyone eating as they're ready. Supper is in two shifts: the kids and then the parents. Lilly always eats with the kids, leaving Dean and Sandy sitting and eating in silence with nothing much left to be said. Sandy understands that Dean doesn't want to hear about her day. What did Sandy do yesterday? She got the car washed, bought a new pair of sneakers for Tina, Hal went to the dentist: had one cavity (in the back on the right side, one of his molars). So, Sandy's happy just sitting in calm silence for the first time all day, the kids in their rooms, or if it's still light, playing on their bikes with the neighborhood children. Sometimes, between bites of their meal, eyes meet across the table and Dean asks if Sandy has enough money, if the electric garage door is running properly, or, if he remembers, how Hal's dentist appointment went. But this calm is all at the end of the day after the kids are fed, after Dean's home with Sandy.

Now, at this moment, it's morning, and the day has just begun and there's shopping to do. Sandy has to deposit a check at the bank, change the sheets on the beds, pick up the dry cleaning, sort the clothes in the hamper, and prepare dinner for the kids and then for Dean and herself. She switches on the black-and-white portable perched on the counter by the toaster. The *Good Day* show is on, one of those boring but nice and pleasant talk shows. Sandy hears her mother's feet padding around upstairs. Lilly will be down shortly, she loves the *Good Day* show, an integral part of her everyday morning routine, and Sandy is faced with her everyday choice of either leaving her mother a note and rushing out of the house now or waiting and having Lilly tag along, forced into watching Lilly pick through the bargain racks at the Fashion Barn, complaining about the outrageous prices for flowered silk blouses and lace-edged slips.

Sandy wipes down the counter with a sponge, shuts off the TV. She guesses she'll just leave her a note. She'll just go out before she sees Lilly, and Sandy drops the sponge and picks up the pad of paper by the phone, writing, "Mother, out doing errands. Be back before the kids are home from school. Love, Sandy." Sandy places the note on the counter where Lilly can't miss it—under the tall wooden pepper mill—and she walks out of the kitchen to the stairs, looking up. Lilly's in the bathroom at the top of the steps and Sandy walks up, touching her feet down lightly on the shag carpet, holding the banister, listening to the water running in the sink, Lilly moving about in the bathroom, splashing water on her face as Sandy slips past the door and into the master bedroom. Sandy looks about and picks up her brown leather bag and sunglasses. The bed isn't made, and Sandy knows she should make it, but instead she decides to do it when she gets home or maybe not at all since she's changing the sheets later this afternoon anyway. So the bed problem is solved. Sandy's objective is to get out before Lilly sees or hears her.

Sandy simply cannot have her mother with her today, telling her where to go, what to buy, making her feel guilty because Sandy doesn't have to clip coupons whereas Lilly had to clip coupons every day of her life before she moved in with Sandy's family. Having Lilly eat lunch with Sandy's friends because she has none of her own, nibbling her "BLT with mayonnaise on whole wheat toast" and sipping her "peppermint tea with a wedge of lemon and four sugars, please," telling Sandy what it was like for her when she had to make her own way in the world, living with her brother on Monument Street in Brookline. And the worst part of it is that Lilly tells this to Sandy as if Sandy wasn't there with her the whole time it occurred. "It wasn't exactly a pleasure cruise to Hawaii for me either, Mother," Sandy has told Lilly on more than one occasion.

Once, Sandy and her best friend, Terry Koppi, were eating lunch after shopping in Boston on Boylston Street. Lilly came too, tagging along; the three women dining in a nice restaurant near Bonwit's, when during the middle of lunch Lilly opened her purse and reached over and picked up the little bowl of sugar packets, dumping them all in and snapping it shut.

Terry looked down at her salad, pretending it didn't happen. Lilly looked up at her daughter with a smile, pleased with herself.

"Why did you do that?" Sandy asked her.

"Sandy, don't worry, they won't miss them," Lilly replied, patronizing Sandy as if Sandy were the one in the wrong, and so Sandy took Lilly's purse from her lap, opened it, placing the sugar packets back in the bowl.

"You give me that back," Lilly demanded.

"Why did you take them?" Sandy asked her.

Terry excused herself to the ladies' room.

"It's a wonder I have any friends considering the stunts you pull," Sandy told her. "Now why did you do that?"

Lilly pursed her lips. "We are running low on sugar at home and I thought I'd save Dean some money after all you've spent shopping on clothes today."

Sandy handed her mother back the purse. "I think we can afford *sugar, Mother.*"

Lilly closed her purse gently. "Just don't take advantage of Dean, that's all," she warned her daughter.

"He's my *husband,*" Sandy explained.

"I was just trying to help," Lilly offered, "just trying to save where I could. Sorry..." And Lilly looked back at Sandy and took a bite of her sandwich.

Sandy picks up the keys to the VW from her nightstand.

"Sandy!" Lilly calls from the bathroom.

Sandy crouches on the white carpet, hiding behind the bed, breathing quietly, waiting for her mother to return to the bathroom and finish washing so she can leave, so she can get away from her mother, but the bathroom door doesn't close and Sandy hears Lilly step into the hall.

"Sandy? Are you in the kitchen? I need shampoo."

And Sandy hears Lilly moving, moving downstairs, and Sandy slides from behind the bed and pokes her head out the door. Lilly has descended the stairs and is walking through the hall to the kitchen, her big fluffy slippers smacking against the floor with her every step, and by now she's in the kitchen, scanning the room, looking over the counters to the tall wooden pepper mill where she'll find the note and learn that Sandy's not here.

Sandy sits on the edge of the bed, clutching her pocketbook, waiting for her mother's response. Maybe she'll just come back up to the bathroom. Maybe it will be as simple as that and then Sandy will be able to leave.

Lilly's seen the note.

"Sandy? Have you gone out or are you still here?" Lilly calls to the house.

Nothing. Silence.

"Sandy?" Lilly calls again.

Sandy hears her mother moving around downstairs, then nothing, more silence, and Sandy slowly walks downstairs, carefully turning corners, listening for her mother, but still Sandy hears nothing, not even the *Good Day* show, and Sandy moves into the hallway, making her way to the kitchen, when she notices that the basement door is ajar. Lilly has gone down to the garage to see if Sandy's car is there or not—Lilly doesn't trust her daughter's note and has to check up on Sandy. Sandy hears the door slam between the basement and the garage and she hurries upstairs to the bedroom, sitting on the edge of the bed. Lilly walks up the stairs. Sandy begins shaking.

"Sandy? Are you here?" Lilly calls.

Ever since Sandy became a mother, she waited for the kids to grow and be off to school so she could spend her days relaxing and watching TV, leisurely doing the errands and housework as she wished, not as was demanded of her, or maybe having friends over for lunches or going to their homes, gossiping until it was time to be home for the kids after school. Terry and Sandy had secretly dreamed about starting up a business partnership, getting Dean and Terry's husband, Jason, to back them in a small business, although what that business might be they hadn't yet decided. That's how Terry and Sandy thought they'd be spending their days once their kids were grown.

"Sandy, are you hurt? Is something wrong? Where are you, honey?" Lilly asks.

Sandy sits on the edge of the bed, running her hands across the pale green comforter, tracing the quilted lines with the tips of her fingers.

"Sandy?" Lilly asks. "Sandy?"

Lilly walks up the stairs. Sandy picks a book from the shelf above the headboard—*Exodus* by Leon Uris—and tosses it out the bedroom door toward the top of the stairs. She hears it thump to the carpet.

Lilly stops, staring at the book only a few feet before her. "Sandy?" she whispers. "Sandy?"

Sandy stands and tiptoes across the room to her closet, opening the door, then slamming it loudly. Sandy realizes she would give anything to see her mother's terrified face, her hands trembling as she grasps the oak banister with both hands. Maybe I'll scare her to death, Sandy thinks to herself, give her a heart attack that would send her pacemaker into shock. There have been too many mornings when Sandy watches Lilly eat her whole wheat toast with a knife and fork, and for one brief, paralyzing moment Sandy prays for her mother to die as Lilly cuts each toasted slice into tinier and tinier squares. Sandy would love to drive her mother crazy, love to be able to justify to herself why her mother should be sent to a nursing home instead of living with the family.

Lilly retreats to the ground floor.

Sandy walks from the bedroom, quietly following. Lilly has moved from the stairs and must be either in the kitchen, den, dining, family or living rooms, but still Sandy doesn't hear her. Sandy walks down the stairs, carefully searching the house for her mother.

In 1954, having married Dean, Sandy was finally able to leave Lilly and Schroeder's apartment in Brookline. Sandy spent the next eighteen years erasing the memory of her childhood, trying to forget how her mother had raised her, but now, in the past two years Lilly's been living with her, the memories of Monument Street keep flooding back.

When Sandy was a child, she used to have to do all the housework in the apartment; Lilly and Schroeder were too busy with their jobs. Lilly worked at a bank and Schroeder was a trolley car driver on the green line. Every morning Lilly left Sandy a list, a packet of coupons and some money all sealed neatly in an envelope on the kitchen table. After school, Sandy would come home, do the cleaning in the apartment, then pick up the envelope and rush to the market to do the errands. When Sandy was older, in her teens, she'd invite friends over after school and they'd play in the kitchen, making candies and cookies, calling boys on the phone, listening to her uncle's radio. At around four-thirty they'd clean the apartment and her friends would run off to their respective homes. Lilly would be in promptly by five-forty-five, never suspecting that Sandy's friends had been there eating Lilly's food, wearing Lilly's perfume and dancing on Lilly's living room carpet. Sandy believed that if her mother had ever found out, she would have gone into a tirade, jealous of the fact that Sandy got to have some fun in her life while her mother's was joyless.

The Monument Street apartment only had two bedrooms. One for Schroeder. One for Sandy and Lilly; they shared the same dresser, bathroom and double-sized bed.

One night, when Sandy was sixteen, Sandy lay awake, watching her mother sleep, when all of a sudden Lilly's eyes shot open, her body springing up in bed. "Sandy!" she cried out.

Sandy sat up, grabbing her mother's shoulders. Lilly's eyes were wide, tearing.

"Mother?" she asked.

Lilly's skin was pale and cold, her nightgown drenched with sweat. She looked around the room, then scanned Sandy's face. "Were you watching me?" Lilly asked suspiciously.

"I just woke up," Sandy told her.

Lilly lifted her daughter's hands from her shoulders. "Well, don't you ever watch me sleep again. It's giving me nightmares."

"It's not my fault," Sandy replied.

"Please, Sandy," Lilly said and she pulled the covers up, wrapping the blanket above her neck.

"Then maybe I should sleep on the couch in the living room. I'm too old to be sharing a bed," Sandy said carefully, rising to get up, but her mother gently placed a cold hand on Sandy's arm, easing her back in the bed as Lilly lay down, shutting her eyes.

"Don't be silly, just sleep with me tonight. I like to have my family close to me, just don't sit there watching me sleep."

"What was your nightmare about?" Sandy asked.

Lilly's eyes opened. "Go to sleep—it's not morning yet." And she shut her eyes, rolling onto her side, back off to sleep.

After that night, Sandy began sleeping on the far edge of the bed, facing away from her mother, lying underneath her own blanket. At least one night each week Lilly would wake in a sweat from a nightmare whether Sandy was watching her or not. Lilly would bolt upright and call Sandy's name and Sandy would pretend she was asleep, ignoring her mother's calls. Lilly would eventually give up trying to rouse Sandy and murmur, "You were watching me—I know it—I know you were—you were watching me."

Sandy prays her own children don't resent her for deeds done long ago as she does her mother, and she reaches the bottom of the stairs, about to step from the rug onto the tiled floor of the hallway, when she hears her mother moving in the kitchen, then the dialing of the phone. Sandy walks into the living room, gently lifting the phone receiver from its cradle, cutting off the call. Lilly stands in the kitchen, leaning on the counter, waiting for the ring.

"Hello?" Lilly says into the dead phone. "Hello? Is this the police?"

Sandy places the receiver down on the coffee table as Lilly attempts redialing.

On the fireplace mantel sits a large porcelain figurine of two doves standing on a tree branch. Lilly insisted it be placed in the living room, as she's always kept it on the living room mantel of every home she's lived in since she was married. It was a wedding gift, but considering how terrible her mother says Hugh was, Sandy often wonders why her mother clings to this memento of that marriage so adamantly, but Lilly does so nevertheless.

Lilly never satisfactorily explained to her daughter why she had to divorce Hugh. Once they had moved out of his apartment, Sandy never saw her father again. Once in a while, Sandy would hear his low voice screaming at Lilly through Schroeder's apartment door, but that was it—Hugh's fists pounding loudly on the wood as Lilly dragged Sandy off to the bedroom, shoving her in the closet. Sandy would sit there, crouching on the closet floor, crying into the hems of her mother's long wool dresses, fearing that the bad man behind the door would break in and kill her mother, Uncle Schroeder and then herself because, "We were living our lives happily without him," Lilly would explain. As years passed, Sandy was forced to hide in the closet less and less as the man's visits tapered off. By the time Sandy was six, she doesn't remember him ever showing again.

Sandy stares at her mother's birds, frozen on their branch. She hears her mother dialing the phone again and again—"Hello?" Lilly asks. "Hello? Police?" Lilly redials. "Operator?" and Sandy grabs the figurine by one of the bird's wings, raises it above her head and smashes it down on the fireplace bricks.

The figurine breaks into four large pieces. Sandy hears her mother shriek and Sandy runs to the front door, swings it wide and steps outside, swinging the door shut behind her. Sandy races down the brick steps and hides behind a purple rhododendron bush, by a window, careful not to make a sound.

"Sandy!" Lilly calls from the kitchen. "Sandy!"

Sandy peers into the living room. Lilly appears, standing in the doorway, waving a large cutting knife. She holds the knife high over her head like Anthony Perkins in *Psycho,* and Sandy starts to laugh at the sight of her mother standing, ready to pounce on any unsuspecting prowler who may be in the home. Lilly looks around the room, then lowers the knife to her side, walking to the fireplace, crouching and investigating the damage.

Lilly touches the birds, lifting a fragment, then she turns her head. "Sandy," her voice cracks. Lilly drops the knife to the carpet, collecting the broken pieces in her hands. "Sandy?" Lilly asks, her voice cracking again, and Sandy can hardly hear her mother through the glass anymore. Lilly's voice has become quiet; her lips move, quivering as she stands holding the birds. Lilly turns toward the window and Sandy's eyes meet her mother's. Sandy quickly lowers her head behind the bush. When Sandy raises her head back within the window frame, her mother is gone.

The branches of the bush scratch Sandy's arms as she pulls herself from the side of the house, back to the front steps, deciding what she should do now. The only real option is to go back in to get her purse and keys, just tell her mother she was out playing with Philynda in the yard, nothing unusual about that, and Sandy enters the house with a blank expression on her face. "Mother?" Sandy asks. Sandy stands in the front doorway.

Lilly appears before her, the broken birds cupped in her hands, wearing a green terry cloth robe, tears running down her face. "Sandy... Sandy..." Lilly cries and then there are more tears. Lilly walks to Sandy, arms outstretched, hands extended, lifting the birds to Sandy's face. "Sandy..." Lilly cries and the belt of her robe loosens and the fold flaps open, revealing Lilly's sad, wrinkled breasts, the scar on her chest where the pacemaker was inserted. She breathes hoarsely. Sandy puts a hand on her mother's cold shoulder.

"Sandy..." Lilly moans.

"Sit, Mother, sit," Sandy says, and Sandy helps her mother sit on the stairway, kneeling before her, gently clasping her mother's wrinkled hands in her own as Lilly holds what's left of the birds.

"I—I heard noises and the phone wouldn't work and the birds... my birds..." Lilly offers Sandy the broken pieces. "My birds..."

"Oh, Mother, let me get you a tissue," Sandy says.

Lilly lowers her head to her lap. "I don't know anymore, Sandy... I'm sorry... I just don't know what I'm—"

"Mother, I'll be back in a sec." Sandy stands, walking to the bathroom by the kitchen, gathering a bunch of tissues, then handing them to her mother.

Lilly grabs Sandy's arm with her thin fingers. "I'm too old. Don't leave me alone... don't leave me alone..."

"Everything's fine. I'm here. I'm here with you."

"Don't ever go out without telling me," Lilly implores. "Please don't."

"I was only out ten minutes," Sandy explains.

"Someone—someone was here."

"It was the wind, Mother. Just the wind."

"No, it was not the wind. Someone was here. Listen to me," Lilly says and her grip tightens on Sandy's arm.

"No one was here, Mother. It was nothing."

"We need better locks on those doors too," Lilly goes on, her voice gathering back some of its strength. "Anyone could come in. Anyone," she warns.

"We'll buy some glue and fix the birds. Maybe one of the kids put it back awkwardly and it fell."

"I don't know... I don't think so." Lilly shakes her head and she's stopped crying and has regained some, if not all, of her composure. She wipes her eyes, then touches her hair. "Where are you going to do your errands? I need shampoo."

"I can pick it up for you," Sandy says.

"No—no, I can do it. I like to shop for myself," Lilly explains. "You had to shop for me when you were a little girl. Let me do it for myself now that I've the time to."

"I may be out for a while. Are you sure you're up for it?"

"I'll be ready in a jiffy. Help me up." Lilly drops the figurine pieces on the carpet, lifting her arms up toward Sandy. Sandy takes her mother's elbows and Lilly stands, leaning on her daughter's shoulders, then grabbing the banister and pulling herself up the stairs. "I'll be down in a jiffy. Maybe we can go to lunch at Brigham's coffee shop." Lilly turns. "Do you think Dean can fix the doves? He is handy, isn't he?"

Sandy reaches down, picking the pieces off the carpet. "I'm sure he can," Sandy says, and Lilly heads off to her room, the padding of her feet growing fainter as she plods down the hall to change for their Mother-Daughter Day on the town.

Sandy stands in the hallway, holding the broken birds, the sharp edges poking into her palms, wondering what the afternoon has in store for her: a trip to the Fashion Barn, a visit to Reed's pharmacy to watch her mother poke through the many brands of shampoo, and a lunch at Brigham's, where Lilly will order a BLT and a peppermint tea. It takes so little to make her mother happy, but giving her that much drives Sandy mad.

∎

Blane and Tom arrive home from junior high school. Tom drops his books on the kitchen table and Blane walks into the family room to turn on the TV. Blane and Tom always watch *Match Game '74* right after they get home from school; the only thing they do together that they both like.

"Is that you, Tom? Get up here," Sandy calls from the top of the stairs.

"I'll be up in a minute," Tom answers. He opens the snack cabinet, looking over the selections.

"Get up here now!" Sandy yells.

"What the fuck?" Tom walks through the kitchen, into the hall and up the stairs.

Sandy and Kyle wait in Tom's room, a full garbage bag standing between them in the middle of the floor. Tom's bed is unmade, his desk and floor littered with crumpled paper, candy wrappers, soda cans and paper cups. Tom enters, surveys the scene and looks at Kyle, then to his mother. They look back at him expectantly but Tom says nothing.

"You're such a loser," Kyle finally says.

"Keep quiet," Sandy says to Kyle. She looks at Tom. "Now what's all this?"

She stares at Tom and he walks over and grabs the bag, dragging it away from her to the bed, where he checks it over. "It's my stuff, just leave it alone," he tells her.

"Well, what is this stuff?" Sandy asks. "What is it?"

"Duh, Mom, figure it out already." Tom stares at her and Sandy stares back. Tom turns his head, looking out the window.

"Well?" Sandy continues.

"They're my *fireworks*," Tom responds. "So what?"

"Oh?" Sandy says, opening her eyes wide.

"Firecrackers, bottle rockets, Roman candles," Tom explains. He gathers the bag's opening together, refastening the twist-tie.

"Is that so?" Sandy asks, nodding her head up and down. "Is that all?"

"Yes, that *is* all," Tom tells her, mimicking her, nodding his head up and down the way she did. "Yes, Mom, that's really, really all they are."

"You're such a loser," Kyle says again.

Tom stands pointing at Kyle. "And get him out of here. I won't talk about it if he's here."

"*Kyle,*" Sandy says and Kyle leaves the room.

"You're a real moron," he mutters under his breath.

"Yeah, fuck you," Tom calls after him and then Kyle's gone and Sandy and Tom stand facing each other across the garbage bag.

Sandy places her hands on her hips, shaking her head. "I'd like some answers."

Tom picks up the bag, moving it back in the closet. "Forget it. It doesn't have anything to do with you."

"You're not going to keep that stuff here, young man," Sandy says.

"Oh-yes-I-am," Tom informs her. "I paid for them."

"They're illegal," Sandy states. "And that's that."

"They're only fireworks, give me a break."

"And what have you been doing with them?"

Tom smirks, dropping his arms to his sides. "Selling them to kids at school. What did you think?"

Sandy glares, annoyed by his flip attitude. "Besides the fact that it's illegal and someone could get hurt and your father and I would be held responsible, you could also get thrown out of school for this."

"My teachers don't even know I'm doing it," Tom explains. "Besides, I can't believe how dumb you are, you're making it sound as if I'm selling guns and switchblades."

Sandy's face is red with anger. She looks to the garbage bag, to the floor, the bed, the desk, the entire mess of the room. "Honestly, why do you do things like this?" she asks, gesturing to the room. "Do you get a kick out of being so bad? Is that it?" Sandy lowers her head, affecting disappointment in her son.

Tom sits at his rolltop desk and yanks the lid down. "There, it's clean. Happy now?"

Sandy turns, going to the closet, lifting out the trash bag. "Well, if you think you're going to keep on doing this, you have another think coming." And she opens the bag.

"What the fuck do you think you're doing?" Tom is out of the chair.

"These are going in my room until your father and I decide what to do with *them*—and *you.*" Sandy begins walking to the door with Tom's fireworks.

Tom intercepts her, yanking the bag from her hands. "No fucking way, lady, I paid for this shit with my own money and—"

Sandy grabs the side of the bag nearest her. Now they both hold it, tugging.

"We will deal with this later, now let's move it into my room now, please." Sandy gives a good pull on the bag.

Tom pulls back. *"Fuck you, Mom."*

And Sandy digs her fingernails into the bag, splitting it down the seam, ripping it apart, bricks of fireworks and bottle rockets falling everywhere, under the bed, the dresser, the desk.

"What the fuck are you doing?!" Tom stares, furious.

"And I am sick of hearing your dirty foul mouth in my house, you understand that?" Sandy bends over, gathering the packages in her hands. "Now help me pick these up," she says.

"No fucking way."

"Fine." Sandy stands, holding a large bunch of the fireworks in her arms, turning toward the door, which her son blocks. She stares into his eyes and Tom reaches out, smacking her side hard, with force, and the firecrackers drop to the floor.

"Damnit, Tom!" Sandy yells. *"This is my house too, you know, not only yours!"* She looks at him, eyes welling with tears.

"Then keep your face out of my room, bitch."

"Maybe I wouldn't have to be in here if you weren't so much of a bother." She takes a breath, keeping herself from crying, from letting him know he's gotten to her.

"Then ignore me."

"I am trying to *help* you," Sandy says. "Help you." And she bends over, pulling the torn garbage bag around the fireworks, collecting them together. "I'm throwing them all out anyway. That's what's going to happen—you can do it yourself or I'll do it myself."

Tom looks down at her. "You throw any out and I'll fucking kill you, lady."

"Oh? Is that so? All over a bunch of fireworks, you're going to kill your mother?" She bundles the packages together, breaking the stems off some of the bottle rockets.

"Fucking bitch."

"With talk like that we'll see how far you get next time you want me to drive you to a friend's house, buster."

"Yeah, you're such a great mother," Tom counters.

"Best you're ever going to get," Sandy warns.

Tom takes a look at her, one long, last look of hatred, and he's out of there. Bag the bitch.

"You better get back here," Sandy calls, releasing the bag, standing.

Tom faces Kyle and Blane in the kitchen. "Fuck off," he says, a reflex reaction.

"I'm not through yet," Sandy follows, but she's too late; Tom's already out the door.

Tom heads for the utility shed, pulling out his five-speed bike and hopping on it, pedaling off and out of the driveway, onto the road.

Sandy runs across the front lawn, arms waving, weak and defeated. "Get back here! You get back here right now!"

"Fuck you!"

Sandy watches Tom pedal away, furious that he got the last word in—*Fuck you!*—that he has somehow won this round, and she walks up the side steps into the house. Kyle and Blane stand in the kitchen, leaning over the counter, drinking colas, eating potato chips from the bag.

"Did you know he was doing this?" Sandy asks Blane accusingly.

"Doing what?" Blane puts the soda down on the counter.

"Dealing the fireworks, that's what. Do you have any idea how long he's been doing this?"

Blane sits at the table. "How would I know?"

Sandy walks over, facing him. "You go to the same school. You must have known something about this." A statement, not a question.

Blane looks at her calmly, disinterested. "Mom, there are six hundred kids in school. You think I know everything that goes on there?"

"Well *this kid* happens to be your brother, so yes, I think you might know," Sandy persists.

Blane stands. "We're not even in the same grade. You think I hang around with the same group of scrub kids he does? I had nothing to do with this, so don't blame me because you didn't know what Tom was doing." Blane walks from the kitchen, upstairs to his room.

Sandy looks away from Kyle's stare and goes to the sink, rinsing her hands, just something for her to do. She takes the thawing hamburger off the wood cutting block, peels off the plastic wrap and begins forming the chopped meat into patties to be fried later this evening.

"So, what are you going to do to him?" Kyle asks.

Sandy rolls the burger into a ball then presses it down on the cutting board with a spatula. "I don't know. I'll have to discuss it with your father."

"You *are* going to punish him, aren't you?" Kyle asks. "If Blane or I had done this you'd kill us."

"Well, Blane or you didn't do this. Tom did. And your father and I will deal with Tom as is appropriate for him. Okay?"

"You mean you're not going to punish him?"

"I don't know." Sandy keeps her back to Kyle, staring out the window above the sink at the backyard of the house. She spots a squirrel scurrying up a tree, onto a branch.

"Are we going to have French fries with the burgers?" Kyle asks.

Sandy shuts her eyes. "I really don't know, Kyle. Don't you have homework to do? I saw the grade on your last English paper and it wasn't exactly gangbusters."

Kyle stares at the back of his mother's head. "I'm doing fine. I'll finish the term with at least a C."

"A C isn't fine and you haven't touched that book you brought home last week. It's been sitting there by the phone the whole time." Sandy takes a platter from the cabinet by the stove, laying the burgers across it. Kyle walks over and picks up the book by the phone, leaving the room.

Sandy sighs deeply, glad to finally be alone, and she leaves the counter area, sitting at the kitchen table, resting her head on her arms. She hears a school bus screech to a halt by the house. Tina and Hal are home.

Tom slides off his bike by the Sudbury River Bridge and looks down at the calm stream. Across the street, people rent canoes and rowboats. They paddle along the shore down to the battle-ground area—tourist families huddle about that minuteman statue, fathers pointing up to the man with the rifle and saying things like, "This is where it all began—the shot heard 'round the world." Dean and Sandy took the family there for a picnic when they first moved to Concord four years ago. They wanted the kids to learn about history. Blane loved it; loved running around the battlefield, playing in a place where a war had been fought two hundred years ago. Blane ran all over that battlefield and across the bridge, pretending to die about fifty times that day. Dean wanted them to learn where they came from. He told the kids, "If you know what you've been, you'll better know how to get where you want to go." And Blane responded, "I know who I am, so that means I know the best how to get where I want to go, right?"

The only thing Tom learned that day was that if you toss one of his mother's soggy tunafish sandwiches into the Sudbury River his father will smack you across the head. The ducks liked the sandwich though, and they all swam toward it, picking at the white bread with their beaks.

Tom rolls his bike down the embankment, setting it on its side in the tall grass by the river's edge. He sits by the water and tosses stones, making small, perfect circles on the water's surface. He reaches into the pocket of his blue windbreaker and takes out a packet of firecrackers and a lighter. He breaks open the pack and tears one off. It's wrapped in blue paper with white stars all over it and he flicks the lighter to the wick. It catches and Tom tosses it over the river. It explodes with a loud crack and its ashes fall, sprinkling down into the calm water. Tom lights another and tosses it high, watching the flash of its small bright explosion in mid-air as it bursts against the blue, cloudless sky.

"What was that?" a woman's voice asks.

Tom looks down the river at a yellow canoe emerging from beneath the stone bridge by the road. A young man and woman are paddling toward the shore near where he's hiding in the weeds.

"It was nothing," the man says. "Relax." They're wearing flannel shirts and sweaters. The canoe is almost directly in front of Tom and he scoots back a bit so they can't see him. He takes out another firecracker, lights its wick and hurls it over the water by their canoe.

There's an explosion and the woman screams. The man whirls his head around in every direction.

"What was that? What was that?" the woman cries.

"A firecracker. Some kid's getting off on lugging firecrackers by the water," the man answers, still looking around, trying to find Tom, and then the couple make a turn and begin heading away, toward the bridge. Tom quickly lights another and chucks it after them. It blows up by the side of their boat.

"Christ almighty!" the woman screams and she paddles faster, scared to death. The man turns his head in Tom's general direction, then looks away, paddling harder, and soon they're gone and back under the bridge.

Tom lies in the high grass on the damp ground. He takes the rest of the pack and lights it all up at once, throwing it as hard as he can. It flies through the air, landing on the bank at the opposite side of the river. Crack—crack—crack: The fireworks burst, then silence, absolute silence and peace.

•   •   •

"Would you mind telling him it's important and to call me once he has the chance?"

"I'll give him the message, Sandy."

"Thank you, Vicki."

"I'll give him the message."

"Thanks."

"Goodbye."

"Bye." Sandy hangs up the phone. She sits at Dean's desk in the den with the door shut, waiting for his meeting to end— Vicki said it should only be a matter of fifteen minutes—so Sandy waits for Dean to return her call.

Sandy doesn't know how Dean and she will punish Tom. If they ground him he just breaks it anyway. If they take away his allowance, they'll only be forcing him to keep dealing the fireworks in order to have money. Tom's not like the other children; he has no fear of Sandy or Dean. He doesn't view his parents as powerful beings in his life, but only as obstacles preventing him from getting what he wants. Sandy and Dean find it easy to punish Kyle because Kyle respects them, believes they're trying to do what's best for him. When Kyle comes home from school with a bad grade, they ground him, forcing him to study harder. If Kyle stays out past his curfew on a weekend night, the following weekend he has to stay in both nights. And Blane; Blane never has to be punished because he never does anything wrong—a straight A student with no behavior problems.

Hal and Tina burst through the door, Hal holding Tina's Raggedy Ann by the neck, above her head.

"Mom, make him give it to me," Tina cries.

"We were playing and then she said she wouldn't share," Hal complains.

"I'm expecting an important call from your father so I'd appreciate it if you could both play quietly," Sandy says, rising from the desk.

"But I don't want to play with him anymore," Tina says.

"But I'm not done with the game I'm playing yet," Hal says.

Sandy steps into the living room, calling upstairs, "Blane!

Blane!" Hal and Tina follow after her. Blane comes downstairs into the room.

Sandy looks to him, wearily. "Would you mind taking Tina and Hal to the playroom and keeping them busy?"

Blane picks up on Sandy's cue. "I could put on a puppet show with your dolls and stuffed animals."

"Yay, a puppet show!" Tina and Hal holler. Hal hands Blane the Raggedy Ann. "Can you do the one about the Queen of the Dungeon and the head chopper?"

"Do you like that one?" Blane asks Tina.

"She has to be a princess this time," Tina replies, and Blane escorts them from the living room, through the hall and down to the playroom.

The phone rings. Sandy steps into the den, shutting the door, sitting at the desk. "Hello?"

"Is something wrong?" Dean asks.

"*Tom has fireworks,*" Sandy states dramatically, attempting to shock her husband.

Dean doesn't say anything. Sandy drums her fingers on the edge of the desk. "So what do you think we should do with him?" she asks.

A pause, then Dean answers with a laugh, "Sandy, most boys Tom's age play with firecrackers. It's natural. I did."

"*It's a garbage-bagful,*" Sandy replies loudly. "He's dealing them to kids in his school for money. You think I'd call you if it wasn't serious?"

Another pause, then, "Has he been caught?" Dean asks.

"What do you mean *has he been caught?*"

"Did the school call and tell you he was doing this?"

"I found them in his closet—a Hefty Bag–ful and when I confronted him he ran away," Sandy explains.

Dean lets out a sigh of relief. "Well, at least the school doesn't know. That's a blessing."

"Aren't you going to help me deal with this?" Sandy asks, exasperated.

"Sandy," Dean begins calmly, patronizingly. "I'm at work," he explains. "What do you expect me to do now that I can't do when I get home in a couple of hours? He may not even be home by then. You know how he is."

Sandy stands, turning, leaning against the desk, gathering control. "I simply thought that I could talk this through with you," Sandy says. "That's all. I wanted someone to talk this over with and"—she stops—why bother?—"we'll discuss it when you get home," Sandy says flatly. "Goodbye."

"I'll see you then, love you."

"You too, bye." Sandy hangs up the phone. Her son deals explosives and her husband doesn't give a damn. Ka-boom.

■

Hal sits on the couch in the family room between Sandy and Tina. Hal reads *Harold and the Purple Crayon* to his sister while his mother looks on. Tina sits forward, gazing at small Harold as he draws purple mountains, boats and pies for mooses and porcupines.

"—put a frig-het-tin-g," Hal sounds out the long word slowly.

"Frightening," Sandy corrects. "The g and the h are silent in this word too."

"Then why do they keep putting them in," Hal asks, looking away from the book and up to his mother. "Look," he points his finger at the word. "If you took out the two letters you could fit another little word in too. It wastes space in the book." Hal doesn't wait for his mother to respond but resumes reading, his finger underlining each word as he mumbles aloud.

On the screened porch off the family room, Lilly reclines on a lounger. She reads a romantic novel, occasionally looking up from the paperback to oversee the yard, watching Kyle run the mower across the back lawn as he weaves between the trees.

A thud from the fireplace.

Hal stops reading, glancing up at the red bricks, the chimney. "Harold's monster's in there," he laughs. "It's a monster."

"Is it a monster?" Tina asks.

"I'm sure it's nothing," Sandy says and she stands, heading

toward the fireplace to investigate when another louder thud sounds. Sandy takes a step back.

"Mommy—" Tina's off the couch, by her mother's side, holding her hand. A third larger thud and then there comes a thrashing sound, a thrashing growing louder and louder, as if someone or something is beating its way down the chimney and into the house.

Sandy stares, transfixed by the noise. Tina tugs at her fingers.

"Who's in there?"

Hal jumps from the couch, flinging the book aside, running from the room, through the kitchen, yelling to Tom and Blane upstairs, "There's a monster in the chimney! A monster's in the chimney!" His voice caught somewhere between elation and fear.

Sandy backs into the kitchen with Tina as the thrashing noise grows, intensifying. Tom, Hal and Blane march by their mother, listening by the fire grate.

"Get away from there, get behind me," Sandy says from the kitchen. Hal heeds her words, moving behind her. Blane takes a step back by her side, and Tom reaches for the fire poker, picking it up, ready to defend the family.

Sandy speaks, "Tom, you put that—"

Suddenly there's a crash and the fire guard is down and a large black flutter fills the room. Tina and Hal shriek, together running upstairs to their rooms. Sandy covers her head with her hands and runs one room further away, into the dining room. Blane runs out the side door, alerting Kyle, while Tom swings the fire poker in the air above his head, making his way back to the kitchen.

The large black crow, panic-stricken, crashes into the walls, dives into the furniture, then swoops up at the lamps and light fixtures, finally settling on a brass lamp stand, perched, looking over its surroundings. Tom stares at the bird, then hurls the poker at it from the kitchen, knocking the lamp over, sending the crow into another frenzy, flying from the family room into the kitchen.

Philynda, who had been sleeping by the kitchen counter, is now awake, barking, chasing after Tom as Tom chases the large crow with a large skillet he has grabbed from a rack on the wall. Sandy screams after Tom, "Get out of the house!"

Philynda leaps into the air, trying to get at the bird. The crow caws loudly, the dog barks. Sandy covers her ears, heading up after Hal and Tina. Tom grabs Philynda by the collar, dragging the barking dog out the side door of the house. He slams the door shut but Philynda keeps on barking, jumping at the door. Tom leaves her, walking down the steps, joining Blane and Kyle out front where they stand about, unsure of what to do next.

Sandy ushers Tina and Hal downstairs, toward the front door. The crow flies by them, through the dining room and into the living room. Sandy ducks, opening the front door, Hal and Tina rushing ahead of her. The front door is shut and the whole family meets on the lawn, convening in a circle, staring back at the house temporarily seized by an oversized black crow. Philynda, tired of barking at the door, trots down the side steps joining the family, rubbing up against Tom's leg.

"Is everybody okay?" Sandy asks.

"I didn't even get to see it," Kyle says.

"Should we go in there and catch it?" Tom asks.

"I'm not going back in there," Hal says. "It might poke me in the eyes with its beak. Birds' beaks are pretty sharp, you know."

"No one is going back in the house while the bird's there," Sandy states.

"So then what are we going to do?" Tom asks. "The bird's not going to fly out the way it came in."

"Someone will have to kill it," Blane says, deadpan. Sandy turns to him, startled by his remark when "Help! Help!" is heard emanating from the back porch.

Lilly stands, her body flat against the screen, hands held high above her head, mouth wide. "Help! Help!" It doesn't matter that the bird isn't even on the porch; Lilly just hears its flapping throughout the house from room to room, and stands petrified, hollering for the family's aid.

Sandy and the kids walk along the front path down to the driveway at basement level, looking up at Lilly on the porch. "Mother, just shut the sliding glass door between the rooms!" Sandy calls.

"Sandy, there's a bird in the house," Lilly calls.

Sandy turns to Blane. "Will you please go up there through the back way and help her down?"

Blane disappears around the side of the house.

"Blane's coming around back to get you!" Sandy screams to her mother.

The crow flies upstairs, searching for a way out of the house.

Dean has gathered the people servicing Territory 5 (western New York, Pennsylvania, eastern Ohio) into his office.

Through a brief memo from Pat Relig, headman of Territory 5, Dean has learned of the loss of an account, albeit a small one that will have absolutely no bearing on the finances of the division or the company, an account Dean would never have even realized the division had had, had it not been for Pat's memo informing him of its loss.

"I don't care that we lost the account," Dean explains calmly to Territory 5. "I just want to know why we lost it so we can prevent it from happening again, possibly with a larger client; a client that matters."

The six members of Territory 5 sit at the conference table in Dean's office, Dean sitting at its head, his desk and credenza behind him. Dean doesn't recognize any of these people except Pat Relig, usually only dealing with the headman of each territory, but Pat has brought along his entire team to represent him: three regional representatives and their two assistants.

Dean gives them a nod, "So what's been going on?"

Pat folds back a sheet of paper on a yellow legal pad. "Dean, it was a tiny account that slipped through the cracks. I probably shouldn't have even bothered you about it."

Dean places his hands on the edge of the conference table. "Then why did you? I wouldn't have even known if you hadn't written me the memo, you know that, Pat. You know I'm dealing with eleven territories; I don't keep track of things on a small-scale basis but only look at the bottom-line numbers on each territory as they come in weekly. And on a bottom-line basis, Territory 5 looks really great. I think you're a great team. But when you send me this memo about this nothing of a client that you lost, I wonder what's going on in Territory 5 that I have to be concerned about? Why is Pat bringing this to my attention? Is it indicative of some greater problem? I don't know, Pat, I want you to tell me, is something wrong that I need to be concerned about in Territory 5, or is this memo—directed specifically to my attention—just a fluke, a miscalculation on your part?" Dean glances at the memo he's referring to, picks it up, then tosses it on the conference table with a shake of his head.

The three regional reps and two assistants look to Pat for guidance. They know of Dean, have seen him in the office, but have never met him or been summoned before him.

Silence, then, "Give me a minute to think this through, Dean," Pat says, then more silence.

Dean glances at his Rolex. It's three-twenty. A client meeting at four. A short conference with the vice president of the division at five-thirty and he should be out of the office by six-fifteen, latest. He looks back at Pat, all of Territory 5, obviously flustered by Dean's long speech. Dean glances at his watch again, considers dismissing the whole affair, just sending them out of his office and back to their desks in shame, leaving the entire question unresolved. But it nags him. All Dean wants to know is: Bottom-line, is Pat Relig capable of being the headman of Territory 5 or is he losing it? If a family can only be as united as its head of the household is strong, then a territory can only be as successful as its headman is adept, and judging from the puzzled expression on Pat's face, Dean's beginning to believe this guy's a loser.

A buzz on the intercom box. Dean swivels in his chair toward the desk. "Yes, Vicki. I'm in a meeting."

Over the voice box, "Your wife on two. You want to take it?"

Dean scans the faces in the room. Pat stands. "Should we go?"

Dean to Pat, "No, stay, you're fine," then to the box, "I'll pick her up in a minute, thanks, Vicki." Dean stands, walking to the desk, sitting and looking across at Territory 5. "I'll be back with you shortly, thanks, just gather your information together." Territory 5 huddles, mumbling softly.

Dean punches line two, picking up the phone receiver. He spins in the desk chair, facing the credenza, brass-framed photos of the family angled along its top.

"Sandy?"

"I think you're going to have to come home."

"What's wrong? What happened?"

"There's a bird in the house."

"A *bird?*" Dean's voice jumps a level. Territory 5's mumbling ceases. Dean cups his hand around the phone's mouthpiece. "A bird. What kind of a bird?"

"A giant black crow," Sandy says. "It's stuck in the house. Came in through the chimney. We're all at Terry's, now what do you want me to do?" Her tone is becoming more irate.

Dean pauses, wondering if Territory 5 is listening, watching his back. "Well, what do you want me to do?" Dean asks.

"Get home," Sandy states bluntly. "I'm at Terry's," she repeats. "Goodbye."

"Fine," Dean sighs, "I'll see you there." He tries to sound relaxed, casual, and he turns in the chair, hanging up the phone, facing Territory 5.

"Ready to go over everything?" Pat asks.

Dean gives him a wave with one hand. "I think we'll have to postpone. Crisis on the homefront." Dean smirks with a slight smile.

The regional reps and the assistants nod, gathering their papers into manila folders, preparing to leave.

"You mentioned a bird?" Pat asks.

Dean stands, lifting his suit jacket from the back of the chair, draping it over an arm. "Yes, a bird," Dean answers sharply. He takes the car keys from his pants pocket.

"What kind of a bird? One of your kids' pets?" Pat persists.

Dean smiles at the headman of Territory 5, deciding that the guy is losing it: Pat Relig is definitely no longer capable of discriminating the important from the banal. "You know, Pat, I'll draw you up a memo on it first thing tomorrow A.M.," and Dean leaves the office; Territory 5 watching as he goes.

Dean searches the house, rifle in hand. He came in through the garage, has proceeded upstairs to the first floor, and stands in the hallway, midway between the kitchen and first-floor bathroom, poised, ready to take out the crow.

He met Sandy, Lilly and the kids at Terry's, the kids jumping around, wanting to be included in on the shooing out of the crow, however it might be done. Sandy had already phoned the police and fire departments, both offices directing her back to the other. Sandy then contacted the Audubon Society, hoping these bird experts might help her out, but they wanted nothing to do with a common North American black crow. So Sandy faced Dean and told him it was up to him to rid the house of the bird.

Dean didn't tell the family how he intended to get the crow to fly from their home. He just told them that he would take care of the problem himself, as he saw fit, leaving it to their imaginations as to what his intentions might be.

Dean slowly walks into the kitchen, holding the rifle at waist-level, angled toward the ceiling. He hears nothing. He notices the damage the bird has caused: a lamp toppled over in the family room, the fire guard on its side, a picture askew in the dining room, a few randomly scattered feathers across the floor, one on the counter by Sandy's memo pad.

Dean paces the first floor and, finding nothing, heads upstairs to the second story, his heart beating faster with every step. This is Dean's first hunt, never having any reason to use the Wallace family artillery before, and despite the circumstances, this freakish opportunity excites him like nothing else—a duel between man and nature—and Dean parades through the second floor, checking the master bedroom, the two bathrooms, Tina's room, then turning a corner in the hallway to check over the boys' rooms.

He looks down the long hall. At the far end stands the black crow. Dean stops, lowering the rifle to his side.

The crow's head turns, its eyes staring at the master of the Wallace household. The crow's beak opens, letting out a caw that startles Dean, sending him back into the wall. The crow caws again, taking steps toward Dean, fanning its large black wings, its beak open, cawing and cawing as it proceeds down the hallway, heading straight for Dean.

Dean stands rigid against the wall, surprised by how large the crow actually is. Its wingspan almost fills the width of the hallway. Dean carefully lifts the gun to his shoulder, sighting the crow over the ridge centered above the gun's barrel. The crow keeps cawing, strolling toward Dean, head up, beak wide. Dean aims the rifle at the crow's chest, his finger squeezing the trigger, pulling it back slowly. The shot is fired, the gun's kick throwing Dean against the wall. Crow feathers float in the air. Dean looks up, the crow is flying, screaming over his head, then is gone, away down the staircase. Dean looks at the spot on the carpet where the bird had stood, but there's nothing, just a scattering of black feathers and a bullet hole in the wall, two feet off the floor.

Dean takes another bullet from his suit jacket pocket, filling the gun's empty chamber. He hears the screaming crow, its flying through the house, and Dean heads downstairs, rifle at shoulder level, eyes focused, finger on the trigger. He hears the crow in the living room.

The bird is flying in a circle throughout the room, charging at the curtains. Dean takes aim and fires. The bird hits the wall, shot in the side, but keeps on flying, sweeping past Dean and into the dining room. Dean follows. The crow, obviously having trouble flying, veers to one side, drops of blood spilling from under its right wing, falling to the carpet. The bird spins, then crashes into the chandelier, caught between the fixture's brass arms, flailing, flapping its wings wildly. Crystals cut into the bird's body, then shatter down to the table. Dean fires once more at the crow.

A loud caw, then all is silent, the bird's body is still, its wings spread between the arms of the chandelier, hovering over the room. Blood spatters on the ceiling just above the bird. Blood drips onto the tablecloth below.

Dean places the rifle on the table, taking a step back, standing in the entrance to the room. He turns, walking into the living room where he sits on the sofa, dropping his head into his hands. He'll just have to remove the bird from the light fixture, wrap it in the already bloodied tablecloth, enclose it in a trash bag and drive it out to the dump this very afternoon; he doesn't want the dead bird sitting in the garage, waiting for the trash collector, who won't be coming until later this week.

And suddenly it occurs to Dean that maybe the bird would have just flown from the house had he or Sandy left a window or door open, giving it a chance to escape: All the bird wanted was to get out; all the family wanted was for it to leave. But the bird has been shot, the goal has been accomplished, and Dean can now remove the intruder from the house, informing his family that their home is once again livable.

1975

"I can order off the adult menu. I'm twelve and eight months and the kids' menu is for under twelve it says," Tom says.

He waves the menu at Dean, who chooses to ignore him, trying to decide what he's going to have for himself. Most of the food at Howard Johnson's is fairly decent and there's something on the menu for all members of the Wallace family.

"Mom, see, look what it says," Tom says.

Sandy ignores him.

Blane takes Tom's menu. "Read it, it says 'Children's Menu: Twelve and Under.' That means it is meant for anyone under the age of thirteen. And you are twelve and I am thirteen."

"You're lying just because you're old enough," Tom says. "Mom, look what it says."

"You'll order off the children's menu," Dean says. "I spend enough money on lift tickets, the motel and gas as it is. You don't need a big, expensive dinner." Dean had forgotten what it was like eating dinner with the kids; usually they eat before he's home from work. By the time he gets home their dishes are out of sight and it's just Sandy and Dean relaxing at the table together. On weekends Dean does take the kids out to McDonald's while running errands. But ordering then is simple— no arguments over the menu—only burgers, fries and colas— no hassles over who gets to order the most expensive items. But even at McD's it's not the whole family—one or two of the kids are usually missing and Sandy rarely comes with him on the Saturday morning rounds of the hardware store, lawn center, sporting goods shop and whatever else either Dean or one of the kids needs that week. Dean's only real time he spends with the kids is on weekends. During the week he sits around watching the TV with them, but Dean's not certain that that counts as "spending time with the kids." At least Sandy doesn't think it does. Dean usually falls half asleep during the shows and Sandy has to poke him in the ribs to keep him from snoring so they can hear the program.

Sandy scans the menu, looking over the chicken dinners.

"Mom, read this." Tom waves the menu at Sandy, hitting her in the chin.

Sandy takes it. "Blane is right, that is what it means." She hands the menu back to Tom. "Now choose something before the waitress comes back." Sandy folds the menu open, hiding her face.

"But how does the restaurant know how much I can eat?" Tom asks to no one in particular.

"Just order off the kids' menu and shut up," Kyle says.

"Well, I'm going to have the fillet of sole," Dean says. "It comes with the salad bar and—"

"I want the salad bar," Tom says. "My food doesn't come with the salad bar."

"I want salad bar, too," Hal says. "I'm big enough."

Dean puts down the menu. "If you all don't keep quiet I'll pack up the car and this ski trip will be over before it's even begun. This is my vacation too and I'd like to relax without being heckled constantly."

Sandy moderates. "Let's just order off the menus we have." She turns to Tom and Hal. "If you want anything from the salad bar you can come up with me and pick something out. Now, you've always enjoyed the Fearless Fido, Tom, so why can't you have that?"

"But it won't fill me up," Tom whines.

"Then you'll just have to have a bigger dessert, won't you?" Sandy replies.

Tom turns back to his menu. "I'm having a banana split then."

"If he gets one, I get one," Hal says.

Dean looks around the restaurant. "Where is our waitress?"

"Relax, Dean, she'll be here," Sandy says.

Everyone has put down their menus but Hal and Tina, who look at the puzzles in the children's menu provided for their amusement.

"Probably less people working today because of the New Year's holiday weekend," Dean explains to the kids. "Kyle's going to have to start thinking about a part-time job soon."

Kyle groans, making a face.

"What? You think I'm going to give you a weekly allowance for the rest of your life?" Dean asks him. "Work makes you feel worthy, to be earning your own money. Your work is who you are."

"*Dad,*" Kyle complains.

"Well, you do have to get a part-time job," Dean tells him. "Work is good. It makes you feel better about yourself."

"Not now, Dean," Sandy says.

"Will I get to ride on the chair lift tomorrow?" Tina asks.

The waitress finally appears. "Shelley" her name tag reads and the family begins ordering.

"You're a schizophrenic," Blane says over the sound of the TV in the kids' room.

Dean's lying on the bed. The sounds of the boys drift in through the connecting door to their room. Tina lies asleep in the second double bed in Sandy and Dean's room. The boys watch TV, Sandy's in the shower, and Dean reads a spy novel.

Sandy steps from the bathroom, her hair twisted up in a small white towel. Another towel wrapped about her chest clings to her body, coming just above her knees. Steam drifts from the bathroom, mist clinging to her legs.

"Some families live like this," Dean tells her. "Seven people in two rooms."

"That's true, but with Mother it would be eight," Sandy replies, smoothing lotion on her arms.

"Maybe we should try that sometime: Shut off all the rooms in the house but the kitchen and family room," Dean says with a laugh.

Sandy yanks the towel from her hair. "Dean, let's just be grateful we have all the rooms we do and make use of every one of them. I grew up in a four-room apartment and that was bad enough with only the three of us."

Dean looks up from the book. "You look pretty," he says.

Sandy turns her back to him, staring at the mirror, leaning in close and examining her face. She spots Dean watching her from the bed and their eyes meet in the mirror. She combs her hair over her face with her fingers, shaking it loose, breaking the look. "I'm tired. We have to get a bigger car if we're going to take family trips with all the kids."

"I like us close together," Dean offers.

"You don't have Tina squirming around in your lap for three hours," Sandy says. "And with the skis and luggage and equipment in the car, even the boys are tight in the back of the van. At least let's buy a roof rack."

Her towel still on, Sandy walks to the adjoining door and closes their side, shutting out the boys. Their TV's only a murmur now. Just Sandy, Tina and Dean.

Sandy sits in the desk chair, lifting the phone receiver.

"You going to call your mother?" Dean asks.

Sandy dials. "If I don't, she'll only call us, so . . ." She shrugs, listening to the phone ring. It rings once, twice, three times. "She's probably not answering just to frighten me," Sandy says.

"She's your mother," Dean says.

Sandy listens.

Two more rings, then, "Hello?" Lilly asks.

Sandy takes a breath, leaning back in the chair. She hadn't

realized how tense she'd been waiting for her mother to pick
up. "Hello, Mother," Sandy says.

"How was the drive?" Lilly asks.

"Fine. Just calling to let you know we made it all right."

"I was afraid the car might not make it, it was packed so full,"
Lilly says, genuinely concerned.

"Well, we did, Mother. You can relax. What are you up to?"

"I'm watching television."

"Good, Mother, I'll let you go then."

"Talk to you tomorrow."

"Of course."

"Love you, Sandy."

"You too, Mother. Goodbye."

"Goodbye. My love to the kids and Dean."

"Goodbye."

"Good night." Lilly hangs up.

Sandy hangs up, then stands, walking over to the dresser.
"Mother's worried that the van's going to break down and we'll
never make it home."

"The van's fine," Dean says, concentrating on the book.

"We do need a car with a big trunk and a ski rack," Sandy
says, interrupting Dean's thoughts. "The van's too cold in the
winter."

"I've been looking at them," Dean says. "Maybe next year."

Sandy unwraps the towel, revealing her body. Not a young
woman, she turns forty this year, but having had five children,
she's still slim except for her stomach, which is a bit round and
less firm. Sandy pulls a long red-and-black flannel nightgown
over her head. It falls to her knees and she draws up the sleeves,
bunching up the cuffs at her elbows. The buttons on the chest
of the nightgown are unfastened and Dean can see her breasts.
He'd like to reach in and touch one, holding it in his palm as
Sandy looks at him and he looks back at her as he slides his
other hand over her—

Sandy turns on the television, volume low because Tina's

sleeping. She takes a step back, looking at the color picture. "Nice having a color TV in the bedroom," Sandy says, deliberately reminding Dean of a recent conversation. She flips the dial twice and switches the set off, opening the door to the boys' room, stepping in.

Dean stares after her, annoyed at himself for being annoyed by her remark. The black-and-white is no longer good enough; she needs the color, Sandy said one night while they watched the late news from bed.

"I remember when we didn't even have a TV," Dean replied. "We'd sit and talk and drink coffee and laugh."

"We couldn't afford a TV. It wasn't out of choice," Sandy said.

"I thought it was," Dean said. "I thought you liked talking to me."

"You were always too tired to talk, remember? You'd come home after working late, or from school, remember? You were too tired. You'd drop off the minute you came in," Sandy said, but there was no bitterness in her voice; she was just stating the facts, Dean had to admit.

"You were that bored?" he asked.

Sandy moved over, putting her arms around him. "I missed you, that's all. I was lonely for you those nights," and Sandy kissed him.

"Why didn't you tell me?" Dean asked.

"What could you have done?" she answered. "You had to do what you had to do."

And Dean looked at her and knew that she was right. He couldn't have done it any different even if he'd thought to.

"Well, he is—he is a schizophrenic," Blane tells his mother. He's lying on the floor, wrapped in a bedspread by the closet. A pillow beneath his head and a comic book in his hands. Tom, Kyle and Hal watch the TV, sprawled with their faces at the foot of the two double beds, leaning over pillows.

"Oh, he is not, ignore him, Tom. Blane, get off the floor and sleep on the bed," Sandy says. She stares down at him.

"I like the floor," Blane rebuts.

"The bed is better for you," Sandy says, trying to persuade him. "Why can't you share a bed with Kyle like Tom and Hal are?"

"I want the bed to myself," Kyle says, spreading his arms and legs wide as if he needed that much room for himself.

"Blane, get in the bed, please. You'll sleep better," Sandy says again. "The light there's better for you to read."

"I can see fine," Blane protests. "And I don't want to sleep with any of them."

"See, he doesn't want to," Kyle says. "Mom, we're trying to watch TV."

Sandy looks at the television. A cop show she doesn't recognize.

"Why don't I get my own bed?" Tom asks. "If Kyle does, why do I have to share with Hal?"

"If Blane sleeps on the floor every night, which I wish he wouldn't, you and Kyle will take turns having your own beds," Sandy says, settling a potential fight before it erupts.

"What about my turn?" Hal asks.

"You're little, you don't need your own bed just yet," Sandy says. "Good night." She walks back into her room, shutting the door behind her firmly.

"I don't know where Blane gets these things," she says.

"School, I suppose, or books. He reads a lot," Dean says.

"I don't know," Sandy says.

"He's a thinker," Dean explains to both himself and Sandy. "Maybe he makes these things up to fool us."

"He acts as if he knows what he's talking about, but he doesn't I hope. I don't understand him," Sandy says. "He didn't get that from me. *Schizophrenic?*"

"But he's bright," Dean says.

"Yes, he is."

"Aren't all our kids?" Dean asks. "Not all in the same ways, maybe, but they are all fairly bright, aren't they? We did pretty well."

"I suppose they are. I don't know, Dean. We're pretty lucky

to have them," Sandy says and she comes over and sits by Dean on the bed.

"We are, aren't we," Dean says, putting an arm around Sandy and he smiles at her. She smiles and Sandy and Dean kiss. Dean folds his hand between the black-and-red checks of her nightshirt. Sandy's breast is soft. Sandy rolls to him, her hands moving over Dean's chest, her legs parting across his lap, a spy novel falling to the carpet. Tina sleeps and Dean's hand slides across Sandy's stomach as the other caresses her breast.

"Blane says I'm a schizo-frantic," Tom bursts in.

Sandy and Dean pull apart. Sandy rolling to the side and yanking down her nightshirt. Dean sits up in bed, turning to Tom, leaning in front of Sandy as she arranges herself.

"Next time knock," Dean responds, standing. Sandy buttons her nightshirt.

"But Blane says I'm schizo-frantic," Tom says, walking further into the room.

"What's going on?" Dean asks. He puts a hand on Tom's shoulder, leading him away from Sandy and into his room. Dean shuts the adjoining door, giving Sandy some privacy.

"Blane keeps calling me names," Tom says.

"What did you call him?" Dean asks Blane.

Blane turns his head up at Dean from his spot on the floor. "He is schizophrenic."

"You don't know what it means," Dean replies.

"Yes, I do," Blane says. He looks directly at Dean, staring him down.

"What does it mean?" Tom asks his father.

"Who cares?" Kyle calls from the bed.

"What is it?" Hal asks. "Is it a magic word?"

"It doesn't mean anything," Dean says, calming Tom and Hal. "Blane doesn't know what he's talking about."

"Yes, I do," Blane insists.

"You keep quiet and go to sleep. Where did you learn that word anyway?" Dean asks.

"Behavioral science," Blane states proudly. "It's a psychological term for people whose brains are all mixed up and so they act out of control to what really happened to them." He looks up at his father, proud of himself.

"It's science!" Hal exclaims. "I love science!"

Dean looks away from Blane to Hal. "It's not science, so calm down." Dean turns to Tom, "You don't have a mental disorder. That's not what it means anyway, so stop being so concerned about what Blane says. Now all of you go to sleep." Dean shuts off the TV and the boys moan. He returns to his room, figuring that if the kids want to squabble, they'll squabble. It's harmless so long as they don't hit each other.

"Are they asleep?" Sandy asks. She lies under the covers, her eyes shut.

"Yes, they're fine." Dean climbs into the bed beside her, shutting off the lights. The bed's cozy. Dean can feel the heat from Sandy's body.

He puts an arm around her. "What's a schizophrenic?"

Sandy rolls over facing him. "Tom's not a schizophrenic. Go to sleep."

"Is something wrong with him?" Dean asks, concerned.

"With who?" Sandy asks. They look at each other, trying to see each other's face in the dark.

"Tom," Dean says.

"He's moody," Sandy replies. "Has a short fuse."

"Who does he get that from?" Dean asks. "You or me?"

"I don't know. Both of us, I suppose, who cares?" Sandy looks at Dean. "Let's sleep, okay?"

"Sometimes do you think one of them is more yours than mine?" Dean asks. "That they have more of one of us in them than the other?"

Sandy pulls herself into a sitting position, leaning against the headboard. "I don't know. Why are you asking?"

"Just wondering," Dean says. "Don't you ever wonder why they're so different but they came from the same two people?

I was just wondering if it's different combinations of each of us that make them different from one another and which of them might have more or less of one of us in them."

Sandy slumps in the bed, rolling over. "I'm tired, figure it out for yourself. I don't divvy them up between us. They're all yours. They're all mine."

Dean moves up next to her, kissing her neck.

"Dean, I'm tired," she brushes him off. Dean realizes he shouldn't have spoken a word; he should have just gotten into bed and touched her. He shouldn't have broken the mood.

Dean reaches under the covers and tickles her thigh. Sandy shoves him back. "Stop it, will you?"

"I want to play."

"Well, I want to sleep."

"You're no fun."

"Stop whining like the kids."

"I am not whining."

"Yes, you are. You are whining."

Dean leans over to her, his lips to her ear. "You're schizophrenic," he whispers softly.

Sandy shoves him back and slides out of the bed.

Dean laughs. "Sandy, what's the matter?"

"I was trying to sleep and you keep poking me and talking." Sandy stands by the side of the bed.

All Dean can see is a black outline in the dark. "You've been very moody lately, I'm trying to lighten you up, okay," Dean says.

"I am not schizophrenic," Sandy states.

"I think you are," Dean says. "Isn't this what schizophrenics do, act out in weird ways?"

"I'm sleeping with Tina," and Sandy climbs into bed beside her daughter. "Good night." She turns away from Dean.

Dean pulls back the covers on Sandy's side. "Come back, please."

Total silence.

"Now you're acting like one of the kids," Dean tells her.

Sandy keeps her eyes closed, saying nothing.

"Tom gets his moodiness from you," Dean continues. "And his competitive edge and athletic skill from me—his father." Sandy lifts her head from the pillow. "In addition to his immaturity. Now be quiet before you wake Tina." She drops her head, letting silence fill the space between them.

Dean, in response, decides to defy Sandy and divvy up the kids. Kyle, he decides, is his. Blane is up for grabs although he leans toward Sandy in most respects, passive by nature. Tom is Dean's for the most part. Hal will be his, Dean decides, and Tina should be Sandy's, being a girl.

"I count three for me and two for you," Dean calls into the dark of the room, but Sandy doesn't respond and Dean supposes that she probably likes to think of them all as hers because she's the mother and as Lilly repeatedly tells the kids, "Your mother is your one best friend for life." Not your father, Dean hears Lilly implying. The father means nothing compared to the mother, according to Sandy's mother. But Dean has learned to keep thoughts concerning Lilly to himself, never knowing when Sandy might agree with—or turn against—him for ridiculing her mother. Lilly once told Dean, "I raised my daughter alone and look how good she turned out—you married her, so obviously you knew she had a proper upbringing. Only proves you don't need a father to raise fine children."

Sandy lies with her head half on, half off the pillow. She can sense Dean's presence and she closes her eyes tight, shutting him out of her thoughts, feeling wet hair cling to her cheeks.

Dean folds the bedspread over the spot where Sandy would have slept, wrapping his arms around her pillow, resting his head and smelling her scent. Sandy's only one bed away, but when she's not lying next to him, Dean feels as if she might as well be miles away or gone altogether. She's either with him or in Alaska, never anyplace in between.

■

Lilly's alone again. The family away, she's alone for the next several days. She clutches the *TV Guide* in one hand and the notepad with the emergency numbers to the police, fire department and hospital in the other. *Hawaii Five-O* is on the TV screen, but Lilly's distracted, her focus directed to the front window. She stands, walking over, peering out, looking through the trees bordering the front lawn to the neighbor's house across the street. Cars line the road, teenagers running through the snow, in and out of the house. Lilly turns down the volume of the TV and listens. She can hear the music they're playing. She can hear screams of teenagers yelling from the street to the house. She hears a beer bottle smashing, thrown to the pavement.

The house across the street is next door to Terry's, Sandy's best friend's, house. Sandy posted Terry's phone number on the bulletin board by the refrigerator. "Call her if you need anything from the store. Terry said she'd be happy to pick any groceries up for you. There's plenty of food for the dog anyway so you don't have to worry about that and you can either let the mail and newspapers collect in the box or call Terry and have one of her boys bring them in to you. I don't want you walking along the driveway and slipping on a patch of ice." Sandy's directions to her mother, as if Lilly hadn't lived most of her life alone and learned how to care for herself. "Don't worry, go," Lilly replied, already accustomed to the family's winter ski trips, being left alone with the run of the house for a long weekend.

A bark at the side door. Lilly puts the *TV Guide* and notepad in the pockets of her robe and walks to let Philynda in. Lilly opens the door, then the glass-paneled storm door, holding it ajar so the spring won't tug it shut.

Philynda sits on the front step, staring up at Lilly.

Cold air floods the house sending a chill through Lilly's body. Philynda still sits, staring up at her.

"In or out?" Lilly asks, her arm becoming tired from holding the door, goose bumps over her body. "In or out?" she asks again.

Philynda stands and trots in past Lilly to the dog dishes on the kitchen floor. Lilly closes both doors, double-checking the locks, then walks after the dog. The beagle's pushing the empty food dish around the tile with her nose.

"I already fed you today," Lilly tells the dog, but Philynda keeps on poking the plastic dish around.

"You're not getting any more. Drink your water." Lilly points to the water dish. "Drink your water." Philynda begins kicking at the empty food dish with her front paws, knocking it against the walls, cabinets and kitchen chairs.

"You're not getting any more from me," Lilly states and she turns, walking into the family room, sitting on the couch. She looks up at the TV. The volume's down. Buddy Ebsen—*Barnaby Jones.* Lilly stands and turns the volume up, drowning out the sounds of the partygoers and the noise of Philynda in the kitchen.

The eleven o'clock news is over. The party across the street has grown louder, kids dancing on the lawn, tossing snowballs at one another. Philynda's through playing with the dish and lies at the foot of the television, sleeping.

Lilly stands, shutting off the TV, then systematically walking from room to room, putting the house to bed. The dishwasher's turned on in the kitchen, lights out downstairs but for one in the living room and one by the front door, and Lilly heads up to the second floor, leaving the hall light on at the top of the stairs.

She enters the master bedroom, walking over to her daughter's dresser and inspecting its top, sorting through Sandy's jewelry boxes filled with strands of pearls, an opal ring and matching watch, gold chains, silver bracelets, a diamond choker: all gifts from Dean.

Lilly holds her left hand up, looking over her only piece of "real" jewelry: a large rectangular garnet ring, her retirement gift from the bank. Lilly's other jewelry: faux pearl earrings, bracelets, necklaces, a crystal bracelet and several ceramic pendants are put away in an old jewelry box in the basement; toys Hal and Tina use as treasure when playing like pirates or explorers. Lilly's anniversary and wedding rings were sold long ago—Lilly didn't want the rings in the apartment, superstitious that if she kept them Hugh would somehow always be a force in her life, a force to be fought; the selling of the rings being Lilly's final active step to erase evidence of Hugh from both Sandy's and her life.

Lilly draws the bedspread to the bottom of Sandy and Dean's bed, then folds back the sheet, climbing in. Having slept in a double bed for so many years before moving in with Sandy's family, Lilly felt awkward sleeping in the twin bed in the guest room. It took a week before she could lie down to sleep without waking several times before morning.

Lilly switches off the night table lamp and settles back, moving a pillow from the headboard parallel to her body. She curls her arms and legs around the down pillow, holding it close for both warmth and comfort.

■

Everyone has their own room in the house but Sandy. The children and Lilly have their bedrooms, and Dean has his den. The only place Sandy has for herself is her walk-in bedroom closet. She turns forty in three weeks.

"What's on at eight?" Kyle asks. He sits on the couch with Lilly and Tom.

"*The Brady Bunch,*" Blane says from the easy chair.

"No way," Tom says. "They're all repeats. They're on every day." He puts a handful of cereal in his mouth, eating from the box.

"That's what we're watching," Blane says. "Watch it or leave."

"That's the show I like," Lilly adds.

"Let me see the *TV Week,*" Kyle interjects.

"Why? You're not changing the station," Blane warns.

"Give it to me," Kyle says, yanking the magazine from Blane's hands.

"Fine, but you're not changing it," Blane repeats confidently.

"Why do you get to decide?" Tom asks.

"Don't create problems for your mother," Lilly says.

"Keep out of it, Mother," Sandy says. "I think I can handle this."

"Well, so can I," Lilly replies stubbornly.

"Why does Blane decide?" Tom asks again.

"Because I make good decisions," Blane explains.

"I'll decide what show we'll watch, now give me the listings, please," Sandy says, extending her hand, and Kyle passes her the listings. Sandy doesn't actually care what they watch. There's nothing much on on Thursdays at eight o'clock anyway, she thinks, so let them watch the reruns, there's no harm in it. *The Brady Bunch* theme song plays.

"I'm not watching this," Tom says.

"Then leave," Blane says, gazing at the TV screen.

Sandy throws down the paper. "We'll watch this show now and you can choose at eight-thirty," she tells Tom.

"But my show starts now, I'll miss the first half," Tom complains.

"Quit your griping," Lilly says.

"Shut up, you old lady," Tom rebuts.

"Did you hear that?" Lilly snaps at her daughter.

"Yes," Sandy replies, "and maybe you should M.Y.O.B.," and to Tom, "and you can watch your show on the kitchen TV for now."

"That's only black-and-white," Tom grumbles.

"I'm done. This is it," Sandy says, and she sits back in the rocking chair, saying no more.

Tom sits for a moment, staring angrily at the TV with a grimace, then he stands. "This sucks." He leaves the room with a big huff.

Kyle remains sitting with Lilly, Blane and Sandy, attentively watching the Bradys' antics. They stare at the large color TV, which sits on a wooden stand by the sliding glass door leading out to the porch.

A room of her own in which she can establish some life beyond her family.

"What do you want to be when you grow up?" she asked her kids recently.

"Rich," Kyle said.

"A brain surgeon," Blane said.

"A race car driver," Tom said.

"A magician," Hal said.

"A dinosaur," Tina said.

Options never given her, a housewife being all she was ever told she could be, and Lilly made this *career* choice sound better than being a famous singer or Queen of England. *"Career Girl?"* Lilly sneered when Sandy asked her what it was like to have an occupation. "A career is a fancy word for a job and a job does not make a woman happy. Look at me. I have a job. Am I happy? Just because I have to work doesn't mean you'll have to once you marry. Every new generation does better than the last and so I can only hope you marry a man you can stay married to, a man who will be a good provider so you can be a good housewife and never *career* your life away as I have."

On TV, Carol Brady has just entered the kitchen carrying the groceries all by herself. Alice stands at the blackboard by the stove, writing down what the evening's dinner will be. Mrs. Brady sets the bags on the kitchen table just as Marcia and Greg storm into the room, bickering about some football player Marcia's dating. And then Mr. Brady enters and the other four Brady children enter and soon the whole room is in chaos, the entire Brady clan and Alice caught up in a flurry of excitement while Carol Brady's bundles are left unattended, and Sandy can't keep herself from wondering what is it that is in those sacks of groceries that Carol Brady has left sitting there on the kitchen table? What groceries did Carol Brady have to buy today, and if she bought dairy products, does Carol Brady realize they may spoil if she doesn't put them away soon? But the Brady family keeps right on bickering and the show cuts to a commercial before the bags are ever unpacked. Sandy stares at the commercial, a commercial for laundry soap, and sadly realizes that Carol Brady's shopping list is of no concern to anyone in the world but herself. A housewife.

Kyle picks up the *TV Week,* looking it over.

"We're watching *On the Rocks* next," Blane tells him with certainty.

"Maybe I want to watch *Fay*," Kyle says.

"Well, maybe you're not going to," Blane retaliates.

"We're watching *On the Rocks*," Lilly declares.

Kyle turns to Sandy for support. "Blane already got to choose this, now it's time for my turn to choose, right?" Kyle looks at Sandy anxiously.

"Can't we just enjoy the show now? We'll worry about that later," Sandy tells Kyle and Kyle tosses the *TV Week* on the carpet, staring back at the TV.

Lilly reaches over to Kyle, patting his shoulder. "I thought you liked watching *On the Rocks*," she says sweetly.

Kyle brushes her hand away. "I don't know," he says staring at the TV, and Lilly sits on the couch, unfazed by Kyle's response.

"You know, that would never happen in real life," Kyle says, critiquing the show.

"Just be quiet," Blane says and they stare at the TV, enjoying the Bradys. Sandy can never seem to follow the plots of the episodes, always getting too caught up in the way Carol Brady handles her everyday duties of shopping, car-pooling and the kids. Sandy Wallace wishes she could be a mother of conviction like Carol Brady, not just doing the wash or cooking the dinner, but Doing the Wash and Cooking the Dinner. But of course Carol Brady has Alice to help her out whenever she is overwhelmed with the kids. All Sandy has is her mother to point out to her what's wrong so that Sandy can fix it. Yet whatever the facts, and however Sandy turns it around in her head to defend herself, Mrs. Carol Brady remains the mother her children idolize and whom she's supposed to emulate: the newest, greatest, hippest mom in the long-running history of TV mothers. Mrs. Carol Brady can carry in all her groceries by herself while Sandy must honk the horn and have the kids come down to the garage and haul them upstairs for her. Compared to Carol Brady, Sandy can only lose.

When the Wallace family consisted of Dean and Sandy, before

the kids, before Lilly, before color TV and two-car garages, Mr. and Mrs. Dean Wallace lived in a four-room Cape Codder in Newton. White with forest green shutters. They had no washer or dryer so twice a week Sandy lugged their dirty clothes and linen around the corner to the laundromat. "What does your husband do?" was the first question off all the young wives' tongues and Sandy would answer, "He's a salesman for a data processing company," and the other wives would nod, impressed—*Data Processing*—anything even remotely involving computers sounded so up-and-coming sophisticated that they knew this woman had married a man with a future.

The answer to "And what do you do?" asked so often nowadays, does not come so readily to Sandy's lips, and after a prolonged, embarrassing pause, Sandy smiles meekly, responding with, "Oh, I'm a housewife, a homemaker," reluctantly admitting she is no help *to,* no participant *in* the women's fight for equal rights, no "sister" to the working women, but still Mrs. Dean Wallace instead of Mrs. Sandy Wallace or, better yet, Ms. Sandy Burke.

Terry, Sandy's friend, just started her own business, running a catering company. Dean's hired her to do the food for Sandy's fortieth birthday celebration. In fact, Terry says she's so busy cooking for other people that she no longer has time to cook meals for her own family; she brings home McDonald's or Kentucky Fried Chicken every other night. Terry says her kids complain that she's not there for them anymore; that she's not there to serve after-school snacks or monitor who gets to watch which cartoons on the TV all afternoon. Terry had sincerely thought that being busy would make the kids value her more, but now all it seems to have done is make them angry. "If you loved us you wouldn't need to get a job and leave us," her youngest son, Charlie, told her. "Dad makes enough money, why do you have to work?" her older boy, Miller, has said.

Terry told this to Sandy over tea at her kitchen table, inhaling deeply on a cigarette, speaking through the smoke rings she exhaled from her mouth. "The little brats think I'm their slave, for God's sake."

Sandy slowly put down her teacup. "They're your children, Terry. They just love you and want to spend time with you. You shouldn't resent that but should appreciate it."

"I can't talk to you about this if you're going to answer like some perfect housewife."

"I'm not trying to be, but I am sure your kids love you, despite what they say."

Terry stubbed the cigarette out. "Yes, but you'd think that if they loved me they'd also want me to be happy. You would think that, wouldn't you? But nope, not my kids, they'd rather make me a slave than let me be what I want to be." Terry lit up another cigarette. She had begun smoking soon after she'd started working. "You know, Sandy," she continued, shaking her head, "if I hadn't been such a good mother and spoiled them before, they wouldn't be so angry with me now. If only I'd been a shitty mother," Terry said sarcastically, "then they wouldn't give a damn that I'm so busy now."

For lack of having anything to say, Sandy added a second packet of Sweet 'n Low to her tea. Terry kept staring at Sandy, waiting for a response, but Sandy had nothing to say.

"Do you think I'm wrong?" Terry finally asked. "I mean, haven't you ever wanted to do something more than be a housewife?"

Sandy looked up at Terry, then to the trail of smoke ascending from the cigarette between her friend's fingers. Sandy wanted to tell Terry to forget about the catering business, to go back to being a good mother and a good wife. "That is what is important," Sandy wanted to say. "That is all that's going to matter years from now," Sandy wanted to tell her best friend, but instead she just took another sip of tea and gave Terry a weak but supportive smile.

On the TV screen, Greg and Marcia are reconciling their differences. Sandy looks to her mother. "Didn't I want to be a veterinarian once?"

"I couldn't have afforded to send you to vet school," Lilly responds, her eyes never leaving the television. "But didn't I want to be?" Sandy asks. "I thought I did when I was about Tom's age." Lilly ignores Sandy's question. The issue is dead because Lilly is right: She simply could not have afforded it whether Sandy wanted to go or not. Not on her salary from the bank, and Lilly said Hugh never once sent them any money to help them get by. Lilly said Hugh wanted them to starve to death—"Don't blame me, blame your father," was the excuse she usually gave as to why Sandy had to be denied a new toy or dress or pair of shoes. Sandy thought about calling her father during her teen years and asking him if he would pay the tuition for veterinarian school, but she couldn't remember what he looked like. And although Sandy knew he couldn't be the brute Lilly described him as being, Sandy didn't have anything to prove that her mother was wrong, so she just let the idea slide. Sandy could never imagine what it would be like to have a father—to have two parental perspectives on the world balancing each other out instead of having just the one being forced upon you. "It's very fortunate that I have to work," Lilly told Sandy. "It forces you into training to be a good housewife at a young age; gives you time to perfect it under my supervision so that when the right man does come along, you'll be ready."

In seventh grade, when Sandy had to draw her family tree, Sandy's name was on the bottom with her father's and mother's names above hers, and her grandparents' and great-grandparents' names above her mother's. Lilly refused to give Sandy any of the names of Hugh's family, and she erased his name from the chart. "If I'm doing all the work," Lilly commented, "why should he get half the credit?"

The closing theme to *The Brady Bunch* plays.

Kyle looks to Sandy. "Now can I choose what we watch?"

"We're watching *On the Rocks*," Blane argues.

"*On the Rocks* is *quality* television," Lilly says.

"It's my turn to choose, isn't it, Mom?" Kyle asks.

"Then choose *On the Rocks* and there won't be a problem," Blane says.

"We're watching what I want," Kyle says, marching up to the TV set, switching the channel to NBC.

"Mom," Blane pleads.

"Sandy," Lilly reprimands.

And Sandy stands. "Watch *Fay,* watch *On the Rocks,* I don't care what you watch," she says, and she leaves the room without a backward glance, hoping they fight: Let them kill each other over their stupid TV shows; life's that important.

Sandy walks across the house into the den where Dean is sitting at his desk, leafing through a pile of papers. Sandy sits on the brown leather couch, staring at his back. "I need to do something," Sandy says.

Dean doesn't look up from the phone bill, double-checking the long-distance charges. "I thought you were watching TV with the kids."

What are the words he said to Kyle not so long ago? *Work makes you feel worthy, to be earning your own money. Your work is who you are.* Sandy sighs and slumps back on the couch. "I don't want the party."

Dean turns around in the chair. "What are you talking about?"

"I don't want the party," Sandy repeats. "I want it canceled."

Dean stares at her, a gold Cross pen in one hand, the phone bill in the other. "And why's that?" he asks her.

"I don't want to be forty in front of all those people," she answers calmly.

"Then why did you decide you originally did want the party?" he asks.

"So I've changed my mind, I'm entitled."

Dean shrugs, looking down, scanning the bill. "Well, we've sent out the invites. People have RSVP'd. We placed the order with Terry." He looks back at her, tossing up his hands. "What do you want me to do?"

"I don't care," Sandy tells him. "Just cancel it."

"What's wrong?" Dean asks and he puts down the pen and

phone bill and comes over to the couch, sitting by Sandy's side. "Have I done something wrong?" he asks gently, touching her hand. "What did I do?" he asks, and Sandy grips his forefinger in her fist, staring at the ceiling, making out the patterns on the speckled white plaster.

"What's wrong?" he asks again.

Sandy stares at the ceiling. She's afraid that if she looks at him she'll cry. "I have to do something," she explains.

"Do what?" Dean asks and he leans over, hugging her shoulders, brushing his cheek up against her face. It's rough with razor stubble and his hands support her body as she keeps staring away, from the ceiling toward the wall where a photo of a humpback whale hangs. Dean puts his nose to Sandy's nose, staring into her eyes, which stare directly back into his.

"You can do whatever you want," Dean says. "You know I'll always support you. I love you."

"I love you too," Sandy mumbles into his ear. She slowly leans forward, pushing him away. "Thank you, I love you too," she tells him again.

"Is everything all right?" he asks, concerned.

Sandy sits, then stands, leaving him on the couch. "Just needed a little reassurance, that's all," and she touches his shoulder and he takes her hand.

"I love you," he repeats.

"I know," Sandy says and she walks from the room.

"So do you really want me to cancel the party?" Dean asks.

Sandy keeps walking. "No, I do not want you to cancel the party," she says lightly. "Don't worry about it."

"I didn't think so," Dean says and he sits back at the desk, once again immersed in the bills.

Sandy walks through the living room to the hall, then upstairs, tracing a hand along the wallpaper, feeling its bumpy straw texture. She looks in on Tina, who's sleeping.

Tina's room is dark, just a triangular beam of yellow light spills in from the hall and Sandy quietly enters, staring down at her daughter. Tina has pretty, long, light brown hair that she pulls back into a ponytail before she climbs into bed. She's wearing a pair of the boys' old train pajamas, the blue ones with locomotives and cabooses. Unlike the younger boys who complain about being passed hand-me-downs from Kyle, Tina welcomes the used clothes, appreciating the bond they form between Kyle, Blane, Tom, Hal and then, ultimately, her. When Sandy bought Tina a flannel nightgown to wear instead of the pajamas, Tina refused to put it on. "I want to share the boys' clothes like they do," she protested.

There are four oak posts rising around the bed, one from each corner. Sandy leans over and kisses Tina's cheek, then lies down beside her, matching her breathing to that of her daughter's, putting them in sync.

Sandy opens her eyes, stares into the dark and takes a breath, standing. She pulls the blanket around Tina's shoulders, then leaves the room, wondering what her earlier dark mood had been about in the first place. She can barely remember; she has Dean, the kids, a great house, an easy life. She walks into the hallway and down the stairs, wondering what might be on the television at this hour. Is it the *Thursday Night Movie, Ellery Queen* or *The Streets of San Francisco?* It's all so simple. More isn't possible.

■

The time is three-thirty and Dean is eating a late lunch at his desk, quickly scanning the pages of the *Wall Street Journal* as he takes bites from the tuna salad sandwich bought from the vending machine in the company's lunchroom. The vending machine was empty but for tuna salad and egg salad, and Dean chose between the lesser of the two evils.

Dean takes note of an article in the paper regarding college admissions scores. A finding that preparatory courses for SATs can significantly increase an applicant's scores. Dean puts down the sandwich and takes the executive-size Swiss army knife from his pants pocket, flipping the small blade open and tracing it around the column. He peels the cut strip from the newspaper and folds it into his shirt pocket; to be given to Kyle tonight.

Kyle, a junior in high school, has begun reading through college catalogs in search of universities with good international economics programs.

Dean takes a bite from the sandwich and a sip of the diet cola, drinking straight from the can.

"Dean, Sandy on three," Vicki calls over the intercom box.

Dean, his mouth full, "I'll call her back in a minute, thanks." He turns the page of the paper, looking over a book review of the latest Le Carré novel.

A knock on the office door.

"Come in." Dean looks up from the paper.

Vicki enters. "Sorry, but she says it's urgent. Do you want to pick up?" Vicki takes another step into the room.

"Sure—sure," Dean nods. "What line is she on?"

"Three. Sorry for interrupting."

"That's all right."

Vicki exits, shutting the door behind her. Dean folds the paper closed, moving it aside, then lifts the phone receiver, taking line three. "Hello, Sandy," Dean says, cheerful, upbeat.

"You could take my call instead of making me explain things to Vicki." Dean can feel Sandy's controlled anger over the phone.

"I was in the middle of something," Dean answers, attempting to soothe her. "I'm sorry, but I didn't know it couldn't wait."

"Well, it can't," Sandy says abruptly. "We have to drive into Boston and pick Tom up."

"What's Tom doing in Boston?" Dean's leaning on the desk, focusing on the phone as if it were Sandy and she was there in the room with him.

"He's at the airport. He never went to school today but hitchhiked into Logan with a friend. Tom contacted one of his teachers at school and the teacher just called me and explained the situation."

"What exactly is the situation?" Dean asks Sandy. "What exactly is going on?"

Sandy lists the facts for Dean. "Tom is at the airport. We have to pick him up. I don't have a car because Kyle took it downtown to work with him. You have to come and pick me up so we can drive into Boston to get Tom. *There.* Is that specific enough for you?"

"But how did this happen?"

"*What?*"

"*Why* is Tom in Boston? Can't you at least explain that? And who is this teacher who called you?"

"Can't we discuss this on the way to the airport?"

A knock on Dean's office door. He looks up, startled. "Yes?"

Vicki opens the door a crack, sticking her head in.

"Dean," Sandy says into his ear.

Dean looks at Vicki, speaking into the phone, "Please, just hold on a minute."

Sandy continues, "Dean, we have to—"

Dean pushes the hold button, cutting her off. "Yes, Vicki?" he asks.

"Mr. Prennell from Towle Industries is on four. He said it was urgent that he speak with you," Vicki says softly.

Dean looks to the phone, lines three and four both lit and blinking, on hold. He covers his eyes with his hands, blocking out the light, regaining some of the concentration Sandy has broken. He speaks, his voice deliberate, sharp. "Tell Mr. Prennell I'm in a meeting. That I was expecting his call and will return it later. Put him through to Alex if he has any information we need to take down immediately. Thank you."

Vicki leaves. Dean hears the door close and he uncovers his eyes. Line four has stopped blinking and is a steady red. Line three blinks rapidly. Dean puts Sandy back on the line, "Sandy?"

"Still here," she says, an edge to her voice.

"I will be home shortly. I'll see you then."

"I'll be waiting. Goodbye." Sandy hangs up the phone.

Dean watches line three go dead, unlit, and he places the receiver down on the desk. A family can only be as united as the head of the household is strong, and Dean stands, taking a bite of the sandwich, a gulp of the soda, then tossing both in the wastebasket.

Lilly sits at the kitchen table watching her daughter speak over the phone to Tom's teacher for the third time this afternoon. Lilly's eating butter cookies while sipping a cup of tea. Tina and Hal watch cartoons in the family room.

"So he's expecting us at the Eastern terminal? It's all set? Thank you, Mr. Dennis, thanks for your help." Sandy makes a note on a pad of paper writing down exactly where they will be meeting Tom at the airport. Mr. Dennis, Tom's homeroom teacher, has been in contact with Tom and Tom's friend, Edgar Simpson, through a pay phone at the airport. Mr. Dennis said that originally Tom wanted him to pick them up but Mr. Dennis convinced them to let their parents as long as he would act as their liaison. So Mr. Dennis passed the information along to Mrs. Wallace and Mrs. Simpson, finishing off his job of mediating, and handing the responsibility for Tom's and Edgar's problems back to their respective families.

Sandy tears the paper off the pad and places it in her pocketbook, taking out her sunglasses, putting them on, preparing for Dean's arrival. She walks to the closet and takes out her plaid wool jacket.

"You're going to go all the way into Boston to get him?" Lilly asks.

Sandy ignores her, putting on the jacket and taking her purse off the counter. She heads upstairs to Blane's room. The door is closed. She knocks.

"Yes?"

Sandy enters. Blane's lying on the bed facing away from her, highlighting pages of his European history textbook with a yellow marker.

Sandy stands in the doorway. "You can watch out for Hal and Tina; keep them occupied with a story or something if they get rowdy, okay?"

Blane draws an outline around the border of East Prussia, a

map of Europe following World War I. "No problem, I'm almost done anyway."

The honk of Dean's car horn. Sandy walks to the window, looking out over the driveway. "Well, time to go," she sighs, walking over to Blane, kissing his cheek. "Thanks for your help, honey." She leaves the room, downstairs through the basement, bypassing her mother in the kitchen, intentionally avoiding her, as well as Hal's and Tina's questions and long goodbyes.

Dean sits in the driver's seat of the dark blue Cadillac, his brown-tinted sunglasses over his eyes. He watches Sandy approach the car. She opens the passenger's side and slides in, pulling the seat belt across her lap.

"Where to?" Dean asks.

"Huh?" Sandy asks, looking up.

"The terminal. Which terminal?" Dean asks.

"Oh. Eastern," Sandy says. "The Eastern terminal."

"Great," Dean replies, and he shifts the car into reverse, backing out of the driveway.

Kyle glances at the order on the check and tosses a burger on the grill. Some of his friends who work here think it's easier being a waiter than a grillperson but Kyle would much rather run the grill than wait on customers. He finds that the customers are a pain in the ass, changing their orders, never satisfied, complaining about their food to the manager as if Friendly's coffee shop was a five-star restaurant and they doled out a hundred dollars for their meal instead of the five bucks it really cost them. When Kyle was a waiter, sometimes he'd end up taking orders from his friends, who would harass him for free sundaes. Or worse yet, he'd have to wait on his family when Sandy would bring them in for dinner or ice cream. She'd completely embarrass Kyle in front of his co-workers, waving to him when he was in the middle of serving a customer. And then, if Lilly's order was prepared incorrectly, Kyle would have to hear her criticism. Given the choice between waiting and grilling, Kyle leaves the waiting for the waitresses.

The takeout phone in the back room rings. Regina, the waitress on weekday afternoons, walks through the swinging door to answer it. Kyle drops some fries down in the frier, then finishes setting up a BLT platter with cole slaw and potato salad. Regina walks over to Kyle. "Your brother's on the phone."

"Which one?" Kyle asks, handing her the BLT plate.

"How the hell would I know?" she answers in her nasal voice. "And don't be too long because I'm the only one out here." She walks off to deliver the food.

Kyle steps out back and picks up the phone. "Yeah?"

"It's me," Blane says.

"What do you want? I'm working." Kyle leans against the wall, stirring a pot of chicken noodle soup on the gas stove by the phone.

"Tom took off. He thinks he's going to Europe," Blane says, laughing.

"What are you talking about?" Kyle asks, irritated. He has to get off the phone quickly in order to finish the orders on the grill. Blane launches into a long monologue, telling Kyle about Tom, the airport, Europe, their mother and father. Blane is laughing the whole time.

"And you think it's funny?" Kyle asks.

"He went to the Eastern terminal," Blane says, condescendingly.

"So?" Kyle asks.

"Eastern doesn't even fly to Europe," Blane explains to his older brother. "Only to Florida—Disney World country. Can you believe it?" Blane laughs again.

"What? You want him to run away?" Kyle asks.

"If he's going to screw up, he should at least screw up properly. He can't even pick the correct terminal," Blane replies.

"Oh, and you would know what to do?" Kyle looks out over the restaurant. Regina is up by the front counter, taking an order, but everything else is running smoothly.

"He doesn't even have a passport," Blane says. "What's he going to be—a stowaway like that old lady in *Airport?*"

Regina walks to the grill, placing an order by the cutting board.

"I have to go back to work," Kyle says. "I'll see you at home later and I wouldn't laugh at him when he comes in."

"He's pathetic," Blane says.

"Just shut up. Goodbye," Kyle tells Blane and he hangs up the phone, walking out to the grill. He lifts the rack of fries, burned golden in the murky oil. He looks up at the clock above the door to the restrooms. It's four-thirty, too early for the dinner crowd, so the shop's empty except for a few regulars who just drink coffee, smoke and talk. Regina takes care of them while Kyle watches over the grill.

Kyle pictures Blane at home with Tina and Hal, making up some elaborate puppet show that he's always doing to entertain them. Knowing his mother, Kyle expects, Sandy will pay Blane for baby-sitting as well as favor him for taking Hal and Tina off her hands. When Kyle takes responsibility for things and drives someone somewhere, it's expected of him because he's the oldest. Kyle never received any compensation for helping his mother out at his younger brothers' and sister's birthday parties yet when Blane helps out, he's treated like a hero. His family doesn't work the way it's supposed to.

In most families, the oldest child sets an example for the younger children that the younger children must live up to. In the Wallace family, Sandy and Dean have made Blane their ideal that Kyle must live up to:

"Blane helps out the most around the house."

"Blane doesn't fight with anyone."

"Blane's not only the best student in the family, but he's also involved in school clubs for his extracurricular activities."

"Blane never complains when he's asked to do something."

"Blane doesn't use cuss words."

Kyle scrapes the spatula across the grill, cleaning away the grease. He was all scared about getting a seventy-four on his math test, anticipating his father's speech about how Kyle is smart enough to be the student council president two years in a row, but he's still pulling very mediocre grades. "How's that going to look on your transcript?" Dean has often said. "I did very well in high school and got into a good college, so there's no reason you can't."

Kyle looks at the grill, flips a burger, pops down two slices of whole wheat bread in the toaster and drops a slice of Swiss cheese on the beef—BBCB-WWT W/SW-W: A Big Beef Cheeseburger on Whole Wheat Toast with Swiss Cheese, Well Done. The burger will never cook through enough and most likely come out too rare. The customer will complain, but Kyle doesn't care, he just gives them their food as fast as he can; that's his job. And if they do complain, they'll complain to Regina, not him.

Regina walks over to the grill. "What time are you on till?" she asks, really pathetically. She slips a check onto the cutting board.

"Just till five, what about you?" Kyle asks although he doesn't care.

"I was supposed to get off at five, but typical Lynn is late again, so Wally's keeping me on till six or seven," she whines, wiping her hands on her apron. "And it sucks because Lynn's always late for her shift and I'm always stuck covering for her. My mother takes a fit I miss so many family dinners." Regina sighs deeply, then walks away, refilling coffee cups for customers.

Kyle picks up the check. It's for a strawberry shake. "Regina," Kyle calls.

"Yeah?"

"This is a *make*, not a *grill* slip," he reprimands her, holding the check up to her face.

She sneers. "Well, no one's on make and I have to wait on the customers."

Kyle picks up an onion and begins chopping it into bits. "What happens to the grill if I have to do all the ice cream orders too?" he asks her. "And it's not so busy that you can't make one milk shake." Regina has got to be the laziest waitress around.

She nods at him. "*Fine,* no problem, Sweetie," and snatches the slip from his hand and stomps off.

Kyle takes the burger off the grill and places it on the toast, then moves it over to a plate, garnishing it with two slices of pickle. He walks over to B bay and sets the burger down for the customer, a nice old woman.

"Here you are, Carrie," he says.

She smiles. "Thank you. And could I have more coffee, please. From the *fresh* pot," she emphasizes.

Kyle turns to Regina, who's walking by with the coffee pot. "Could you pour Carrie a fresh cup, Regina?"

"Yes, Kyle-honey," she says, smirking.

"Are you sure that's the *fresh* pot?" Carrie asks.

"I'm certainly sure it is, sweetie," Regina says with a nasty smile.

Kyle walks back to the grill, wiping down the cutting board with a rag. He's the best grill person on the staff here. Wally, the manager, told him that. Kyle can handle the most orders alone without screwing up. Kyle's had about twenty orders going on the grill at once: burgers, fish fillets, fries, clam boats, grilled cheeses, chicken patties—and not one mess up on anything. He even gets all the side orders right.

Kyle looks off across the entire floor of the shop, making sure everyone has been attended to. The near booth in A bay is where his family always sits. Years before he'd ever worked here, Kyle remembers one dinner sitting in that booth with his mother and brothers and sister, all six of them jammed in, three on either side with a chair pulled up on the booth's outside edge for Lilly. On another occasion, Hal toppled a cola across all their meals. On another, Tina flung catsup-soaked French fries into Sandy's hair. On another, Kyle, Blane and Tom argued about burgers, fries, sodas, ice cream and who their parents wanted most.

Wally walks onto the floor from out back. "You off now, guy?"

Kyle turns and looks at the clock. "Seems that way."

"Okay, I'll take over the grill. Thanks," Wally says. He steps around Kyle and looks over the orders.

"See you tomorrow, same time, buddy," Kyle tells him.

"Thanks, guy," he answers, slicing a tomato.

"Bye, Regina," Kyle says with an insincere smile.

"Yeah, bye," she says, still pissed at him for making her do the milk shake. Every time she scoops the ice cream she's afraid she'll break a fingernail. So what if she's pissed at him—it's about time someone made her do her job correctly.

Kyle walks to the back room and gets his jacket off the peg in the closet. He heads out to his mother's car. He can't imagine what his parents talked about the whole ride into the airport. He can't even imagine what the three of them are saying to one another the whole trip home. What he can imagine is that his mother and father are probably wishing they had stopped having children after him, or maybe after him and Blane if it would have spared them having Tom. For years he's only proved himself to be the family's bad seed. When Tom was only twelve, Sandy came across a bag stuffed with bottle rockets, firecrackers and M-80s in Tom's bedroom closet. Tom had been dealing them to kids in the junior high. Sandy and Dean's punishment was that Tom couldn't sell them anymore, but he could shoot them all off on the Fourth of July to entertain the family and neighbors down at the beach house on Cape Cod. Tom became the most popular kid in the neighborhood that holiday weekend, impressing everyone with the show.

"This is a punishment?" Kyle asked his mother, amazed.

"This is *his* punishment, not yours, so mind your own business," was Sandy's only response.

Kyle pulls out of the parking lot and heads home, turning onto a side street that winds through the woods. He turns the radio up loud, drowning out the sound of the car's engine as he drives faster, jamming his foot down on the accelerator, taking the sharp turns in the road. He wants to get home, change out of his work uniform, then watch Tom's reaction when he walks through the door and sees the entire family—Kyle, Blane, Hal, Tina and Lilly—all standing there, looking at him with disgust. Tom will stare back, angry and humiliated, and then Sandy and

Dean will enter, tired and annoyed. They won't even care about that C on Kyle's math test. Sandy and Dean will never even notice it because compared to Tom's stunt, Kyle's C is an A.

"Yes, you can go outside." Blane sits at the kitchen table, eating Lucky Charms cereal from the box while reading a chapter of *Dibs: In Search of Self*, his social studies homework. Tina and Hal leave their older brother's side and rush into the hall, grabbing their jackets from the hooks by the door.

"Hal, zip Tina," Blane orders.

"Yeah, yeah," Hal answers.

"What's all this?" Lilly stands between Blane's seat at the table and Tina and Hal's position in the hall, her hands shoved deep in her bathrobe's pockets.

"We're going outside to play," Tina says. "Blane said we could." Tina turns to Hal, extending her arms straight out to her sides. "Zip me."

Hal zips Tina and they go to the door when Lilly says, "Just hold on a minute. Don't you think it's a bit late to be playing outside at this hour?"

Blane glances at the kitchen clock, the big hand on the tomato, the small hand on the bunch of three carrots. "It's four-thirty. What's the problem?" He keeps his back to his grandmother.

Hal's hand rests on the doorknob. "We're going out now."

"Fine, just stay in our yard," Blane responds over his shoulder.

Lilly walks off down the hall, seizing Tina's hand. "Now, I told you I think it's too late for you to be going outside." She walks Tina back into the kitchen, causing Hal to release the doorknob and follow after. Tina pulls her hand from Lilly's grip and aligns herself with Hal, who has taken a stance at Blane's side. Blane closes his book and looks to his grandmother's stern face. "Why can't they go out? What's the problem?"

"Your mother's not home and I'm in charge so—"

"Mom said Blane was in charge of us," Hal cuts her off.

"Blane's our baby-sitter," Tina insists, "so he's the decider."

Lilly looks to Blane to back her up but Blane looks to Hal and Tina and says, "If you want to go out, go out, just stay in our yard."

"We know that," Tina says.

"Tina cannot go out," Lilly commands.

"Why not?" Blane asks.

"Can we go?" Hal asks.

"I want to go," Tina says.

"Why not?" Blane asks his grandmother. "They'll be in our yard. She'll be with Hal." Tina and Hal start for the door.

"Don't you go out," Lilly says to Hal and Tina and they stop, looking to Blane for help in dealing with their grandmother.

"Nana, they'll be fine. They'll be in the driveway and I'll put on all the outside lights," Blane comforts, and he stands, walking down the hall, flicking on the series of light switches by the side door. "There. Now the entire front yard and driveway will be lit. When it's dark, you'll still be able to see them."

"I don't think they should be out there unsupervised," Lilly contends.

"Can we go out yet?" Tina asks. Hal stands by the door, dragging his zipper down then up then down then up.

Blane faces his grandmother. "Then go out with her if you don't think it's safe."

Lilly walks to the stove, lifting the kettle, giving it a shake to check if there's enough water standing in it for tea. "It's too cold for me and since you're doing your homework, she should settle down and watch TV with me. If Hal wants to go out, he can go."

"They want to play together, Nana."

Lilly turns the burner up high and opens a cabinet, lifting out a mug, a red-and-green rooster painted on its side. "Look at the time. It's nearly five. Why don't they just stay in and keep me company while you work?"

"We don't want to keep you company," Hal states. "We want to go out."

"You're not in charge of us anyway," Tina argues with her grandmother.

Blane looks to Hal and Tina waiting anxiously by the door in their jackets. He reaches over lifting his jacket from a hook, then grabbing his book off the kitchen table. "I'll go out with them, okay? Tina will be supervised by me just in case a kidnapper comes along so I can save her." He heads down the hall, slipping on his jacket. "Come on, let's get out of here, midgets."

Lilly stands in the kitchen, mug in hand, tea bag in mug, waiting for the water to boil as Blane, Hal and Tina leave the house for the yard. Did she win or lose over Blane? Did her rule govern the situation or was Blane the one who made the decision and is thus "in charge" of Hal and Tina?

The kettle whistles and Lilly pours the boiling water into the mug, filling it two-thirds full, then resettling the kettle on the burner, whereupon it promptly whistles until Lilly relocates it to a cool burner.

She carries the mug of steeping tea to the bay window overlooking the driveway. Blane sits on the steps leading to the driveway, reading his book while Tina pedals her pink-framed bike with training wheels in circles around the driveway. Hal practices dribbling a basketball and shooting hoops at the basketball net hung on a pole at the back corner of the driveway.

Blane now being old enough to watch over Hal and Tina as well as young enough to play and keep up with them, Lilly sees herself being displaced as Sandy's great, helpful baby-sitter. And the displacement took place without a word said to Lilly, Sandy just placing Blane in charge as if her mother no longer existed.

Hal shoots a basket and misses. Tina pedals on her four wheels, taking a curve. Blane turns a page of his book. Lilly places her mug on the bay windowsill by a potted violet, looking out, the five o'clock news playing on the TV in the background.

"Do you have change for the tollbooth?" Dean asks, the first words spoken since they've begun the drive back to Concord after picking Tom up at the airport.

Sandy opens her purse, taking out the change and handing it to Dean, dropping it in his extended, open palm. Dean closes his fingers around the coins and lowers the electric car window with the other hand, tossing the change in the basket. The light turns from red to green and Dean drives on, into the underground tunnel connecting the airport to the city.

The ride into the city was filled with silence, only to be broken by an occasional outburst—a statement or fact spoken by either Sandy or Dean, directed less at each other than into the air between them:

"The leaves are beginning to change," Sandy observed.

"I wonder how much I could get off if I traded this car in for one of next year's models?" Dean asked.

"Boston has a pretty skyline," Sandy said as they drove along the Charles River.

"The traffic isn't that bad," Dean said.

Tom spotted his father's car as he waited on the terminal's sidewalk. "DW1" the license plate reads. Sandy's new wagon is "DW2."

Dean pulled up by the curb, Tom climbed in the back seat, and father, mother and son were headed home.

When they reach the rotary, Dean takes Route 2 west to Concord.

"So," Sandy begins, turning her head to Tom, "what do you think we should do with you?"

Dean's grip tightens on the steering wheel.

"Whatever you want," Tom replies easily.

Sandy faces forward. "Of course, thanks. What do you think, Dean? You do have an opinion, don't you?"

"Not at this moment, no, I don't," Dean says. He turns on the radio. A Muzak rendition of "What's New Pussycat?"

"This sucks," Tom says.

"You bet it does," Sandy says.

Dean wants to shut his eyes, wants to shut it all out, but he can't—he's driving—so he stares at the road, pressing his foot down harder on the gas pedal. The faster they're home, the faster he can retreat to his den, Tom can retreat to his bedroom, and Sandy can prepare dinner in the kitchen.

"So how should we handle this?" Sandy asks. "Dean?"

Dean says nothing.

"Tom?" Sandy asks.

Tom says nothing, stretching out and reclining across the back seat.

"Anyone?" Sandy asks.

Silence.

The radio plays a Muzak rendition of "The Candy Man."

1976

" I T ' S a lot of fun, you'll like it, trust me," Dean says play-
fully. "You liked Disney World, didn't you?"

The family is driving along a Tampa highway. Sandy, Dean and
Tina in the front seat of the rent-a-car, a large dark brown Oldsmobile four-door coupe. The boys squeeze into the back seat,
thighs and knees bumping up against each other with every
twist in the road the car takes. Dean bought each member of
the family a Mickey Mouse sweatshirt, insisting that everyone
wear the matching sweatshirts tonight.

"What is it like?" Hal asks.

"They have rides and games and nice shops for Mommy,"
Dean answers.

"I like other activities besides shopping," Sandy interjects.

"What kind of rides?" Hal asks.

"A water ride for everyone, and big-boy rides for Kyle and
Blane and Tom like a corkscrew roller-coaster."

"I can go on the roller-coaster too," Hal says.

"I'm going on the roller-coaster first," Tom states emphatically.

"Well, we're all going to do something together," Dean says.
"This is a family vacation. We don't have to be split up the entire
day."

"I am going on the corkscrew first," Tom repeats.

"I promise you will," Dean says and he rolls down the window
a crack. A cool breeze blows through the car.

The roller-coaster is at Busch Gardens where the family will be visiting tomorrow. They arrived in Florida on Tuesday night. Spent Wednesday, Thanksgiving-Thursday, and Friday at Disney World, and left Orlando this morning for Tampa. They had Thanksgiving dinner in the Polynesian Village, eating shish kebobs, watching fire dancers and wearing shell necklaces. During dessert, an assortment of tropical fruits and sherbets, Sandy and Dean began dancing on the floor by the Hawaiian band, waltzing to the bongos and guitars. Mr. and Mrs. Wallace were the only couple on the dance floor and the Wallace children ate their dessert furiously, refusing to acknowledge their parents' presence they were so embarrassed. A few minutes later, a crazy fat woman wearing a muumuu ran out onto the dance floor, hulaing, waving one arm in the air and shaking her belly while taking sips out of the coconut shell she balanced in her other hand. Next to this spectacle, Sandy and Dean's performance became immaterial; the boys didn't even bother them about it when they returned to the table.

In Disney World, the family didn't spend a great deal of time together. Sandy and Dean paired off, Hal and Tom buddied up, Kyle took along Tina, and Blane ventured off on his own, each of the family groups leaving the hotel as each pleased, the sole restriction being that they meet up for lunch. "One P.M. on the nose at the steps to Cinderella's Castle," Dean proclaimed.

Lunches and dinners were family time; time spent around restaurant tables comparing notes on the best attractions to be seen in the park. Hal loved Mr. Toad's Wild Ride, insisting that Tom take him on it each of the three days the family spent in Orlando. Tom loved Space Mountain and Tina It's a Small World. Kyle thought Pirates of the Caribbean was the best and Blane argued that the Jungle Cruise won out over everything. Dean and Sandy were just thankful that there was enough of a variety at Disney World to keep all the children entertained. No complaints in Orlando except for Kyle and Tom's nightly argument over who got to sleep single in the double bed since Blane always slept on the floor by the closet wrapped in a bedspread.

"So, are we going to drive around forever or decide upon a place to eat?" Sandy asks. She brushes her hands through her hair, refastening her ponytail with a large scrimshaw barrette.

"I'm enjoying this drive," Dean says, stretching an arm along the back of the seat. "It's pretty. Maybe we should just drive for a while and take in the sights."

The kids stare out the window at the scenery. It's a thick forest of trees, then every so often a large restaurant appears out of nowhere surrounded by an even larger parking lot.

"The kids are hungry, Dean," Sandy says, correctly reading everyone's boredom with the drive. "What would we like to eat?" She twists her head around to the back seat, facing the boys.

"Pizza," Tom says.

"We had pizza last night," Kyle complains.

"Shut up," Tom says. "Pizza's the best."

"We're not having pizza," Sandy decides. "We'll all have pizza coming out of our ears if we keep this up."

"I saw a nice fish place back a bit," Dean says.

"That sounds good," Kyle says.

"I don't eat fish," Tom reminds everyone.

"Does everyone agree to that?" Dean asks.

"I don't," Tom says. "I hate fish and Blane hates fish."

"I'm sure they'll have other things too," Dean reassures him.

"I'm sure they'll have something for everyone," Sandy confirms and she turns to face the windshield as Dean makes a U-turn on the highway, heading back toward the restaurant.

"I don't want fish," Tom asserts.

"Then order something else, idiot," Kyle says.

"Blane doesn't eat fish either," Tom says.

"I don't care," Blane says. "Just get me out of this car. It's making me sick."

"I'm not going in if we go there," Tom threatens.

"Oh, we'll really miss you," Kyle says.

"Shut up, asshole," Tom says.

"You cut that out now. All of you," Dean declares.

"I didn't say anything," Hal says quietly.

"You're fine, honey," Sandy says.

"Am I fine?" Tina asks.

"You're terrific," Dean replies.

"I'm not going in," Tom repeats, as if no one had been listening the first time.

"Then you'll sit in the car," Dean responds without missing a beat.

"Dean," Sandy warns.

"I'm not taking any of his whimpering," Dean says, turning to face her. "If he wants to sit in the car, he can sit in the car for all I care."

"Then I will," Tom dares him.

"There'll be plenty of other things on the menu he can have. He shouldn't be acting like such a baby," Dean says and the restaurant comes into view. A large red neon lobster hovers over the huge parking lot, pointing a claw toward the restaurant. The lobster smiles with large white teeth bordered by blue neon.

The Oldsmobile pulls into the gravel parking lot. Dean parks by the highway, next to the woods. The huge restaurant is designed to resemble a log cabin from the nineteenth century. The parking lot is filled.

"This looks fine," Sandy says, trying to sound upbeat.

"I'm still not going," Tom says.

"Fine," Dean says and he gets out of the car, as do Sandy, Tina, Kyle, Hal and Blane. Everyone slams their car doors but Sandy, who leans in at Tom, "Don't be silly. You'll be hungry later. I'm sure they'll have chicken or a burger or something."

"Sandy," Dean calls.

Sandy shuts the car door and the family (minus Tom) heads across the parking lot toward the restaurant entrance, the gravel crunching under their feet, their faces glowing yellow from the harsh overhead lights. No one says anything until they arrive at the entrance's overhang. They stand on the large green welcome rug and Sandy turns and looks across the parking lot toward the car. "We can't just let him sit there for a couple hours, Dean."

"He'll come in if he wants," Kyle says.

"I don't want him sitting out in a car while we're eating. He doesn't know where he is," she persists. "What if something happened?" She looks directly at Dean.

"Fine, you're right, I'll go get him," Dean says and he gives his wife a kiss on the cheek and walks across the parking lot to the rent-a-car.

Blane shoves his hands deep into his jean pockets. "We should have just gone out for pizza. It's much easier than putting up with this."

"We shouldn't have to give in to him," Kyle says.

"It always ends up his way anyway," Blane comments. "Why even bother to go against him in the first place?" He kicks at the welcome mat with his sneakers.

"I don't care if we have pizza," Hal says.

"We're not giving in to him this time," Kyle says.

"Yeah, sure," Blane says. "I bet Dad's over there right now promising him a present so he'll come in with us."

"Both of you stop it now," Sandy blurts out suddenly, and Kyle and Blane look back at her, surprised by her angry tone. Blane looks away, down at his sweatshirt. They stand by the glass doors, silent, their Mickey Mouses all smiling with wide eyes, large, black noses and exaggerated grins. Tina stretches hers down to her knees. "See my Mickey. I saw him real in person," she says happily.

"Do you remember what he said?" Kyle asks.

"He liked me lots," Tina replies with a laugh.

"You like Mickey Mouse, don't you?" Sandy says, looking back at the car. Dean's leaning into the rear seat, his back to them.

"I like him the most," Tina says.

"He likes you too," Sandy says absently, and Tom's door opens and he leaps out, backing away from the car. Dean slams the car door. They face each other across the hood of the car.

"Go fuck yourself," Tom yells and it echoes across the parking lot. Dean moves quickly around the car toward Tom. Tom ducks for a moment, disappearing from sight. When he stands, Dean

is coming at him fast and Tom lifts an arm, tossing a handful of gravel at his father's face.

"Fucking asshole," Tom yells.

Dean's hands fly up to his eyes for an instant and Tom stares at him, doing nothing. Dean reaches out and grabs Tom's arm, smacking him alongside the head. Tom reels from the blow and Dean lifts his hand high, bringing it down across Tom's face. "You stupid, fucking—"

"Dean," Sandy calls and she turns to Kyle. "Run over there to—" and she heads off toward the car with Kyle.

Tom has now wrestled himself free of his father's grip. Dean goes at him, chasing Tom back to the patch of grass bordering the parking lot. Tom grabs at the grass and dirt, hurling it at his father's face.

"Dean!" Sandy calls. She's wearing heels and every time she attempts to run, her ankles give and she stumbles in the gravel.

Blane takes Hal's and Tina's hands. Their father is now down on his knees, rubbing his eyes as Tom stands above him repeatedly shoving the earth into his face, scrubbing it into his father's mouth and nose.

"What's happening?" Hal asks, scared. "What's happening?"

Tina worries, "Where's Daddy?" Both are too short to see over the tops of the cars.

Tom has shoved Dean to the ground. Kyle is on Tom's back, pulling him off their father, Kyle's arm locked around Tom's neck as Sandy yanks at Dean's arm, crying his name. Kyle wrangles Tom off Dean, shoving him away, but then Tom takes a swing at Kyle, knocking Kyle to the ground, and dashing into the woods. Suddenly Tom is gone from sight and there is a beat of silence.

Dean stands, his face a shocking dirty black in the parking lot light.

"Where's Tom?" Sandy asks, bewildered. "Tom!" she calls and she begins running at the woods, again twisting an ankle, falling to the grass. Dean and Kyle plunge into the woods, between the trees and brush. Sandy pulls herself up on her knees, cupping her hands to her mouth like a megaphone as she alternates screaming the names of her husband and the two of her sons who have disappeared into the woods along the side of the highway.

Blane grips Tina's and Hal's hands tightly, still standing by the side of the restaurant's entrance as other families enter for dinner. Hal looks up at Blane. "What's happening?"

"What's happening?" Tina asks, and "What's happening?" they keep asking and Blane tells them that it's fine, that everything's fine and he slowly leads them away from the restaurant, back to the car where they see their mother on her knees at the side of the woods. They begin crying. There is no sign of the others except for an occasional shout from Kyle for his father or Tom.

"Why don't we just let him go?" Blane mutters under his breath. "How can they even muster up the energy to care?"

Hal looks up at his brother, staring. "What?" he asks. "What?" and Blane ignores him.

Kyle reappears from the woods first, his face and clothes dirty, his Mickey Mouse sweatshirt smeared with mud. He runs to his mother, helping her stand. Grass stains spot the front of Sandy's white cotton skirt. She leans against Kyle. He supports her, his arm around her waist. A moment later, Dean appears with his arm gripping Tom's shoulder, their faces red, angry and crying. Tom's brown corduroys are torn at the knees and thigh. They're not struggling anymore, just standing, looking exhausted and weary. Sandy, Dean, Kyle and Tom look less like tourists than survivors of some disaster in the middle of the Everglades. They've only now emerged from the woods, back to civilization for the first time in months and their faces are worn with anguish and grief. Tom pulls away from his father, but they keep walking side by side. The entire family slowly gravitates toward the car. They will not be eating seafood tonight.

The doors of the car are opened in silence. Kyle helps his mother into the passenger seat. A sigh escapes her lips as she falls against the cushion. Tom slides into the middle of the front seat beside her. Dean sits on the driver's side. He grips the steering wheel tightly with both hands, leaning his forehead against its center. The rest of the kids sit in the back. Kyle by the window. Hal in the middle. Tina sits on Blane's lap, his arms locked around her waist.

"I'm a failure as a father," Dean mumbles into the dashboard. "I've failed my family... I have." His back heaves up and down as he speaks.

"No, you're not, Dad," Kyle says.

"No," the family murmurs in unison. Dean's hunched up, leaning over the steering wheel, covering his face.

"We have to get some counseling," Sandy says out of nowhere. Tom's head rests on her shoulder. She's stroking his hair lightly.

"No, we don't," Kyle says.

"*I* don't need any help," Blane says.

"We all need help together," Sandy emphasizes.

"We're fine," Kyle says.

"I hate it here," Hal says. "I want to go back to Disney World."

Tina sits up in Blane's lap. "Disney World," she says. "Let's go back to see Mickey Mouse."

"No," Sandy argues desperately. "We have to see someone. We have to."

Tom lifts his head from her shoulder, wiping his face on the sleeve of his sweatshirt. "It's just this place, let's just get out of here, that's all."

And Kyle and Hal and Tina murmur a chorus of "yes" and Dean lifts his head, putting an arm around Tom. "Maybe we should just fly home tomorrow," he sighs.

"Maybe we should," Sandy agrees sadly. "Maybe we should."

"This place bites," Tom says.

"But when we do get back," Sandy adds, "we are going to go to a family counselor."

The kids moan.

Dean stares out the window. "I don't know what I've done wrong, I just don't know." He shrugs, then turns and kisses Tom's forehead. "I love you," he says quietly.

"I love you," Tom mumbles and they hug and cry some more, pulling each other close. Sandy and Kyle and Tina and Hal begin crying too. Blane stares out the window, holding Tina, reaching around and wiping her tears away with the cuff of his sweatshirt.

Ten minutes later, Dean sits back in the front seat, grips the steering wheel and starts the car, driving back to the hotel. He's decided the family will order up room service.

■

After all the hassles Sandy went through to get them here, now, looking at the family in the psychiatrist's office, she sees that their faces are completely bored and annoyed. She's beginning to wonder if maybe this was a mistake. Maybe she was wrong and they were right. Maybe the family doesn't need counseling. Maybe Sandy's the only one with the problem.

This is Sandy's third session with Dr. Taulman. She saw him once a week for the past two weeks, getting to know him and discovering if he is a suitable man for the family. And having decided that she likes and trusts him, Dr. Taulman and Sandy set an appointment for him to meet the entire family. Not a "session," but an "appointment." Sandy's family meeting the doctor and adjusting to the situation while the doctor has the chance to observe the family as a unit. "A brief session," Dr. Taulman told Sandy last week. "Just a half hour to say hello. Since they seem very hesitant about coming, we should make it as nonthreatening as possible, building up the time as the therapy progresses." Dr. Taulman spoke very confidently, self-assuredly, and Sandy said, "Yes, that sounds exactly right."

Now, seeing all of them sitting in a circle of folding wooden chairs, Sandy has her doubts. She takes a sip of tea, then a deep breath. She has made the family so angry by forcing them to come here that she wonders if she's only aggravated the situation instead of calming it. Everyone made a huge fuss, even Dean.

"Ninety dollars for fifty minutes of time?" Dean asked Sandy after she'd seen the doctor the first week. "Ninety dollars?"

They stood in the basement's laundry room; Sandy unloading towels from the dryer, folding them into a stack, Dean watching, pulling on the tie around his neck, loosening the knot.

"He wants to help us sort things out," Sandy explained. "He can give us a perspective on things we can't see ourselves."

"Ninety dollars? And for how many weeks?"

Sandy looked into the dryer, pulling out a stray washcloth. "Dean, I don't know. And we can afford it so what does it matter? This is important."

"But seriously, how much time are we talking about?" Dean asked.

Sandy stared down into the overflowing laundry basket, everything folded neatly, smelling fresh. Dr. Taulman told Sandy that family therapy could take a couple years at the very least. "A few sessions," Sandy said, answering Dean's question. "I don't think any more than that."

The kids were worse, afraid their friends would find out and make fun of them for going to a "brain-picker," as Blane named Dr. Taulman. "He picks your brain the way other people pick their noses," Blane announced to the family when Sandy told them she'd set the appointment.

Earlier, late this afternoon, the kids and Lilly began changing from their everyday clothes into sports jackets and dresses. They thought they should dress well so as to make a good impression on the doctor. Sandy had to stop them and explain that therapy wasn't like that. "The doctor wants you to be yourselves," she told them, and they changed back into their sweaters and jeans.

Dr. Taulman sits in a brown leather chair, staring at the family. He's a thin, wiry man, gaunt-looking. He balances a yellow legal pad on one knee, giving the family a nod of recognition. "Why don't I go around the room and get your names first," he says in his soft, low voice.

He starts at his right.

"Kyle," Kyle says firmly.

"Hal," Hal says.

"Tom," Tom says.

"Lilly," Lilly says.

Blane leans over a notebook that he holds on his lap, studying papers from school. He looks up. "Blane." He returns to his books.

"Blane, do you mind putting your books down until after the session?" Dr. Taulman asks. "I'd appreciate it." He looks over at Blane with a smile.

Blane looks up at him, very calm and controlled. "I told my mother that if I came here I was going to study for a test I have tomorrow morning and that is what I intend to do." He looks back to his books.

The family stares at Blane, waiting for the doctor's response, and although Sandy is sure Blane does have a test tomorrow, she feels like yanking his books from his hands and tossing them out the window. The rest of the family sits attentively watching Blane. Dean half hoping that Blane will continue studying his notes—one hell of a lot more practical than sitting here staring at one another. But then he looks at Sandy, her hands shaking as she lifts the tea cup to her lips, and a wave of guilt hits him and he resolves himself to playing along with this for Sandy's sake. He looks down to the wood floor, listening to the doctor deal with Blane.

"I'd rather you put them down," Dr. Taulman responds simply.

"I'm sorry," Blane says, "but I have to study for my test." He flips open a manila folder, taking out a sheet of paper with a diagram of the human body. He doesn't even know why he has to be here. Tom's the fuck-up, not him.

The doctor turns to Tina, casually putting Blane aside. "And what's your name?"

"Tina," she says softly.

Dean's turn. "Dean. I'm the poppa." He smiles nervously.

Sandy leans forward in the chair. "Sandy," she says, smiling, she too nervous, and the family sits, waiting for the doctor to do or say something, but all he does is look down at his notepad.

A minute passes.

That's about two dollars for sitting silent, Dean thinks, consciously keeping himself from glancing at his watch.

The doctor slowly looks up, raising his pen to his mouth and chewing on its tip. "So, how does everyone feel about being here?"

Sandy moves nervously in her seat. The eyes of the family shift toward her. She clears her throat. "Well, we're here," she answers lamely. "That's what's important, isn't it?" She directs her attention to the doctor.

"Okay," Dr. Taulman says. "But I hope as time goes by and you get used to me, you'll find that I'm no longer a stranger, but we can all speak the truth. And maybe, one day, after a month or two you'll actually look forward to coming here." He smiles.

"I don't think our problems are so severe that a *month* of sessions will be necessary," Dean volunteers.

"I think one's more than enough," Tom says.

"Not for you," Lilly jumps in with a laugh.

"What are you laughing about," Tom sneers. "You're the only crazy goon here."

"Maybe we should listen to what the doctor recommends," Sandy says, attempting to soothe the family.

"So then how long does he expect us to come here?" Lilly asks her daughter. "Any other doctor fixes a problem in one visit. How many visits does it take this man?"

"Mother, why don't you ask him, he's sitting right here with us?"

"I'm not going to repeat myself. He heard me."

The room is silent, the Wallace family focusing on the doctor, waiting for a response; even Blane looks up from his studies.

"Based on what Sandy, your mother, told me, I think it might take some time to sort out all the issues involved." He looks around the room, meeting the eyes of each family member. "The dynamics are complex."

"Could you approximate how much time that might be?" Dean asks. "Roughly. It doesn't have to be exact."

The doctor smiles. "How about as much time as is necessary?" "That's pretty vague," Dean replies, also assuming a smile. Her idea that therapy can help the family is dying. "Dean, it's not the sort of thing he can answer for us. He's only just met us."

"I'm sure he has some idea how long this sort of thing takes on average," Dean says.

Sandy shakes her head, looking to Dr. Taulman for help. Dr. Taulman glances to his notepad, then up quickly. "Two years. That's what I expect it will take. How's that?" He doesn't smile, the doctor isn't joking.

"Two years?" Tom asks incredulously.

"I go to college next fall," Kyle states, then laughs. "I guess I'll just have to miss out."

"I'm not going if he doesn't," Tom declares.

"Me neither. No way," Hal says.

"Two years seems awfully long," Lilly says.

"What's in two years?" Tina asks her mother.

"Nothing, honey," Sandy replies.

"You bet *nothing,*" Dean states definitively. "We're not coming here for two years. Of that I am certain."

"Thank God," Blane mutters and Dean feels the family coming together around him, uniting under the condescending scrutiny of this self-serving, self-believingly omnipotent doctor. "I think that's one item we all can agree on," Dean adds, and Sandy says nothing, invisible, lost, forgotten, and when Dean reaches out and takes hold of her hand, Sandy is repulsed, wants to slap it away but all she does is hold on, hold on tight.

The car ride home from Dr. Taulman's office is silent, all family members staring out the station wagon's windows into the darkness of this late December evening. Sandy's new Chevrolet Impala station wagon. A navy blue exterior and red vinyl interior. Dean drives, Hal sits in the middle of the front seat, Sandy at the passenger side. Lilly, Kyle and Tom sit in the back seat and

Blane and Tina ride facing backward in the third row of seats by the tailgate door.

The doctor couldn't help her family or the family couldn't let themselves be helped by the doctor or maybe they don't really need all this help and all Sandy's done is alienate herself from the family. The odd woman out, the only one who wanted to go, reaches into her purse for her lip balm, applying a coat of the wax, hoping it will keep her from chewing on her lower lip. Walking from the office to the parking lot, Dean offered his wife this support, "It wasn't a bad idea. It just wasn't the right idea for us." Sandy supposes he's right, that the family she was trying to help just isn't the family she has and the family she has has no way of being helped. Everyone else in the family so adamantly knew this was a stupid idea yet Sandy took a stand and, headstrong and determined, forced them all into visiting this psychiatrist. All the other Wallaces saw how wrong therapy was for the family but for Sandy and she could kick herself for making such an issue out of "saving the family" as if they were on a sinking ship.

"Every family has arguments," Dean explained to Sandy while in bed last night, "some far worse than ours. Look at how you grew up for instance. And my parents fought sometimes and sometimes I argued with my father. But none of that means the end of the world is coming."

"I feel like it's all out of control," Sandy admitted, hesitantly. "I just don't understand and I can't control it and I'm afraid, that's all."

Dean laughed a small laugh, cupping his wife's cheek with a palm. "We're a big family, the kids growing up. We all love each other. Relax."

Sandy stares out the car window as they drive past a Chinese restaurant. She is reminded of dinner. She thinks about asking if they should pick something up on the way home but is afraid to. Afraid the family will disagree—Tom wanting pizza, Kyle wanting Chinese, Lilly wanting deli sandwiches, etc., etc. Another family argument propelling the Wallaces further over the abyss Sandy believes her family has fallen over but no one else recognizes; the end result of the fight being her husband crumpled over a steering wheel, once again crying, "I'm a failure as a father." Sandy never asked Dean why he said that, what he meant by it, and she wonders if he remembers saying it or whether he said it like something out of a dream, spoken out of a haze, a fog.

"Should we stop and pick up some dinner?" Dean asks, and quicker than a flash of lightning, before one of the kids can utter a sound, Sandy replies, "No, that's all right, I was just going to make us all spaghetti tonight anyway," and she's averted a crisis.

1 9 7 7

T H E lawn needs raking. Dean stares down at it from the master bedroom window, watching for more members of Sandy's group to arrive. Sandy's friends from her "housewives support group." Sandy is downstairs in the living room entertaining the first of her guests. Dean watches out the window, careful not to let them see him as he stares out across the lawn.

Brown pine needles cover the grass. Dead leaves blow through the air. During the spring and summer months, the yard is well kept. The grass is green and trimmed and the hedges are clipped into neat cubes. The flower beds by the walkway bloom without weeds. Now that it's autumn, keeping the yard in shape takes a lot more effort. The grass, pine needles and leaves are dead and brown. The flowers aren't blooming. Weeds sprout from the cracks in the walkway.

Dean's kids refuse to help keep things in order. They fail to understand that if they don't keep the yard up in the fall, it won't grow back well in the spring. The kids are too shortsighted and just won't look six months ahead to when the ground is thawing and the roses will be preparing to bud. Dean's even offered them money to do the raking, but they don't care about the compensation; they say they have more important things to do now that they're back in school. Blane has an endless amount of papers due. Tom always has plans with friends. Hal has soccer practice with the junior league. And even Tina, only eight years old, has an excuse. She claims that her grandmother wants her to watch TV with her because Lilly doesn't like watching it alone. Kyle used to be the one to help Dean keep up the yard, but now that he's at Clark University in Worcester, an hour and a half away, Dean's left in Concord to care for it himself. The front, the back and the sides of the house, not to mention the flowers, the walkway, the area by the mailbox and the stone fence bordering the road.

"We all live here and we all have to pitch in to keep the place up," Dean asserted at breakfast this morning.

"I don't care how it looks," Tom said.

"It's going to be covered with snow in a month anyway," Blane said, justifying his idleness. "No one will see it."

Dean truly doesn't understand how he—a man who had to work so hard for everything he has achieved—could raise children who are so lazy and spoiled, taking everything in life for granted.

Sometimes Dean wishes he had a house like the one his father owned. His father never had to landscape a lawn this large. Phil Wallace's house in Somerville was small: two bedrooms, a living room and kitchen. The houses sat almost on top of the road, lined up alongside each other with only a narrow path separating them just wide enough for a car to squeeze through. The yard was nothing but a scrap of grass a yard deep and ten yards across. Lynda Wallace kept a small flower bed by the front of the house. Petunias, pansies and marigolds decorated the short path from the street to the door. The backyard was a foot or two deeper than the front, but it was more dirt than lawn. Dean's mother kept a vegetable garden growing back there with tomatoes, cucumbers, turnips and parsley. Phil never had to pay his son for raking because there were no trees in the yard, only that small empty expanse of grass.

Dean's huge lawn sweeps around the front, sides and back of the house. Pine and maple trees are everywhere. Rhododendrons, hyacinths and lilac trees decorate the walkway and entrance to the driveway. Boxwoods are by the front of the house. The flower beds are filled with rose bushes, tiger lilies, mums, irises and geraniums. Endless care is taken to keep it looking beautiful.

The doorbell rings and Sandy answers it. Dean wasn't paying attention and has missed seeing whoever it was who's arrived.

"Hi, Sylvia," Sandy greets her guest.

"You look pretty today," Sylvia says.

"Thank you. Everyone's in the living room, join us."

"I'm the last one?" Sylvia asks.

"We're just having tea, don't worry," Sandy says sweetly.

Dean hears vague murmurings through the bedroom floor, above the living room. Sandy's group. Housewives gathering at one another's homes every Saturday afternoon for two to three hours, discussing family issues, how to make being a housewife more manageable. Following a fight on the day before Kyle left for college, a fight in which Kyle and Tom squared off in the kitchen, Kyle with a steak knife and Tom with a large skewering fork, a fight in which Sandy, trying to break up her lunging sons, got caught in the arm by the points of the fork, the fork puncturing the skin and drawing blood, Sandy called a social services agency, who referred her to this group of housewives who cannot adequately handle their home lives.

"You're a good housewife and mother. Why do you need to meet with these people?" Dean asked.

"You have conferences with other businessmen to work out management techniques," Sandy offered. "This is just my way of doing the same thing for our family."

Tina and Hal run into the bedroom waving their hands in the air.

"All the zombies are here," Hal says with a laugh.

"They're witches," Tina says, baring her teeth.

"They're not witches," Dean tells them. "They're your mother's friends. It's her class."

"They're funny," Tina says.

Dean laughs. "Yes, they do some kooky stuff, I admit, but your mother's a kooky lady." Dean walks over and sits in the armchair by the side of the bed, picking up the day's paper.

"I think they're brainwashing her," Hal says. "She says we have to start helping her with stuff not even on the chore chart."

"I'm not, no way," Tina says. "I did all my jobs already and that's enough."

Dean opens the paper to the local news section. "Where are Tom and Blane?"

Hal and Tina don't say anything.

"Well?" Dean asks again.

"Tom's out with the Simpson brothers," Hal says nervously. Dean has a feeling that Tom probably told Hal not to tell him this. Daniel Simpson is the delinquent with the black Corvette who leaves skid marks on the driveway. His younger brother, Edgar, is the friend Tom ran off to the airport with a couple years ago.

"Where's your Nana Lilly?" Dean asks, lowering the paper to look at Hal.

"Watching TV," Tina answers, sitting on the bed. "She watches the most TV."

"They didn't have TVs when she was a young girl like you, so she has to make up for what she missed," Dean says humorously.

"That's a rude remark," Lilly says. She's standing in the doorway, glaring. "And whose business is it if I want to watch TV? Whose is it?"

Dean stands and lets out a laugh. "Relax, Lilly, no one's stopping you from watching the TV."

"And I was not watching TV, Tina, you shouldn't lie," Lilly complains, a sneer on her face, and she looks over at Dean. "She's picking up bad habits from Tom. Tom is teaching her to disrespect me."

Tina sticks out her tongue. "Blah!"

Dean grabs Tina's face by the chin.

"See that," Lilly says. "Tom all over again." She leaves the room.

"Don't you ever do that to her. You respect her," Dean says.

"She's always ordering us around," Hal says. "And she's not our mother anyway."

Tina gets off the bed and walks over beside Hal, both of them now staring at Dean.

"She loves you," Dean explains. "She worries about you."

"She's mean," Tina says. "She says to me I act like a boy. She says girls can't play outside but can only sit and read and watch TV."

"She's tired and old, be kind to her," Dean says. "She can be a very nice lady. She's your mother's mother and look how good Mom came out." But somehow, in Dean's own thoughts, he cannot attribute Sandy's personality to Lilly's good mothering, however appropriate it does sound to say to the kids.

"How long has Nana Lilly been living with us?" Dean asks Hal.

Hal looks back at him, a puzzled expression on his face.

"I think it's been about five years, hasn't it?" Dean asks.

"I don't know," Hal says. "Maybe."

"Since I was a baby," Tina says.

"Well, whatever it is, she is living here and she's a member of this family, so treat her nicely and with respect," Dean tells them.

"She's a pain," Tina whines.

"Well, she's still going to live here. It's what your mother wants."

"Why?" Hal asks. "She's always fighting with Tom. She isn't happy here."

"She hates me and Hal and everyone," Tina says.

"I think she's happy," Dean says unconvincingly, then adds, "and your Mom thinks it's best that Nana Lilly stay with us, so that's that. She's old and needs your love."

"I don't love her," Tina says and she walks over to Sandy's dresser and opens the jewelry box, looking over the rings and necklaces. A burst of laughter comes up from the living room. Dean takes a deep breath. Maybe they're swapping recipes, but he always feels as if they're ridiculing their husbands and children.

Hal looks at him. "Dad, why does Mom have these weird new friends?"

Dean turns away from his son toward the window, looking out at the lawn. "Go rake the leaves, please."

"Tina and me are going to the Jacobs'," Hal replies.

"Fine, go. Go," Dean tells them. "We'll do it next week." Dean continues staring out the window. He hears Hal and Tina scramble out of the room.

"Hold your breath as you pass the living room or the spooks will get in you," Hal says softly.

Sandy fears she is not the perfect housewife, and no matter how hard Dean tries, he cannot convince her to be happy with the near-perfect status she has achieved. "You're a better mother than your mother. You're a better mother than *my* mother and my mother was a great mother, so why must you overreact because the kids have a few squabbles?"

Sandy shrugged in response, a sad look in her eyes. "I just want us to be a happy family."

No one speaks for a moment, the six other members of the group considering Christina Greco's question carefully before responding. The women, mostly in their mid to late thirties and early forties, sit in a circle, some on furniture and some on the Oriental carpet, legs crossed Indian-style. A sidecart sits by the fireplace where thin wafer cookies lie fanned across a white porcelain dish with gold-leaf edging. Also provided are a coffee urn and a pot of hot water for tea. Sandy's first week as group hostess, her fourth week as a member of the group.

Frances Bartulocci shakes her head. "I don't think money has anything to do with it."

"I do," Roberta Kulkert disagrees. "If our husbands couldn't have supported us so well we'd have to have had careers. They couldn't have afforded to let us be housewives and have litters of kids."

"And then once you have the kids, they can't afford not to keep you a housewife!" Diane Sugarman, the oldest member of the group at forty-six, cries loudly. She stands, punctuating her statement by strolling to the sidecart and selecting three more cookies and a second cup of coffee.

Sandy, hoping Dean hasn't heard Diane's explosion, surveys these women, all so discontent with their lives, wanting careers, wanting fewer restrictions, blaming their parents, their kids, their husbands for all they haven't done in their lives, just like her. "Maybe I don't understand, but Dean isn't always happy with his job and his job puts pressure on him and restricts him but he sacrifices so we can have a nice home, so how can I *not* sacrifice too?"

"You feel guilty for being in this group, don't you, Sandy?" Diane Sugarman asks, not expecting any answer. "You have no idea how great the societal forces are that make you think the way you do."

Dean picks up the paper. Dean picks up a magazine. Dean picks up a book or watches the television and whatever he tries, he still cannot concentrate, for all he can think about, all his mind is focused upon is the band of seven not-so-merry housewives in his living room. "Once you have the kids they can't afford not to keep you a housewife," one bellowing bag of a woman screamed and Dean was close to marching down those stairs and throwing the half dozen women out of his house. He never *forced* Sandy into being a housewife. He never *forced* Sandy into having their children. They have the life they wanted and it's one thousand times better than his or her parents' lives or homes. A person shouldn't be greedy. A person should only want as much as they need to live a good, solid, comfortable life and to want more would be selfish. Must he now add *Sandy* to the list of people in his life who don't appreciate how hard he's worked to give them all they have? The yard work is never

going to get done before the first snowfall and Dean hates the
thought of having to hire a landscaper to do the job when he
has three sons in the house capable of knocking off the work
in one or two weekend afternoons.

"Yes he gives you *money*, but it's *grocery* money or money
for the kids' *sneakers*, but that's certainly not a *salary, Roberta!*"
Again, the loud, bellowing voice and Dean can't bear to hear it
anymore, these clucking chickens, and he walks out of the master
bedroom, down the hall to Blane's room to see how his second
son is doing. Blane's door is shut and Dean listens, hears nothing,
then knocks.

"Come in," Blane says, rather unenthusiastically.

Dean walks in. Blane's sprawled across the carpet reading a
book.

"What are you reading? Is it good?" Dean asks.

"*L'Assommoir* by Zola," Blane says.

Dean sits at the desk. "Is it good?"

"It's for school."

"Maybe I'll read it when you're through," Dean tells him.

"I doubt you'd like it, Dad," he says.

"You may not know it," Dean says, "but I do like other books
besides spy novels."

"Fine," Blane says, shrugging. "Read it when I'm done."

Dean looks over the desk. Blane's always writing papers, but
he doesn't see any lying about to read. He looks down at his
son on the floor. "Why don't you ever show us anything you're
working on? I'd be interested in reading one of your papers."

Blane looks up from the book, keeping his place with a finger.
"They're just school papers. They won't make any sense if you're
not in the class."

"Still," Dean persists, "I'd be interested in reading one."

"Dad, they're not that interesting. I'm doing fine, so don't
worry about it."

"All right, all right," Dean says, letting the subject drop. Dean
stands, deciding to let Blane do his reading. He'll just go into
the den and catch up on some office work. But then it hits Dean

that to enter the den he has to walk through the living room where Sandy's group meets. And so Dean sits back down at Blane's desk, wondering what to do with the remainder of the afternoon. He supposes he could always drive in to the office and proofread the divisional status reports he had Vicki type up on Friday afternoon. There are bound to be many typos, as Vicki has just become engaged to one of the men who works in the computer room, her mind now occupied with bridal dresses and honeymoon plans.

"Do you plan on working after you're married? I'd hate to lose you after twelve years."

"Oh, I'll be here," Vicki comforted. "You think I'm going to let my new husband go off to work all day and me not know what he's up to? Uh-uh."

Blane reads his book, seemingly oblivious to his father's presence.

"Are things so bad that your mother really has to join this kooky group?" Dean asks.

Blane's eyes don't leave the page. "If it's what she wants to do, it doesn't bother me."

"But are things that difficult when I'm not around?" Dean persists.

Blane holds an expression of complete annoyance for this subject. "I don't know. I don't have anything to do with anyone's problems."

Dean nods, then smiles at his son. "You're right. You're a good kid, our perfect child. No problems with you. You can take care of yourself." He stands, reaches out and ruffles Blane's hair with a hand.

Blane smacks his father's forearm back. "I'm trying to read. This *is* due Monday."

Dean walks to the window, observes the state of the backyard. It's worse than the front. More needles, more leaves, broken twigs scattered about that fell during the last storm. "The back needs cleaning up. You want to help me out with that, pal?" Dean suggests.

"I'm not your pal," Blane explains.

Dean slaps him on the back. "We're good friends, aren't we?"

"You're my father," Blane clarifies.

"We can also be friends," Dean says. "Now come out and help me. We'll have it all knocked off in a few hours and I'll take the family out for dinner."

"I told you I have to finish this book," Blane says.

Dean nods. "Right. School has to come first. You have your priorities set. Don't have to worry about you." He walks to the door. "You want it closed?"

"Please," Blane says.

Dean steps out, closing the door. On the wall, down to his right, a couple feet off the floor, remains the bullet hole, left unpatched these past four years, a permanent mark of Dean's heroism in shooing the intruding crow from his home.

Dean leans over, poking his small finger in the hole, feeling the smooth plaster against his skin. "I'll patch it one of these days," he's told Sandy countless times when she's asked for the repair to be done. "I'll get to it soon," Dean has often replied.

Dean retreads his steps down the hall to the master bedroom, opening the closet and taking out his gloves and parka. He can't really go downstairs without running into a member of Sandy's group or Lilly, so he figures he might as well get some work done on the yard. If he leaves it for too much longer he'll have to have the whole lawn redone next spring.

Dean heads downstairs, passing the living room's entrance. A woman speaks. "Sometimes I just think there's my version of the family and my husband's version. It's almost like we're not even in the same family when I hear him talking about us," Dean hears this woman say, this woman who is his wife who is Sandy, and Dean steps outside onto the front step, shutting the door behind him, the brass knocker rapping against the door with a thud.

Saturday afternoon sports shows are all they have on the television at this hour and Lilly decides that now's as good a time as any to start reading that new book Sandy gave her. *The Thorn Birds,* over one thousand pages in an Australian family's history. "Did you give me this to exercise my arms? The book weighs at least twenty pounds."

Lilly walks through the kitchen, approaching the stairs when she spots the sidecart in the living room and decides she'll just sneak in and steal herself a cup of tea and plate of cookies, and Lilly enters the room, ignoring the ladies' conversation.

As long as she's in and out in a minute Sandy doesn't mind her mother's being here and Sandy directs her focus back to the group when Melanie Cushman, a health care volunteer in a senior center, leans in to Sandy's ear, "Wouldn't your mother like to join us," then up across the room, "Lilly? Wouldn't you like to join us and share your opinions?"

Lilly looks to Melanie, holding her cup and plate. "Oh no. No thank you, I've got what I came for." She smiles warmly, heading for the door and Sandy can only applaud her mother's behavior.

Melanie continues after Lilly. "Might be nice having the perspective of a homemaker who's more experienced than us."

Lilly stops and turns, her previous smile broadening into a grin. "Oh. Well, then you wouldn't want *me.* I don't know if Sandy told you, but, you see, I was never a homemaker. Sandy did all the housework, as I had to work for a living. Five days a week, Monday through Friday." Lilly lifts her cup of tea and plate of cookies higher in the air. "Nope, I was too busy on most Saturday afternoons to chat and enjoy tea and cookies so now I'm making up for lost time." And Lilly leaves the room.

The women shrug Lilly off and resume a discussion about the best ways to inform a husband about a day's events in the home. "Hand him a list like a memo," Christina volunteers. "Pin it to the toilet lid."

Sandy isn't listening, still stuck on her mother's comment, "too busy to enjoy tea and cookies."

Sylvia laughs hysterically. "Or better yet, tape it to your crotch."

And Sandy takes a bite from the cookie on her plate, thinking perhaps her mother *does* deserve it more.

■

An argument has broken out between Tom and Hal on the front lawn. Tom tosses the baseball bat to the ground, quitting, accusing Hal of cheating. Hal yells that Tom's only leaving because for once his younger brother is beating him.

"That's because you fucking cheat," Tom says and he walks up the side steps, into the house, through the screen door.

"Asshole," Hal calls, walking after him.

Tom turns, watching his brother come up the steps. He flicks the latch on the screen door, locking Hal out. Hal reaches for the handle and attempts to pull it open. Tom smiles at Hal through the screen.

"Unlock it, asshole," Hal says.

"Say *please*," Tom says.

"Asshole," Hal says.

Tom walks away, into the kitchen, opening a cabinet and looking in. Blane and Lilly sit in the next room watching a *Green Acres* rerun on TV.

Hal raps his fist against the aluminum frame of the door. "Fucking let me in, asshole."

Tom tears open a bag of semisweet chocolate morsels, downing a handful.

Hal presses a finger on the doorbell, holding it, letting it ring over and over.

"Will someone please get the door!" Sandy calls from upstairs.

Blane stands and walks into the kitchen, seeing Tom at the counter. He turns, looks down the hall and sees Hal at the door still ringing the doorbell, then turns back to Tom. "What the hell's the matter with you?" Blane walks to the screen door, unlocking it. "Now quit ringing that," he tells Hal and he returns to the family room.

Hal walks into the kitchen, facing Tom. "You're such an asshole."

"No, you are, faggot face." Tom turns his back to Hal.

"No, you're the faggot face," Hal says, shoving Tom's shoulder and Tom swings an arm back, throwing an elbow into Hal's chest, sending Hal down to the tile floor with a shower of chocolate bits.

"Will you two keep quiet?" Blane calls from the family room. "Go back outside."

Hal stands and grabs the salt shaker off the kitchen table, hurling it at Tom. Tom steps out of the way, easily avoiding its path, and he laughs as the salt shaker hits the refrigerator, falling to the floor.

"What's going on in here?" Lilly walks into the room.

"Tom's being a fucking asshole, that's what," Hal says, heading toward his brother.

Tom picks up the salt shaker and throws it at Hal, but it misses, bypassing him and striking Lilly on the knee. She collapses to the floor, grabbing a kitchen chair for support. "Sandy! Sandy!" she calls.

"Shut up, you old bat," Tom says to her. "You're fine."

Hal goes at Tom, catching him off guard, shoving him, and Tom's head snaps back, hitting the corner of a cabinet. Tom grabs his forehead, momentarily stunned. Hal backs away from his brother, but Tom quickly regains control, reaching out, grabbing Hal by the neck, forcing him to the floor and pinning him under his knees while wrapping both hands around his neck, thumbs pressed into his throat.

"Sandy!" Lilly calls, "Sandy! Sandy!"

Tom squeezes Hal's throat tighter. Hal's face turns red. He gasps for air.

Sandy hears Lilly's calls and hurries into the kitchen, surveying the scene. She quickly goes after Tom, taking him by the shoulders. Tom lifts a hand off Hal and turns, punching his mother in the stomach. Sandy recoils for a moment, then is back on Tom, pulling at him.

"Blane! Blane! Help your mother," Lilly calls from her spot on the floor.

Tom and Sandy are in a wrestling match; she continues pulling at him while he fends her off while grappling with Hal.

"Blane! Blane!" Lilly continues calling, and Blane appears in the room, standing in the entrance. He looks at Lilly, Sandy, Tom and Hal. The scene looks both scary and vaguely comic like an old vaudeville routine. He moves to separate Tom from Hal but Sandy waves him off.

"No, go away. I don't want you to get hurt. Go upstairs and check on Tina."

Tom smacks her along the side of the face. "Fucking bitch," Tom says, and Blane disappears upstairs.

Lilly keeps calling after Blane.

"Shut up, Mother!" Sandy calls and she drags her fingernails across Tom's cheek.

Tom lets out a yell, releasing Hal and turning on Sandy, grabbing her hair, yanking her to the floor. Three thin, red lines cut Tom's face from his right eye to the corner of his jaw. "I'm going to fucking kill you, bitch."

Hal, now free, bends over on his knees, holding his stomach, vomiting on the floor.

Tom slaps Sandy's face.

Lilly's at the phone. "I'm calling the police! I'm calling the police!"

And Tom stands, grabs the receiver from her hand and tears it from the wall. "You fucking old hag." He takes one last look around the room and heads out of the house.

Sandy sits in the bathroom off her bedroom, toilet lid down, looking into her compact as she reapplies blush. She tries to imagine what advice any of the women in the housewives support group might give her but her imagination fails her. And now, two months after Sandy let her family pressure her into quitting the group, she doesn't have the courage to phone one of the women just to talk as friends.

Every Saturday morning before and Saturday evening after the group's meetings, Dean, Blane, Tom, Hal, Tina and Lilly would launch into jokes and criticism about Sandy's new friends.

"I simply don't know how I can mop the floors *today*," Tom

mimicked. "There's a big sale going at Saks, I *cannot* miss."

"Remind me of the witches in *Macbeth*," was Blane's pretentious insight.

"Those women don't know how lucky they are," Lilly said. "All feeling sorry for themselves as if they weren't married and living in pretty homes."

"I don't know how any of them could be married they all look so weird," Hal commented.

"Your mother doesn't look weird," Dean defended.

"She's acting weird," Tom responded. "They just haven't completely infected her yet. Like vampires."

"Are you a vampire," Tina asked with a scream. "Are you sucking blood like Dracula?"

A knock on the bathroom door. Sandy closes the compact and stands. "Yes?"

Another knock on the door. "Sandy, are you all right?" Lilly asks.

"I'm fine, Mother, go away, please."

"I need to see you, Sandy, please."

Sandy slides open the medicine cabinet and takes out the aspirin. "I'm fine. Don't worry." She takes a dixie cup from the dispenser, filling it with water.

"We can't keep living like this," Lilly continues. "It's not good for any of us and I know you know that." Lilly takes hold of the doorknob, rattling it, trying to get in. "Are you sure you're all right?"

Sandy swallows the aspirin. "Why don't you go lie down and rest. You sound tired."

Lilly rattles the doorknob again. "I want to see you; see that you're all right."

"I'm going to the *bathroom,* Mother!" Sandy exclaims. "Must you bother me here?"

Lilly sighs. "Well, as long as you're all right." And she walks away.

Sandy steps onto the bathroom scale. One hundred five. Only a few pounds more than when she was a teenager; exactly seven pounds more. She sits on the toilet seat, wondering if she'll ever get used to this, if she's supposed to get used to this or if she's supposed to change it, and, if so, how? They can't go on living like this, her mother said, and Sandy knows she's right. What is it when a child kills his parents? Patricide? Matricide? Would Tom ever become angry enough to go that far: matricide and/or patricide? Sometimes, during fights between Dean and Tom, Sandy can almost envision it: one of them crossing the blurred line between hurting and actually killing. At what point do all the blows add up to an attempt at murder?

She wishes she could remember if there were fights like this in her own childhood. Sandy pictures a young Lilly and a hazy image of her father having it out in an apartment she cannot remember. Hugh beating Lilly as Lilly has said he did. Sandy half wishes that Hugh had somehow scarred or disfigured her mother, giving her tangible evidence of the alleged abuse, but none exists. Only Lilly's stories and her own memories of her father pounding on the apartment door while she sat in a closet, her strongest childhood memory, and she wonders whether Hal's and Tina's memories will be tainted with violence and emotional upheaval. Will they remember Disney World or that Tampa evening the following day?

Sandy stands and unlocks the bathroom door, walking out and leaving the bedroom. She checks in on Tina, who's happily playing in her room, arranging the plastic furniture in her Fisher-Price house. She looks in on Hal, who's at his desk leaning over a math textbook. She walks further down the hall. Lilly's room is empty, indicating that she must be downstairs. Sandy knocks on the closed door to Blane's room.

"Come in."

Sandy opens the door. The room is dark, with shades down and curtains drawn. Blane lies on the floor by his stereo, leaning on a pillow looking up at his mother. He takes off the headphones, dropping them to the pillow. He stands and turns off the turntable.

Sandy steps into the room, leaving the door slightly ajar for light. "Were you sleeping?"

"Just listening to music." Blane switches on the desk lamp, his eyes squinting from the change from dark to light. He sits at the desk.

Sandy shuts the door and walks across the room, sitting on the edge of Blane's bed, crossing her legs. She sees her reflection in the mirror on the back of Blane's closet door. Her eyes are bleary and red, her blouse wrinkled, half untucked from her denim skirt. No shoes on her feet, only beige stockings. She looks and feels older than her forty-three years. "I certainly look a mess," she says to Blane with a thin smile, trying to read him. "How are you doing? Are you all right? Tina looks fine."

"I'm fine," Blane answers. "Where'd he go?" He looks away from his mother to the desktop, embarrassed to be seeing her this disheveled.

"I don't know," Sandy says, "have no idea." She runs a hand through her hair, pulling it back from her face. Blane picks up a pen and begins doodling on a notepad, drawing lines, circles, squares, rectangles.

"What do you think we should do with him?" Sandy asks. "What do you think?"

Blane puts down the pen, looking at her. Sandy looks back. She rubs her eyes.

"Do you really want to hear what I think?"

"It could help," Sandy says.

Blane shrugs. "Well, I think it's too late for him, but if you don't toughen up Hal and Tina will end up the same way."

Sandy nods slowly. Blane looks away, back to the desk, picking up the pen and scribbling rings around the paper's border. Sandy stands, looking herself over in the mirror, tucking her blouse into her skirt. "Okay, thanks."

"I'm sorry, but that's how I feel. You asked." Blane draws a hangman's stand and then a noose with five boxes for letters underneath.

Sandy opens the door, looking out into the hallway. "Remember, he's my son too, just like you. I love him just as much and can't believe it's ever too late." She walks out of the room, closing the door behind her. And Sandy stops, hears Dean's car pull into the driveway, the sound of the garage door being pulled up by its electronic motor two floors below.

The school radio station plays music for the town via a weak transmitter. Blane sits next to Miller in the DJ booth, having taken his father's car out and driven to the school to sit in on Miller's radio hour, just somewhere to go to get out of the house. Blane is the only one of his friends who doesn't have a radio show; doesn't feel the need to make himself sound like an idiot before all of Concord, in his opinion. Miller puts *Greetings from Asbury Park* next to the turntable.

"This is going to be a Springsteen hour," Miller says.

"You always have a Springsteen hour," Blane says.

"Quiet or I'll smack you," Miller says.

Blane raises his hand to Miller's face, moving thumb to fingers, making a mouth for a puppet. "Violence and violins," Blane says in a high-pitched voice, "they sound so close, but they are oh so very different."

"I hate that fucking hand thing so if you're going to do it just get out of here," Miller says. "When I'm on the air you better shut up or I'll get into trouble."

"It's just Mr. Hand." Blane grins.

"Yeah? Well, tell Mr. Hand to fucking shut up then."

"I'll try," Blane says and he continues watching Miller spin records. Miller is Blane's best friend. Blane's known him ever since his family moved to Concord about eight years ago and through Miller he met all his other friends. Their mothers are best friends too and sometimes Blane suspects that the only reason Miller and him are friends is because Sandy and Terry kept lumping them together in the cold basements of their houses while they chatted upstairs in the living rooms sipping tea and coffee. The two kids spent so much time together, sitting bored, waiting for their mothers, that they became friends out of necessity, playing games like Careers, Battleship, Stratego, and Life for hours to keep themselves occupied.

Miller's father is dying of cancer. He's been sick on and off for a few years, but lately it has become a constant in his family's life. And although Miller is Blane's best friend, they've never once spoken about Miller's father's cancer and impending death. Blane only learns about its course through messages relayed by his mother. Sandy and Blane were in the car; she was dropping him off at work. "Miller's father's going into the hospital again next week, has he told you anything about it?"

"No," Blane answered.

"Does he ever talk about it with you?" Sandy asked.

"No," Blane said.

"I thought you were best friends?" Sandy commented.

"We are, Mom, maybe he's just not ready to talk about it yet."

Blane looks over to Miller. Miller studies the album jacket to "Greetings." Blane wonders if Miller's mother fills him in on the stories of the Wallace family the way his mother tells him about Miller's father. Miller doesn't act as if he knows anything about Blane's family, but then again Blane doesn't act as if he knows anything about Miller's. So Blane says nothing about either. Miller has enough to deal with with his father dying without being burdened with hearing the Wallace Family Saga.

Miller stacks records, giving Blane the order of the songs. Blane notes the artist's name, the song title, the album title and the song's playing time on a sheet of notebook paper, totaling the list to make sure the show won't run over or under its sixty-minute time limit.

"Give me the list already," Miller says. "How'd it come out?"

"A-okay here, buddy," Mr. Hand squawks. "A-okay here."

Miller snatches the list from Blane. "Just give it to me. You don't have to make it into a fucking joke." He looks over the list. "Looks pretty good so far."

Blane sits back in his chair as the first chords of Springsteen's "Blinded by the Light" play.

"The Boss!" Miller exclaims, giving Blane the thumbs-up sign.

Philynda's howling at the moon. Dean leans out the bedroom window, yelling down to the dog, "Hey! Hey! Hey!" But Philynda's head remains turned up toward the full moon. Dean pulls his head inside the window, closing it fast. "Christ, it's cold out there." He rubs his bare arms, only wearing pajama bottoms, and he walks to the closet, taking out his heavy terry cloth robe.

Sandy sits up in bed, watching. "Can't we have this conversation? You've been avoiding me all night. Dean?"

Dean slips on the robe, shoving his hands deep in the side pockets. "The neighbors are going to kill that dog if I don't drag her in." He heads out of the room, downstairs.

Sandy slides out of bed, pulling down her nightgown and going to the window. The lamp above the side door lights up and Dean emerges from the house in his robe and workboots, laces untied and dangling on the frost-covered lawn. Philynda stops howling and stands, wagging her tail and trotting over to him. Dean grabs her by the collar and gives the dog a yank toward the door with one hand, pointing with the other. He releases Philynda and she scurries up the side steps ahead of him. "Good dog," Dean says, proud of himself for taking care of this so easily. He enters the house and the lamp above the side door goes out. Sandy returns to the bed and climbs in.

Dean has been avoiding this conversation all evening. Too tired to talk when he came home, he took a shower. Too hungry to talk it over during dinner. Too much office work to do in the den to talk all evening. Sandy sat at the kitchen table reading a magazine when Tom returned home at ten o'clock. He casually stopped in the kitchen, taking the time to grab himself a two-liter bottle of soda and a box of Oreos. Sandy watched him, expecting him to say something, if not "I'm sorry" then at least something to hurt her feelings, but he said nothing, heading straight up to his room for the night.

Sandy pulls the covers up around her chest, folding them under her arms, waiting for Dean.

He enters the room, closing the door and hanging the bathrobe over the closet doorknob, letting its hem drag along the shag carpet. "That's done." He rubs his hands together. "I don't know why the dog was staying out there. It's so damn cold." He gets into the bed, rubbing a hand over his bare chest, then sliding down and resting his head on the pillow. He looks up at Sandy, who's still sitting with the covers tucked up around her. "So what's up?" Dean asks.

Sandy looks at Dean, her big, strong husband who so easily took care of the situation and calmed their dog. She's waited all night to have this conversation but now fears starting it, fears his reaction to her question.

"Well, what's up?" Dean folds his arms around his head, palms cupping his scalp.

Sandy leans on an elbow, chin resting in palm. "Today Blane said that Tom is a lost cause and that if we don't toughen up, Hal and Tina will end up the same way."

Dean shrugs his eyebrows. "Will end up what way?"

"Like Tom."

"What does that mean? They'll end up like Tom? What's so wrong with that? Tom's a bright, assertive kid. I'd be thrilled to hire a kid with Tom's qualities. As it is too many of my salesmen are weak-spined, not nearly tough enough to tackle their assignments." Dean shuts his eyes. "All set?" he asks his wife.

Sandy stares at the pattern of dark hair across her husband's chest and she reaches over, playing with a curl at its center. "All set," Sandy answers quietly and she lays her head against his shoulder, seeking warmth and comfort.

1 9 7 8

A W R O N G turn was taken somewhere within the last half hour of this journey or maybe Dean has had the directions wrong from the start, but as of three o'clock, Dean and Sandy are over an hour late for Vicki's wedding.

Sandy, patient throughout the drive, not once asking if perhaps Dean is lost, glances at her watch, acknowledging their tardiness. "You could always tell her something came up at the last minute."

Dean grips the sheet of Xeroxed instructions to the steering wheel, reading. A two-hour drive up into New Hampshire, over an hour spent trying to locate Vicki's apparently nonexistent hometown. "I swear to God, there is no such place. Did we miss a turnoff somewhere? I didn't see any turnoff."

"Do you really think she'll miss us?" Sandy didn't even want to come to this event. Her husband's secretary's wedding. She likes Vicki and all, but they're hardly close, hardly close enough so that Sandy feels obligated to get lost in the woods of New Hampshire on a cold winter afternoon.

"Maybe we should stop, get a bite to eat and just aim to get there for the reception."

"But if we can't find the town of the wedding, how can we find the reception?"

"I don't know. We'll ask directions at the restaurant. I think I saw a Burger King a few miles back off the interstate."

"Dean, let's go home. I need to be with Terry now." Jason Koppi could die anytime within the next week. Sandy wants to be there when her friend needs her, is actually surprised by how distant Dean has been to Jason, considering they too are friends.

"For all we know, the church could be within a mile of here."

"Please, Dean."

"I'm going to get directions at the Burger King. Relax. I'm sure we're almost there."

"Aren't you concerned about Jason?"

"Of course I'm concerned about Jason, but I can't think about him and figure out where we are at the same time." Sandy has been so involved in Jason's declining health and Terry's grief that Dean half believes his wife is actually enjoying the Koppi family's disaster, enjoys being on the inside of another family's distress, being depended upon for help and comfort and love.

"Must be hard being around them so much with all that emotion," Dean says.

Sandy's pleased that Dean's finally showing some interest in her feelings. "It is sad, but how could it be anything else? They're good friends of ours. Their kids with our kids, Terry, me, you and Jason. It's a tough thing to understand. It all seems so arbitrary."

Dean pulls off the highway onto the exit leading to the Burger King restaurant, adjacent to a Mobil station. Sandy stares at her husband, so intent on attending this wedding, avoiding the oncoming death of Jason as he avoids all else. Last night she tried to talk to him about her mother and Tom, how unbearable it was living with both of them. Dean's response: "I'm sure Tom will grow out of it."

The car's motor is shut off. "Should we go in?" Dean asks, opening the door, a waft of frigid air blowing at his pants legs.

Sandy opens her car door and steps out onto the icy pavement. Could she have said, *"No. No, I don't want to go in"*? Sandy wonders. She steps carefully along the icy slick tar in her high heels, making her way to the front grille of the car where Dean waits. He puts his arm around his wife's shoulder, escorting her along the sidewalk. "Easy does it," he says.

By the time Sandy is done in the ladies' room, Dean is sitting at a booth by the window overlooking their car, a tray of two drinks, two burgers and two orders of fries before him. Sandy sits, pulling off her coat. Dean places a cup of tea, a pack of fries and a burger before her. "Here you go," he says. "I have extra catsup packs if you need them."

Twenty-four years of marriage and he cannot remember she doesn't eat hamburgers, cannot remember she only eats the fish fillet sandwich when they eat out at McDonald's or Burger King. Holding up the unwanted burger. "I think they'll let me exchange this for a fish sandwich, don't you?"

"I thought you wanted a burger?"

"You know I don't eat burgers."

"You eat them sometimes. You like them. But go exchange it if you want." He reaches into his pocket, placing a few single bills on the tabletop. "Why don't you just buy the fish. I'll eat the other burger."

Sandy glares at the three crumpled bills lying on the counter between her burger and fries. She feels like one of the kids, being doled out an allowance for a meal, and wonders what it must be like to actually receive a paycheck and earn the money one's spending instead of having it passed out to her in weekly installments. Three dollars—Dean's three dollars—disdainfully handed over to his wife because she refuses to eat a burger but must have a fillet-o-fish sandwich. Sandy shakes her head. "You really can't remember that I don't eat burgers? I don't know how many times I've told you."

Dean looks up from his food, had been thinking through the directions the cashier gave him to Vicki's hometown. "I forgot. I was concentrating on other things."

Such a busy man. "Sorry I'm such a distraction to you," and Sandy regrets saying it instantly. She sees that Dean is startled, but the words said, she might as well continue with the thought. "You really don't take me seriously, do you? Everything I do and say and feel about the family is all a joke to you, isn't it? A *distraction?* Don't you realize something's wrong?"

Dean collects the three dollars, smoothing them across the table, looking Sandy squarely in the eyes. "Do you want me to get you the fish fillet? Is that what this is all about?"

And Sandy stares at this man, the stupidest man she's ever met in her life—*Why did she marry him?*—for a moment she cannot remember, then it hits her—*to get away from her mother, to be able to move out of that awful apartment*—and Sandy shoves her arms into her coat sleeves, standing, fastening its belt. "I'm going to call home and check up on things. Forget it, I'm not hungry, I'll eat at the reception."

"Mr. Koppi's dead," Blane said over the phone and now Sandy and Dean are headed south, away from Vicki's wedding reception.

The last time Dean saw Jason was in the hospital three days ago. Tubes running in and out of his arms, an air tank standing by the side of the bed, Jason stared up at Dean, a two-week growth of beard on his face. Dean had wished Jason was already dead. Jason too easily reminding Dean that this could happen to him. Jason and his family taking too much of Sandy's time away from him and their family. Dean took Jason's hand and gripped it firmly, wanted to say something, anything, but didn't and he was thankful when the nurse entered, asking him to leave. "It'll be hard to think of Terry without Jason," Dean says to his wife. Jason could be me, he thinks, Terry could be Sandy.

"We never knew one without the other," Sandy answers and it occurs to her that no one she knows but her own mother knows her without Dean, whereas all of Dean's office workers know him without her. "I guess we saw them both as always one," Sandy says.

Dean reaches a hand off the steering wheel, taking Sandy's hand in his own. "I love you. I like being part of our one."

When the "one" that they are is defined almost exclusively by Dean himself, Sandy cannot see how he *wouldn't* like being a part of *their* one, and she at once feels guilty for having this thought at the rare odd moment when Dean is humbly expressing his feelings, vulnerable and true.

■

"Go away! Will you go away already!" Tina stands at the side of the street, hands at her sides, glaring at her grandmother ten yards off. "Mom lets me go to Debbie's alone! It's only six houses away already!"

Lilly keeps walking toward her granddaughter, slowly making her way to Tina, hoping Tina will remain still so she can catch up with—instead of follow—her.

"Stop walking this way!" Tina screams, her face red, almost in tears. "Go home!"

Lilly keeps walking her slow walk toward Tina and Tina folds her arms across her chest, frowning at her grandmother. Lilly reaches Tina and stops, putting her hands to her cheeks and inhaling deeply, smiling. "Oh, I'm not used to walking so much. Let's rest a bit and then we can turn around and head home."

"I'm going to Debbie's, you dumbhead." Tina takes a step, walking backward in the direction of Debbie's house.

"You have to stay at home today. You know that." Lilly takes a step forward, bridging the gap between them.

"Mom said this morning I could go to Debbie's."

"Well, she forgot to tell me before going out this afternoon so to be safe you should stay home with me, I'd say."

Tina uncrosses her arms, pointing to the dark green house across the street. "Mom's right in there with Mrs. Koppi. Why don't you just call her to find out it's all right?"

"Now, I don't think that's—"

"You just don't want me to leave because then you'll be left alone in the house and you don't have any of your own friends. That's only why you don't want me to go to Debbie's."

"That is not so."

"Then why not?"

A car approaches. Lilly backs against the stone wall bordering the road. Tina keeps her place, watching the car drive by.

"That wasn't safe," Lilly criticizes. "You didn't even step to the side."

Tina turns and continues on her walk.

Lilly takes a step, then stops, her left knee aching, unable to continue. "You come back here with me!" she calls. "You come back here, Tina Wallace!"

Tina doesn't even turn her head, doesn't even slacken her pace.

"Come back and help me to the house!" Lilly cries. "I need you to help me to the house!"

Tina walks past two houses, her grandmother now fifty yards behind her. Tina turns her head slightly and sees Lilly leaning against a telephone pole, Lilly's hands gripping the pole as she shakes her left leg in the air a foot or two off the ground. Tina faces forward, spotting Debbie's house through a row of pine trees at the corner.

1979

B L A N E has his headphones hooked up to the stereo. He's lying on the floor, his face pressed into a pillow. The shades are down, his door is closed. Billy Joel's *The Stranger* is beating into his head. He turns the volume up high, as high as he can stand it, but he can still hear them downstairs.

Screams. Sandy's and Lilly's. Yells from Tom and Dean. Cries from Tina. Loud banging noises as chairs are toppled over and objects thrown. Crashing noises and the sound of a dish breaking. All heard by Blane but with no real idea of what exactly *is* taking place. Blane was reading over the curriculum information to Hampshire College, the school he'll be attending in the fall, when he heard screams coming from downstairs. Once the shouting became louder, threatening, Blane put the college pamphlets aside, plugged his headphones into the stereo receiver jack, switched on the turntable and lay down on the floor. The music pounds into his ears.

Blane's greatest fear is that the fight won't end before the record side is over, which means that during the time between sides, while he's flipping the record, he'll have to hear the fight continuing. Blane finds it bad enough having to hear the screaming between the songs. He finally becomes a little less tense as the song ends, the music lulling him into a false sense of security when, during that ten-second break between songs, he hears furniture being thrown or a voice yelling at a high pitch and Blane's as tense as if he were down there watching it.

Side A of *The Stranger* ends and Blane hears nothing. Sometimes this is a good sign, a sign that it's over, but sometimes Blane gets this eerie feeling that this time *it* happened. That this time Tom went over the edge, killed the entire family and is now marching upstairs to hunt Blane down with a large kitchen knife in one hand and a hammer from his father's toolbox in the other. The Wallace family's own Charles Manson.

Blane puts on Side B and returns to his position on the floor, his face buried in a pillow.

Only once did Tom and Blane come close to having a fight. It was a night earlier this winter. Tina and Hal were asleep, Lilly watching television in her room. Sandy and Dean were away for the weekend at the Cape house and Blane stood in the kitchen making a sandwich, Tom watching. "Yes, can I help you?" Blane asked his brother, folding the sliced turkey on the roll's bottom.

Tom leaned across the counter, staring at his brother. "I'm okay."

"Glad to hear it." Blane folded the plastic wrap around the stack of sliced turkey meat, putting it away in the refrigerator. "Are you so bored you have to stand here annoying me?"

"Am I annoying you?"

Blane returned to the counter, peeling lettuce off the head and placing it on the turkey. "No more than you annoy everyone else."

"Is that right?" Tom said.

"You think you don't annoy everyone in the family? You think we're all not sick of you?" Blane sliced the top off the tomato, dropping it in the disposal, then cutting two thin slices for the sandwich.

"You think we're not sick of you?" Tom rebutted.

"I'm not the problem in the family." Blane rinsed off the knife, putting it in the dishwasher. "You don't think the family would be better off without you? The only thing you contribute to this

family is shit." Blane unscrewed the cap to the mustard jar.
"You're fucking useless. You're the cause of all our problems.
You don't think if you left we'd be better off?" Blane took a knife
from the silverware drawer.
"Aren't you Mr. Perfect," Tom said.
Blane spread the mustard across the bread, knew not to look
his brother in the eyes. He just picked up the sandwich and
turned away. Tom shoved Blane's shoulder but Blane kept going,
ignoring Tom, eating his sandwich as he walked upstairs to his
bedroom, closing the door, finishing the sandwich, then un-
dressing and climbing into bed. A few minutes later the door
opened and Tom walked into the room, around to the side of
the bed.
Blane turned to him. "What do you want?"
Tom held a large kitchen cutting knife. "I'm going to fucking
kill you. You think you're so smart and perfect."
"That is not what I said. That's what you said." Blane turned
away toward the wall. "Now get out of here."
"I'm going to kill you, shithead." Tom laughed.
"Then go ahead and do it and shut up."
"Go fuck yourself, you fucking wimp. You fucking smarty ass
wimp. Mom and Dad's perfect asshole. I should fucking chop
you up into bits."
"Then go ahead. I really don't care." Blane stared at the wall,
watching Tom's shadow, waiting for Tom to move toward him
or leave, but Tom just stood there, holding the knife in one
hand, swinging it around, slashing at the air. "I'm going to fucking kill you, kill you, kill you." Blane heard him move around,
shuffling papers on the desk and then the shadow grew smaller
and Tom left the room, shutting the door behind him. They
haven't fought since. Neither ever told anyone what happened.
Side B ends and Blane takes off the headphones, shutting off
the stereo, returning the pillow to his bed and sitting at his desk,
taking out his college information, dreaming of the day when
he'll move out of this pit his mother and father call home.

• • •

Tina sits on the bed, looking at the opposite wall where her father painted a huge rainbow against a sky blue background, the rainbow rising from one corner, arching to the ceiling, then descending into the door frame, just above the doorknob.

She has four brothers and Kyle's away in college and always acts like a parent when he comes home. Blane plays with her toys with her, plays games with her, read books to her before she could read them herself and still does these things with her even though he's almost eighteen. Tom and her play outside together, he teaching her baseball, lacrosse and soccer. In the family room they play Godzilla vs. Mega-Godzilla, a game in which Tina is Godzilla and she wants to stay on the couch and Tom tries to tear her off the couch and they wrestle and throw cushions and pillows at each other and if Tom gets her off the couch, she dies unless she can get all the way across the room and tag the handle of the sliding glass door. Hal and Tina play together but it's not like with the other boys because Hal's closer to her age so when they play together they're the same and not like Kyle, Blane and Tom, who are always older and in charge.

Tina doesn't know what to do or where to go so she stays on her bed, trying to decide. She didn't have anything to do with the fight, but once it ended, her mother and father sent her up to her room, Hal to his room, Lilly to her room and they stayed downstairs. Tom drove away somewhere.

Tom never gets mad at Tina because she's the only girl, the "specialest." If Tom or Kyle or Hal or Blane ever have candy, all Tina has to do is say, "You'll be my favorite brother if you give me some," and they always give it to her and then she gives them a hug and a kiss on the cheek. They all want to be her favorite brother because she's the "specialest," the one their parents wanted the most and everyone in the family knows that's true.

Tina gets off her bed. She doesn't want to do anything but she should clean her room. After school today her friend Gwen came over and they cut all the hair off Tina's three Barbie dolls, then painted their bodies with different color poster paints. She should probably wash them off and hide them in her closet, and so Tina walks over, picking the three dolls off the newspaper Gwen and she had spread out. Tina doesn't care that the dolls are ruined because she hates dolls, especially Barbies because they're so girlie and her Nana Lilly gives Tina a new Barbie every birthday, Christmas and Easter. "A girl can never have too many Barbie friends!" That's what Nana Lilly says about Barbies and so Tina goes to her bedroom window, opening it halfway and tossing out the yellow-painted Barbie.

The doll falls past the kitchen window where Sandy and Dean sit and Tina wonders if they saw the doll fall by the window or heard it hit the ground. Tina pushes the window further open and leans her head out but it's already dark so she can't see the Barbie. Tina picks up the Barbie she painted blue, purple and green, throwing her hard, and Barbie lands on the porch roof, just outside Blane's window. He doesn't come to the window or anything so she picks up the third Barbie, red, black and orange.

Gwen went to Disney World last February vacation and today she wore a Minnie Mouse sweatshirt. Tina's old Mickey Mouse sweatshirt is too small for her and was given away to the Goodwill clothes collection. Gwen talked about going in the Haunted Mansion and seeing the Bear Jamboree. She asked Tina what her favorite ride was when she went and Tina said that since she was only seven, It's a Small World was her favorite.

"What else did you like? I liked the Dumbo flying ride. Do you remember that?"

But Tina can't even remember It's a Small World, she only knows it was her favorite because her mother and father have told her it was. Crying in a parking lot, her whole family crying in a parking lot with a big lobster is how Tina remembers Florida.

"It's not every girl that gets to have three Barbies," Lilly exclaimed when Tina opened the present on Christmas morning, and Tina leans her body out the window, raising an arm high over her head, throwing the third Barbie deep into the night.

"As awful as things were between me and Hugh, they were never as bad as this."

"Then why don't you move out of here like you did with us then," was Sandy's response, and Lilly marched up to her room.

"Don't ask for my advice while your family falls into disarray," she called over her shoulder.

Lilly lies in bed, leaving the light on but shutting her eyes. Life with the Wallaces, nothing but a long, painful humiliation at the hands of her daughter and grandchildren. The exceptions: Dean, who isn't cruel, patronizing but not cruel, and Blane, who says and does nothing. On a daily basis Lilly is called an old lady, a granny-witch, a whore, a skank, a brittle old bat. No longer ever called Nana Lilly by the children, in casual conversation they refer to her as the old lady as if she were a stranger.

"Do you hear them? Did you hear what Tina called me and all I did was ask her if she'd like some more *juice?* An old crank. And Tom encourages her, eggs her on."

Sandy told her mother not to talk to the kids anymore if she didn't like what they had to say.

Lilly can see the glow of yellow light through her eyelids. Warm and yellow like the daffodils on her faded sheets. Move out, her daughter told her, and Lilly only wishes she could but has nowhere else to go. Where *would* she rather live her life? What would her ideal dream life be?

Lilly opens her eyes, sitting up in bed, seriously pondering the question. Having never lived or visited outside of Massachusetts, her knowledge of the greater world limited to what she's viewed on the news and through the eyes of *The Love Boat* crew, Lilly has no idea where she would rather be or who she would rather be living with. But then again, there *are* no other options so why tease the fantasy? Lilly shuts her eyes.

• • •

"A Biography of the Wallace Family" by Hal Wallace. Hal's seventh grade social science class project due on Friday. Enjoying science and math more than English and history, Hal decided to make his biography a biological family tree, relating blood types, eye colors, skin tone, hair color and texture, height, weight and the number of fillings in each family member's mouth.

Hal spent the last week looking in everyone's mouths, measuring everyone with his father's tape measure, and pricking everyone's finger with a pin in order to draw a tiny blood sample he could test for type with the chemistry set his parents gave him for Christmas. Hal had to have Sandy prick Tina's finger and Lilly said her blood type was none of Hal's business and to leave her alone. Kyle, being away at college, couldn't participate in the test so Sandy looked his blood type up in the family's medical file she keeps in the bottom drawer of her bedroom dresser.

"Is this what kind of biography your teacher wants?" Sandy asked, proud of her son's interest and ambitions but unsure if he'd misunderstood the assignment.

"It tells how we're related and who we are and where we came from so it's our biography," Hal replied in earnest.

Hal finished all the family trees of characteristics over the weekend and yesterday he finished drawing the combined family tree detailing all their traits. Tonight, while he has some time to waste in between the fight and when his parents call him down to dinner, Hal sits at his rolltop desk, the final tree before him, writing his conclusion.

"You can see where my family came from because if you see the different things that make us up, you see that they are all very alike. Most of all the hair in my family is straight or only a little not straight. Our blood is all the same except for my mom's and mine which is B positive. Our hair is all brown or black. Our heights and weights are all different because we are different ages. Most of us have brown eyes but my grandmother has green and Kyle has green. Our skin is light and tans but for Kyle and

Blane who burn more. Our teeth have different numbers of cavities. These are my conclusions. Other families have some of these things too but because my family has all of them like this together that means this can only be my family's biography."

Hal rereads the paragraph, then flips through the eight charts, looking each over, observing the lines connecting the names, the characteristic outlined written beneath each person's name.

Early this evening's event. Sandy Wallace's *brown and straight* hair was pulled by Tom Wallace. Tom Wallace's *type O blood* was scratched out of his arm by Lilly Burke. Dean Wallace's *light skin* was punched by Tom Wallace. Tom Wallace's *brown eye* was punched by Dean Wallace. How the Wallaces are connected. Hal closes the report, straightening pages, aligning corners and stapling.

Kyle hangs up the phone in his dorm room and immediately turns to his roommate, reading on his bed. "You know," Kyle says, interrupting Andrew's studies, "my father has no trouble spending money on me for gifts he wants me to have that I don't want but the minute I ask him for something I actually need he tells me that I should work more hours and make the money myself. For Christmas he bought me new Rossignols, new bindings, poles and boots when I already had my K2s but now I ask him for a hundred extra dollars for the month and he acts like I'm trying to rip him off. Maybe I should just sell my old skis at the student union. I'm sure I could easily get two hundred for them and then if he asks me where they are I'll say they were stolen. But what I can't believe is that he treats me like I'm the spoiled one when he's letting Blane go to Hampshire, which easily costs twice as much as tuition here. He lets Blane go there but can't give me one hundred extra bucks the only time I've asked all year. Christ, I knew I shouldn't have called him at home. He's always in a bad mood when I call him at home because all those other idiots are hassling him. Fine. Maybe I'll just call him again at his office tomorrow. He's always in a better mood when I talk to him at his office than he is when he's at home. I knew I shouldn't have . . ."

His head resting in Eva's jean-clad lap, lying across the front seat of his father's black Cadillac, armrest up and knees bent up against the steering wheel, he feels his head rise and fall as Eva inhales and exhales. She lays a hand underneath Tom's chin, the other rests on the back of his head, playing with his hair. "I feel like your mother when we sit like this," she says, a bit too loud, a bit too annoyed, and Tom instantly sits, swinging his legs under the dashboard.

"You're fucking sick."

"Well, I do when we do that."

"Why don't you just go back inside your house."

"I thought we were going out. You said you wanted to."

"I lied. Forget it."

"Jesus, you're such a fuck to me tonight."

"Only tonight?" he asks, a joke, and the joke works and Eva smiles, breaking her anger.

"Right. Every night." She leans across the seat, kissing Tom. "I hope the Rents are done fighting. God I wish they'd just separate and fuck each other over." Eva smirks and opens the car door. "Call me later. Promise. You want to come in and get something for your eye?"

"Fuck my eye. I'll call you later."

She shuts the door and Tom starts the car, watching Eva walk up the path to her front door, letting herself in.

Tom drives, keeping the radio silent, wanting peace. I feel like your mother she said and Tom knows that's not what it's like because his mother is no comfort to him like Eva is. His mother's a comfort to Tina and Hal and Blane and Kyle and his father, but all she is to him is wary.

"I don't think you really love me. I think you want to think you do but I don't think you do," Tom said to her.

"I know I do," Sandy replied. "I don't like all the things that you do, but that doesn't mean I don't love you."

"You *hate* everything I do, and what I do is who I am."

"I think you want us to hate you because you're afraid to face how much you really do want us to love you and help you. I think it's easier for you to fight us than to ask us for love and help."

Sandy's library books are left on tables and countertops and the kids' desks, all over the house. She began reading self-help psychology books and has now begun passing them on to her family, sticking bookmarks between pages and underlining passages in pencil. Tom came home drunk and stoned late one night to find *The Middle Child* lying on his pillow. He pitched the book out his bedroom window, hurling it onto the front lawn.

The bruise around the side and bottom of Tom's eye begins throbbing and Tom pulls the car into the elementary school parking lot where Tina goes to fourth grade. He steps out of the car and strolls onto the playground, looking over the slide, the swings, the tree fort, the teeter-totter, the blacktop where the girls play hopscotch and the boys play four-square. Tom scoops a handful of snow up in his gloved hand, pressing it to his eye, letting it cool the sting. Tom and Eva had sex for the first time in the tree fort on this playground three months ago. No home to go to, Eva brought a blanket and they climbed up the creaky ladder to the tree fort, spread her father's old army blanket and made love. "Just imagine," Tom said, looking up after sucking Eva's breast. "My sister's going to be playing up in here in less than twelve hours with her other little friends." After they were dressed, Tom carved "Tina Wallace Fall '78" into the side of the tree fort with his ivory-handled jackknife. When Tina came home from school the following day, she was elated, proud to have her name cut into the side of the tree house for all her friends to see. She gave Tom a hug, telling him he was her favorite brother.

Tina's favorite brother then, but doubtful her favorite brother this evening, Tom guesses, after witnessing his attack on their parents.

"What's wrong with you?" his parents repeatedly ask him and the answer that Tom replies with is Blane's explanation of years ago. "I'm schizophrenic," Tom answers with a smirk. "My brain doesn't work like it's supposed to, like Mr. Fuckhead Blane's does."

Tom once asked Blane why he acted so perfect, why Blane had to do everything right and never misbehave.

"Maybe I have to act so perfect in order to make up to Mom and Dad for how bad you are," Blane replied coolly. "Maybe if you weren't running away to airports, selling fireworks, swearing all the time, beating up on the family and dealing drugs to all the kids in high school, maybe then I *wouldn't* act so perfect."

"You have to be good in order to make up for how bad I am," Tom challenged. "That's bullshit."

"That's not what I meant," Blane corrected his brother. "I act perfect in order to get back at you. After all, the better I become to Mom and Dad, the worse you look in comparison. Do you understand *now* or do I have to explain it some more?"

And Tom doesn't understand why it's so, can't figure out how it came to be, but he believes Blane is the one who has made him so angry and violent toward the family. "Maybe if Blane wasn't so smart and didn't do everything right, maybe then I wouldn't have to be so bad," he argued with his mother.

Sandy shook her head. "You're going to blame the fact that Blane does well in school for why you have to swear at me?"

And Tom can't explain the logic of it, but perhaps if Blane wasn't who he is, Tom wouldn't have to be who he is either, but he can't figure out why this is so, but it is.

Sleet falls from the sky, grains of ice, and Tom drops the slush from his hand, shaking it out from between the fingers of his glove. His cheekbone is cool and numb and he can see out of the eye fine and he walks off the playground, around the school.

Passing the third-grade classroom window, Tom peers in at the dark school. Small wood desks, red plastic chairs, a map of Washington, D.C., hanging under the clock by the door, and white construction paper snowflakes taped flat against the window. Tom can't remember which desk was his, if he sat in the front, middle or back—*I was once a cute nice little kid, sitting in there and cutting out construction paper snowflakes,* Tom thinks, and he tries to remember which seat it was that was his, when his feet suddenly feel a biting cold and he gives up, walking off to the car.

"Why does our family fight? I can't live like this anymore. Is something wrong with us? Don't we love each other? Did we raise them all wrong? Are we bad parents?" Sandy sits across the kitchen table from Dean. He holds a bag of ice against his swollen jaw.

This week is Tom's week to handle the garbage responsibilities and when Dean saw these being neglected he reprimanded his son, words were spoken, a shoving match ensued, and punches were thrown. Tom may have shoved at Dean first but Dean threw the first punch and after Dean gave Tom a blow to his eye, Tom gave Dean a blow to his jaw. Sandy intervened, Tom grabbing her hair and shoving her away, Lilly came out from the family room, batting Tom in the head with her fist, then grabbing and scratching his forearm, trying to loosen it from Sandy's head. Hal was pulling at his father, trying to distance him from Tom, and Tina watched the whole episode standing in the door of the family room, *Gilligan's Island* playing in the background.

"Earlier this week, Tina called me a bitch when I forgot to buy a box of Frankenberry cereal. When I told Hal to go to his room after he and Lilly fought about the TV, he told me to fuck off. I can't live like this anymore. Between Tom, Hal, Tina, my mother—I just can't do it anymore. Something has to change."

Dean is thankful Sandy has finally stopped complaining, his mind more focused on Kyle's recent phone call than the fight of a half hour ago.

"It's only a hundred dollars, Dad," Kyle said so casually.

"Think of me in college," Dean responded, "I didn't have a father to call up and ask an extra hundred dollars or even *one* dollar from. What do you think I did?"

Silence from the other end of the phone.

"You can't expect something for nothing," Dean expanded on the issue at hand. "Life doesn't come that easy. You make decisions. You make sacrifices."

Sandy stands, walking to the stove, shutting off the burner under the corn niblets. "Dinner's almost ready for the second time this evening."

Not only has Dean had enough of the kids, but he's had enough of Sandy as well and he says nothing in response, taking in the silence, savoring his home at peace before he must reply to his wife's complaints. Dean's childhood home was always silent, never any fights breaking out between his father and mother or himself and one of his parents. The Phil Wallace family argued but never fought. Phil Wallace came home from work, listened to the radio and smoked his pipe. Lynda served dinner, Dean cleared the table and helped his mother wash the dishes before going to his room to finish his homework. Monday, Wednesday and Friday nights the family sat in the living room around a fold-out card table and played Monopoly, Yahtzee or Scrabble. Phil, Lynda and Dean Wallace all knew who they were and what they were supposed to do, and when Dean examines this family he has raised, their refusal to be who they're supposed to be and act in accord with the norms that guide family life, when he analyzes his children's greedy, spoiled attitudes and their smart-ass mentality, Dean knows these behaviors could not have come from his family but could only have their origins in the side of the family that has a history of familial upset.

"Are we going to discuss this or are you going to sit there annoyed with me?" Sandy looks to him for an answer, giving up on her own. Maybe if three years ago she had just forced the family to remain in therapy she wouldn't have the scars of three fork prongs on her arm and Dean wouldn't be clutching a bag of ice to his face. Maybe if fifteen to twenty years ago she hadn't let Dean convince her to bear child upon child upon child . . .

"*So?*" Sandy presses her husband, irritated by his silence.

"I'm thinking things through if you'd let me." Dean can't understand how he can preside over three hundred and twenty-five employees all day and solve problems involving millions of dollars within minutes yet cannot manage a minor family crisis.

"Dean, I'm afraid someone's going to get killed, that one day someone will go too far. I walk around this house and I live in constant fear of a fight breaking out and I don't know what to do or say so we won't fight. I'm afraid to talk to Tom, and Hal and Tina are more difficult and my mother's always at me. I just can't—"

Dean slams a fist down against the table—anything to shake Sandy out of this strange panic. "*No one* is going to get killed, Sandy," Dean says with a laugh, and when he sees Sandy take a breath, her eyes glassing over, he stands, putting down the ice bag and going to her at the sink, taking her hands. "We all love each other. We're not killing each other, we just need to learn how to better communicate and establish modes of communication."

He caught her off guard, but she doesn't believe him for an instant. Her husband keeps bailing into the role of respected, appreciated patriarch when all those around him don't respect or appreciate him. Sandy releases Dean's icy-cold hands, walking to the hallway closet, putting on her winter ski jacket.

"Where are you going?" Dean asks.

"Terry's. Keeping her company for a couple hours this evening."

Dean's happy to see Sandy's back to being her good self. "Send her my love," he says.

"Great," Sandy says and she opens the door and steps out, shutting it behind her. She strolls across the lawn, sleet pelting her skin. She tried. Has been trying for years, and if her husband says their family life is loving and stable, then it's loving and stable, and if he ever decides it's not, then it's his problem. She's had it, has been trying for years, and she steps to the side of the road, walking in the direction of the Koppis' house.

■

"Mother, come out of the bathroom. I can't talk with you like this." Sandy stands outside the bathroom door, hands braced against the frame, head down, eyes fixed on the slit of light shining from under. "Won't you let me explain," Sandy asks.

A crash against the bathroom door and Sandy lurches back, backing into the railing above the stairs. "Mother? Are you all right?" Sandy waits, approaching the door, an ear pressed against the wood. Sandy hears nothing, then the sound of water running in the tub. Her mother's going to take a bath and Sandy sighs, relieved. "I guess we'll talk about it later then." She walks downstairs to finish the lunch that was interrupted. Sandy can't be sure how Lilly's taken the news because once Sandy told her mother, Lilly had very little to say, uttering only a few angry sentences before picking up the Filene's shopping bag and excusing herself upstairs to the bathroom. Sandy resumes picking at the lump of tuna salad in its bowl, the half-eaten BLT she prepared for Lilly glaring at her from its plate.

The silk robe her daughter bought her hangs on a hook on the back of the bathroom door. A royal blue painted with purple, pink and red tulips with green stalks. A morning of shopping with Sandy, trying on new lipstick colors at the cosmetics counter. Lilly chose the Ambrosia Rose and Sandy tried on the Pink Coral Blossom. And when Lilly commented on how beautiful this new designer silk robe was, Sandy bought it for her mother in a snap. A fun morning at the mall and then mother and daughter returned home, Sandy fixing them up a nice lunch. A morning too good to be true for Lilly, and as Lilly took her second bite of the BLT sandwich, the toast all warm and mayonnaissey the way she likes it, Sandy told her mother that they— Dean and her—had decided it would be best for Lilly to be moved into a nursing home. In fact, they'd already picked one out and reserved her a room.

Lilly sits down hard on the toilet lid, leaning against the commode, kicking her shoes off and onto the tile floor. The tub's half filled with steamy warm water and Lilly pulls at the buttons on her shirt, wrestling them through the small holes.

"So this is it for me? Treat me nice all morning, buy me a new robe and now you're telling me I'm no longer welcome in *your* home? So where have I been living all these years? Wasn't it ever *my* home? Wasn't it ever *mine?*"

Sandy had nothing to say and Lilly was so disgusted by her daughter that she picked up the shopping bag and marched upstairs, securing herself in the bathroom.

The homes Lilly has lived in during her life. The apartment on Commonwealth Avenue where she grew up with her parents and her brother, Schroeder. The apartment in the North End where she lived with Hugh for the three years they were married. Schroeder's apartment in Brookline where she moved with Sandy after leaving Hugh, and, finally, Sandy's home in Concord where she's been living since Schroeder died and she became incapable of taking care of herself. From her parents' to her husband's to her brother's to her daughter's and now to a nursing home. Never having a home of her own but always a burdensome accessory to someone else's.

Her blouse and skirt and nylons hang over the towel rack, and Lilly stands, kicking aside the plastic soap dish she hurled at the door. She peers into the tub, the clear water reaching the full level, water lapping at the tub's rim, and Lilly unhooks her bra, unfastening it in the front and letting it fall to the bath mat. She then unhooks her girdle, letting this too fall to the floor, and then Lilly bends over, shoving down her undershorts, dragging them across her thighs until they are below her knees where they can drop smoothly away to her ankles. Lilly steps back, the undershorts sliding off her feet, and she grips the bar along the back and side of the tub, lowering her bulk into its depth.

Water surges over the edge, gushing out of the tub in a wave, crashing on the floor with a clap as Lilly settles against the tub's bottom. Her feet rest beside the drain, toes feeling the ripple of warm water as it jets from the faucet. Water sloshes out of the tub in a constant roll, soaking the bath mat, Lilly's underclothes, the tile and the edge of the hallway carpet peeking under the door.

"We think it's for the best," Sandy explained. "It'll be more peaceful for you there. Something has to change. It was a difficult decision and..."

Difficult but not so difficult her daughter couldn't make it. Lilly inventories the state of her body, her pale skin, soft, listless flesh, her muscles, limp on the bones, her breasts, stomach and thighs nothing but a series of wrinkles and falling folds. A nursing home is where Lilly Burke belongs because the Wallace family is sick of her and she's not yet dead but remains inconveniently alive. An old lady, old hag, old bat just as her grandchildren have always said, and Lilly lifts a hand from the tub, slapping her palm down tight against the water's surface, creating a ripple.

At one-thirty, preparing to go over to Terry's to help pack Jason's old clothes to give to the church, Sandy picks her pocketbook off the kitchen counter and turns to go upstairs to inform her mother of her plans. To go out without telling Lilly where she's off to only causes chaos, and Sandy is heading out of the kitchen when her eye is caught by a thin trickle of water beading down the door of Dean's suit closet at the end of the hallway.

Sandy advances to the door and opens. Water spews down from the closet's ceiling. The whole ceiling of the closet apparently so soaked through and drenched that the water is raining down on all of Dean's business suits. Five-hundred-, six-hundred-, seven- and eight-hundred-dollar suits dripping with water. Flecks of paint and plaster sticking to the coats' shoulders, sleeves and lapels.

Sandy yanks four hangers in each hand, lifting them off the rack, but the suits, laden with water, drag her arms to the floor and she has to struggle to get them into the next room atop the kitchen table. Four more trips and all Dean's suits, slacks, sports coats and ties are out of the closet and hanging over the backs of the chairs around the kitchen table. Dean's business shirts, placed high on a closet shelf, folded in cardboard boxes straight from the cleaners, are soaked through. Sandy will just have to bring them all back down to the cleaners to be rewashed and pressed—the price of putting her mother in a nursing home— and Sandy hurries upstairs, immediately pounding a fist on the bathroom door.

Lilly sits on the couch wearing the new silk robe. It's late after-noon and Donahue's on the television. Hal and Tina went to their friends' homes so they're not in yet. Blane's up in his room, reading. Lilly waited silently in the tub until she heard a footstep on the stairs that wasn't Sandy's. She called out, asking if Sandy was still home, Lilly waiting for her daughter to leave before daring to depart from the bathroom.

"I promise you she's gone. She left a note downstairs saying she went to Mrs. Koppi's," Blane replied, and Lilly rose from the tub, her body wrinkled by both age and water.

Donahue's topic is transvestites, men who dress like women. All very silly, all nonsense to Lilly. Lilly has never once seen a man dress like a woman even on Halloween, and here, on this show, these men say they do it every day. "It's obviously a big put on, Phil," she says aloud to the television.

The side door opens. "Hello?" Lilly asks, worried that it's Sandy.

Tom pokes his head into the family room. "Hey there, granny-puss, what's all this here in the kitchen? Having a rummage sale? Selling my father's clothes to buy yourself more Ben-Gay?"

"Very funny," Lilly replies. "What a comic you are." She looks back to the television. Tom enters the room, strutting about in his jean jacket and jean pants. "So what happened to the stuff?"

"They're wet. There was a leak. If you want to know more, ask your mother. I'm busy."

Tom looks to the TV, how busy his grandmother is, a grin

breaking out across his face. "You know, Grams, you're almost as pretty as those guys."

Lilly doesn't give him the satisfaction of a response, she keeps her eyes fixed on the screen.

Tom sits on the chair by the couch. "I guess I'll watch this with you," he says loudly.

"I'd rather watch it alone, thank you," Lilly tells him.

"Then go up to your room," he says. "You have a TV there, don't you?"

"I'm already watching it here, if you don't mind," she answers.

"Then we'll have to watch it together," Tom says, and he drapes his legs over the chair's arm.

Lilly stares at the TV. She can't concentrate on the show now that Tom's in the room.

"I heard that you were leaving here in a month," Tom teases. "Maybe if you were prettier and nicer like my Mom instead of an old biddie you wouldn't be divorced and all alone now."

"*I* left *him,* he didn't leave me," Lilly asserts, but her mind is on the other thing Tom has said. She hadn't realized Sandy told the kids of the nursing home plans before informing her. "Besides, it's not next month anyway," Lilly corrects Tom. "It's before the summer, your mother even said so, so there." She sticks her chin up at him, then looks back to Donahue.

Tom laughs. "Next month *is* before the summer."

"Sandy would have told me if it was going to be next month," Lilly argues. "So don't think you're so smart."

"Where are you moving to?" he asks. "I hope it's not too far. I'm going to miss you."

"Yes, miss bullying me around. No other seventy-six-year-old ladies to beat up in the neighborhood," Lilly snaps back. "Why if your mother and father had any brains you're the one they'd be sending away. The way you treat them." Lilly shakes her head in shame, glad to have gotten a punch in but all Tom does is laugh and stand.

"Yeah, you're just lucky my father's paying for it. I'd have thrown you out on the street with nothing." He walks over, blocking the TV from Lilly's view.

Lilly waves a hand. "Move away from there, don't be mean, Tom, please."

He laughs and walks nearer. "I'm gonna miss you."

Lilly holds up her hands. "Go away, please, Tom," she asks.

He laughs again. "I'm glad you're getting out of here 'cause no one of us'll ever have to see you again." He leans in close to Lilly, baring his teeth, breathing in her face.

Lilly lets out a cry, then spits in his eyes.

Tom pulls back. "You fucking bitch!" He slaps the side of Lilly's head.

Her hands fly up to protect herself. "Sandy!" she cries. "Sandy!"

Tom slaps the back of her head. "Fucking crazy bitch!"

"Sandy!"

"Fucking bitch." Tom walks away from her. "Fucking crazy bitch." He wipes the spit from his face. "You're lucky I don't kill you now, you fucking bitch." He flips her the finger.

"Fuck you too!" Lilly cries out at him. *"Fuck you too!"* she cries and Tom grabs at his groin.

"Yeah? Then come and get it, granny." He laughs and leaves the room. The screen door opens and snaps shut. A car starts and he's gone.

Lilly stands and walks to the kitchen, noting the small circular puddles forming on the floor around the damp hanging clothes. She puts a pot of water on the stove to make tea, then walks into the bathroom and looks in the mirror, checking her face for damage. A small lump has appeared on her forehead, but that is about all she sees, nothing more. Just one small bruise. She can't help but think that Tom should have just beaten her to death, possibly rescuing her from the nursing home, ending her miserable life here and now, having it all done and over. But all the damage amounts to is one small bump.

■

"Twenty-five years!" Dean exclaims proudly. "A quarter of a century!" He smiles brightly at Sandy, his face shining pink as the sun sets behind the cliffs along Cape Cod Bay. Sandy and Dean relax on the rocky beach, on a small flat patch of sand from which the kids cleared away the many boulders. The summer house sits one hundred yards above them, set back from the edge of the cliff.

Sandy smiles at Dean, handing him the fuel to light their makeshift grill: large stones gathered in a circle, a steel rack balanced over them, driftwood for kindling. Dean saturates the wood with the fluid and tosses in a match. A flame bursts up through the rack, bright and fiery, then quickly settles, burning and crackling the dry wood. "It looks like it's caught," Sandy remarks, opening a package of franks. "Are you sure we have enough branches? Should I have the kids collect more?"

"This should be plenty," Dean says and he puts the aluminum foil-wrapped onions and potatoes on the grill to cook.

Sandy sits on a blanket holding a platter, arranging franks, burgers, shrimp and swordfish fillets. Tina and Hal climb over the rocks and boulders that line the beach's edge, searching for buoys that have been torn loose from their lobster traps and washed upon the shore. Philynda runs by the water, barking and chasing seagulls in flight.

The bay has grown dark, quiet. Tonight is a weeknight, so the Wallaces' neighbors aren't around—they only come down on weekends, whereas the Wallaces live in their beach house the summer through. Dean commutes back and forth to the office daily. Sandy stays in the summer house caring for Hal and Tina, keeping them occupied during their two-month school break. Kyle, too, stays on the Cape. Off from college, he waits tables at a tourist restaurant along the canal. Only Tom and Blane remain in the suburbs. Tom, working as a lawnboy for a landscaper, alternates between spending time in Concord and at the summer house. Blane, however, absolutely refuses to visit the Cape, claiming he hates the beach, the sun, the sand, and the smell of the salt air. He continues working at the coffee shop in the town center. And Lilly, no longer a problem, was moved into the nursing home five weeks ago.

A flash and the beach is lit with the dull orange lights strung along the stairs that wind through the brush and rocks down the face of the cliff. Kyle can be heard walking the wooden planks.

"Need any help?" Dean calls up to him.

"I'm okay," Kyle responds and his clomping continues. He appears on the final landing, resting, then continuing down the steps with the cooler in his arms. He carries it over to Sandy, setting it down by the blanket. "Christ, that's heavy," Kyle says.

"You should have asked for help," Sandy says.

"I managed it," Kyle says. He opens the lid and takes out a beer. "Dad, you want one?"

Dean prods the potatoes with a stick, rolling them over. "All set for now, thanks. Why don't you bury the champagne in the sand by the water's edge. It will give it a nice chill for later."

"It'll keep cold in the cooler," Kyle says, sitting on the blanket, twisting the beer's bottlecap off. "Don't worry about it."

"Please, Kyle," Dean says and Kyle takes the two bottles of champagne to the bay, wedging them between the rocks so they won't get lost with the incoming tide.

"Would have been nice if Blane and Tom could have made it down," Dean says.

"Well, Tom says he'll probably be down this weekend," Sandy comforts. "And Blane. Blane just doesn't like the beach. Dean, are you ready for the burgers yet?"

"Almost."

Kyle places a thumb over the mouth of the beer bottle and gives it a shake. He quickly inserts the bottle into his mouth, letting the beer spray to the back of his throat. Foam drips down his chin.

"Is that what you learn in college?" Sandy asks.

"It's better than learning nothing at all," Kyle says with a grin.

"You better plan on learning more than that," Dean says.

"Tina! Hal! Come! It's getting too dark to be climbing around there!" Sandy can barely see them as they're walking further and further away down the beach.

"We're all right!" Hal calls. "Tina and me found a dead horseshoe crab!"

"We each get two!" Tina yells.

Sandy turns to Kyle. "Will you go after them, please? Tell them supper's almost ready."

Kyle drops the empty beer bottle in the cooler and takes a second, walking off. Sandy looks at Dean. Twenty-five years, twenty-five years, twenty-five years, she can't help but think. Twenty-five years keeps echoing in her head and she doesn't know what it means, these twenty-five years past since she's been Mrs. Dean Wallace. Some kind of accomplishment for twenty-five years, she thinks.

"Twenty-five years!" Dean reiterates, "Twenty-five big ones!" Dean announces to the sky.

"I know how many years it's been, Dean. You don't have to shout it to the world. It's twenty-five years, I'm happy about it too." Sandy opens the bag of hotdog rolls and begins splitting them apart.

Dean looks over at Sandy. "I'm just proud of how long we've been together, that's all."

"Why? Is it an endurance test?" Sandy asks. She looks away from Dean, staring into the fire.

Dean laughs, poking her in the side with the tip of the charred stick. "Come on, you know I love you. Now pass me the burgers, I'm ready for them."

The heat is stifling and Blane's bedroom windows are open. He lies in bed on his back, arms folded over his face. There is no breeze in the air, just heat—the three Hs: hazy, hot and humid, the sun in a cloudless sky, mid-afternoon on a weekday. Blane got off work an hour ago. He had the opening shift, six A.M. to two P.M. The customers utter that phrase, "It's not the heat so much as it's the humidity." Blane bad-mouths them to his co-

worker friends: "It's not the heat so much as it's their stupidity."
Blane's just glad that these are his last few weeks working at the
coffee shop. By summer's end he'll be off to college in Amherst.

Blane came home from work, tossed his uniform in the
washer, took a shower, then planned on having lunch and taking
a nap before going out with Cindy, his girlfriend, this evening.
However, by the time Blane had toweled dry, Tom had returned
home with three of his friends and besieged the downstairs,
turning on loud music, yelling to one another, and sitting out
on the porch drinking beer and smoking pot from Tom's four-
foot-high purple acrylic bong. Blane gave up the prospect of
going to the kitchen for food and went straight to his bedroom.

Tom Wallace: habitual pot smoker and dealer. The past three
years of high school, Tom's friends were always calling out to
Blane in the halls: "Hey, where's Tom? You know if he got any
bags with him?" "Where's your bongo-bro?" "Where's weed-
whacky Tom at?"

Blane's friends, once informed that Tom sold "good stuff,"
asked Blane to pass money along to Tom so he could make the
deal for them. "Forget it," Blane refused. "I'm not my brother's
fucking courier." And so soon thereafter, Blane's friends began
dealing with Tom directly. On more than one occasion Blane's
friends visited the Wallace home under the pretext of hanging
out with Blane, but once inside and having said hello to Mrs.
Wallace, they'd make a pit stop by Tom's bedroom before continuing down the hall to Blane's.

"Will you put on the Aerosmith!" Tom calls. He reclines on the
chaise lounge, out on the porch.

"Just mellow out already," Dave calls back. "I want to hear my
new tape again." He stands in the family room, rewinding a
cassette on the tape deck.

"Put on the Aerosmith!" Alan hollers, exhaling a puff of smoke
with a cough. "This tape you bought is shit."

He passes the bong to Henry, who takes it, inhales deeply,
holds the smoke in his lungs, then exhales. "Ah, that was good.

I mean, we really, really *do* need the Aerosmith on now, Dave."

Tom takes the bong from Henry, speaking to Dave. "You're not getting any more hits till you put it on, asshole."

"Fuck you," Dave says, coming to the sliding glass door. "It's my pot."

"It's my pot. You haven't paid me yet, asshole."

"I told you I'd pay tomorrow."

"Then put on the Aerosmith."

"Do it, asshole."

"See, we all want it on but you."

"Fine, fuck you all." Dave walks back to the tape deck, taking out his cassette. "So which one do you want on?"

"*Toys,* of course," Tom replies.

Dave puts the tape on and returns to the porch, sitting on one of the cast-iron chairs surrounding the matching dining-room-size table. Tom hands him the bong. Dave takes it, shaking his head. "You guys, you really brought me down with that talk, man."

"Just take a hit and pass it on," Alan demands.

"Mellow out," Dave says. "Relax."

"Fuck *mellowing out,*" Alan tells him, glancing at his watch. "We only have twenty minutes before we have to be at the Leventhals' to do their lawn."

"Is there any more pizza left?" Henry asks, standing.

"It's gone," Dave says, "and my stomach's the fucking Grand Canyon."

Tom takes the bong from Alan. "Just go in the kitchen and take whatever you want. I think my brother did the shopping yesterday."

"*Food!*" Henry exclaims with a clap of his hands, and Dave and he head into the house.

All is quiet. Blane walks downstairs, into the kitchen. A large pizza box sits open on the counter surrounded by half-eaten pizza crusts, spatters of tomato sauce, crumpled, greasy paper towels, crushed beer cans, dirty finger-stained glasses and an ice cube tray, half the cubes missing, the other half quickly melting into small pools of water. A pile of plates and bowls are stacked high in the sink topped by an empty half-gallon container of chocolate chip ice cream. The kitchen table is covered with three boxes of cookies, opened, plastic wrappers torn, crumbs all about. An empty bag of barbecue flavor potato chips, peanut shells and an unwrapped rectangle of cream cheese with a large bite taken from its side. The TV is on in the family room—*Tic-Tac-Dough*. Magazines, newspapers and mail-order catalogs, pushed off the coffee table, lay spread across the shag carpet. Four empty plastic sandwich bags and a scattering of pot seeds decorate the coffee table's top. The purple bong stands on the porch in the center of the room.

Blane turns off the television and sits on the hassock in front of the recliner. He wants to leave the mess, hoping that maybe Tom will clean it himself, but that means that while he waits for Tom to do it, Blane will be too depressed to leave his room and come downstairs. Heightening Blane's irritation is the fact that once the house finally does become too much for even Tom to bear, Tom just gets into his car and drives down the Cape to be pampered by Sandy and Dean. Blane, left alone, then has no other choice but to clean the first floor of the house, putting it back in order and restocking the food supply with the weekly grocery allowance his parents give him. Three or four days later, Tom, annoyed and fed up with his parents, returns to Concord to get back to his landscaping job, get back to his dealing, and meet up with his friends.

Blane slides off the hassock, onto his knees on the carpet. He gathers the magazines in his hands and places them on the corner of the coffee table. He then heads into the kitchen for a sponge.

1 9 8 0

L U K E Hall says, "It's nice to have someone to eat with, thank you."

Sandy smiles at him from across the dining room table, taking a bite of the fruit salad she made for lunch. Usually Luke and Sandy meet at his house for their hospice sessions, but this week Sandy decided to have him see the house, letting him see how the Wallaces live so he would become more comfortable with her. They're eating a light weekday lunch, just fruit salad, cheese, bread and an assortment of sliced raw vegetables.

She got the idea from a TV movie last fall. The show concerned a woman whose father was dying from cancer and the woman seeks help and support from a hospice agency in her community. Thus, Sandy arrived at the idea of becoming a hospice worker herself and the following morning she phoned the nearest office and drove down to interview for a volunteer position. On the application, under "Applicable Experience," Sandy wrote a paragraph about her experience with the Koppis.

Luke Hall's wife, Nita, died in January from breast cancer. Nita was a tall, beautiful woman. Luke is thirty-eight and she was thirty-four. They had been married three years and were planning on having a child within the first year of marriage, but once Nita found out she had the cancer, the illness soon eclipsed all else in their lives. The thought of the child was, if not forgotten, at least looked upon as an impossibility.

Sandy observes Luke eating at the dining room table, looking very handsome in a dark blue suit and red paisley tie. With Kyle and Blane off in college and Lilly in the nursing home, Sandy didn't have to convince Dean that she had time to spare for volunteer work. "There are three less people living here. The kids are older and more independent. I think a little outside activity might be fun for me."

"But *hospice?*" Dean asked. "Why there?"

"I'll be helping people who need help," Sandy responded, and Dean, observing his wife in a cheerful, perky mood at the prospect of this new adventure, could only approve of her wishes.

"Will it make you happy to do that?" he asked.

Sandy kissed Dean on the cheek, a victory won. "I like to help people."

When Luke and Sandy met at his home in Acton last week, he said the thing he missed most about Nita was not having anyone to hold him, not having any family to hold him when he cried. Sandy and Luke sat on the couch in the living room. Sandy moved closer and held him in her arms. He collapsed on her shoulder, heaving. She held him for half an hour as he sobbed, his arms locked around her waist, their legs pressed together, Sandy's knee folded up by his groin. Luke had an erection pressing against Sandy all the while he was crying. When they pulled away from each other and Luke had stopped crying, Sandy noticed a dark, wet spot at the top of his fly. She blushed and looked away, neither of them saying anything. Luke just led her to the door. After a quick goodbye hug, Sandy left, telling him she'd see him at her house for lunch on Tuesday as they'd previously arranged.

Luke picks at the fruit salad, pushing the grapes around on his plate. He keeps looking down at the table, saying very little. When he finally does look up at Sandy, he blushes, embarrassed.

"What's wrong?" Sandy asks. She lowers her fork.

He shakes his head. "Nothing," he says, looking to his plate of food.

"Come on," Sandy urges. "What's wrong?"

He looks up. "I'm sorry about last time. I didn't mean—"

Sandy holds up her hand. "No, it's *all right,* I *understand.*"

He goes on. "I didn't mean that—"

Sandy stops him. "It's *all right,*" she says. *"Please,* I *understand,"* and now Sandy's beginning to blush.

They each take a bite of bread. Sandy's glad that's over with. Her heart's racing.

"How are your kids? You have five, right?" Luke asks.

"Yes, five. The two oldest, Kyle and Blane, are in college. Tom, my middle child, is finishing up high school. And my youngest boy, Hal, is in the eighth grade. Tina is in the sixth."

"That's quite a few kids," Luke says.

"I suppose."

"The youngest is the girl?" Luke asks.

"Yes," Sandy says with a nod. "Our one and only. I'm just glad we finally got her. I think I might have had a dozen kids until I got the girl."

"I'm glad it worked out," Luke adds. He takes a sip of water. "You have a nice bunch of kids then?" he asks.

"Oh, they're fine," Sandy says. "They keep themselves busy. It's nice to have the house to myself all day." She takes a slice of banana from the plate with a spoon and puts it in her mouth. Sandy's plate is empty and Luke's plate is empty and they sit in silence, saying nothing, half glancing at each other every few seconds. Sandy takes the napkin from her lap and folds it on the table. Luke takes the napkin from his lap and drops it down by the plate.

"That was nice," he says. Luke looks around the room. "You have a lovely home. A beautiful yard."

"Dean takes care of the outside and I take care of the inside," Sandy says. She stands, picking up the plates. "The children each chose the wallpaper in their rooms. Would you like to see the whole place?" She walks into the kitchen, placing the dishes on the counter as Luke follows. "These can sit," she says and she takes Luke's hand, leading him into the family room.

• • •

Sandy shows Luke the last of the kids' rooms, then leads him toward the master bedroom. They step into the room and Sandy releases his hand. Luke walks around, looking out the windows at the views of the front, back and sides of the house. The sunlight falls in through the windows of the room and Luke gazes out at the street. Sandy sits on the edge of the bed, holding her knees in her palms, over her pink skirt. "I find it pleasant. It's nice during the day when I can just lie back and listen to the trees sway against the house. The sound of the pine trees' needles against the windows."

Luke looks over at her with a small smile and walks nearer, standing by her side, his hand by her face. Sandy reaches up and takes his forefinger, clasping it in her fist. Luke sits down beside her, taking his hand back, then replacing it on Sandy's shoulder. Their thighs touch slightly. Luke stares at her. His hand tightens on her shoulder. Sandy grips the edge of the bed, staring down at her feet. She's wearing white flats and taps the toes of the shoes into the carpet. Luke continues staring, their thighs still touching gently, his pants leg against Sandy's skirt. She can hear his breath pass through his lips. He touches her chin with his fingertips. "Sandy?" he asks. "Sandy?" he says and she can't look at him. She keeps staring down at her feet, tapping the carpet with her toes.

"Sandy?" he asks and his breathing stops. He leans over kissing her cheek. He slowly leans back, his lips a soft, light brush against Sandy's skin; a tear rolls out of one eye and Sandy wipes it away with a finger.

Luke lies back on the bed, arms folded over his chest, eyes looking up toward the ceiling. "I'm sorry," he says.

Sandy, still sitting, her back to Luke, reaches out and slides a hand up the inside of his thigh. She rubs Luke's leg from knee to groin then groin to knee, feeling the soft flannel trousers. Luke sits up, rubbing Sandy's shoulders from behind, then slowly undoing the pearl buttons down the back of her silk shirt. Sandy feels his breath on her shoulder blades. She has stopped massaging his leg and has wrapped her arm around Luke's waist, leaning against him as he unfastens her bra. Sandy turns to face him, her blouse and bra slipping down her arms, to her elbows and into her lap. Luke cups Sandy's breasts in his hands. He sighs, shutting his eyes, and Sandy eases him back on the bed, kicking off her shoes and leaning over his chest, loosening his tie and unbuttoning his shirt. Luke pinches Sandy's firm nipples, rubbing them between thumb and forefinger as she unfastens his belt, slowly drawing down the fly of his suit pants revealing pale blue boxers. Luke's hands leave Sandy's chest and gently trace down her spine to the skirt's zipper. Sandy reaches inside the fly of Luke's boxers. He's only semihard and Sandy holds him, feeling the blood rush into him, and she rubs her hand between his legs as he becomes fully aroused. Luke fumbles with the zipper on the back of Sandy's skirt, unable to reach around and get it down all the way.

Sandy smiles at him. "I'll take care of it," she whispers. She moves to stand, pulling her hand from around the base of Luke's penis when she realizes her engagement ring has become caught in Luke's pubic hair. Sandy stares into Luke's fly, twisting her wrist, trying to get the diamond ring free but the silver setting just becomes more tangled. Frustrated, Sandy gives a sharp tug, hoping to loosen the hair knotted around the ring.

Luke grabs Sandy's arm. *"Jesus—what the—"*

Sandy looks away from him, at a painting on the wall. *Blue Winter in the Woods.* She speaks. "It's all right, sorry." Luke's grip loosens on her arm and Sandy grits her teeth, giving another pull. "Damnit," she mutters.

Luke grabs Sandy by the elbow. "Hey—hey there—" He sits up, staring at the back of Sandy's head.

Sandy lays her hand flat against Luke's crotch. Her breath is coming fast, she feels dizzy. "I—I—I—"

Luke takes her wrist, attempting to extract her hand from his boxers when he sees the problem. Sandy turns toward him and their eyes meet. Sandy can feel Luke's dick lying limp across the back of her hand. A shiver comes over her and her skin is covered with goose bumps. She looks away from Luke to the carpet where her shoes, bra and blouse lay scattered by their feet. She notices Luke's black-socked feet, that during the course of this he must have kicked off his burgundy tassel loafers, but Sandy doesn't remember hearing them drop to the carpet.

"Can . . . can you get the ring off maybe?" Luke asks, gripping Sandy's wrist firmly lest she attempt to make a sudden move.

"It doesn't *come off,*" Sandy explains. "It's been on my finger for years and—*and* my finger has grown in around it. And my wedding band," she adds as an afterthought.

Luke hands Sandy back the scissors and Sandy returns them to the appropriate pocket in her travel sewing kit. She stands, facing away from Luke, immediately picking up her blouse and putting it on, then nudging her bra under the bed with a foot. She shakes out her left hand, bending fingers. "That feels better." She reaches around and buttons up the back of the shirt. The zipper on Luke's pants goes up and Sandy looks back at him as he fastens his belt. His shirt is still open, chest bared. A small patch of dark hair runs between his pectoral muscles down across his stomach to between his legs. He swiftly buttons and tucks in the shirt. He *is* handsome, Sandy thinks. As bad as this turned out, he *is* handsome and she can't keep herself from desiring him.

Luke looks up and catches Sandy's look. "Something wrong?"

"No, sorry." She turns away, blushing, and walks to her dresser, taking off her earrings, dropping them gently into their appropriate jewelry box and placing her hands on the edge of the bureau. A stray strand of hair is wrapped around the engagement ring and Sandy quickly plucks it away, letting it fall to the carpet by her stockinged feet. When she turns back to Luke, he is fully dressed, shoes, shirt, tie and jacket.

He glances in the mirror, runs a hand through his hair. He looks to Sandy, sees her blank expression, and runs a hand across his scalp again. "I look okay?" he asks.

"You look great," Sandy says. She attempts to smile, shrug this whole mistake—*was it a mistake?*—off, but the smile doesn't come, only a shake of her head. "Well?" she asks him.

"I'm sorry we started this. It shouldn't have happened, shouldn't have let it happen . . . It was a mistake to think . . ." Luke stops, slowly heads to the bedroom door. "I guess I'm still in love with my wife."

He leaves the room and Sandy walks after him. "Don't think I don't love my husband," she says, then regrets it.

Luke, halfway down the stairs, keeps walking. The front door opens, he steps out and he's gone.

Sandy stands at the top of the stairs, leaning on the banister, watching the door swing shut. Not exactly how she'd envisioned this afternoon turning out; no romance, no sex, no love. Just fruit salad, sliced vegetables, cheese and bread.

I'm still *in love* with my wife, Luke Hall told Sandy Wallace, and Sandy keeps staring down at the front door, guiltily hoping that Luke will return to her, but knowing full well that he is gone and that the next man through that door will be Dean Wallace, her husband and the only man she's ever made love to.

Sandy strolls into the bedroom, letting her robe hang loose, off one shoulder, hoping to attract Dean's attention. She's just come upstairs from watching *Hart to Hart:* Jennifer and Jonathan Hart, a wealthy, jet-setting, super-romantic, super-sleuthing dynamic duo whose only concerns are their love for each other and their love for adventure. The inseparable Harts and their dog, Freeway.

The dishwasher roars in the kitchen as it switches into the rinse cycle. Hal and Tina are asleep in bed. Tom is out on the town somewhere.

Sandy closes the bedroom door. She hangs up her robe, displaying a sheer blue lace nightgown falling to her mid-thigh. She kneels on the bed, watching Dean read, leaning over his shoulder. "Almost done?"

Dean is reading *The Stand* by Stephen King, completely engrossed in King's apocalyptic tale of a biological armageddon, good versus evil. "This book is incredible. You'll have to read it when I'm done."

"Can't you just put it down for tonight?" Sandy reaches over and begins unbuttoning Dean's pajama top.

Dean turns a page, reading on. "Come on, Sandy, what are you doing?" He brushes her hand away. "It's cold." He looks at her, sees the negligee, the outline of her breasts against the thin cloth, then looks back to the book, pretending to read although his thoughts have already been interrupted by this surprise diversion, unsure of whether he welcomes his wife acting like a harlot or not. "So, what is this? What's going on?" he asks.

Sandy sits on her heels, hands on her knees. "Huh?" She attempts playing dumb.

"What is this?" Dean asks.

Sandy slides out of her position, her back to Dean, fluffing up the down pillows at the head of the bed. "What is what?" she asks him in return.

"The nightgown. The light nightgown in early spring. Aren't you going to be cold?"

Sandy stands, walking to the dresser, opening the middle drawer. "Maybe you're right. I was warm earlier, but maybe you're right and I should change."

"If you think you'd be more comfortable."

Sandy gazes into the drawer, her hands resting on a knee-length cotton New England Patriots jersey. Red, white and blue. The air in the room filters through the flimsy nightgown she wears, caressing her skin. She thinks about Luke's penis, the only one she's ever touched besides Dean's. She compares the two. Whose is bigger? she wonders. Luke's, for the minute or so it was fully erect, was pretty long, maybe an inch longer than Dean's, although Dean's, Sandy is sure, is thicker. In a magazine she once read that thicker was better than longer, that thicker felt better, so Sandy supposes she's lucky to have Dean but—

"What are you going to do? I've just finished the chapter." He places the book on the night table, ready to switch off the reading lamp. "Are you going to change or not?"

"I'm deciding."

"Why don't you come to bed? If you're cold you can change later." Dean switches off the lamp, tired, and hasn't the time for this game. The room is black and stars appear in front of his eyes. He can't see Sandy, only hearing the sound of the drawer closing and the soft padding of her feet as she approaches the bed. He closes his eyes, falling off to sleep.

Sandy climbs in beside Dean, lying still on her back, eyes open, facing the dark. She's reminded of those nights with her mother, lying awake beside her mother as Lilly slept having her nightmares. At these times, Sandy can feel herself becoming her mother, afraid in the night, her passion turned inward into cynicism and hate. Lilly, with no pleasure in her life, is living her final years in a nursing home, bitterness and resentment filling every hour of every day. As far as Sandy knows, and Sandy is quite sure this is the truth, Lilly has not had sex or been loved by a man since she left Hugh over forty years ago. Sandy does know Dean loves her, and she does get sex from him—once a week, every Saturday for as long as they've been married—so in some respects she is definitely not like her mother, but Sandy worries. She still wants Luke Hall: the strong, young, brooding, sensitive widower, a man whose need for love has only grown stronger through the death of the one he loved. She pictures him as a hero from a romance novel, realizes it, but can't help herself from thinking so.

Sandy leans on an elbow, her head propped against a pillow, and she observes Dean as he sleeps. Passionless Dean, good husband, good father, good provider. Sandy has seen segments on television magazine shows: how to put the spark *back* into your marriage, how to *re*ignite the flame, but Sandy doesn't believe there ever was a flame to be reignited.

Dean's face, gentle and fragile, the skin gathered in small folds around his eyes, mouth and under his chin. His features have softened as he's grown older. But he's still handsome, and Sandy reaches out, lightly touching a fingertip to the center of his forehead. Dean doesn't respond and she takes the finger away.

Lilly never mentioned sex to her daughter. The way Lilly saw a woman's situation was that if a woman got married, her husband ought to teach her what he wanted from her. Lilly saw no need in coaching Sandy into being a sexual person. Like his sister, Schroeder Burke, too, never had any relationships during his adult years. A family completely asexual, Sandy observes, and she speculates that Dean grew up similarly despite the fact that his parents remained married. Sandy has seen photos of Phil Wallace, broad-shouldered with a mustache and pipe. Photos of Lynda Wallace, short, thin and small-breasted in a dark, drab dress. A dispassionate couple, Sandy conjectures, and she has the fleeting image of Tina in thirty years, lying in bed with her young husband, thinking sadly of her Betty Crocker–like mother and Mr. Business Suit Dad. Is that how the Wallace children view their parents? Is that who Mr. and Mrs. Dean Wallace are?

Sandy can't imagine Luke Hall ever went to sleep without making love to his wife. Luke Hall loved his wife—was *in love* with his wife—and Sandy wants to be *in love* with Dean but isn't sure how—or even if—that's possible, and she draws the nightgown above her hips, quietly rolling over and sitting atop Dean's thighs, her hands pulling at his pajama bottoms.

Dean is startled awake and grabs Sandy at the waist. "What are you—"

She wraps a hand around his penis, giving it a squeeze, shoving a finger into Dean's mouth. "Shhh, quiet, just close your eyes and relax." Dean says nothing, shocked, his tongue swirling around Sandy's forefinger, then her middle finger as she shoves that too in his mouth. He becomes hard and can't stop his hips from arching off the bed, pressing into Sandy and Sandy swings her body up, then down, sliding Dean inside her, pressing her hips against his pelvic bone. Dean stops licking her fingers and gasps. Sandy rides him, leaning over him, her breasts in his face, rocking back and forth across his body. Dean cannot believe that this is his wife and his hands roam over Sandy's breasts, stomach, to between her legs where he shoves his fingers inside her with him. Sandy moans, dropping her entire weight on Dean, letting him fill her, and this isn't Dean Wallace, she thinks, this isn't anyone but Luke—*Luke Hall*—and she's taking all of Luke inside of her—*all of him*—and Sandy cries out in pleasure.

■

Dean surveys the kitchen table, looking over the food: a bowl stacked with baked potatoes, five Shake-and-Baked chicken breasts, and a green salad tossed with cucumber and carrot slices. "I don't think there's enough food here." Dean sits wearing his shirtsleeves, his suit jacket hanging over the back of the chair, his tie draped loose around his open collar.

Sandy lifts a baked potato from the bowl, dropping it onto Dean's plate. "There's plenty enough for everyone. Really." She lifts another potato, dispensing it to her mother's plate at her left. She too wears her workday clothes, a pale yellow blouse and black skirt.

Lilly stares at the potato, doing nothing, and Sandy reaches across, taking Lilly's fork and knife, stabbing the potato, slicing, then folding open the halves.

Tina and Hal serve themselves the chicken and salad and potatoes they prepared for dinner. Dean contemplates the potato, barely cooked around the edges and hard at its core, "This certainly isn't done."

"I cooked it for how long Mom said," Tina says. "Thirty minutes."

"I said fifty to sixty minutes, honey," Sandy corrects. She serves Lilly a piece of chicken and portion of salad, can't believe how quickly her mother has deteriorated in the one year she's been away in the nursing home. Lilly didn't even want to come out for a visit this weekend, kept hollering, "No! No! No!" until Sandy told her they'd only make it for tonight, for dinner, and would drive her back to the home right after.

"You said thirty minutes," Tina insists. "Don't lie."

"You did, I heard you," Hal concurs.

"I would never say to cook potatoes for thirty minutes. *Never,*"

Sandy adamantly declares. She serves herself the food—the chicken and salad, bypassing the one remaining potato.

"This chicken could use some help," Dean sneers. "It's as dry as kindling for Christ's sake."

"Don't blame us," Tina says, defending Hal as well as herself. "We didn't want to be the cooks. We didn't want to have to cook dinner every night."

Sandy peels the skin from the chicken, laying it along the side of her plate. "It is not *every* night that I'm asking you to cook dinner. Only Mondays, Wednesdays and Fridays, so I'm still cooking the majority of the week's meals, okay?"

"And I'm supposed to starve when I come home from work every Monday, Wednesday and Friday?" Dean asks. "I am tired, I'm hungry and I don't like sitting down at the table and gambling that dinner's going to be edible."

"Fuck you," Hal says. "We did our job so fuck off. I can't even get my homework done 'cause of cooking this shit."

Dean points a finger at him. "Upstairs! Out of here! I won't have that!"

Hal smiles, drops his fork to his plate with a wave. "You think I want to eat this? I hope you all get botulism." He stands, still smiling, and exits upstairs.

"*There,* are you happy now?" Sandy asks her husband.

"I'll be happy when things return to normal." Dean shoves his plate away, walking to the refrigerator.

"*Dean,*" Sandy stresses, her voice hard. "This *is* our normal. Our new normal, so nothing is returning to anything." She takes a bite of the chicken. The white meat is dry and tasteless—she'd spit it out into her napkin if Tina, the cook, wasn't sitting right here at the table with her.

The *new* normal began two months ago, one evening as Dean was working in his den. "The hospice is hiring me on a full-time basis with a salary," Sandy excitedly told her husband. "I'll need a work wardrobe now that I'll be at a desk in their offices."

"Full-time? Don't you think that's a bit excessive?" She landed this on him as he was going over charge card bills at his desk.

Charge card bills for the cards he gave Blane and Kyle when they went off to college, to be used only in case of emergency. "I can't believe this." Dean shook his head, holding up both Blane's and Kyle's charge statements. "Strawberries Records? The Daiquiri Factory? Their need for music and alcohol constitutes emergencies in our sons' minds?"

"Are you listening to me? I'm happy about this. I want to do it."

Dean put down the bills, realizing his wife was serious. "But what about the kids? Someone has to be here for them. You know that."

"There's only Tina and Hal now that Tom's moved out and they'll just have to learn to help out more in the house. You're going to have to too because I'm doing this." She wasn't asking his permission, she was just informing him, and their new normal began shortly thereafter when Sandy drew up a new chore chart detailing the cooking and cleaning duties to be handled by Tina, Hal, her husband and herself.

Dean stares into the refrigerator, searching for a leftover that does not exist.

"Gonna catch a cold standing there so long," Tina mimics her father, and Dean shuts the refrigerator and returns to the table, sliding his plate back before him, picking at the chicken with his fingers, stripping the meat from the bone.

Sandy, in lieu of scolding her husband for acting like a child: "Honestly, you're taking this worse than the kids. You act as if I were torturing you." She turns away from Dean, to her mother, who she finds busy rolling a baked potato in the hem of her dress.

Sandy unrolls the potato from her mother's flower-print cotton dress. "Mother, it belongs on your plate!"

"What's she doing?" Tina asks.

"I want to take it back with me," Lilly says sternly to her daughter. "I'm taking it back," and Lilly grabs the potato from her plate, folding it into the hem of her dress, cracks of white potato splitting from the sides and falling over her lap.

"Mother, no." Sandy takes Lilly's hands, which hold tight to the dress-wrapped potato.

"I'm taking it back!"

"What's she doing?" Tina repeats.

Sandy's hands still on her mother's, furious: "She's rolling her potato up in her dress! Okay?"

"What!" Tina laughs uproariously. "What a gas!"

"That's enough out of you," Dean disciplines, ignoring his wife's struggle with Lilly, finishing off the chicken and now working on his salad.

"Give it to me," Lilly demands, but Sandy wrestles the potato free from her mother's grasp, holding the crushed potato to the side and away from Lilly, placing it on the kitchen counter behind her. "Eat the rest of your meal," Sandy says.

"I didn't want to come here," Lilly complains. "You wanted me here and I can't even have a potato."

Tina drops her uncut potato on Lilly's plate where it lands with a thud. "Here, have mine. Roll it all you want."

"Tina, why do you have to—" But Sandy stops as Tina laughs at her grandmother, who is once again rolling a potato in her dress. Sandy gazes down at her mother's hands on the cloth, watching as her mother gathers the material around the potato, drawing it into her lap.

"Done," Lilly says happily.

Tina stands, coming around the table to get a good look at Lilly's lap. "Good work, Grandma, congratulations."

Sandy sighs.

Dean pushes his chair back, dinner completed. He stands. "Thank you, ladies, for an unforgettable and relaxing dinner." He aims for the kitchen door with the goal of reaching his den.

"Sorry every meal can't be perfect for you, Your Majesty," Sandy calls after him.

Dean stops, turns and returns to the table, standing above Sandy, Tina and Lilly. He moves in close, hovering over the table, looking over its aftermath. "I am a good father. I am a good husband. I don't ask for very much . . ." And he redirects his speech from Sandy, Lilly and Tina to his own reflection staring back at him from the window set into the kitchen wall. He sees himself as he is in this scene as he stands there talking to his family: a man, his wife, his daughter, his mother-in-law and the spoils of a meal gone bad. "Is this all I should get at the end of the day? Is this it?" He nods his head to his reflecting self, who nods back in acknowledgment, and Dean turns, this time making it out of the room and into his den.

Tina and Sandy look to each other.

"I told you it wouldn't work if you started working all the time," Tina says. "I told you it wouldn't."

Sandy takes a look at Tina, a look at her mother and stands, leaving the room as Dean has, speaking over her shoulder. "Call Hal down to help clean up. I'm taking a shower, then driving your grandmother back."

Tina watches her mother leave the room. "Fuck you," she calls out after Sandy.

"Fuck yourself," Sandy replies, her voice flat, and Tina lifts a plate and a bowl from the table, clearing dishes as Lilly eats the salad with her fingers.

■

One A.M. the morning of Christmas Day, the only lights in the Wallace home coming from the Christmas tree lit with hundreds of tiny white bulbs.

"Make them blink," Tina cheered. "Make them blink!"

"The blinking makes me nervous," Sandy said. "Keep them still."

"Blinking lights are tacky anyway," Kyle added and so the lights on the Wallaces' blue spruce do not blink but shine bright and steady, reflecting off the ice cubes in Dean's glass of scotch.

The family sleeps but for Dean, sitting in his festive red-and-green-striped pajamas, drinking his fourth scotch on the rocks, staring at the tree, and Tom, out somewhere with Eva, his girl-friend for the last few years. They share an apartment in Boston, Eva attending Boston University and Tom waiting tables in an expensive restaurant. Eva's spending Christmas with the Wallaces, as her parents have divorced, her mother moving to Minneapolis and her father relocating to Seattle.

"And she'll be sleeping in the same bed with me there," Tom informed his father over the phone last week.

"Don't you think Tina and Hal are too young to understand that?" Dean asked, standing in the kitchen, Sandy at his side, listening in.

"To understand *what?*"

Dean gripped the phone tight in his fist. "About you and Eva sleeping together."

"Then you'll explain it to them. I don't care. Otherwise we're not coming," Tom declared, his ultimatum delivered, and Dean relented, allowing Tom and Eva to cohabit under his roof.

"I just hope there'll be enough room for you both in that twin bed," Dean warned. "One of you might just have to sleep on the floor."

The Wallaces plus one with Eva joining the family, but minus one with Blane absent. Dean and Sandy's number two son refused to come home. He refused at Thanksgiving and now again at Christmas, preferring to spend the holiday break in Amherst with college friends who also opt not to return home to their families for the season. Dean and Sandy argued and fought, but Blane remained sure. "The family has survived worse things than me not showing up for X-mas."

Sandy sleeps. Tina sleeps. Hal sleeps. Kyle sleeps in Blane's old room now that Sandy has made Kyle's old bedroom into her den. She has redone the room, painting the walls eggshell blue with white trim, ripping up the wall-to-wall carpet and leaving the polished wood floor exposed, purchasing a desk, bookshelves, lamps, tables, chairs and an easel where she can hang paper when painting watercolors. She has moved all her books out of the bedroom and onto the shelves in her den. She put a lock on the door to which she alone has the key.

"Why do you need a lock on the door?" Dean asked, standing in his wife's den as she reread a book titled *On Death and*

Dying. "What is it that needs to be locked in here?" Dean asked. Sandy kept reading, careful not to let the smallest hint of uncertainty show on her face. "It's my private den just as you have yours. You have a lock on that door." Dean looked at the painting hanging on the easel. A blotch of blue, a blotch of pink and a line of yellow. "So you need to keep the kids out of your things like I do. Is that it?" *"Exactly,"* Sandy replied, not missing a beat. "Just as you do." And her voice had an edge to it, an edge she didn't even bother to explain to her husband.

Dean had thought that once Lilly was moved out and Tom graduated high school and moved out, Sandy would become the old easygoing wife she'd been when they first married, when the older boys were young, but now with Lilly off Sandy's back and Tom out of the house no longer stirring up fights, Sandy has only become more unpredictable. In the eighteen months since her mother's departure, Sandy has made the family's life flip topsy-turvy, first becoming a volunteer at hospice, then introducing aggressive, new sexual antics into their life (last week, asking him to do it doggy-style), then increasing her work hours to full-time, then creating a den for herself, and all the while delegating more and more of her household chores to Hal and Tina. She has established a life for herself beyond the family's needs, *without regard to* the family's needs. Sandy rarely prepares an entire meal anymore: most nights it's either burgers or spaghetti or pizza taken in or Chinese eaten out, and over a year's passed since his wife last baked a sheet of cookies or pan of brownies.

Dean gulps down a large swallow of scotch, then sets the glass down on the coffee table, missing the coaster but not caring. Let the ice melt and the glass stain a ring on the table. Let it happen— he bought the table—he owns it—it's *his*—and Dean stands, walking across the room to the Christmas tree, sitting on the edge of the Oriental carpet. Piles of gifts spill from under the tree's boughs, branches hanging heavy with brilliant crystal ornaments. Eight piles of gifts and if Dean's counted correctly (and he double-checks to make sure he has), excluding Eva's pile, he has the least amount of gifts. Each of the kids buys a gift for one of their siblings, names having been picked out of a hat the preceding Thanksgiving. Each member of the family received one special present from Sandy that she bought with her own earned income. Each of the kids received four to five gifts paid for by Dean but chosen by Sandy and Dean. Sandy's pile contains four gifts from Dean, one gift from Kyle, and one gift from Tom and Eva. Dean's pile consists of three boxes, all from Sandy.

"Your mother is your one best friend," Lilly often told the children, and the evidence of her statement is laid out before Dean early on this Christmas day. As years have gone by and the kids have grown, Father's Day has often been celebrated with nothing more than a gift chosen and purchased by Sandy and a card chosen, purchased and inscribed with the kids' names by Sandy. No matter where the kids are on Mother's Day, they never fail to send a card, a bouquet of flowers, or—at the very least—phone their mother with love and thanks in their voices.

His own most memorable Father's Day gift: a wooden deer that no longer exists. A wooden deer that Tom, several Christmases back, in a fit of fury over not receiving a large check as a gift instead of boxed presents, hurled atop the burning logs in the fireplace that snowy morning.

Dean stands, a rush overcoming him, and he stumbles across the room, settling on the couch, pouring himself another scotch from the bottle, mixing the alcohol in with the near-melted ice cubes. It may be better to give than to receive, but when Dean has given so much and received so little in return, his giving feels more like an exercise in masochism than generosity. Spending hundreds and hundreds of dollars to bring joy to the faces of the children he loves, yet they will not spend one thin dime to bring a smile to his face. If his family can acknowledge the pleasure they receive when given gifts from a loved one, why can they not acknowledge the pain they inflict when denying a loved one the same?

The side door opens and Dean hears Tom and Eva entering,

laughing in hushed tones. "Go in the family room. I'll be in in a sec," Dean hears his son say, and a moment later Dean hears the refrigerator door being swung shut hard, salad, catsup and soda bottles rattling on their racks.

Silence again but for the sound of scotch pouring onto Dean's tongue and the swallowing in his throat. The ice is gone, the tree's lights sparkle in Dean's eyes. Strings and strings and strings of lights, tangled and untangled every year in celebration of the birth of Christ, pages of charge card bills and a score of canceled checks galore in celebration of this gala holiday, and Dean stares at the many packages, boxes covered with green, gold, red, silver wrappings, and he sips the scotch, *warm,* and decides it's time to take a trip to the kitchen for ice. He clutches the glass in hand, stands and walks into the hallway, about to enter the kitchen when he hears a low, quiet moan.

Dean stops, listening, taking a step forward so his body is aligned with the kitchen's door frame. Heavy breathing, sighs and gasps and more low moans and Dean leans his head with the door until he can see through the kitchen all the way into the family room where Eva lies nude on the carpet, Tom's hands on her breasts, his bare ass thrusting between her spread legs. Dean is mesmerized and his hand holding the scotch glass shakes. He braces himself against the wall, watching as his son rides this girl, lifting her legs, placing a calf over each of his shoulders.

Dean's pulse quickens, his penis growing as Tom mounts Eva's face, slipping the head of his erection past her parted lips, Dean's free hand bringing his own erection through the fly opening of his pajama bottoms, his dick standing stiff in the air as he strokes it furiously. Eva is busily, greedily, spitting and licking at Tom's dick and when it is covered with a dripping, slick coat of saliva, Tom moves down her body, quickly pumping it into her, scooping Eva off the floor so she is sitting on his thighs, his cock buried deep within her. Tom eases Eva back and Eva slides to the floor, her hands massaging her full breasts, playing with her nipples and a building tension grows deep within Dean, a growing tension he cannot control and he is suddenly about to come, about to come any second now but cannot, realizing he simply cannot because he simply cannot shoot his semen on the tile floor of the kitchen and Dean spins away from his son and Eva, his mind racing, his body spasming and he grabs hold of the railing to the stairs, his body convulsing, jerking as he shoots three thick strands of semen onto the dark blue Oriental runner.

His body stops shaking and Dean shivers, composing himself, reaching a hand into the dark and touching the stairs, feeling spots of wetness. He opens his palm and rubs the semen into the carpet, the carpet so old and worn, Dean guesses a few new spots will hardly be noticed. Tom and Eva are still quietly going at it, quietly, rhythmically going at it, and Dean cannot believe they have the daring, the indecency to do so in the family room where possibly Hal or Tina could discover them if either ventured down to the kitchen for a late-night glass of juice. Dean wipes his hand on the leg of his pajamas, returning to the living room, refilling his glass with scotch and drinking it warm, no longer able to hear the faint cries of ecstasy coming from the family room.

Tom and Eva. Dean recollects a picture of Tom with Eva, Tom's dick lowering into Eva's waiting mouth, and *who is bigger?* springs into his thoughts: *Who is bigger? Himself or his son? Or his father or himself or his son or are they all the same since they're all related?*—and Dean takes a huge swallow from the glass, obliterating the thought, refocusing on the very few gifts he received from his selfish, callous children.

Is *that* where the next generation of the Wallace family will be conceived? By Tom, out of wedlock, on the floor of the *family* room?

Dean swigs back a mouthful of scotch straight from the bottle. *Dean Wallace,* Dean thinks, *Dean Wallace* created this mess of a family, put the seed in his wife that brought forth these awful, ungrateful brats—and the scotch roars through him, glittering Christmas tree and presents a blur before his eyes—brought forth these unappreciative, ungrateful, hedonistic, materialistic brats he cannot unlove, cannot stop himself from trying to win the love of, no matter how hard he tries.

1981

T H E Y never made it to Busch Gardens on their first Florida trip five years ago, so this visit Dean decided they'd *start out* in Tampa and *then* go on to Disney World for the vacation's finale.

The Wallaces drive along a Tampa highway, Sandy and Dean in the front seat of the rent-a-car, a mid-size midnight blue Crown Victoria. Tina and Hal sit in the back seat, each by a window, between them lie their carry-on luggage bags filled with a magnetic chess game, comic books, find-a-word collections, school books, two Snickers bars and a bag of Cheez Doodles.

Sandy and Dean sat down with Hal and Tina in early January, asking them where they might like to travel for their February vacation, and both Sandy and Dean were surprised when their two youngest concurred on Disney World.

"Why there?" Sandy asked nervously. "You've been there before."

"Wouldn't you rather go to Washington, D.C., or New York City?" Dean proposed.

"What's the matter with Florida?" Hal asked. "Me and Tina hardly even remember it."

"At least if I go now I'll be able to remember it," Tina commented, and observing how optimistically their children regarded Florida, observing their children held no superstitions concerning the chances of having a second disastrous Florida trip as *they* did, Sandy and Dean respected Hal and Tina's vacation choice.

A mid-morning plane brought them into Tampa early this afternoon, leaving near-zero Boston wind-chills for tropical Florida weather.

"Are we ever going to eat?" Tina asks. She dangles an arm out the window, fingers catching the air, wind rippling the sleeve of her white cotton jersey.

"We're going to wait till we get to the hotel," Hal tells his sister.

"Can't you just wait a little longer," Sandy says.

"I'm hungry," Tina whines.

"We're all hungry," Dean says. "We'll be there in a few minutes."

"I'll probably be starved by then," Tina says.

"Do you want one of my candy bars?" Hal asks. "I'll give you one if that'll shut you up."

Tina brightens instantly. "Sure, hand it over."

"Get it yourself."

Tina reaches for Hal's bag and Hal snatches it away. "Hey, don't touch, baby girl." He opens the duffel, hands his sister a crushed Snickers bar.

"Looks like you ate it already, thanks."

"Then give it back."

"No way," and Tina bites into the bar, chewing wrapper and chocolate together and swallowing.

"You're a sicko," Hal laughs, then to his parents: "She's eating the wrapper."

Dean drives, Sandy speaks to the windshield, "Don't eat the wrapper."

Tina takes a second large bite, wrapper, chocolate, nougat and peanuts.

"You're a *sicko*," Hal repeats and Tina grins, opening her mouth wide, displaying the chewed food, leaning close into Hal's face. Hal looks away to the window, amused and disgusted. "Get away from me."

Tina leans over his body, her head by his, and she spits the chunk of candy out the window. Hal watches it hit the side of the car, then bounce off to the road. The two of them break up, laughing hysterically.

Sandy flips down the vanity mirror, looking at her children. "What's going on?"

Hal sits up straight, pushing Tina away. "We're just having fun. This is our vacation."

Sandy folds the mirror up. "Sorry for interrupting."

The car rounds a turn and there in the distance is a large red neon lobster. The sign hovers over a huge parking lot, the lobster's claw pointing toward the restaurant. The lobster smiles with large white teeth bordered by blue neon.

"That's the lobster from last time," Tina exclaims. "Look!"

Dean, Sandy and Hal look, immediately recognizing the lobster, a mythic presence in their lives.

"That's it all right," Dean says, wishing Tina hadn't identified it, not wanting to dredge up the misfortune of their last trip south.

"I remember that place," Hal says.

"We could go there for lunch," Sandy suggests mischievously, half joking.

"I thought we were going to wait until we get to the hotel," Dean says.

They are fast approaching the restaurant.

"Do you want to go?" Sandy asks.

"Let's go!" Tina shouts.

"I'll go," Hal agrees.

"Why don't we wait," Dean says.

"Pull in! Let's go!"

"Dean, why not?"

"I'm hungry!"

"Come on, Dad."

And against Dean's better judgment, he takes a hard right, throwing Sandy against the side of the car, pulling into the parking lot of the seafood restaurant, tires kicking up gravel as he quickly brakes and glides into a parking space close to the restaurant's entrance.

"It's not too busy," Sandy comments, observing the two-thirds empty lot.

"Well, it's too late for lunch and early for dinner," Dean explains. He shuts off the motor, sitting, waiting for one of the others to open a door and step foot on this familiar terrain. Hal and Tina wait for one of their parents to click open the electric door locks and Sandy stares across the lot, recollecting the scene of almost five years past. "Do you remember what happened here?" she asks her children, sounding more like a tour guide than their mom, as if this was a famous historical site.

Dean cannot believe his wife is playing counselor at this time, at this place, and he clicks open the door locks, signaling Hal and Tina to open their doors, which they do and he does. Sandy's question remains unanswered and they've bypassed memory lane.

"I hope there's no wait, I'm hungrier than I thought," Dean says and he walks to the restaurant, followed by Hal and Tina.

"There better not be any wait," Tina says.

Sandy stands by the side of the car, staring off across the expanse of the parking lot to the exact spot where she had knelt in her white skirt, where Dean and Tom emerged from the woods. She walks off in that direction, away from the restaurant, and Dean, Tina and Hal watch their mother, waiting by the entrance.

"Mom, I'm hungry," Tina moans.

"What the hell's she doing," Hal asks his father. "What's her fucking problem? We're hungry."

Dean looks to Hal sharply. "I don't want to hear you cussing on this trip, got that? I don't like it one bit." He walks off, going after Sandy. Hal and Tina look to each other. Hal shrugs. "What's their fucking problem?"

Tina rolls her eyes. "They're both crazy." She goes after her father and mother.

"If you wait here they'll come back sooner," Hal informs his sister but she keeps walking. Hal slumps down by a post under the restaurant's overhang, sitting on the rough green welcome rug.

Sandy stands by the side of the woods when she hears Dean and Tina approaching from behind. "Looking around here in the bright of day it's hard to ever imagine anything happened here to us. But I look around here and I keep seeing ghosts of us reenacting the event."

Dean stares at his wife. *So what?*

"Doesn't it interest you that here we are again?" Sandy asks.

Tina grabs her mother's arm, dragging her forward. "We're eating, now come on."

Dean turns, walking ahead of Sandy and Tina off to the restaurant.

"What is it you always tell the kids, Dean," Sandy asks to the back of his head, attempting to make her point known and force him into enlightenment. "What is it you're always telling them?"

"Shut up, Mom, let's just eat." Tina keeps a hold on her mother's arm lest she attempt to escape back to the patch of grass by the woods, and Sandy yanks her arm free from Tina.

"Will you let me go? I'm coming already."

"What a bitch," Tina says quietly and before Sandy can reply, she's already run off across the parking lot to meet up with Hal.

Sandy notes the stiffness in Dean's shoulders. "What is it you're always telling the kids?"

He sighs, listening to the crunching gravel as he walks. "You tell me," he tells his wife.

Sandy speaks. "You're always saying that if you know what you've been, you'll better know how to get where you want to go. Now what do you think of that while standing here in this parking lot?"

"I don't," Dean replies and the family enters the restaurant for a seafood lunch.

Dean raises his voice. "That was almost five years ago! Haven't you gotten over it yet?" He picks up the beer he got from the self-serve mini bar in the hotel room and walks onto the terrace overlooking the bay. The sun sets, a cool orange-red burning a trail across the water, and if his wife would just keep quiet for more than—

"Nothing has changed. That's all I'm trying to show you. Here we are, five years later." Sandy tosses up her hands. "Nothing has changed."

A young woman and man jet-ski across the water, onto the shore. "*Well,*" Dean begins humorously, "I'm not in the woods searching for my son and you're not screaming for us. I'd say that's an improvement." He smiles to himself, waiting for his wife's bitter reply.

Sandy says nothing, watching her husband sip his beer while staring out at the water. She steps back into the room, shutting the sliding door behind her, locking her husband out on the balcony. She picks up her purse and the rent-a-car keys.

Why does she stay with Dean? What keeps her there? Why doesn't she leave him? Sandy sits on the dirt ground in the forest bordering the neon-lobster-lit restaurant. Evening has arrived and the parking lot is lit with glowing yellow overhead lights. All very eerie, déjà-vu-like, and Sandy looks out upon the parking lot from her vantage point, leaning against the trunk of a thin tree, her knees bent up to her chest, low branches and leaves brushing up against her cheeks.

She never thought the family could survive after that night after Disney World, never thought they'd stay together, but today, years later, they remain a family intact and what keeps them together is being apart. Kyle then Lilly then Blane then Tom. As each family member departs, Sandy finds living in the house increasingly tolerable, even more so now that she's working and not trapped in it all day.

Why Jason Koppi died from cancer and her husband has not is a puzzle Sandy cannot figure the answer to. Three years after Jason's death, Terry still mourns. Her eldest boy off in college, her other to graduate high school in a few more years, Terry fears growing old alone, living in that house alone with only the memories of a happy family life. "I never realized how lucky I was, how I took it all for granted until it was gone. I'm selling this house once Charlie's in college. I can't live here after he's moved out. You're so lucky you have Dean you have no idea."

"You could always start dating again maybe," Sandy comforted. "I don't mean now or anytime soon, but eventually, when you're ready."

Terry waved the thought off. "Men our age don't want women their own age. They're looking for younger women, that's what they want. They don't want a widow who's still pining away for her lost husband."

Just last week Sandy was at the supermarket, picking up a few necessities before returning home from work, when she ran into Diane Sugarman for the first time in years.

"Oh, the group's dissolved," said Diane, responding to Sandy's inquiry. "Almost all of us are separated or divorced. Me, Melanie and Roberta. And they've both got apartments in Boston. Frances's husband took her with him when he took a new job in Nebraska. And Sylvia! Oh God. She got so depressed, Randall had to put her in Silver Hills. A mental hospital! I think it's only you, me and Christina still in town now but she's not with her husband either. He moved out on her when she told him she was a lesbian and now they're fighting for custody of Dorothy. It's nasty. Men don't like being left and unless you get a generous settlement you can live your old age on the street. But Jeff and I are considering a reconciliation so it's not all bad news. I'm certainly not going to give up living in my nice country home for a tiny one-bedroom in the city."

A wind picks up from off the bay, rustling the trees, branches blowing in around Sandy and she watches as two elderly people, a middle-aged woman and two boys and a girl, all in their teens, walk from their car to the restaurant. Where is the middle-aged woman's husband? Is she divorced, did he die? Sandy wonders.

"Although I think you should, you don't have to marry him," Lilly told her daughter when Sandy was nineteen, after Dean had proposed. "A woman doesn't have to marry to be happy." Sandy responded with, "I love Dean and want to marry him and I don't see you having such a great time not being married." The thought dawns on Sandy that it has taken her twenty-seven years in this marriage to reach the point her mother arrived at in three, but whereas Lilly left her husband, Sandy, sitting in the woods, her husband still locked out on the balcony unless the kids let him in, realizes she will never leave hers.

"I can't imagine what it would be like without Dean," Sandy told Terry. "I mean, if he were to die suddenly in an accident or something. I'm not always happy about who I am with him but I'm afraid of who I'd be without him."

The two women ate lunch in a restaurant in the Chestnut Hill Mall after spending a Saturday morning shopping in Bloomingdale's, Terry purchasing new kitchen appliances, preparing to start up her catering business again.

Terry stubbed her cigarette out in a hollowed-out cherry tomato cut to look like a flower. She immediately lit up another. Sandy watched, knew not to comment, but then decided to do so. "Do you have a death wish to die like Jason?" She plucked the cigarette from between Terry's fingers. "Is that what this is?"

Terry snatched the cigarette back, inhaling deeply. "I'm really not in the mood for your earnest lectures, okay? Just let's enjoy this lunch."

Sandy settled back in the booth as Terry intentionally blew smoke rings in her direction.

"You know what, Sandy?" Terry asked.

"No, what?" Sandy asked.

"Stop complaining about your husband to me all the time, okay? So what if he doesn't understand you? You going to resent him all your life because of a decision you made to be a housewife? Who cares? I don't. Dean loves you and lets you do whatever you want. Isn't that enough already?"

Sandy wasn't sure but out of respect for her friend she nodded. "Maybe it should be," she replied.

A beetle crawls on Sandy's neck and she swats at it, standing quickly, shaking it away.

"Something's in there! An animal's in there!" a child cries from the parking lot, and Sandy peers through the trees, spying a mother, father and son standing by a car, the young boy pointing toward where Sandy stands in the woods.

"Can you see what kind of animal it is," the mother asks her son. "Is it a deer?"

"What do you see?" the father asks.

"I think it's a crocodile," the boy answers gleefully.

"We'll have to watch and see," the father says.

The family stands, silently waiting. Sandy doesn't move a muscle lest she make herself visible.

"Why don't we go eat," the mother says but the boy steps forward onto the grass, advancing toward the trees. "I want to see it," the boy says and his mother smiles and sighs with resignation.

The father leads the boy to the edge of the woods. Sandy keeps her body rigid, observing the family, the boy and man no more than a few yards distant, and when she looks to the man's face, their eyes lock for an instant and then he takes his son's hand, looking down, away. "Let's go, it's nothing," he says.

They walk off the grass. "What was it?" the woman asks.

"There's a woman in there. Just standing in there."

"A woman?" the mother asks. "Is something wrong? Does she need help?"

A pause, then, "Richie, take your Mommy's hand." The man proceeds to the forest and Sandy rustles back further into the trees, hopefully out of sight.

"Do you need any help? Can we get help for you?" the man calls.

Sandy grips a tree trunk with a hand, fingers digging into the bark.

"I don't see her anymore," the man says to his wife.

"Call again to be sure," the woman says.

"If you need help, we'd like to help," the man says. "If you're not okay, we could call the police or a hospital."

"Maybe she was in a car accident," the woman says. "Maybe she's in shock."

"Are you sure we can't help you?" the man gives a last call. Sandy's eyes water. She grips the tree firmly, breaking a fingernail, a tear spilling from an eye.

The man turns back to his wife, walking onto the lot. "She's gone. I don't know where she went." He puts his arm around his wife's waist. "Let's go eat. She was standing so obviously she can get help for herself if she needs it." They walk off to the restaurant, the man and woman side by side, and their son running ahead, swinging his arms.

1 9 8 2

S A N D Y hangs up the phone, sitting at the kitchen table, waiting, anticipating tears. First there was her mother's funeral yesterday and now this. Sandy sits at the kitchen table, watching the *Today* show. Jane Pauley introducing a segment on a man who can speak backward. The segment ends. The time is nine o'clock. The *Good Day* show begins. Lilly's old favorite. Dean and all the kids are still sleeping. Kyle, Tom and Blane all returning home for the funeral of their grandmother. An hour passes and the time is ten o'clock. This is the first time in three years the whole family's been together. The year Sandy and Dean celebrated their twenty-fifth wedding anniversary, the year Lilly entered the nursing home, Blane entered college and Sandy began volunteering at hospice.

Dean walks into the kitchen wearing his blue-and-white-striped terry cloth robe, white tube socks on his feet with yellow-and-green stripes. Sandy immediately stands, shutting off the TV. Dean is at the stove, picking up the coffee pot left warming on the burner. "How are you doing?" he asks.

"Philynda was run over," Sandy replies.

Dean and Kyle park the station wagon alongside the road on Pine Ridge Path in front of the Kanes' house. Les Kane stands on the front lawn. By his feet is the body of Philynda, covered by a dirty, pale yellow blanket. "Sorry about this," Les says. He holds a mug of coffee in one hand, sipping. "I found her here this morning. Must have dragged herself here sometime last night."

Dean and Kyle walk across the dew-covered lawn. A sunny, warm, late May day. The three men look down at the form under the blanket, making out Philynda's legs, body and head. A small, dull spot of red stains the yellow blanket above the dog's rear legs.

"Can we take the blanket?" Dean asks.

"Sure, go ahead. Sorry about this."

Dean turns to Kyle. "Go and open the tailgate."

Lilly died three days ago at the age of seventy-nine. Her heart had been beating regularly with the help of the pacemaker for the last ten years but late Tuesday afternoon her heart gave out and she died. A nurse phoned the Wallaces just as Hal was serving dinner to his mother, father and sister. Hearing the news herself, Sandy hung up the phone and immediately told the family.

"How do you feel about this?" she asked her children.

"I'm all right," Tina replied.

"She was old," Hal offered.

Sandy theorized that the children's casual response to their grandmother's death was because they hadn't seen her in so long. To them, their Nana Lilly ceased to exist two years ago, since her last visit to the Wallace family homestead. Indeed, none of the children visited Lilly in all the time she spent in the nursing home.

Sandy, on the other hand, visited her mother once each week since her admittance to the facility. Every Saturday before embarking on the visit, she would ask Hal and Tina if they would like to go. The two kids would be sitting in the family room watching sitcom reruns, eating the donuts Dean had picked up in town earlier that morning.

Sandy would dangle the car keys from her fingers. "Would either of you like to come with me?"

"No, Mom," they would answer each week, too ashamed to look away from the TV screen.

"She'd like to see you," Sandy would say.

"You said she can't even recognize you anymore," Hal would reply, "so how would she even know who we were?"

And Sandy would look at him and know he was right, acknowledging to herself that the only real reason she wanted them there was because she was afraid of visiting her mother alone.

During Lilly's final year in the nursing home, she not only couldn't remember Sandy, but sometimes she couldn't remember herself either. Sandy would sit by the bed and ask her mother who she thought she was and Lilly would don new personas, creating new lives for herself. "I'm Josephine Hanover, the wife of a fur trader," Lilly once told her daughter, and another time, "Why, I'm Celeste Beaumont. My husband was a naval officer killed in the Great War. I was a very young bride." And Sandy would respond with a simple, "Yes, of course, I remember," and she'd sit and watch her mother dream life away.

Following these episodes, instead of conversing, which became increasingly impossible, Sandy began reading her mother a chapter from *The Wind in the Willows.* Sandy would sit by the side of the bed while Lilly absently stared at the wall. Sandy didn't think her mother listened to the story, but then again, Sandy read it less to entertain Lilly than to give herself something to do while visiting. As the months, years passed, Sandy found herself realizing that the faster Lilly deteriorated, the more she felt a sense of love for her again.

Kyle, Hal and Tom dig into the soft earth with shovels, piling the rocky dirt on one side of the hole that is to be Philynda's grave. They dig the hole just off the lawn in the backyard, a few yards into the woods. Dean is driving down to the hardware store to pick up a couple bags of lime.

Tina walks onto the lawn barefoot, wearing shorts and a baseball shirt. Not having seen Tina since Christmas, Kyle was surprised to discover that his sister's developing breasts, had never before thought of her as being sexual, a woman. Seeing her in the baseball shirt, braless, he looks away quickly, resuming his shoveling.

"How deep does it have to be?" she asks.

"Five or six feet," Kyle replies.

"You want to take a turn?" Tom asks.

"Where's she anyhow?" Tina asks.

"In the garage," Kyle replies, head down.

Hal lifts a shovel of dirt, piling it on Tina's toes. Tina kicks it away. "Aren't you a regular prankster."

Hal shrugs his eyebrows. "Pardon me, miss."

Tom hands his shovel to Tina. "Your turn to dig. She was your dog too."

Tina lets the shovel drop to the ground. "I only do the chores for inside the house. Hal does the outside ones."

Tom lifts his sister by the waist, her feet leaving the ground. "Yeah? Well, maybe we should bury you alive," and Tina kicks at him and he drops her in the three-foot-deep hole, Tina landing on her butt.

"Will you get out of there?" Hal pokes her in the side with the tip of the shovel.

"He put me in."

"Just come on and get out," Kyle says. "We have to get this done."

"Philynda's dead. I think she can wait," Tom observes.

"If it gets too warm, she'll start stinking," Hal says.

"I bet Nana Lilly really smells bad," Tom says.

"They sprayed her with chemicals so she wouldn't," Hal informs his brother, drawing on his knowledge of science.

"I was afraid they'd put the coffin open and we'd have to look at her," Tina says.

"That's disgusting," Hal says.

"No matter what the Reverend said about her with all that nice stuff, she was still a cranky old maid." Tom digs a rock out of the ground with his hands, hurling it deep into the woods.

The Reverend met with the family on Thursday morning, the day of the funeral. On Wednesday, Kyle flew up from New York, Tom took a train out from Boston, and Blane drove east from college. Kyle and Tom were good about coming, Kyle taking a couple days off from his job at an investment banking firm and Tom taking two nights off from waiting tables. Blane originally resisted coming home for the funeral when his mother asked. "My senior thesis is due next week and it's not even done yet," he said, leading Sandy to say, "We've put up with you not coming home anymore for holidays and other family gatherings, but this is non-negotiable."

The Reverend asked each grandchild to give a thought or feeling they had about their grandmother, "Some way in which you remember or think of her for being who she was."

"She tried as best she could," Blane said.

"She loved to watch TV," Kyle said. "She wouldn't let anyone watch anything that wasn't one of her favorites."

"She may have been a pain but I think she loved us," Hal said.

"She used to drive me crazy," Tina said. "Following me down the streets to my friends' houses to check up on me."

"She was my mother's mother," Tom said, "and I'm glad she had my mom so I could be her son."

Sandy, listening to the children's less-than-glowing reports on Lilly, reminded, "When you stayed in her apartment, you all liked that with her."

"I never did that," Tina said.

"I didn't," Hal said.

"That was fun," Kyle remembered. "I liked visiting the city."

"The ballgames were good," Tom admitted.

Sandy continued acting as cheerleader for her mother. "And Blane, I know you enjoyed baking cookies with her. As did both of you, Tina and Hal. She did that here too with the both of you, remember that? You did enjoy that."

The Reverend looked to Hal and Tina and Blane. "Shall I say

you enjoyed spending time baking cookies with your grandmother?"

"Sure," Tina replied easily. "The cookies were good."

Philynda is bound in several blankets, the corner of the blankets knotted and secured with rope. Her body lies in the homemade grave. Lime dusts the hole in the ground, the old blankets
and Philynda herself. Dean pulled back the blankets and tossed
several cupsful of lime over the dog before the boys wrapped
her up.

Kyle, Blane, Tom, Hal, Tina, Sandy and Dean stand by the
gravesite. Hal picks up a spade, shoveling dirt in on Philynda's
body. Dean winces at the sound of the heavy ground falling
against the dog's side. "She was a good dog," he says.

"She was a good dog," Sandy repeats.

"She grew up right along with us," Kyle says.

"I remember when she was as big as me when we first got
her," Tina says.

"I remember the night Dad brought her home," Hal says.

Tom takes the shovel from Hal, scraping dirt off the pile and
into the grave. Kyle moves alongside him, lifting another shovel,
pitching it into the pile of dirt and tossing it down on the family
pet. Blane stares down in the hole, Philynda's body almost completely covered. "I'll miss her," he says.

"She was a part of this family," Dean says, remembering for
whom he named Philynda, *Phil* after his father, *Lynda* after his
mother. "She was getting old," Dean says. "Almost ten years.
Seventy in dog ages."

The family walked through Lilly's funeral ceremony with little
sentiment. When Sandy first told the family of the news of Lilly's
death, she concluded with, "I suppose this is for the best for
her. She wasn't a happy woman. She had a pretty lonely life."
Standing at the gravesite, Lilly buried in a plot alongside her
brother, mother and father, Sandy felt no sadness, only relief,
as if she had been holding her breath underwater for forty-
seven years and could only now breathe freely. "I feel guilty

over thinking it," Sandy told Dean late last night, "but I don't think I'm going to miss her."

"You can't choose your parents," Dean responded, then added quietly, "but I do miss my parents. They died so long ago."

"That's probably why you love them," Sandy responded. "Maybe in twenty years I'll miss my mother too."

The grave is now two-thirds full.

"Pack it in good," Dean says. He turns to Sandy. "Remember when your mother ruined all my suits?"

"My mother always did get her revenge. On us for putting her in the home. On my father by keeping me from him." Sandy stops, remembering the hours she spent trapped with her mother in the house after the kids and Dean were gone for the day. Trapped in the house with Lilly or trapped in the car with Lilly or trapped in a mall or a restaurant— With Terry and Lilly after shopping at Bonwit's on Boylston Street, Lilly opening her purse, reaching over, picking up the little bowl of sugar packets and dumping them all in and—

"She made quite an impact on this family," Dean says with a nod.

"Like a dent," Sandy says. "God, I'm glad she's gone."

Dean looks to Sandy, taken aback by her gross anger, displaying her fury toward Lilly in front of the kids. Kyle and Tom stop shoveling dirt into the grave. All the children, Kyle, Blane, Tom, Hal and Tina, watch Sandy closely, surprised by their mother's ridicule of Lilly after having coerced them into saying nice things about her yesterday morning.

Sandy folds her arms across her chest.

Dean moves to take Sandy's shoulders but she pushes him back. "I can't help it if I hated her," she says to the family, "I can't help that but I do. I think we all do. She was a lousy mother. A lousy person. *There.* It's been said." Sandy picks up Kyle's abandoned shovel, using its back side to pack the dirt firmly into the ground. "It's easier to love a dog than a parent."

1 9 8 3

W A T C H I N G old home movies, Sandy is struck with the notion of three Wallace families. There is the Wallace family on the screen. Sandy, Dean, Kyle, Blane and Tom. There is the Wallace family watching the home movies. Sandy, Dean, Hal and Tina. And there is the Wallace family between these two poles, the larger family that existed between these two families and exists again every so often on holidays and family ski vacations. Sandy finds it peculiar that only after having been married for twenty-nine years have Dean and she created their ideal family, their nuclear family of a husband, wife, son and daughter, the way they had originally planned it all those years ago when they were young and childless.

Kyle is seven years old, Blane is five and Tom is four. They swing from the branches of the oak tree on the front lawn of the house in Wayland. Sandy, thirty-one years old and very pregnant with Hal, walks up to the tree, taking Tom in her arms, lifting him away from the tree and swinging him through the air. Sandy wears a kelly green skirt, a sleeveless white blouse and blue tennis shoes, no socks. Her hair is cut in a flip. She drops Tom to the ground and he runs off, out of the camera frame. The screen goes white.

"Okay, Tina, the lights." Dean shuts off the projector and the room is momentarily black until Tina switches on the lamp by the sofa. Dean rewinds the reel the family's just seen. "That's what we were like before you two were born," Dean says. He sits in a chair by the projector; opposite him, at the far end of the room, stands the movie screen, in front of the love seat. "That's what you were all like back then?" Hal asks. "Always laughing and playing on the lawn?"

"I think the house we live in now is better," Tina comments.

"You can't even remember that house," Sandy says.

"Duh, Mom, I just saw it in the movie."

"I remember," Hal says. "And Tina's right. This one is better."

"Tina, the lights, please." Dean switches on the projector. The lights go out. The screen flickers with the image of Sandy, Kyle, Blane and Tom walking through the gates of a petting farm. Tom carries a plastic walkie-talkie, holding it up to his face. Kyle and Blane wear identical red-and-yellow-striped jerseys and blue jean shorts. "The Wayland house was nice," Dean says. "We could use a house that size now, now that most of you kids have grown." Never mind the spare rooms in the house, but Dean can't quite believe how much of his salary he's able to save now that Kyle, Blane and Tom are out on their own, supporting themselves. Kyle earning a great salary as a bond trader on Wall Street. Blane, living in Chicago, making his way through graduate school in psychology by working as a research assistant and teaching undergraduate intro psychology courses. He even took out his own student loan to make up the difference between financial aid money and tuition costs.

"I'd be happy to pay for it," Dean volunteered, but his son would have none of it. "I want to do it myself," Blane said and Dean had never been more proud of his son.

Even Tom, still working as a waiter, earns his own living. Dean and Sandy can't help but be concerned for his future. Tom has no desire to attend college but his parents can't complain so long as he's happy with his life. Dean's just thankful having him, as well as his two older brothers, off his payroll; much easier having his kids around when they're not regarding him as a billfold.

A farmhand holds a sheep and Kyle and Blane reach their

hands out tentatively, lightly stroking the animal's wool with their fingertips. Tom hovers back by Sandy, clinging to the hem of her pale pink cotton maternity dress, the walkie-talkie antenna poking her in the calf. "See what your older brothers were like then?" Dean asks. "And now they're all grown and independent. I'm very proud of all of them. Of all of you. See that?" He points to the screen where Sandy is pouring breadcrumbs from a brown paper bag into the outstretched palms of her three boys. Kyle, Blane and Tom sprinkle the crumbs through a wire mesh fence where a group of brown ducks wait.

"Look at that," Dean says. "How cute they all were."

"We see, Dean, we see," Sandy says. "We're all sitting right here with you." Sandy can't quite believe how perfect a housewife she was in the sixties. Perfectly pretty and nice. The perfect accessory to her husband the businessman, completing and complementing his life. When the screen shows a picture of her sitting on a fallen tree, legs crossed at the ankles, smiling and waving with her huge belly and utter sincerity, Sandy considers stealing all these films later this evening while Dean sleeps. Stealing these old 16mm films, burning them and erasing the evidence that she once sincerely strived and succeeded at being a perfectly pathetic little homemaker.

"God, Mom, you looked like such a dork," Tina says. "You got happy over anything." And Sandy should be offended by her daughter's remark but is actually thankful Tina looks down on who her mother was, glad her daughter won't turn out the same way.

"We've always been a happy family," Dean says.

"If we're all so happy, why won't Blane ever come home?" Hal asks, "if we're all so happy and everything?"

"He's just very busy in school," Dean replies without a thought. "You'll see yourself when you're in college."

"I hope not," Hal answers and he watches the small reel of film spin on the projector, watching his father's face as Dean watches these scenes of a family that no longer exists. This is an insight into his father's mind, Hal believes. This is the way

Dean Wallace views his life and these are the moments he has selected for his family to remember. Other events, the events Dean Wallace hasn't recorded either in film or photo, can be forgotten, best left unrecollected in the minds of his children. Life before Hal and Tina were born appears as simple, warm, uncomplicated—nothing short of splendid. But then, if life before Hal and Tina was so utterly perfect, what then accounts for the resulting chaos that ensued? His and Tina's births? Hal thinks not. Hal hypothesizes that between the reels of footage his father projects, there lives another family. A family of Sandy, Dean, Kyle, Blane and Tom that appeared calm on the surface, as calm as a dormant volcano, but underneath that placid exterior, deep at its core . . . "So why aren't there any home movies with Tina and me in them?" Hal asks. "Why didn't you take any with us?"

"Yeah," Tina pipes in. "Didn't we matter as much as them?"

"Because if there aren't any of us," Hal says, "as I'm sure there aren't because I've never seen any before, Tina and I want to go out for ice cream."

Sandy defers to Dean, finds Hal and Tina's relationship interesting in that they are constantly backing each other up, whereas the older boys were always competing with one another. And although Hal and Tina are hardly easily disciplined, have foul mouths and are always ready with a verbal jab to throw at their parents, they're certainly not the trouble Tom was, and for that Sandy is very thankful.

Tom, Blane and Kyle sit in the back of a large red wagon. A hay ride and the boys bury themselves up to their chins in the straw. The wagon pulls them off, down a path between a cow pasture and a corn field.

"The reason there are no films of either you or Tina," Dean explains patiently, "is that on the day I was bringing Mommy home with you from the hospital, as we walked up the front steps, your mother was holding you in her arms, Hal, and that little boy you see milking the cow up there," Dean points to a picture of Tom on the screen, "took the camera and tried to film us coming up the walkway from his bedroom window.

Unfortunately, his little hands slipped and he dropped the camera onto the front steps, smashing it to bits." Dean smiles at Hal, his face half lit by the light from the projector. "Just be thankful he didn't drop it when your mother carried you under the window, otherwise you might not be here today."

"Or he'd be retarded," Tina jokes and Hal laughs, standing. "So there aren't any of us then. Let's go, loser."

Tina stands, slipping her bare feet into the Topsiders by the coffee table, "We're outta here," and they walk from the room, Hal stopping momentarily at the door.

"We'll be taking your car, Dad."

"This is your family, for God's sake. Now sit down and watch these with your mother and me," Dean pleads.

"We're not even in them, Dad," Tina moans, then, taking a different tack, "and anyway, this only became my family when I was born. Before that how can it be if I wasn't here? Okay? We're outta here." She leaves.

"I'm taking your car, right?" Hal says.

"I'd rather you stayed," Dean replies.

"But we're not," Hal states.

Dean shuts his eyes, waving his son off. "Fine, go. Do you want us to wait and watch the rest tomorrow?"

"I grew up with them," Hal says. "I don't need to see the years I was fortunate enough to have missed." He leaves.

"You don't mean that," Dean calls after his number four son. Silence in the room but for the projector's soft whir. Dean reaches over and shuts down the film. The room is black.

"We can still watch them even if they're not here, Dean," Sandy says, lying across the couch, her head against the armrest.

"Do you really want to?" he asks. He had planned on this being a family thing.

"I haven't left with them, have I?"

The film reappears, the world of the Wallaces from 1966 flashing before Sandy's and Dean's eyes in 1983. The kids and Sandy sit at a picnic table. Blane and Kyle eat Hoodsie cups, half chocolate, half vanilla. Sandy gently lifts the top off Tom's ice cream cup, handing him the treat he eats with a small, flat wooden spoon.

"We have been a happy family all these years, from beginning to the present." Dean says this with certainty, as if there were nothing he could be more sure of, and Sandy, watching the scene before her, cannot deny that there have been many happy moments in her life with Dean. These boring films, if nothing else, are evidence of that. The farm visit ends, the film runs through, and the screen shines white across their faces.

"Why is it that you have such a short memory for the bad and such a long memory for the good, whereas I have such a long one for the bad and a short one for the good? Why is that?" Sandy stares at the blank screen, not expecting any answer, only wanting to think through her own thoughts, but Dean comes over to her, stroking hair back from her eyes, touching a finger to the tip of her nose.

"That's why you need me," he says, and Sandy can't quite believe it but he's right.

1984

T H E Salvation Army is sending a truck over this coming Tuesday to pick up the Wallace family's unwanted belongings. Sandy, Dean, Hal and Tina wear T-shirts and shorts as they spend Labor Day weekend cleaning the house of accumulated articles from over the years. Already the basement is packed with stuff to be taken away. Lilly's clothes, furniture and knick-knack collections, the children's games, stuffed animals and Fisher-Price toys they've long outgrown, bicycles, sleds and archery and boccie ball sets. The four Wallace family members sort through personal items, deciding what is necessary to keep for either practical or sentimental reasons.

Hal stacks comic books, collected by both him and Blane, in his closet, refusing to give them away, sure they will be worth something in years to come despite their wrinkles and torn covers. Thousands of baseball cards, collected by both him and Tom, are bound with wide elastic bands, separated by year, classified according to team. These are kept in plastic milk carton crates in a corner of the closet. So far the only thing he's come across to donate is a child's night table lamp in the shape of a walrus.

Tina fares better, discarding clothes that actually fit her, clothes in perfect condition. She hopes that by sacrificing enough to the collection agency and exhibiting her generosity, she'll be rewarded with a new wardrobe. Two garbage bagsful of pastel-colored sweaters, corduroys and cotton blouses sit on the floor of her room alongside a short pile of Sesame Street albums found lining the bottom "trash drawer" of her large dresser.

Sandy and Dean, having given up the prospect of going through Kyle's, Blane's and Tom's rooms for fear they'd give away some relic the boys treasure, resigned themselves to doing their own room. The couple sit cross-legged on the floors of their separate walk-in closets sorting through worn-out shoes, out-of-style garments and boxes of personal effects.

"I don't really want to abandon any of these things," Dean calls to Sandy as he examines a large clam shell painted with a barn on its inside. "I think we have some pretty interesting stuff here we should keep." He stands, walks from his closet and enters Sandy's. "See this?" He holds up the shell.

Sandy tosses a pair of Dr. Scholl's sandals in the give-away pile, then scrutinizes the object in Dean's hand. She has absolutely no idea where it came from. "That shell?" Sandy asks. "Probably from the Cape sometime." She picks up a pair of pink high-heeled shoes, doesn't remember ever wearing them, wonders if perhaps she borrowed them from a friend and never gave them back, wonders if maybe a guest left them in the house and never bothered to reclaim them. The pink shoes are dismissed to the give-away pile.

"But when did we buy it? What was the occasion?" Dean's curiosity is piqued by the appearance of this mysterious shell.

"Please, just pack it in a box. We can't puzzle over every little thing we come across."

"But I like this shell. It's interesting—think of it—why paint a barn on a shell?"

"Then keep it." The summer heat is too oppressive to want to converse. Sandy opens another shoebox. No shoes in it, the box is empty and Sandy places it by her side.

"Do you think one of the kids gave it to us?"

"I don't remember."

"I wouldn't want to throw it out if one of the kids gave it to us. It wouldn't be right."

Sandy extends a hand. "Here, let me look at it." She takes the shell from Dean, searching the design for a possible clue, a mark of recognition informing them of when it was bought. None is evident. Sandy vaguely remembers her mother giving Dean a shell for a birthday one year. This could be that shell. She hands it to Dean. "My mother gave it to you for a birthday. So are you going to keep it?"

Dean stares at the brown barn in the field of yellow grass. He doesn't recall receiving it from Lilly, but he accepts Sandy's reply as truth and returns to his closet, sitting, deciding whether to get rid of it. The painting is ugly, he admits, crude and sloppily done, not even simple enough to have the charm of a child's handiwork. His mother-in-law had terrible taste; he hopes she didn't spend more than a few dollars on this gift although he is sure she did. Lilly always was one to be taken advantage of when shopping. Dean suspects she probably noticed he never put the shell on display in either the Cape or Concord house, that being the kind of thing Lilly tended to look out for. He feels a pang of guilt about that, about not appreciating the gift more, and considers keeping the shell, as if by valuing it in the present, his past sin of thanklessness will be forgiven. "Did your mother pick this up in a tourist trap, you think?"

"Most likely."

"I can't say it's very pretty." Dean smiles at the sad, pathetic shell.

"I never claimed she had good taste."

"You couldn't say that, no."

Sandy removes the lid from a box containing the kids' letters and postcards from camp.

Dean places the shell in the garbage pile, not even giving it the distinction of ending up in another person's home via the Salvation Army. The thought of some poor soul spending money on Lilly's shell and displaying it prominently in his home depresses Dean. If it's too ugly for the Wallaces, it should be too ugly for anyone.

Sandy counts the letters. Kyle wrote the most, closely followed by Hal and Blane, then Tina, and finally Tom, who only wrote a total of two for each of the three summers he spent away. She selects one—one of Blane's—and reads:

> Dear Mom and Dad,
> I like it here. I do tennis and swimming and am learning to water ski. It is like snow skiing but they do it on water and with waves instead of hills or moguls. The food is good and we drink a lot of bug juice. Next week we do our bunk sign and ours will be in the shape of a soda bottle with our names on it. Signed, Blane Wallace

Not exactly the warmest letter Sandy's ever received. She carefully folds the creased paper back into its envelope, returning it to the box. She notes that Blane hasn't exactly changed all that much since this letter was written. Once friendly yet distant, he is now simply distant. Blane refused to return home for Hal's high school graduation this past spring and they haven't heard from him since. *Signed, Blane Wallace,* he wrote on every letter he wrote from camp. The other children—Tom included, however seldom he may have written—closed their letters with *love,* but not Blane. Blane *Wallace,* as if they wouldn't have remembered their son otherwise.

A shadow falls on Sandy, blocking the overhead light, and she looks up to see Hal standing in the closet doorway. "This is a real fun way to spend my last weekend before going to college, you guys. Can't you do this next weekend after I'm gone?"

"We're doing it *now,"* Dean contends. "Your mother and I shouldn't have to do this ourselves. It's already hard enough trying to decide what to do with the boys' stuff."

"Would you like us to decide for you what to keep or throw away?" Sandy asks, backing up her husband.

"Why can't we just keep everything?" Hal persists in his argument. "It's not as if you don't have the room. Why does it matter? Are you going to be selling the house soon?"

"Can't you do what we ask without making a fuss?" Dean asks.

"No."

"Well, then keep it to yourself. And could you please reach up to that shelf," Sandy says, "just take those and put them on the bed."

Hal lifts a number of assorted-size boxes from the uppermost shelf in Sandy's closet and does as he was told. "Is this fine?"

"Thank you." Sandy stands, walking to the back wall of the closet, looking over her dresses from decades past, laughing to herself at the ancient styles. Dean rakes through sport shirts, relegating those with yellowed armpits, torn pockets or more than two buttons missing to the Salvation Army.

Tina enters. "I'm done." She eyes the items on the bed, a nice assortment of dress, scarf and hatboxes. Hal lies on his back, spread out across the bed, resting before his parents order him to do something more, which he is sure will be shortly.

Tina opens a dress box, yanking out a long, floor-length black-beaded gown. "Why are you getting rid of this?" she asks. "If you don't want it, I'll take it for a costume."

"Maybe I'm not getting rid of it," Sandy answers from the closet, not bothering to see the article Tina asks about. "And please don't go through my things before I have."

Dean walks from the closet carrying an armload of shirts. "Grab that pile of shoes off the floor in there," he directs Hal. "Let's make a run to the basement."

"I'm on break," Hal mutters, refusing to budge an inch, shutting his eyes.

Dean glances at him, gives up and heads downstairs. Tina opens a hatbox, lifting a white straw hat tied with a black ribbon. Plastic cherries decorate the brim. "Nice choice, Mom." She puts it on. "Look at this." She taps Hal on the foot and he sits. Tina swivels her hips and marches around the room, impersonating her mother. "And don't forget to clean the kitchen after yourselves. I don't want to have to do it when I get home from work."

"That is not how I sound," Sandy informs her children.

"Is so."

"That is how you sound."

Tina stares in the mirror, arranging the hat and untangling the string of cherries. Hal opens a second hatbox, this one decorated on the outside with a pattern of yellow roses. He looks in, staring at the large book lying facedown in the circular box. He turns it over. *The Joy of Sex,* the title reads.

Hal flips the book front-side down, hiding the cover, and he folds the back cover open, quickly skimming through the pages from index to table of contents. Sketches in black-and-white and watercolors show a hippie couple engaged in sex in every way possible. Oriental etchings decorate other pages, depicting a man and a woman fornicating, the man with a huge phallus, the woman with her legs wide. Hal reads section headings in bold print: Quickies, Fellatio, Al Fresco. The book itself doesn't disturb him, he's seen it many times before, having glanced at it in bookstores; however, the fact that *his parents* have the book is shocking. He never denied the fact that they probably had sex, but he never thought they'd need a manual to do it.

Tina puts the cherry bonnet away and leans over Hal's shoulder inspecting his discovery. "What the hell is that?"

"Just keep quiet," he tells her and he shuts the book, closing the box lid.

Tina grabs at it. "Let me see it."

"We'll look at it when they've gone out," Hal tells her. "Now forget about it."

Tina keeps her hands on the box. "But what if they decide to give it away?"

"You don't give books like this to the Salvation Army, idiot," Hal explains. "What are you? Stupid?"

Tina sees Hal's point. "Okay, but make sure you watch to see where they put it." She releases her grip on the box and Hal places it on the bed, as it was.

"Hal, will you come down here and help me?" Dean calls from the kitchen.

"Can't we do it later?" Hal complains. "I'm tired."

"*Goddamnit, Hal!*"

And Hal gets off the bed, going downstairs to appease his father.

Tina takes *The Joy of Sex* from the hatbox, opening it across her lap, carefully scrutinizing the details of the woman giving the man a handjob. She's never seen this before, has surely never done this before, and is curious as well as intrigued in understanding how to perform the act correctly if ever the situation presents itself.

"I hope you're not going through my things." Sandy's back is to Tina. She sifts through a small wardrobe case of gloves in leather, woolen and lace varieties, some antique and some relatively new. Sandy checks for holes and broken seams.

Tina ignores her mother, doesn't care if she finds her reading this book. After all, Tina thinks, who's actually going to be the one to be embarrassed? Tina holds her hand up, fixing its position to match that of the woman's in the picture who grips the base of the man's cock.

Dean enters the room and Tina is startled, her hand still poised in mid-air. She drops the book in the hatbox and stands.

"What was that?" Dean asks her. "Is it something we're keeping?"

Tina shrugs. "I don't know, just some book of Mom's."

Sandy calls to Dean, "Is she still going through my things?"

"Everything's fine," Dean tells Sandy and he turns to Tina. "Why don't you go help Hal order things in the basement?" Tina says nothing, walking past her father and out of the room, hoping her parents don't move the book to a new spot in a different box.

Dean approaches the bed, interested in the book Tina hid. He lifts it from the yellow-rose-covered box, holding it up to chest level.

"Some of the things here might be valuable," Sandy mentions, examining a gold brooch pinned to a scarf. "We might want to have them appraised."

Dean stares at the white glossy cover, the small cursive red letters printed in its center. *The Joy of Sex,* he reads and his hands clutch the book firmly. He has absolutely no desire to peruse it, has a very good idea what's inside this one-time best-selling "cookbook of love."

Sandy and sex. Sandy and *The Joy of* sex. Dean cannot fathom how the relation came to be. Dean cannot fathom *when* the relation came to be and he lies in bed wondering about Sandy's sex life or the lack of it. Not Sex *and* Sandy, but Sex *with* Sandy— that is the topic that occupies his thoughts—where did he go wrong in his sex *with* Sandy to drive her to buy this book? Has he failed her in bed? How long ago was it? Has this book helped or does she still remain—if the existence of this book indicates that she once was—unhappy?

Dean retired to the bedroom early, leaving Sandy watching TV with Hal and Tina. He obsesses. He lies under the thin cotton sheet wearing a pair of boxers and nothing more. The head-board's reading light is on and he stares at the door to his wife's closet, the shadow of his body thrown up against it. Dean said nothing to Sandy concerning the book. He set it in the hatbox and waited to see what she would decide to do with it. Would it be kept or given to the needy? Or is *she* the needy one in the case of this book? However, Sandy never got around to inspecting the boxes Hal had carried out to the bed; late this afternoon they were returned to their spot high on the closet shelf.

Dean rises from the bed, sweat running down his back, stain-ing a V at the top of his shorts. He refuses to purchase air conditioners for the Concord house. Since the family spends the majority of the summer months on the Cape, he sees no point in it, and the room swelters in the early September heat. Dean enters the closet, reaching into the yellow-flowered hatbox and taking the book in hand. He returns to the bed, sitting back against the headboard, propping the hard cover against his bent knees.

Dean stares at a page, scrutinizing the couple's stance, the woman astride the man in the dominant position. Dean remembers when Sandy began taking this position, when Sandy began initiating new sexual practices into their old routine, and, as Dean turns more and more pages of the book, he observes more and more activities that Sandy has brought into their bed. He has seen *Sandy* do what this woman is doing. He has seen *Sandy* take his hands and position them on her body in such a manner. He has heard *Sandy* whisper into his ear what she wants him to do to her. And Dean had always believed she was acting spontaneously, out of the throes of passion, but now he sees she calculated it, planned these new exploits to better please herself. And although he is annoyed that she has been consciously working on their bedroom encounters, he, too, has become more excited at the prospect of engaging in sex with his wife. Their sex life *has* never been better and it roils him to know his wife manipulated it out of him through the help of a guidebook; he feels duped. This has been going on for several years and Dean can only wonder how often Sandy referred to this book when she became dissatisfied with his own sexual tactics.

Dean hears his wife's footsteps on the stairs and quickly runs to the closet, placing the book in the hatbox and closing the closet door.

Sandy enters, immediately taking off her robe and draping it over the chair before the vanity. Dean stands before the closet door in his boxers, his arms folded across his bare chest. Sandy looks at him, puzzled. "What's the matter?"

"Sit down. I think we have to have a talk."

"A talk about what?"

"Sit."

Sandy sits at the foot of the bed, crossing her legs, folding her arms across her chest as Dean has. "I'm ready."

Dean opens the closet, walks in and lifts the hatbox from its spot on the top shelf, carrying it to his wife. "Do you know what's in here?"

Sandy stares at the hatbox. "A hat, I suppose."

Dean places the box on the floor between them, at Sandy's

feet. "There is a book in this hatbox," Dean says stiffly. "A *book.*"

Sandy uncrosses her legs, unfolds her arms, suddenly remembering the book placed in the hatbox long ago, over a decade past, taken out occasionally for a number of years but eventually abandoned and forgotten altogether, and Sandy, rather than act the role of the guilty housewife, decides to feign a casual air about the whole thing. She smiles, placing her hands flat atop the box's lid. "Yes, it's a book. I bought it years ago and then forgot about it. Is that a problem?" Having never once had a discussion concerning sex with her husband, she has no idea what to expect and she presses her hands tightly against the box's sides to keep from trembling. She recrosses her legs, lifting the box and balancing it atop a knee.

Dean stares hard at his wife. "I looked in that book. I saw what was in there."

"So?" Sandy holds her smile, attempting to keep this light.

Dean thinks back to last week. Last week Sandy positioned her hips above his face, wanting him to lick her but Dean resisted, touching her with his fingers instead. He takes the box from his wife. "The book goes. *Tomorrow.* I'll drop it off in a dumpster on my way to work. That will be the end of it." He opens his closet door, setting the box down by his shoe tree, then closing the door.

Sandy stands. "That's fine. I haven't looked at it in years anyway." She heads into the bathroom, closing the door, securing the lock and twisting on the hot and cold knobs at the sink, letting the sound of rushing water fill her ears.

Dean slides back under the covers, his mission accomplished—no more book and no more sex outside of their established routine of Saturdays at nine-thirty A.M. Through keeping to the ritual, there will be no more surprises, each will know what they are expected to do and each will know what they are bound to receive in return—and Dean switches off the light, shutting his eyes, glad to feel that he's put a halt to his wife's practices before they progressed any further, glad he nipped this problem in the bud.

■

The hostess at Moriarty's steak house seats Richard Myers, Jim
Thorne, Andrea Peakes and Kyle Wallace at a circular table in
the corner of the main dining room. Kyle flew up to Boston to
be interviewed by Lagenbach, Inc., an investment banking firm
that's trying to steal him away from his present position in New
York. Kyle, although not actively seeking new employment, chose
to scope out the offer, if not for now, then possibly for the future.
He saw no sense in thumbing his nose at Lagenbach when he
may need these people at a later date. So, after a tour of the
firm's downtown Boston facilities and a meeting with several
key personnel, the trio of Richard, Jim and Andrea whisked their
prospect off to the best steak house in Boston for an informal
chat; a quick dinner before Kyle must fly south on the nine
o'clock shuttle.

Kyle sits in the corner seat, facing into the dining room, facing
Richard Myers, one of the many senior vice presidents at Lagenbach. To Kyle's right sits Andrea Peakes, a vice president in
the bond department, and at Kyle's left is Jim Thorne, Andrea's
assistant. The four businesspeople sip drinks carried over from
the bar. Glenlivets on the rocks. The members of the circle lift
their drinks in a toast to good health, exposing Rolex watches
on each of their left wrists.

Richard signals the waiter.

"May I take your order?" the waiter asks. The voice registers
in Kyle's memory.

"Kyle," Richard says, and Kyle looks up from the menu. The
waiter is Tom, his brother. The Wallace brothers' eyes meet for
an instant, a split second, just enough to signify joint recognition
of the situation. Tom's about to speak, to say hello to his brother,
but Kyle's eyes return to the menu. Tom glances down at the
check pad in his hand. Kyle hides his face in the menu, isn't
sure whether he should acknowledge his waiter brother—certainly doesn't *want* to acknowledge his waiter brother—and
then he realizes that at this moment he can't. Now that he's

postponed his recognition of Tom, identifying him at this point would appear foolish. The Lagenbach people would most surely find Kyle lacking, although lacking in *what* Kyle cannot ascertain. "Do you need a minute, sir?" Tom asks. He's opted for anonymity, not bothering to force his brother into performing awkward introductions with his business friends. He has a good idea of exactly what thoughts are running through his eldest brother's mind and Tom hopes that by playing it very cool, he'll be able to keep Kyle on edge, fearful. All Tom would have to do at any time during the meal is admit that he is Kyle's brother, throwing a wrench in Bond Trader Wallace's carefully studied demeanor.

"Yes, I'll take the filet mignon. Well done. Make sure it's *well*, please. A side of asparagus in lemon butter for the table. Is that fine with everyone?" A collective nod from the group. Kyle has won them over, has taken command and won, and he proceeds. "Good. Then how about adding a hefty portion of the browns as well. *Well browned*, please." Kyle taps the rim of his drinking glass with the tip of a forefinger. "And another scotch on the rocks. Glenlivet." Kyle looks his brother in the eyes while ordering, aware that strong eye contact is something the Lagenbach people search for in leader material.

Tom's eyes hold Kyle's gaze with equal intensity. "Anything to start off with?"

"What do you recommend?" Kyle asks, demonstrating to the Lagenbach people that he can both command a situation as well as leave himself open for suggestions.

"We have a special appetizer of a giant mushroom sautéed in olive oil and laid over with fresh crabmeat. I recommend it." Tom knows Kyle hates crabmeat, wonders if his brother will take the bait to impress his business associates.

"Sounds great," Kyle says, unfazed, and he hands Tom the menu. Tom folds it under an arm and resumes taking the table's order, giving them his best servile, docile manner.

"What a pretentious asshole," Tom tells Derek, a fellow waiter at Moriarty's. "I should go out there and tell them about when *he* used to wait on *me* at Friendly's. He was a *peon,* fry oil in his hair, dried ice cream coating his forearms. I used to watch him cram his fingers in the bottom of tall, fudge-filled sundae glasses just to get out a dime tip. And he's sitting there like such a fucking blowhard."

"Do you want me to switch tables with you?" Derek asks. "I'll give you number five. Same number of people, also out on business."

Tom won't even consider it. "No, I want to keep them. I enjoy making eye contact with him, making him uneasy."

Mary, the assistant chef, approaches Tom. "Come on, soldiers, get with it already. We're not serving the crabmeat app tonight."

"Don't you have enough left over to make *one?*" Tom pleads.

Mary huffs. "Swell. *One.* But don't screw up again." She walks off to dig through yesterday's leftovers in the refrigerator.

Tom makes his way out front to the bar, placing the order for the table's second round of drinks. "Four Glenlivets on the rocks, thanks." He leans on the brass railing, pulling at the black tie around his neck, stuffing its tail in the gap between the third and fourth buttons of his heavily starched white shirt. He watches his brother talk, gesturing, waving his arms in excitement about some financial matter. How Tom would love to go up to the table and kill his brother, lop that rich asshole's head off with a meat cleaver from the kitchen. Such a big-shot-shit asshole. Tom is sure he could flatten Kyle in a fight situation, would love to take him out right here in front of his friends, but it would cost Tom his job, and Tom knows, above all else, he cannot afford to lose his job no matter how low it makes him feel at this particular moment. Yes, Derek did propose a table switch, but switching tables would only serve to prove Kyle had won, that Tom was ashamed of himself and had to hide from his brother. Kyle, a twenty-five-year-old bond trader earning one hundred and fifty thousand a year, and Tom, three years younger, a steakhouse waiter earning approximately twenty percent of that including tips.

Tom carries the drinks to the table, placing the fresh glasses down, then removing the old.

"Which town is your family from?" Richard asks Kyle. Tom plucks a drink stirrer from the table, placing it on the tray.

"Concord. A beautiful town." Kyle lifts his empty glass to Tom and Tom takes it, dispensing the new drink into Kyle's hand.

"I like Concord," Richard says. "My wife and I almost bought there but we settled in Lincoln instead."

"Lincoln's great," Kyle says. "We had a good rivalry going with Lincoln's football team."

Richard nods, pulling at his chin. "That's right. Of course."

"Do you play any sports?" Andrea asks.

Tom finishes serving the round. Kyle speaks, "I play a bit of—"

"Can I get you something more?" Tom asks, deliberately interrupting.

The conversation stops. The table looks to Tom. "I think we're all set," Richard says with a smile, and he turns to Kyle. "I like this restaurant. Very careful, attentive service. They treat you well."

And Kyle can only agree.

Kyle wishes he could pay the bill, but being the guest of Lagenbach, Richard, the senior employee, picks up the tab. Kyle wishes he could have picked it up, putting it on his Amex, leaving his brother zero dollars and zero cents in tip.

The crabmeat appetizer was terrible. Much too lemony-tasting, it puckered Kyle's lips. The steak, charred on the outside, was blood red on the inside—not the well he had ordered. Kyle sent Tom back to the kitchen *twice* before the steak was prepared correctly. "Sorry about that, sir," Tom politely replied each time he returned Kyle's plate to the kitchen, and Kyle was left eating nothing while Andrea, Jim and Richard sliced their steaks with zeal, all "cooked to perfection," they told Tom. Kyle waited, smiling with good charm as his dinner companions ate, insisting that they do so while fuming underneath at the inherent hostility of his brother's behavior.

"Can't blame the waiter when it's the cook who errs," Richard said good-naturedly to Tom the second time Kyle had the filet mignon sent back. If Kyle hadn't emphasized he wanted the steak well done, that would have been one thing, at least then there would be no issue at hand, but Kyle *did* order the steak well done. It would have cheapened him to accept it rare—or even *medium*—the Lagenbach people observing him caving in, giving up and eating the pink meat when they knew—*they heard him say*—he wanted it brown. The Lagenbach people would most surely think Kyle was the kind of guy who backed down from confrontation, settled for mediocrity, for second best. And Kyle couldn't let them think that. He persevered, and in the end he won, finally receiving the well-done steak. He ate it with a broad grin, giving his heartfelt thanks to the waiter for his patience, telling his comrades that the wait was worth it, the steak was great.

"I'm sorry it wasn't served correctly the first time," Tom replied meekly. "I'm sure it will never happen again."

"I'm sure it won't," Kyle said graciously. "Mistakes do occur."

Richard fills in the charge card slip and tears out the customer receipt. Kyle eyes the number under the tip heading. Seventy dollars. More than twenty-five percent of the bill including bar tab and tax. Kyle feels like standing up, pointing at Tom, making a dramatic scene: "He's my brother. He intentionally ruined my meal to make me look bad in front of you. He's jealous of my good life. Look at him. He's a waiter. A *waiter,* for God's sake. And he intentionally ruined my meal." But all Kyle does is take his overcoat from the hat check girl, hand her a dollar and head out into the night with the Lagenbach people.

Tom, finished with his work shift, heads into the kitchen, waving his night's winnings. "My brother must have been shitting bricks the entire dinner."

"He'll probably kill you next time he sees you," Rachel, a waitress, points out. "You made him look like an idiot. What was he here for anyhow?"

"Looked like a business thing."

"Christ, if I was him I'd have killed you. You deserved it."

"It's his own fault," Tom argues. "He should have said I'm his brother instead of hiding it. It was his place to do so. He treats me like I'm shit, I'll treat him the same."

Rachel cocks her head to the side. "What a fucking mature attitude," and she carries a tray of salads out front.

Tom counts out seventy dollars—three twenties and a ten. He considers what Rachel said. No, his behavior definitely wasn't mature, however humiliating Kyle was perhaps necessary. Did it get Tom something more that he needed? Yes, seventy dollars, Tom thinks quickly, but then even Tom grants that the tip was an entirely separate matter. He saw the Amex slip. It wasn't on Kyle's card. The middle-aged guy at the table paid it. So, *what*— if anything—*did* Tom's humiliation of Kyle accomplish? Tom lists the answers: 1) It made Kyle uneasy, 2) It gave Tom a sense of power over his older brother, and 3) It was fun.

On the other side, Tom poses, what then did it accomplish for Kyle?

Tom picks at a plate of steamed vegetables with his fingers, eating a slice of zucchini. He refuses to answer the question he asks of himself, feels the response inside him, but refuses to bring it into his consciousness. The bad feeling hovers over him, casting a cloud of gloom over the seventy-dollar tip. Tom can't quite believe he's tearing himself up over this small incident. It was a joke, that's all it was. Fuck Kyle if he can't take a joke.

Tom enters the manager's office, selecting his time card and punching out on the clock. Kyle earns one hundred fifty thousand dollars a year including bonus money, and Tom, on an hourly clock, is feeling increasingly shitty for treating his snotty rich brother poorly, possibly even costing Kyle a big business deal, Tom guesses.

He stares at the time clock, listening to the minute hand click as each sixty seconds passes and Tom crumples the tip money into a ball, shoving it deep in a pocket and holding it there. Even when he wins, he loses, and Tom hears a minute pass.

1985

Dear Blane,

Receiving a letter from me may be a surprise, but I have been wanting to communicate with you for a while and you have ceased to return messages left on your machine and I am no longer sure what to think. It hurts me very deeply when I think that you don't care to speak to your father and me, so I'm writing this letter having many things to tell you, but no way to reach you. I'm not sure what has happened that you've drawn the curtains, as it were, on our relationship and cannot be with the family. Hopefully this letter can be a first step toward rectifying the situation.

How long has it been since you've come home? How long has it been since we communicated? That, too, has been quite a while. It was just before you had completed work on a paper for school. You sounded hurried, busy and eager to end our conversation. I assumed that was because you were under pressure to get your paper done. Maybe I was wrong. I expect I wanted to believe it wasn't me, or Dad and I, or just Dad. Again, I don't know.

I am afraid to ask you for a specific event or time when we can speak, because you may say no and a no should not necessarily mean you are too busy to speak to me but may indicate that you just don't want to speak to me. I feel sad beyond words that we, Dad and I, have created a climate you find unbearable. This is unbearable for me. You and I, to some extent, are capable of understanding the psychological dynamics of what is going on. I know I understand, because I have tried to know myself. I know you understand, because you too have studied psychology and are an intelligent man. I hope this helps you to empathize with my feelings about the distance you have put between us.

At present, I am feeling the pain of loss in terms of a comfort level I thought you and I have had with each other. An ease of communication both verbal and silent. I miss you. Maybe what I miss is the you that has probably not existed except in my mind for a long time now. It is time for me to catch up with the here and now and what that means to me. I hope you'll give me the chance.

I feel as though I am getting bogged down in words, but I am trying to figure out what to do or a way to let you know what I'm thinking and feeling so I will continue.

We have a good, caring, loving family and it upsets me to see you rejecting us. I say "rejecting" because that is how it feels. Your brothers, your sister, your father and I all feel abandoned by you. Lost to you, and we don't know why or what we've done to deserve such punishment. If you refuse to provide us the answer, we can't solve the problem for you or us. But then again, maybe you don't want it solved and have your own agenda that precludes us. I find myself angry—angry at this situation. Three thoughts: #1—If I lived here alone or only with your siblings, you would be here. We could talk and resolve our differences. #2—Maybe you would be more comfortable if we visited you in Chicago, on your own home ground. #3—You are not comfortable in Concord with your family around you and have thus refused returning home for holidays, vacations or even a short visit. This is sad.

When I fantasize about what has driven you away, I look back and attempt to pinpoint a moment when I did something wrong, said the wrong thing, gave the wrong advice. Should I have forced you to come out of your room and spend time with the family when you wanted to be alone? Should I have noticed you were having difficulty with things when you gave us the appearance that all was well? But then again, how could I have known? I did the best I could with what I knew of you. How could I do more than that? Maybe I want to be absolved of these sins I feel I must have committed toward you? I only wish I knew what they were. It's the not knowing that scares me, making me feel I've failed you. At least try to remember that I am a person too, just like you, subject to failures. More fallible than perfect. What I find perplexing is that I don't know of any way we treated you that we didn't treat Kyle, Tom, Hal or Tina. We raised and loved you all as equals—*and that remains so* whether you choose to contact us or not. I will always love you and I want you to know that.

My wish for you is that you have close, loving relationships with people who feel the same for you. I wish you to have a full, satisfying life with a woman to whom you are number one, totally and unconditionally. Whether you choose to share that with me, I can only hope, but I still do wish that for you.

When I think about you, I think of your incredible smile, your bright eyes, your laughter, your deep sensitivity, capacity to feel, your good nature. I think of your determination to do things the way you want to do them. I think of how well you have done in school, in college, and am proud to see you on the threshold of your career in psychology. It lets me know you do care about people and I hope you can give some of that to your family. Maybe what you've learned through your education will help you to forgive us for anything we may have done but remain ignorant of.

I remember reading stories to you when you were young. I remember puppet shows you put on for Hal and Tina. I remember you sucking your thumb with Snoopy bunched up by your side close to your face. I remember your gifts to me, a vase from a pottery boutique, a flower-patterned silk scarf to tie my hair back given for one Mother's Day, a large fluffy blue rabbit made out of dyed bird feathers. I am so grateful to you for all of your gifts—for all of you. Sometimes

I feel myself remembering you as if you are someone from my past. I remember you, and I love and want you back. Writing this letter is a big thing for me to do. Now that I am concluding I feel a sense of relief but also that I have gone out on a limb. Please respond.

With deep love,

Mom

Several months pass and Sandy still hasn't received a response from Blane. She considers writing a second letter, sits in the hospice office at her desk and takes a pen in hand to do so, but this time the words do not come. The feelings, having already been delivered previously, lie dormant. She no longer has any idea of how to communicate with her son. He is lost to her, to the family, and she puts the sheet of stationery away in the top drawer of her filing cabinet, pours herself a cup of tea from the pot in the reception area, and returns to her desk, picking up the phone and calling Dean at his office.

Dear Blane,

I have been lenient toward you because you have always been independent and I respect that. However, one thing I cannot let continue is your blatant disregard for the family. Not only has your neglect disappointed us greatly, but it is rude and I find it intolerable.

I had Vicki examine my past year's calendar of appointments. I had Vicki examine the year before that's calendar of appointments and then the year previous to that. Did you know it has been approximately *three years* since we last saw you? *Three years!* At your Nana Lilly's funeral. I myself am a very busy man with a great understanding of the demands of making a living, but even I cannot fathom why we have not seen you in three years. You refuse to phone and return our phone calls (it has been over a year since we last spoke over the phone), so here I sit writing a letter to you. Writing a letter to my own son! I find this difficult to comprehend, but here I am doing it.

Your mother took the time to write you and you failed to give her the satisfaction of a reply. Why? What has she—what have I—what have *any* of us done to deserve such a hostile silence? The answer is, clearly, nothing. We have done nothing to deserve such silence. If you are unhappy with us yet refuse to address the issue with us maturely, then obviously no solution can be achieved. I refuse to take the blame for acts I have no knowledge of having committed. I refuse to feel guilty through your silence.

You have walked away from your family and shut us out. That is your choice, not our doing. I can only hope that you reach some degree of rationale so that you may realize you can negotiate any peace with us you feel you have lost. I am not a dictator. I am a fair man and if you have been wronged by us, then it can be corrected. However, if you refuse to sit down at the bargaining table with us, as I wrote before, a hospitable outcome is clearly not possible.

I hope you are well. Love,
Dad.

Dean's letter is returned, unopened, three weeks later. The envelope is tagged with a yellow mail label reading, "Return to sender. Wallace, Blane, no longer listed at specified address. No forwarding information available."

1 9 8 6

M A T T ' S going to be at the house in less than fifteen minutes and Tina still hasn't finished her chores. She vacuums the Oriental rug in the living room, cleaning it quickly so she'll be done by the time Matt arrives. Once the chores are completed, Tina will be able to be with Matt without worrying that her mother will get mad at her for cleaning the house improperly. Matt's been Tina's boyfriend for the last five months. He's seventeen, just the same age as Tina is.

Tina glances at the grandfather clock in the corner of the room. It's three-twenty. Matt should be at the house in ten minutes and she switches off the vacuum and drags it to the hall closet, putting it away, then taking out the furniture polish and a dust rag. She's already cleaned the kitchen, so at least that's done.

Tina's been keeping the Wallace house in order for the last several years. At first, when Hal was living at home, he took care of the outside of the house under Dean's supervision while Tina took care of the inside under Sandy's. However, for the past year and a half since Hal's been in college at the University of Connecticut, Tina takes care of both the inside and outside of the house.

"Why do I have to do everything?" Tina complained at supper last week.

"The boys helped out around the house, why can't you?" Dean asked.

"But there's only one of me and they did it together and I'm doing it alone," Tina argued.

"I cleaned the house for over twenty years," Sandy said, "and now that I'm working, I don't have the time for it anymore."

"Then can't we hire a maid?" Tina asked. "I mean, there are plenty of empty rooms upstairs she could live in."

Sandy and Dean gave Tina a look, letting her know that they were weary of this conversation.

"I think the few tidbits you do around here is very little compared to what you're getting," Dean told her.

"And what *am* I getting?" Tina asked, knowing she shouldn't have, knowing her father would have an answer.

"You are *getting*, My Darling Princess, the car you now drive as well as your college tuition."

"Can't we just use my college money to hire a maid?"

Sandy and Dean ignored her query and began talking about the interesting days they'd each had at work.

Tina interrupted her parents. "You know, I can't wait until I'm in college, then no one will be here and you'll both have to do all the cleaning yourselves."

Sandy looked at Tina, then smiled at Dean. "*That* is when we will hire a maid." And they laughed in unison.

Tina walks into the living room, to the mantel, and dusts, moving her parents' art objects, wiping underneath everything. One day, when Tina first started cleaning the house, she only dusted around the objects, not bothering to move them. When Sandy inspected the job Tina had done, she had a fit. "Come on, Tina, you can do better than this."

"Why don't you do it if you think you're such a perfect house-wife and mother," Tina rebutted and Sandy fumed, making Tina redust the entire room.

Upon doing the laundry each week, Tina intentionally leaves out washing Sandy's pale blue silk panties with the lace trim.

Tina folds them neatly and redeposits them back in her mother's dresser as if they'd been cleaned and then delights each week when she finds them in the hamper, waiting to be washed but only to be put back in Sandy's underwear drawer yet again.

Tina dusts the ornaments on the mantel, the pewter candlesticks, the brass eagle, the crystal elephant, Lilly's porcelain doves. Cracks cut the figurine across the wings and around the neck of one of the birds. When Dean fixed the piece, he put the broken bird's head on backward, facing it in the wrong direction, making the already gaudy object look even cheaper. Nonetheless, Lilly insisted it remain on the mantel. Even now, after she's passed away, Sandy keeps it on display. "One day, when you're married, I'll pass the birds on to you," Sandy told her daughter.

Tina looked at her mother as if she was crazy. "Do you really think I want them? Be serious."

Sandy laughed. "I guess it is a pretty ugly thing, but it has been in the family for a long time so you'll just have to take it whether you like it or not."

Tina finishes the mantel and sprays polish on the coffee table, writing out M-A-T-T with the foam, rubbing it into the dark wood. The doorbell rings and she drops the rag and spray can on the carpet, rushing over and opening the door.

Matt's standing on the front steps in his red letterman's jacket, wearing a button-down shirt and corduroys. He smiles at her. "Hi." He steps into the house.

"Hi," Tina says. He reaches out and holds her shoulders and they lean together and kiss.

She takes his hand, leading him into the living room. "I have a bit more to do, okay? But you can watch me, it won't take long."

Matt sits on the couch, facing his girlfriend across the coffee table as Tina polishes. He slips off his jacket and leans forward. "Aren't you a happy homemaker?" He reaches out and takes Tina's hand off the table, clasping it in his own.

Tina takes her hand from his. "I just have a little dusting to do, that's all."

"Your hand smells like lemons," he says.

"I kind of like it." She polishes the table legs.

Matt sits back, leaning on the arm of the couch, looking over the end table at the photos of the Wallaces. He picks up a portrait from years ago, when the boys were still living at home.

Tina walks to the grandfather clock, polishing one side. "You know, it pisses me off, Mom always did the cleaning when the boys were here, but now that she wants to work, I have to do it all. It really sucks."

Matt puts the picture on the end table, angling the frame as he found it. "Do you want me to help you finish?" He stands and walks to her.

Tina tosses the cloth and polish on the couch. "Oh forget it, I'll just finish later. Let's go upstairs. We have two hours till my mom gets home."

■

"Hal, go help your mother carry the food in from the kitchen," Dean says.

Hal gets up. "I always have to do it because I'm the youngest guy in the family."

Tom smiles at him. "Well, when you become the oldest, you won't have to anymore."

They're all sitting in the dining room, awaiting Sandy's Thanksgiving dinner. Kyle and Tom are down at one end of the table, opposite their father, smoking. Tom smokes Marlboros and Kyle inhales Dunhills. Dean finds it sad that his children smoke, regards it as a personal failure that he never stressed how bad it is for them, but if he wants them to come home, he realizes he has to let them do what they want despite his opposition. He carves the bird while Sandy and Hal carry in large bowls brimming with vegetables, sauces, stuffings and gravy.

"The room looks nice since you've redecorated it," Kyle says. "Much nicer."

"Your mother and I think it's a bit more sophisticated," Dean says.

"Sophisticated?" Tom asks incredulously, stubbing out a cigarette on the edge of his plate.

"Yes," Dean says. "Your mother and I have become very social and sophisticated now that we've gotten rid of all of you but the girl there."

"Hey, no one told you you had to have us," Tom informs his father and he pours himself a second glass of the white wine Kyle brought up from New York.

Dean shakes a drumstick at his middle child. "Thank you for that reminder, Tom-Boy, thank you very much." He places the turkey leg on the platter with the slices of white meat he's cut. "Your mother and I just got to thinking that now that you kids and Philynda are gone, we no longer had to worry about things getting ruined. Don't have to worry about any dog or kid dirtying the carpet, or the walls getting messed with finger or paw prints. We thought we deserved a bit more luxury in our lives."

"I'm not sure you deserve it," Tina says.

"Philynda was a great dog," Kyle says.

"Well, I certainly miss having her nosing around the Thanksgiving table whining for turkey scraps," Dean says.

The Wallaces pause. A minute of silence, recognizing the absence of their beagle.

"So," Dean breaks the moment, "it *would* be nice if you kids could help me out in the yard a bit this weekend."

"Hey, I didn't come here for that, old man," Tom states.

"What are you complaining about?" Tina says. "They make me do most everything here now that all of you are gone."

"Poor baby," Kyle teases.

"Yeah, you have it so bad," Tom says, giving his sister a light punch on the shoulder.

She punches him back. "You watch it there, boy."

Tom laughs at her. "You watch it yourself, girlie."

Tina sticks her chin up at him, mockingly. "But I'm not a *girlie,* I'm Dad's princess, aren't I, Dad?"

"Of course you are," Dean says. "Now go help your mother in the kitchen, princess."

Hal walks in and sits at his father's side. "We're all done, so forget it."

Sandy follows Hal, lifting a shopping bag in the air. "I have a little something for everyone," she announces and she walks to the end of the table between Tom and Kyle, opening the bag.

"Gifts for everyone?" Dean asks.

"Everyone. Even you." Sandy smiles and she withdraws six identical books from the bag, distributing them among her children and husband.

"Bradshaw on: The Family" Dean reads, then to Sandy, "Can't you leave off even on Thanksgiving?" He places the book on the sidecart by the table without another thought.

Sandy ignores her husband. The Wallace children all flip the book from front to back to front to back again.

"So what's the point?" Tina asks, placing her book on the carpet under her chair.

"The point," Sandy says, taking her seat at Dean's side, "is that I read this book and it has a lot of things in it that apply to us. We never worked our issues out in therapy because you all didn't want to go so I thought that reading this book might help make it easier for you to understand things. It has to do with liberating the child within and dealing with the shame we all feel."

Tom breaks into a grin. "Help me!" he cries in a tiny, baby voice. "Help me! I'm the child within! Help me! Get me out!"

Tina and Hal and Dean laugh out loud. Kyle conceals his laughter behind a cough, forcing himself to keep a straight face, not giving his brother the benefit of approval.

"I'm serious about this," Sandy says. "It's important that we learn to get over the shame we feel for our past."

"Mom," Tina implores. *"What* shame?" Tina shrugs, completely uncomprehending of her mother. "I don't feel any shame about anything. I feel fine about us, so what's the point?"

Hal, Kyle and Tom drop their books to the carpet. Dean begins serving himself dark-meat turkey from the heaping platter.

Sandy gazes at her daughter. "Then I'm very, very glad for you. You're very lucky," and she looks away to the center of the table, reaching for the bowl of mashed potatoes—she gave them the books, she delivered her message, she must let it go—"Now let's all eat up before it gets cold. Everything's hot and ready."

Tom drinks almost every night at the club he manages; Kyle drinks with clients during long business dinners; Hal drinks beer at frat parties a few nights each week; and Tina occasionally drinks with high school friends on weekends at the house of whoever's parents happen to be away on vacation.

After dinner, after the table was cleared, the dishes cleaned and Sandy and Dean had retired to bed exhausted from over-eating, Tom brought out a bottle of Stolichnaya and another of tequila. Kyle feigned disgust, initially reprimanding his brother for being a bad influence on Hal and Tina, but since it *was* Stolichnaya he gave Tom credit for having good taste and decided to take a shot or two.

Soon after, the four Wallace children were sitting in the family room, watching television. Late-night reruns of *I Love Lucy* and *The Mary Tyler Moore Show,* and the late movie, *Portrait of a Teenage Hitchhiker.*

Kyle, in the recliner, drinks a steady flow of vodka on the rocks. Tom, at one end of the couch, shakes salt in a palm, licks it, downs a shot of tequila, then quickly takes a bite from one of the many slices of lime he's cut. Hal tries to keep up with Tom's pace, but he's not used to drinking tequila and can't quite get the timing down correctly between salt, shot and lime. Tina, on the far end of the couch, drinks screwdrivers, her brothers insisting that she is too young to be drinking her alcohol straight up.

"So what if that guy's killing those hitchhikers," Tom says. "Those girls aren't even pretty. I'd never let them into my club."

Kyle leans over to Tina, shaking an authoritative finger. "Let this be a lesson to you," he says, imitating their father. "I hope you're paying careful attention to what's happening to those girls."

Tina laughs. "No way, man, tomorrow I'm outta here and I'm gonna hitchhike all the way to San Diego."

"That's not funny," Tom says, acting as their mother. "This is a serious situation. Those girls need guidance." He pours himself another shot, then another for Hal. Kyle walks into the kitchen to refill his glass with ice.

"You're lucky Mom's asleep," Tina says. "She'd have a fit if she saw this alcohol in the house. She gives me lectures about drugs and drinking every single day. She even tries to get Dad to not bring any beer into the house anymore so it won't be around to tempt me."

"I'd go crazy living here alone with them," Tom says. "They'd drive me nuts."

"You think I like it," Tina says. "I can't wait to go to college next year."

Kyle returns, picking up the vodka bottle, staring down at Tom, giving Tom a hard look. "I hardly think you're the one who should be complaining about living with *them.*"

Tom glares at his older brother, downing a shot. He doesn't reach for a lime, but clenches his jaw tight. "Oh fuck off, who cares?"

"What?" Kyle asks. "You think you were such a great person to live with?"

"I'm easy to live with," Tom replies, glancing about, wishing he had a beer handy. "I never was any trouble to anyone."

Kyle sits, sipping his drink. "Only running off to airports and stabbing Mom with a fork. No problem at all."

"You just still wish you were an only kid. That's why you're always so pissed."

Kyle waves a hand at him. "Give it up. Pass me the vodka," but he reaches over and grabs it himself.

"All I know is that when they get old like Granny did, they're not moving in with me." Tom slices two wedges of lime, one for him, one for Hal.

"You think they'd want to?" Kyle asks.

"They'll probably make me do it because I'm the girl," Tina complains.

"We'll all hav'tado-it," Hal says, slurring his words, his face a drunken, flushed red.

"But at least they'll have enough money to take care of themselves," Kyle says. "At least they have enough money to pay for their own nursing homes and funerals."

They all sit silent, contemplating the distant future when their parents will be gone.

"How much money *do* they have?" Tom asks.

Kyle places his drink on an end table. Tina, Tom and Hal, no longer paying attention to the TV, focus on their eldest brother, waiting for an answer.

Kyle speaks confidently. Dean and Kyle have had many talks about the family's financial matters, Kyle being the eldest, the most "business-minded" of the children. "This house is worth at least half a million," Kyle says. "The house on the Cape, although small, is on waterfront property, so that's probably worth about another half mill or so; the land *is* nice. Dad's stocks and bonds are worth two to three million. And depending upon how he dies, that could kick in some money, but probably nothing too significant. In total, I estimate that by the time he's gone, assuming he lives to be about seventy, he'll be worth close to four million." Kyle lifts his drink, taking a sip, pleased with his detailed account of their father's financial status.

"That's not true," Hal says, shocked.

"No way," Tina says. *"Him? Our Dad?* Why doesn't he give us any of the money? Why do we have to go to college and get jobs?"

"Because he wants us to learn the value of earning a dollar," Tom says sarcastically.

Silence. Tom reaches over and takes a sip of Tina's drink.

"Are you sure?" Hal asks Kyle.

"Don't talk about it," Kyle replies. "I wasn't supposed to tell any of you."

"Why not?" Tom asks. "Is he giving it all to you?"

"Maybe," Kyle laughs. *"Maybe."*

"He wouldn't do that," Hal says, shaking his head drunkenly. "I used to help out around the house. I deserve some of it. I used to rake the leaves." He slumps back on the couch, closing his eyes.

"I'm sure Dad will split it evenly between the four or five of us depending if Blane ever comes back," Kyle states, and he stands, walking into the kitchen, putting his glass in the dishwasher.

"If it means getting a lot more money, I hope he never comes back," Tina half jokes, thinking over what she could do with her percentage of the take. "I mean, it's been so many years since we heard or saw him I bet Dad's cut him out already."

Kyle calls from the other room, "You better clean up that stuff so they don't find out."

On TV, the teenage girl has just been rescued from the crazed-killer driver. Her parents decide to buy their daughter a car so she will never have to hitchhike again.

"So what if they find out?" Tom calls back to Kyle. "What can they do to us, we don't even live here anymore."

Kyle stands in the entrance to the room. "Fine, do whatever you want, I'm going to bed." He turns and leaves.

Tom finishes off the last of Hal's drink, then picks up the remote control, clicking off the television.

Tina collects the glasses. "After Mom and Dad die, which one of us will get stuck making Thanksgiving dinner?"

Hal wakes, lifting his head, dazed.

"Probably Kyle," Tom answers. "He'll probably want to, then tell his wife to cook it."

Tina nods. "Yeah, probably."

1987

T I N A ' S only been away at Lehigh for three weeks, yet to Sandy and Dean it feels as if she's been gone for decades, the change is so dramatic. The first time in twenty-eight years when there hasn't been a child in the house, neither of them having to act as "parent" all day and night, but both able to be just "husband and wife," "Dean and Sandy," or "Sandy" and "Dean."

"Don't you want to watch the movie?" Sandy asks. She takes a handful of popcorn from the bowl on the nightstand, placing each kernel of corn in her mouth individually, one by one.

"This is fine," Dean says. "I'm tired, that's all."

"Well, then next time you can choose the tape."

"I'm fine." His eyes are completely closed.

Dean and Sandy lie in bed, watching a cassette on the VCR Dean moved up from the family room over the weekend. Once the kids were all out and gone, it made more sense to hook it up to the master bedroom's television. Now when Dean falls asleep halfway through the movie, he's already in bed; Sandy doesn't have to bother waking him, trying to get him to move upstairs.

Sandy pokes Dean in the side.

He sits up, his eyes opening wide. "What's the matter?"

"Nothing, just watch the movie with me," Sandy replies. "You're the one who wanted to see one."

"What did you pick out?" he asks. Dean stares at the bright

TV screen, then slowly begins slouching down under the covers.

"It's *Out of Africa,*" Sandy tells him.

"And what's happening?" he mumbles, his head resting on a pillow.

"Just watch it and find out."

"Didn't we ever see this in a theater?" he asks, yawning, facing away from the television.

Sandy sighs, watching the movie as Robert Redford and Meryl Streep play out their drama across a vast landscape of plains, fields and brush; a lion roars, a fire erupts, and a coffee bean farm burns to ashes. Sandy takes another handful of popcorn. Dean snores by her side.

ABOUT THE AUTHOR

Lawrence David was born in 1963 and grew up in Sudbury, Massachusetts. He was educated at Bennington College and New York University's Tisch School of the Arts. He lives in New York City.